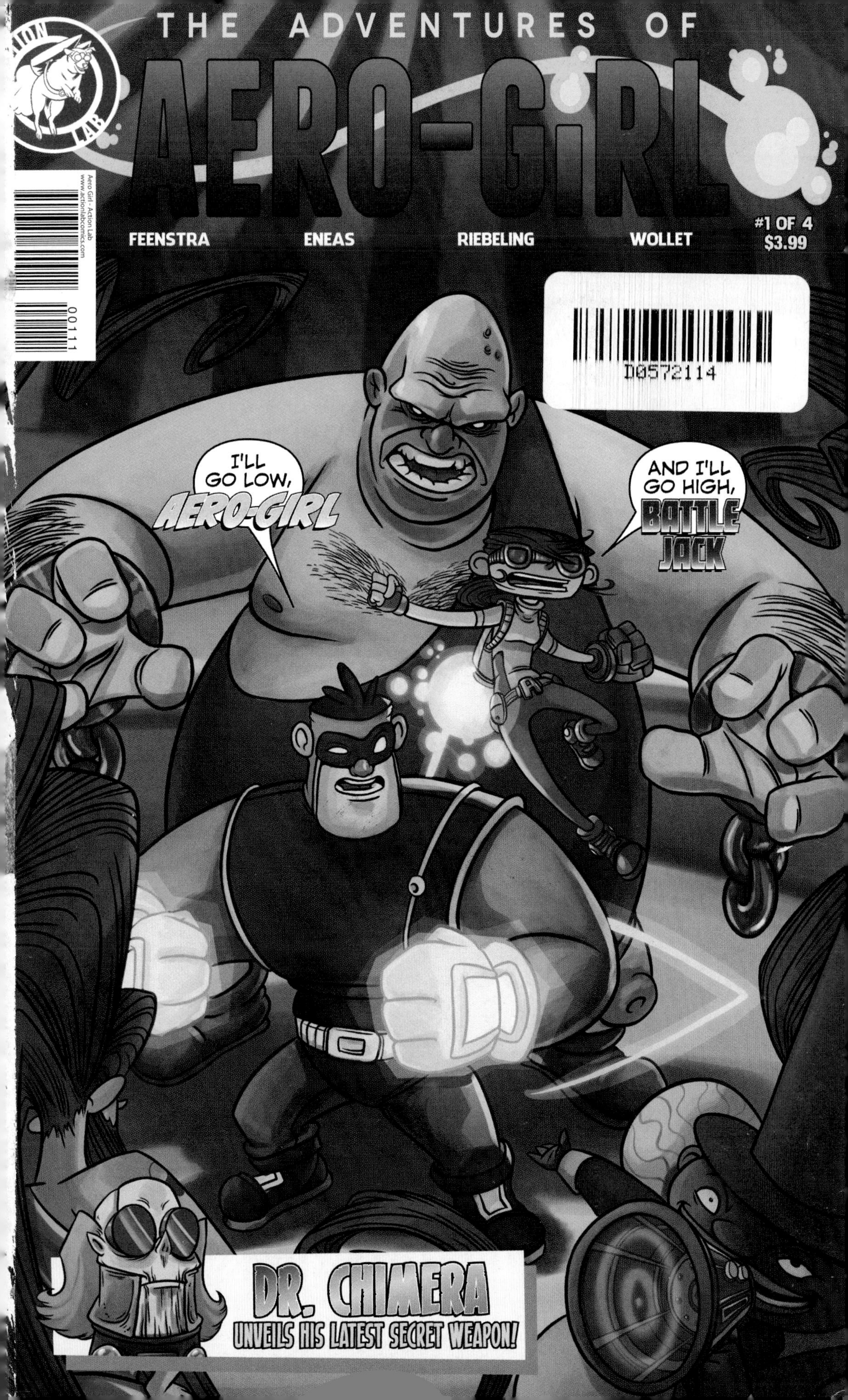
THE ADVENTURES OF
AERO-GiRL
FEENSTRA
ENEAS
RIEBELING
WOLLET
#1 OF 4
$3.99
Aero Girl - Action Lab
www.actionlabcomics.com
D0572114
I'LL GO LOW, AERO-GIRL
AND I'LL GO HIGH, BATTLE JACK
DR. CHIMERA
UNVEILS HIS LATEST SECRET WEAPON!

FROM JAMES WRIGHT & JACKIE CROFTS

NUTMEG

AVAILABLE IN FINER STORES EVERYWHERE

Vol. 1 "Early Fall: Taste Buddies" collects issues 1-3 of Nutmeg, following 8th-grader Poppy
Pepper's partnership with new girl Cassia Caraway and their plan to sabotage rich girl rival
Saffron Longfellow's brownie fundraiser, taking their first steps toward a life of crime.

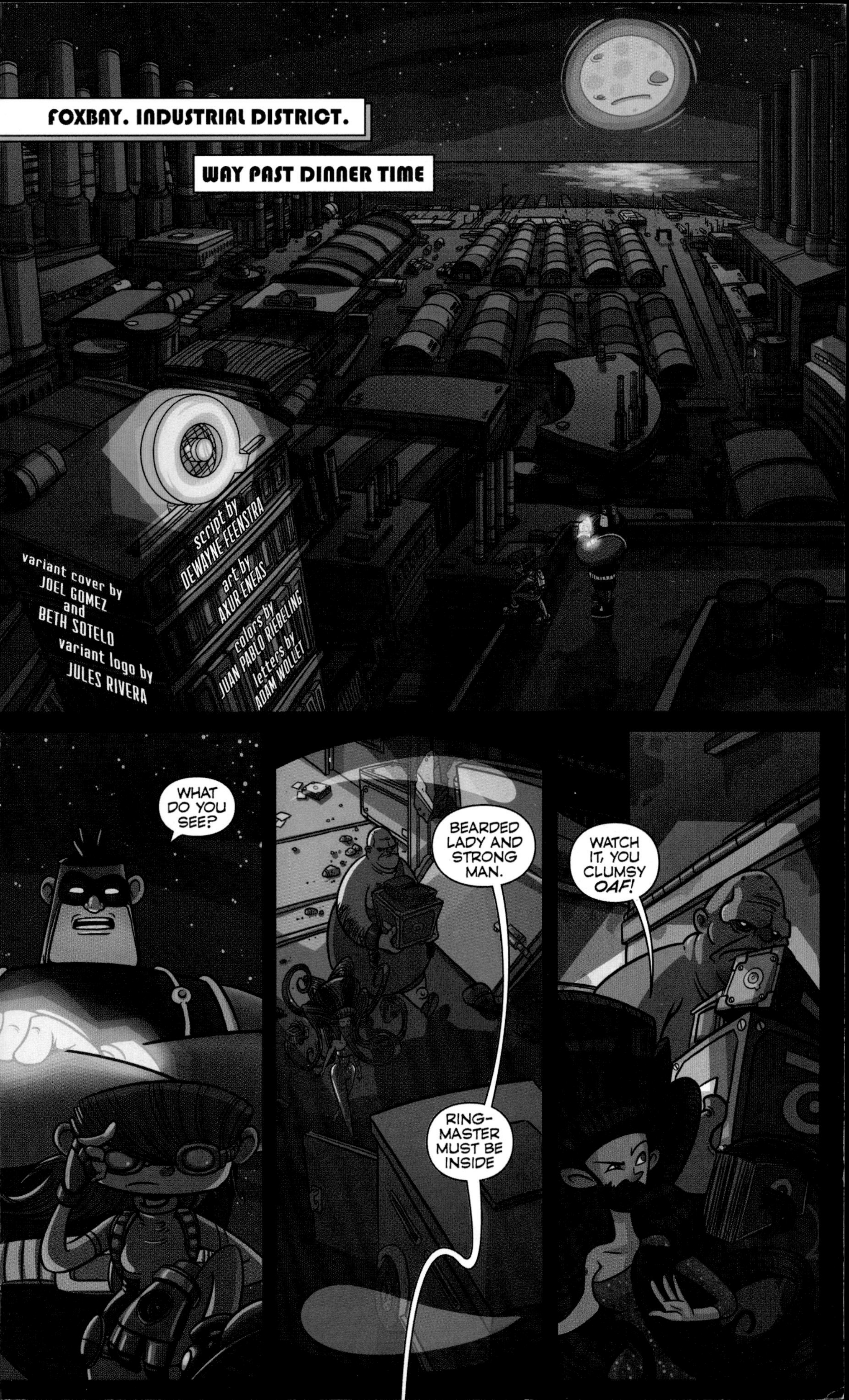
FOXBAY. INDUSTRIAL DISTRICT.
WAY PAST DINNER TIME
script by DEWAYNE FEENSTRA
art by AXUR ENEAS
colors by JUAN PABLO RIEBELING
letters by ADAM WOLLET
variant cover by JOEL GOMEZ and BETH SOTELO
variant logo by JULES RIVERA
WHAT DO YOU SEE?
BEARDED LADY AND STRONG MAN.
RING-MASTER MUST BE INSIDE
WATCH IT, YOU CLUMSY OAF!

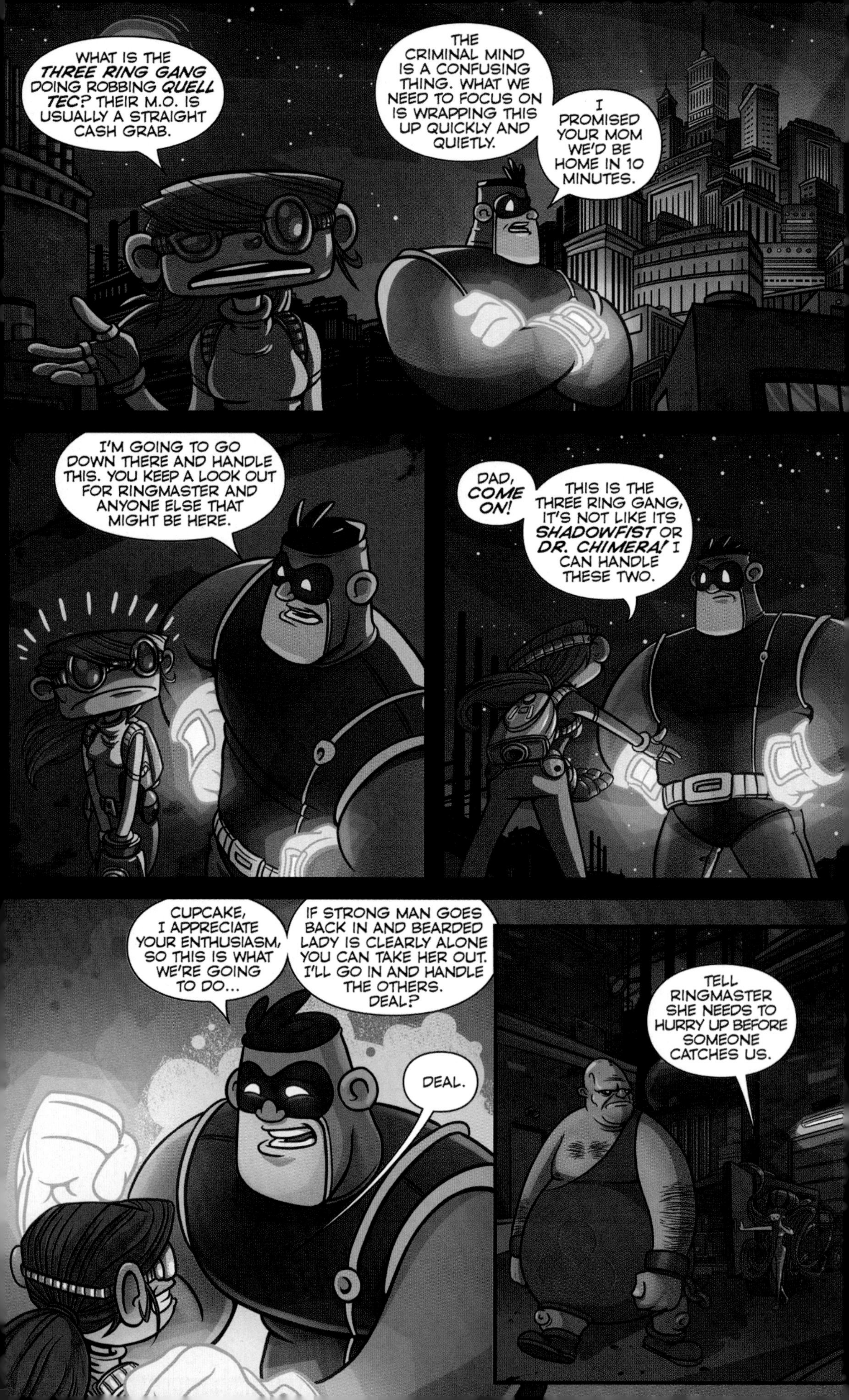
WHAT IS THE THREE RING GANG DOING ROBBING QUELL TEC? THEIR M.O. IS USUALLY A STRAIGHT CASH GRAB.
THE CRIMINAL MIND IS A CONFUSING THING. WHAT WE NEED TO FOCUS ON IS WRAPPING THIS UP QUICKLY AND QUIETLY.
I PROMISED YOUR MOM WE'D BE HOME IN 10 MINUTES.
I'M GOING TO GO DOWN THERE AND HANDLE THIS. YOU KEEP A LOOK OUT FOR RINGMASTER AND ANYONE ELSE THAT MIGHT BE HERE.
DAD, COME ON!
THIS IS THE THREE RING GANG, IT'S NOT LIKE ITS SHADOWFIST OR DR. CHIMERA! I CAN HANDLE THESE TWO.
CUPCAKE, I APPRECIATE YOUR ENTHUSIASM, SO THIS IS WHAT WE'RE GOING TO DO...
IF STRONG MAN GOES BACK IN AND BEARDED LADY IS CLEARLY ALONE YOU CAN TAKE HER OUT. I'LL GO IN AND HANDLE THE OTHERS. DEAL?
DEAL.
TELL RINGMASTER SHE NEEDS TO HURRY UP BEFORE SOMEONE CATCHES US.

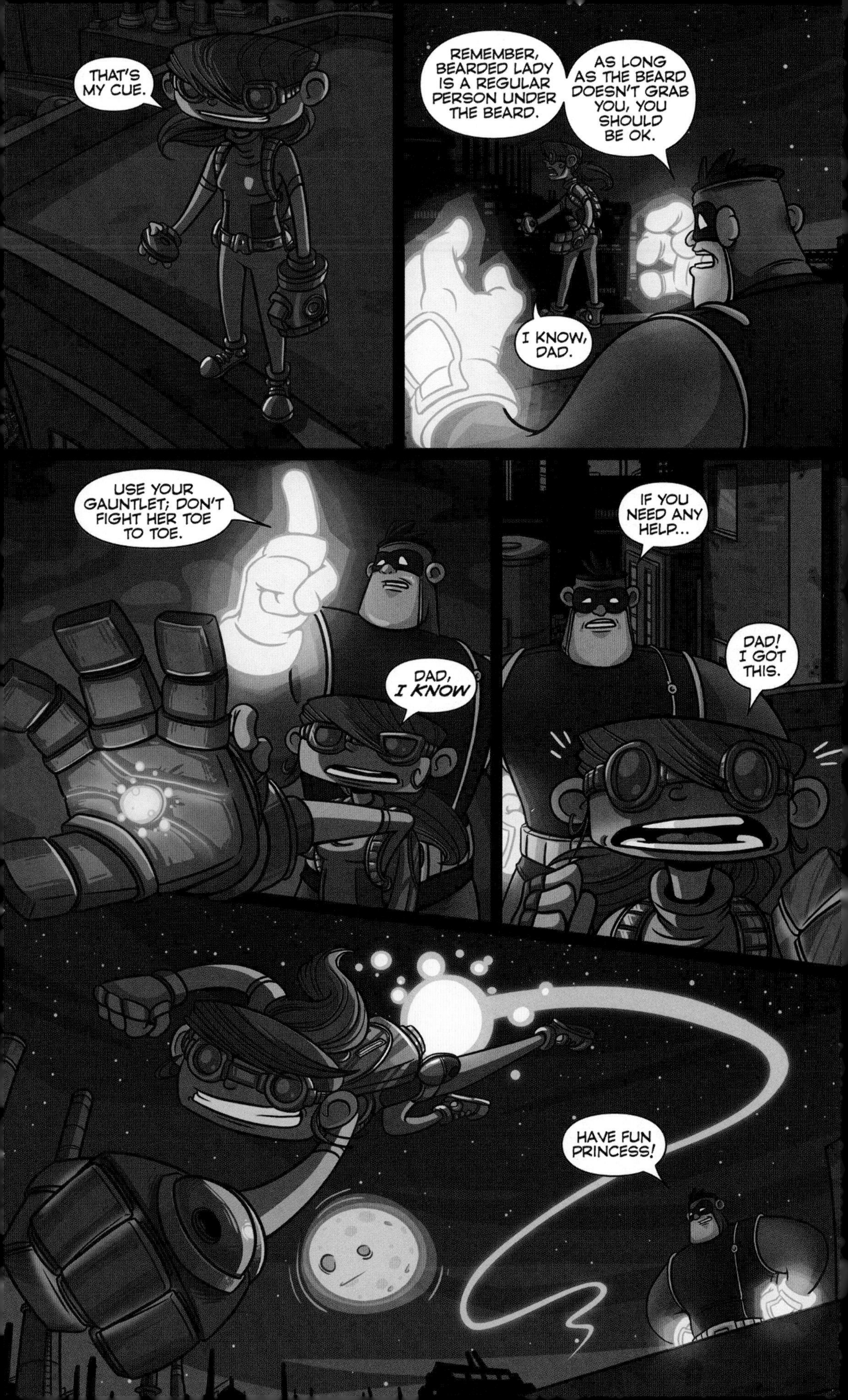
THAT'S MY CUE.
REMEMBER, BEARDED LADY IS A REGULAR PERSON UNDER THE BEARD.
AS LONG AS THE BEARD DOESN'T GRAB YOU, YOU SHOULD BE OK.
I KNOW, DAD.
USE YOUR GAUNTLET; DON'T FIGHT HER TOE TO TOE.
DAD, *I KNOW*
IF YOU NEED ANY HELP...
DAD! I GOT THIS.
HAVE FUN PRINCESS!

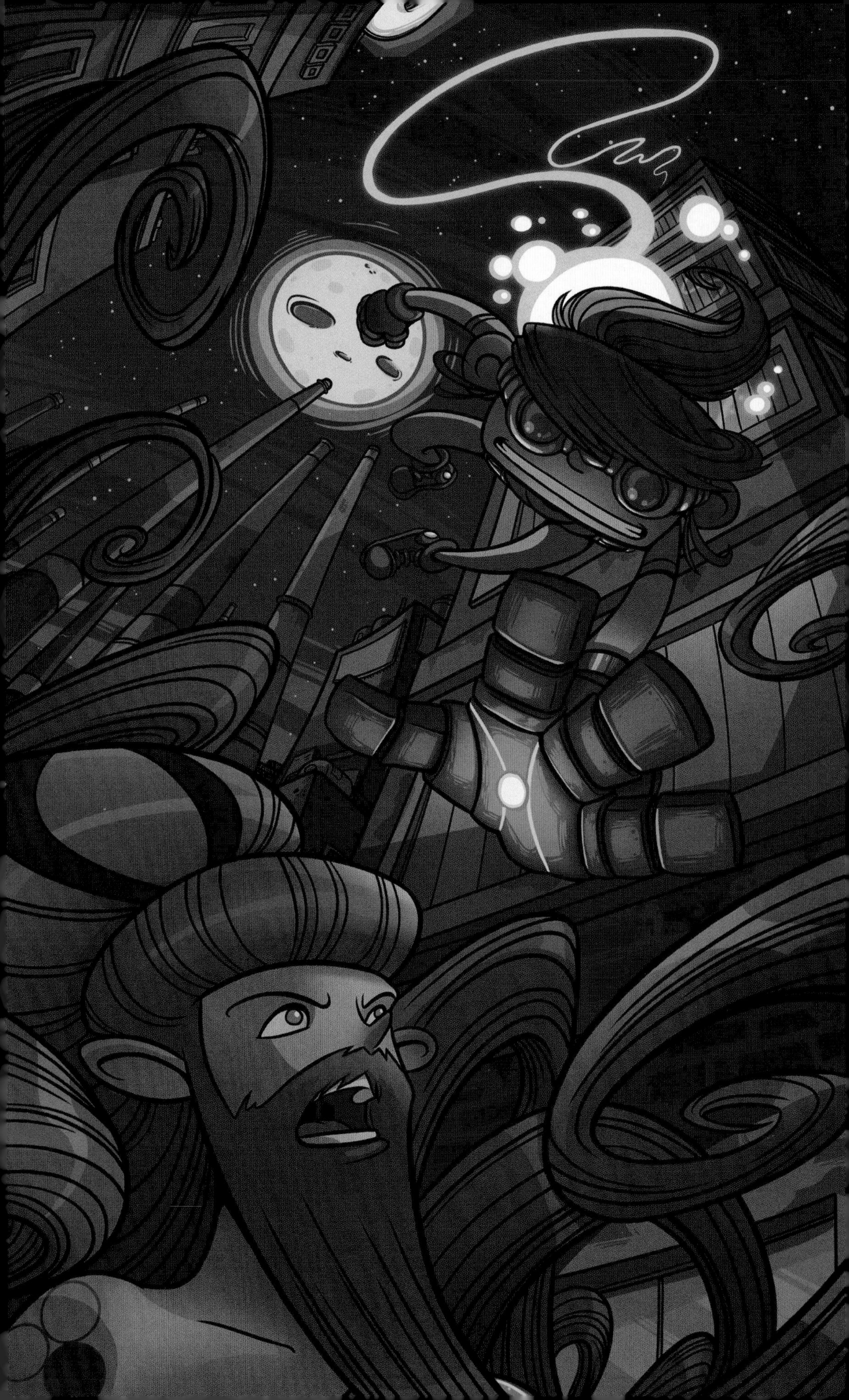

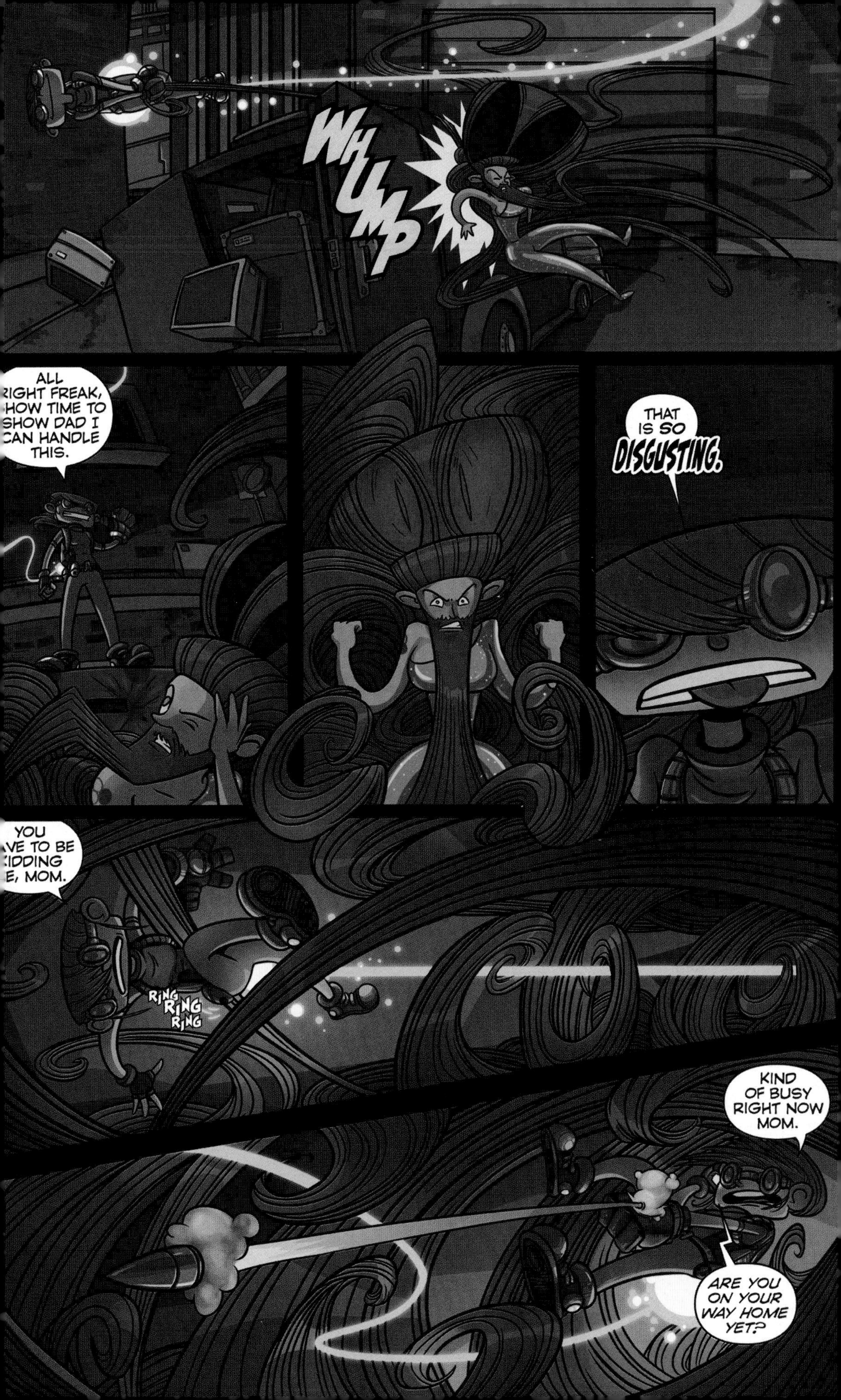
WHUMP
ALL RIGHT FREAK, NOW TIME TO SHOW DAD I CAN HANDLE THIS.
THAT IS SO DISGUSTING.
YOU HAVE TO BE KIDDING ME, MOM.
RING RING RING
KIND OF BUSY RIGHT NOW MOM.
ARE YOU ON YOUR WAY HOME YET?

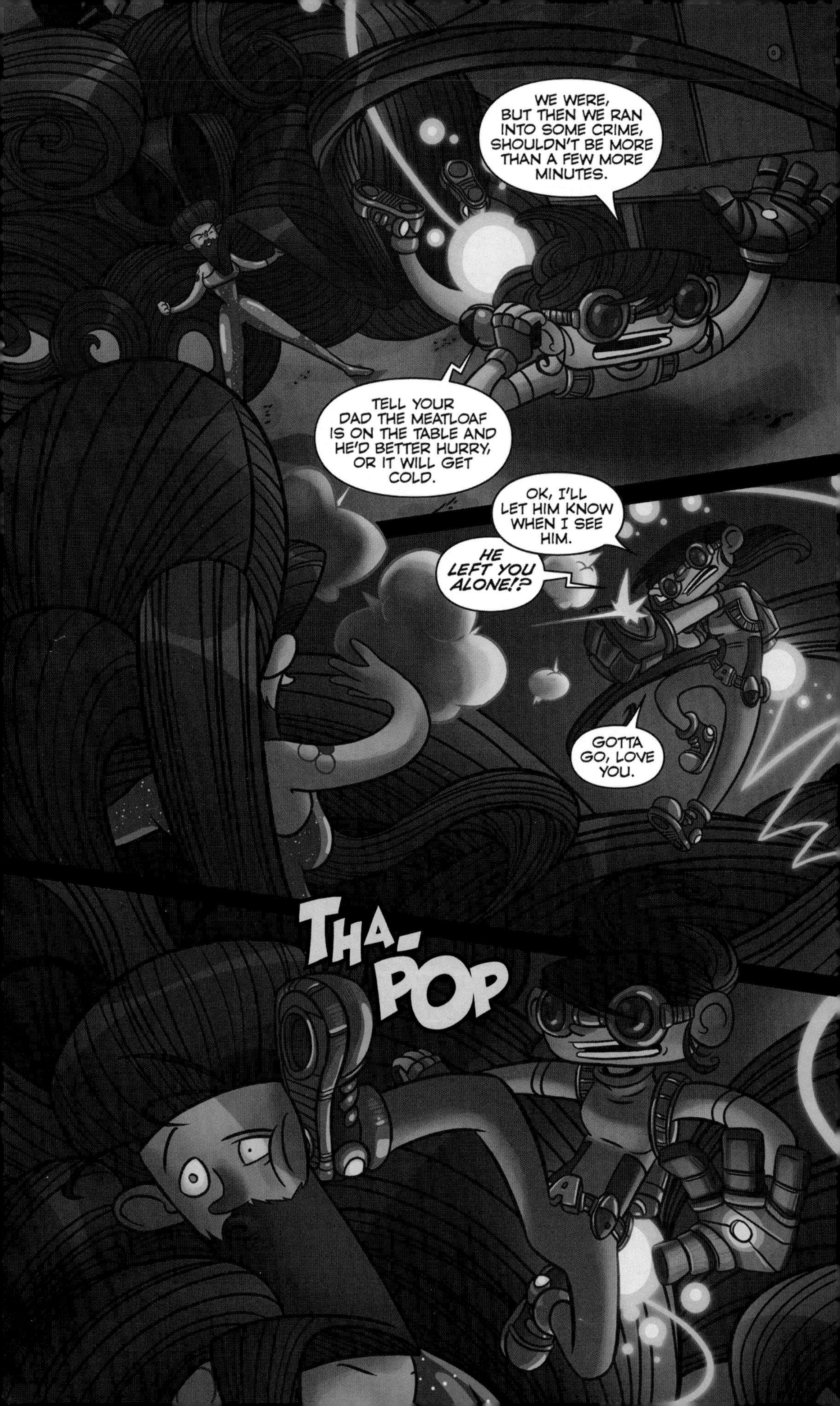
WE WERE, BUT THEN WE RAN INTO SOME CRIME, SHOULDN'T BE MORE THAN A FEW MORE MINUTES.
TELL YOUR DAD THE MEATLOAF IS ON THE TABLE AND HE'D BETTER HURRY, OR IT WILL GET COLD.
OK, I'LL LET HIM KNOW WHEN I SEE HIM.
HE LEFT YOU ALONE!?
GOTTA GO, LOVE YOU.
THA-POP

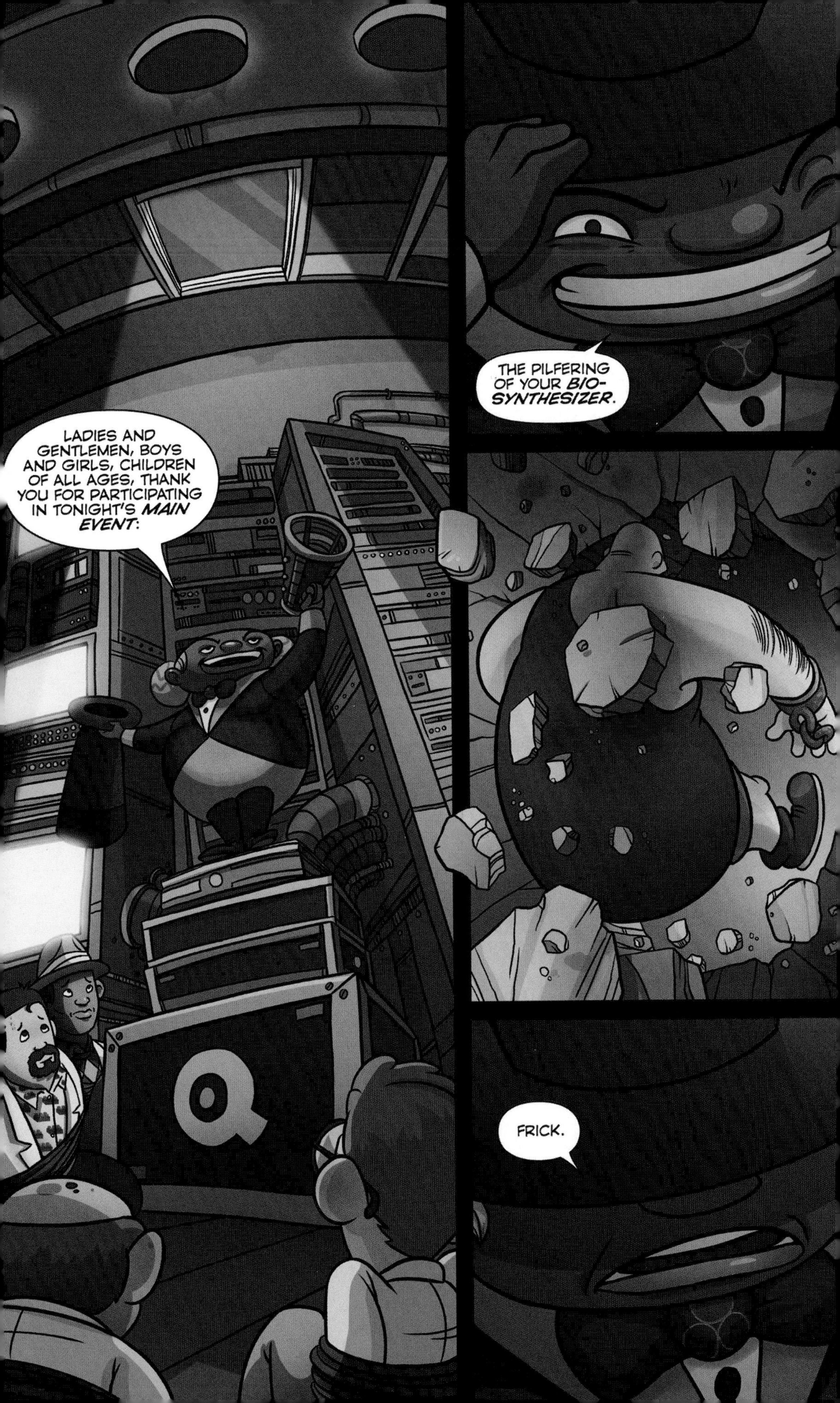
LADIES AND GENTLEMEN, BOYS AND GIRLS, CHILDREN OF ALL AGES, THANK YOU FOR PARTICIPATING IN TONIGHT'S *MAIN EVENT*:
THE PILFERING OF YOUR *BIO-SYNTHESIZER*.
FRICK.

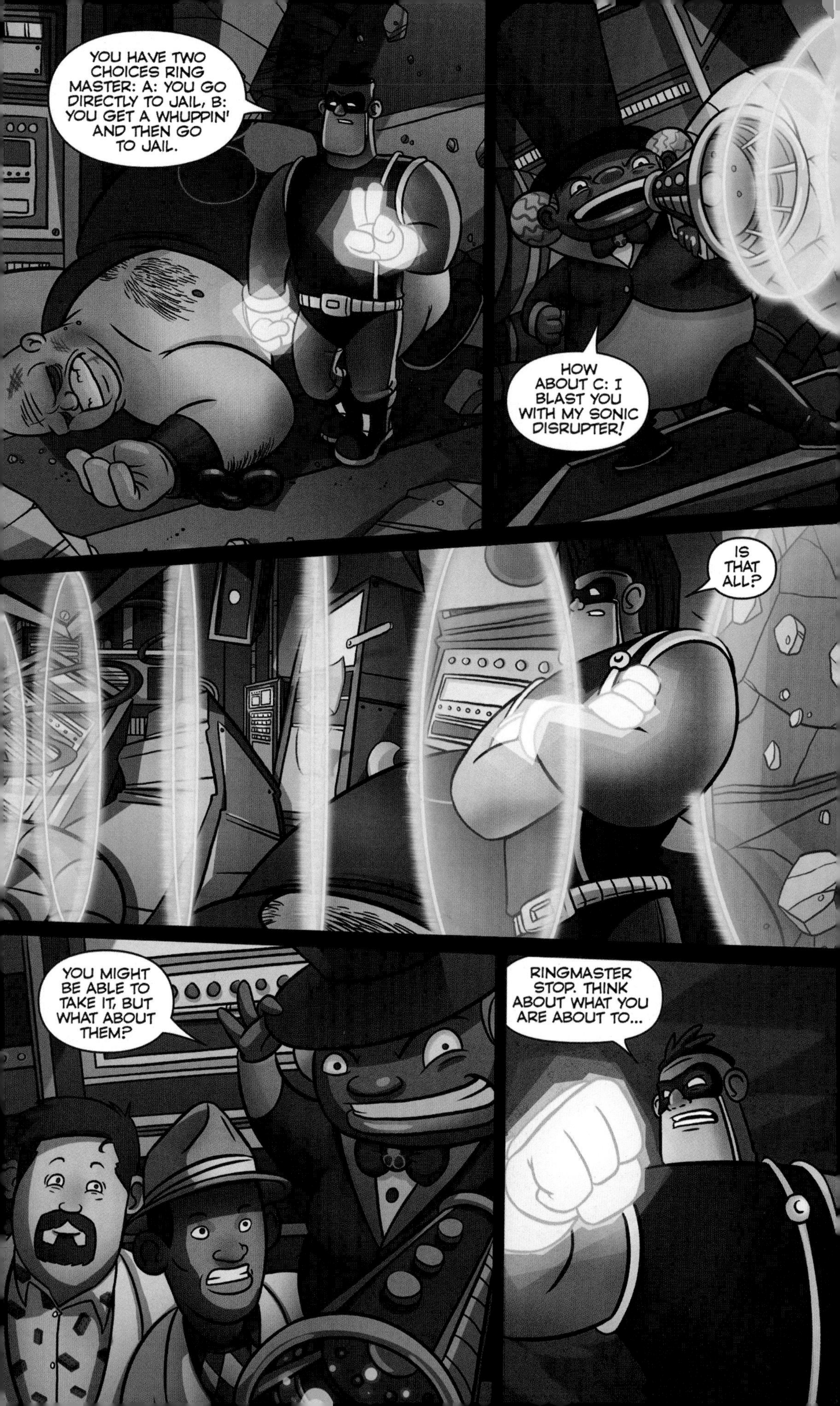
YOU HAVE TWO CHOICES RING MASTER: A: YOU GO DIRECTLY TO JAIL, B: YOU GET A WHUPPIN' AND THEN GO TO JAIL.
HOW ABOUT C: I BLAST YOU WITH MY SONIC DISRUPTER!
IS THAT ALL?
YOU MIGHT BE ABLE TO TAKE IT, BUT WHAT ABOUT THEM?
RINGMASTER STOP. THINK ABOUT WHAT YOU ARE ABOUT TO...

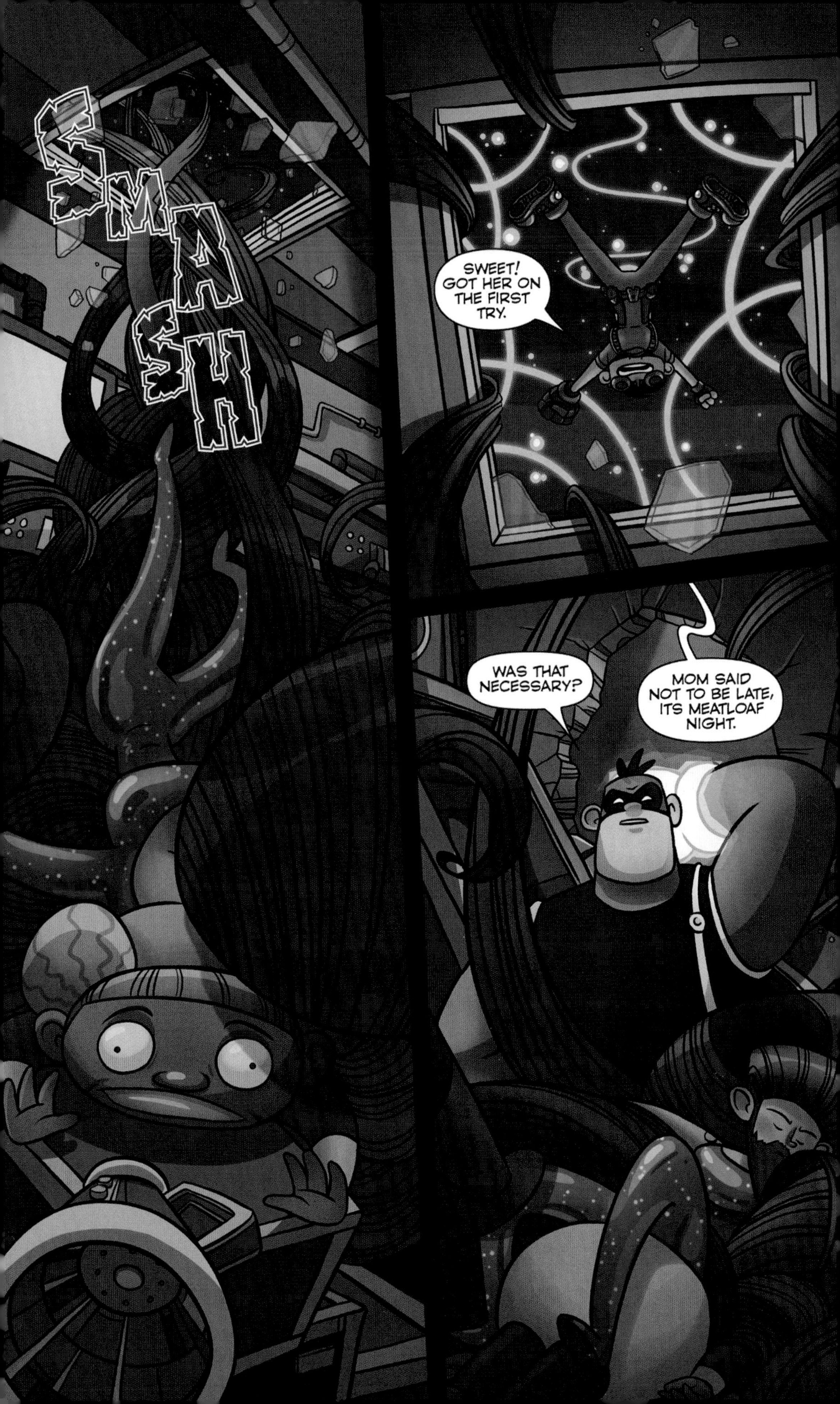
SMASH
SWEET! GOT HER ON THE FIRST TRY.
WAS THAT NECESSARY?
MOM SAID NOT TO BE LATE, ITS MEATLOAF NIGHT.

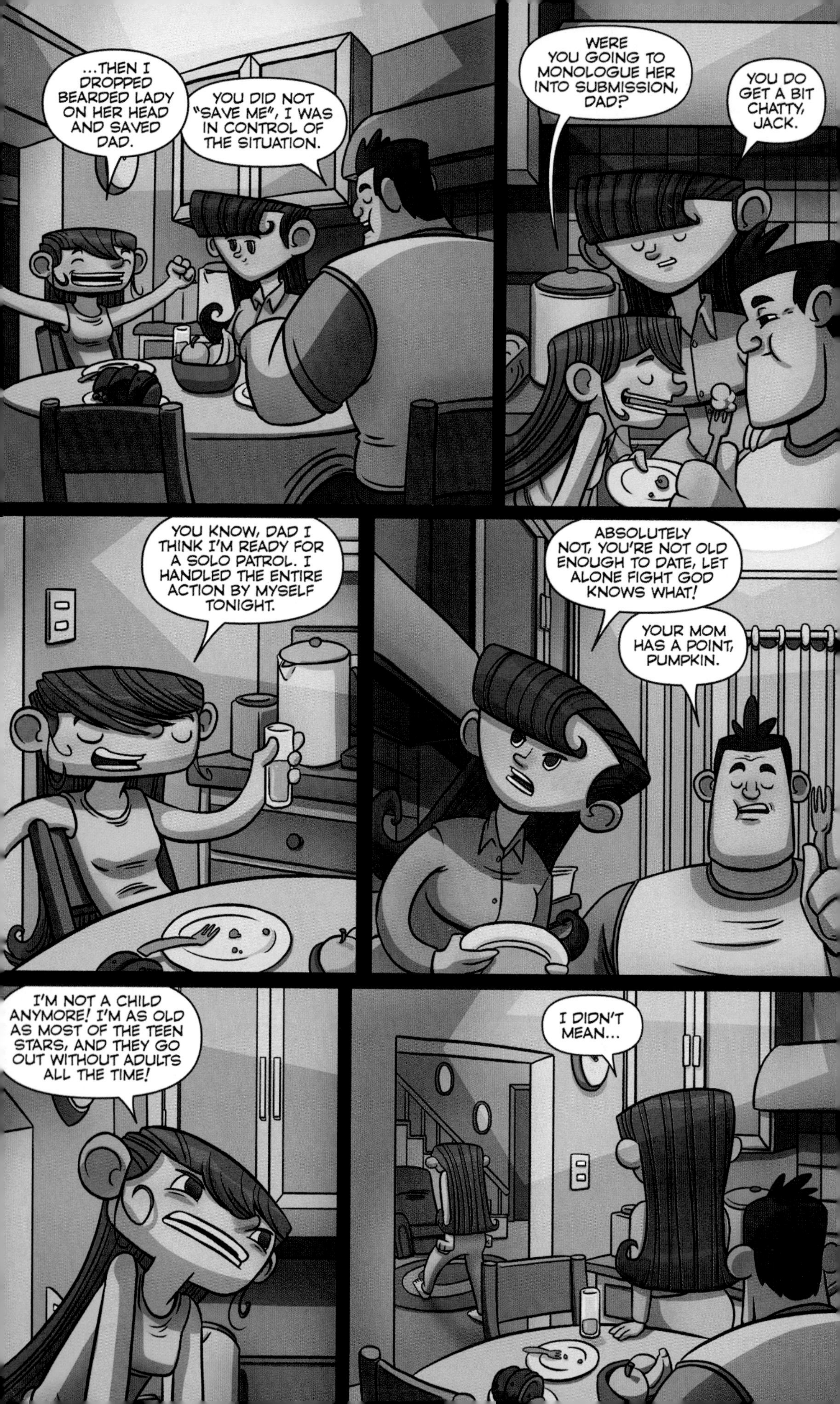

...THEN I DROPPED BEARDED LADY ON HER HEAD AND SAVED DAD.
YOU DID NOT "SAVE ME", I WAS IN CONTROL OF THE SITUATION.
WERE YOU GOING TO MONOLOGUE HER INTO SUBMISSION, DAD?
YOU DO GET A BIT CHATTY, JACK.
YOU KNOW, DAD I THINK I'M READY FOR A SOLO PATROL. I HANDLED THE ENTIRE ACTION BY MYSELF TONIGHT.
ABSOLUTELY NOT, YOU'RE NOT OLD ENOUGH TO DATE, LET ALONE FIGHT GOD KNOWS WHAT!
YOUR MOM HAS A POINT, PUMPKIN.
I'M NOT A CHILD ANYMORE! I'M AS OLD AS MOST OF THE TEEN STARS, AND THEY GO OUT WITHOUT ADULTS ALL THE TIME!
I DIDN'T MEAN...

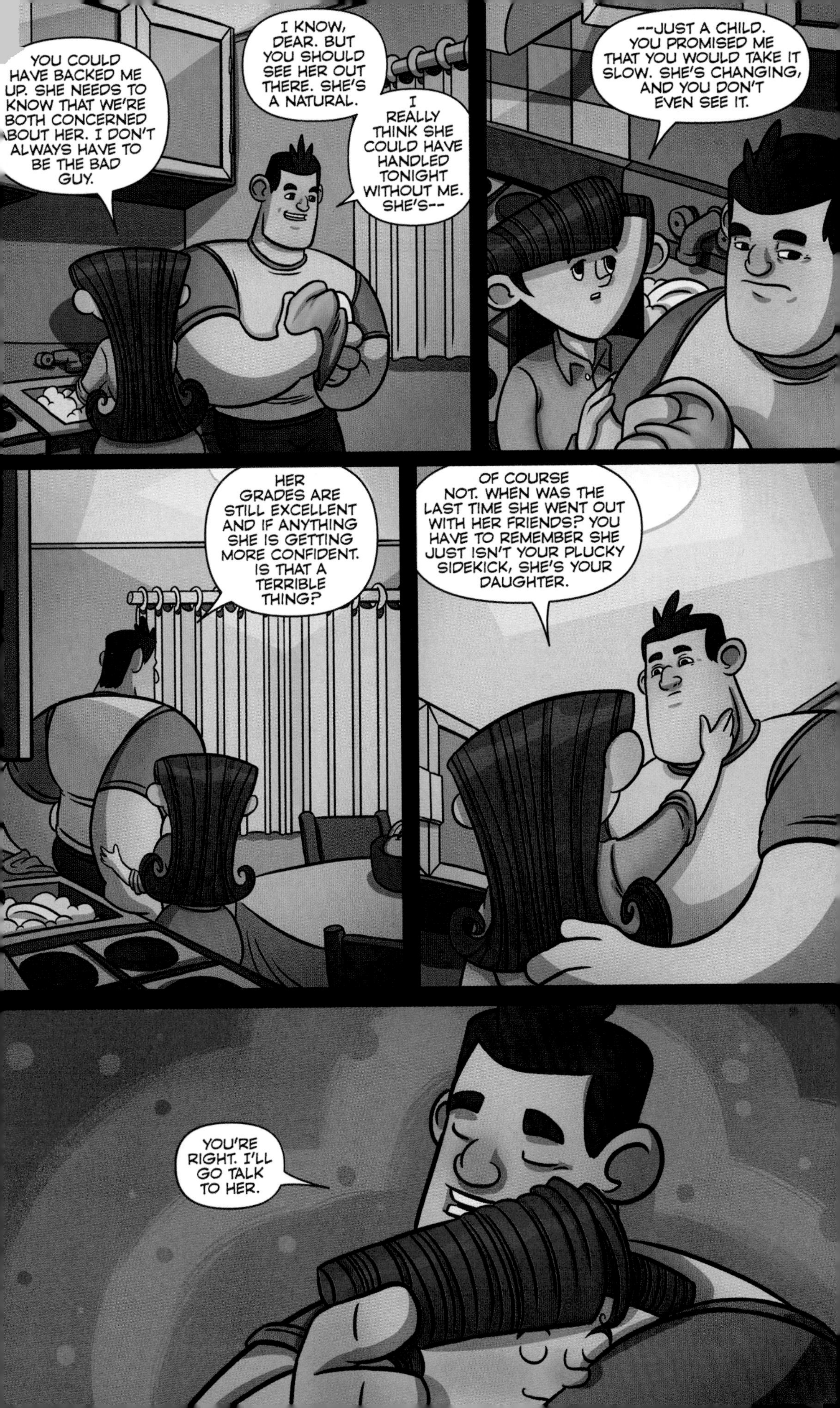
YOU COULD HAVE BACKED ME UP. SHE NEEDS TO KNOW THAT WE'RE BOTH CONCERNED ABOUT HER. I DON'T ALWAYS HAVE TO BE THE BAD GUY.
I KNOW, DEAR. BUT YOU SHOULD SEE HER OUT THERE. SHE'S A NATURAL.
I REALLY THINK SHE COULD HAVE HANDLED TONIGHT WITHOUT ME. SHE'S--
--JUST A CHILD. YOU PROMISED ME THAT YOU WOULD TAKE IT SLOW. SHE'S CHANGING, AND YOU DON'T EVEN SEE IT.
HER GRADES ARE STILL EXCELLENT AND IF ANYTHING SHE IS GETTING MORE CONFIDENT. IS THAT A TERRIBLE THING?
OF COURSE NOT. WHEN WAS THE LAST TIME SHE WENT OUT WITH HER FRIENDS? YOU HAVE TO REMEMBER SHE JUST ISN'T YOUR PLUCKY SIDEKICK, SHE'S YOUR DAUGHTER.
YOU'RE RIGHT. I'LL GO TALK TO HER.

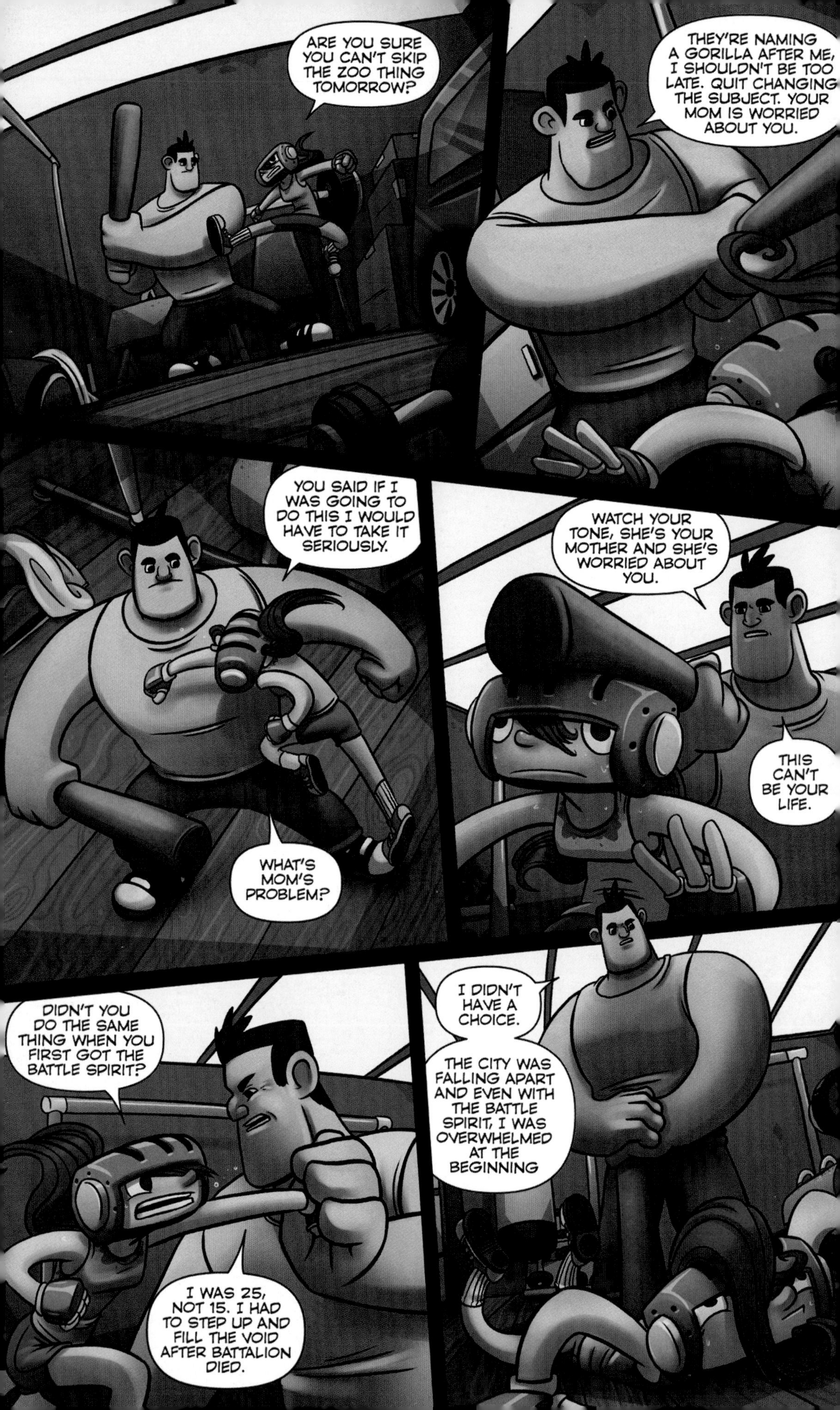

ARE YOU SURE YOU CAN'T SKIP THE ZOO THING TOMORROW?
THEY'RE NAMING A GORILLA AFTER ME, I SHOULDN'T BE TOO LATE. QUIT CHANGING THE SUBJECT. YOUR MOM IS WORRIED ABOUT YOU.
YOU SAID IF I WAS GOING TO DO THIS I WOULD HAVE TO TAKE IT SERIOUSLY.
WHAT'S MOM'S PROBLEM?
WATCH YOUR TONE, SHE'S YOUR MOTHER AND SHE'S WORRIED ABOUT YOU.
THIS CAN'T BE YOUR LIFE.
DIDN'T YOU DO THE SAME THING WHEN YOU FIRST GOT THE BATTLE SPIRIT?
I WAS 25, NOT 15. I HAD TO STEP UP AND FILL THE VOID AFTER BATTALION DIED.
I DIDN'T HAVE A CHOICE.
THE CITY WAS FALLING APART AND EVEN WITH THE BATTLE SPIRIT, I WAS OVERWHELMED AT THE BEGINNING

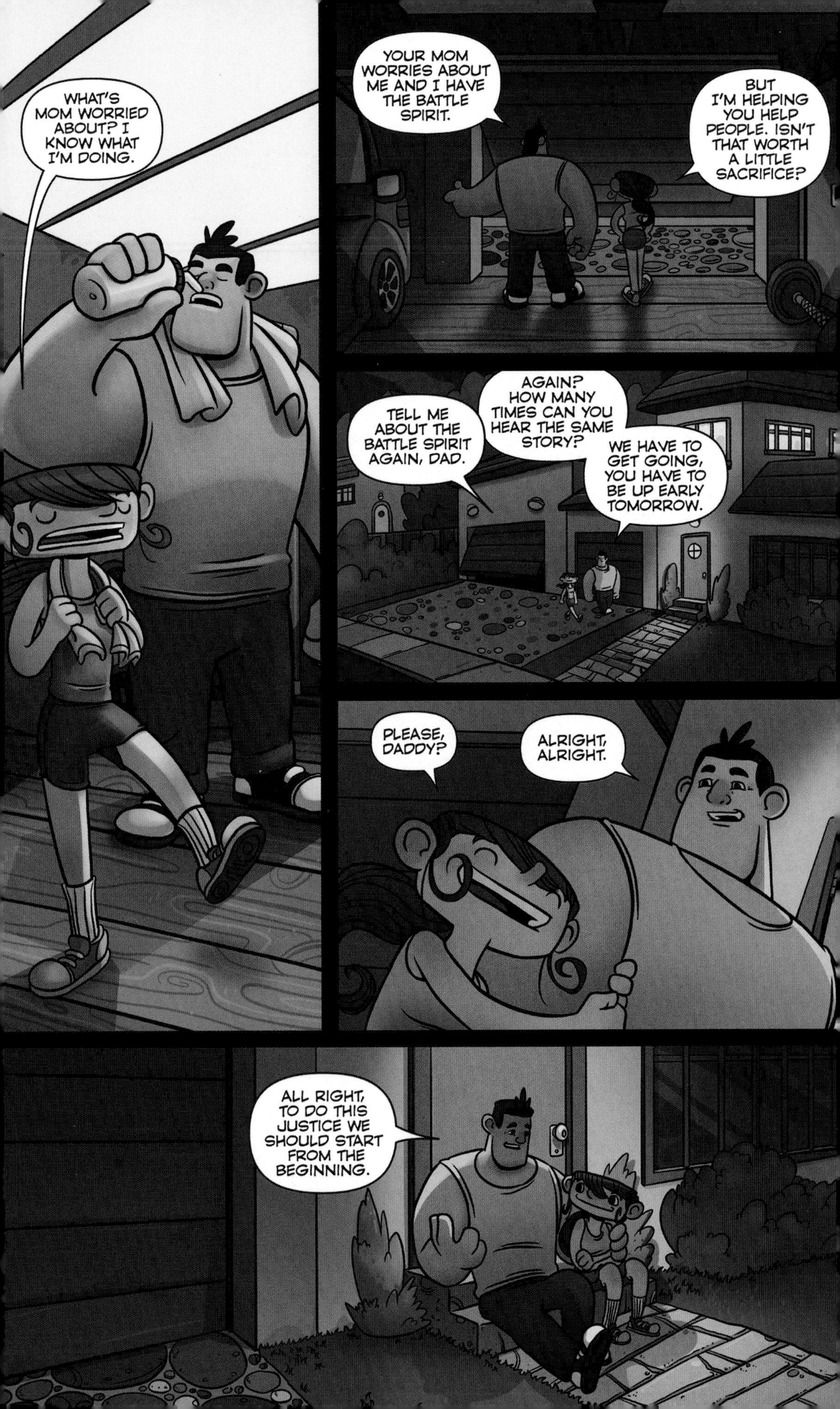
WHAT'S MOM WORRIED ABOUT? I KNOW WHAT I'M DOING.
YOUR MOM WORRIES ABOUT ME AND I HAVE THE BATTLE SPIRIT.
BUT I'M HELPING YOU HELP PEOPLE. ISN'T THAT WORTH A LITTLE SACRIFICE?
TELL ME ABOUT THE BATTLE SPIRIT AGAIN, DAD.
AGAIN? HOW MANY TIMES CAN YOU HEAR THE SAME STORY?
WE HAVE TO GET GOING, YOU HAVE TO BE UP EARLY TOMORROW.
PLEASE, DADDY?
ALRIGHT, ALRIGHT.
ALL RIGHT, TO DO THIS JUSTICE WE SHOULD START FROM THE BEGINNING.

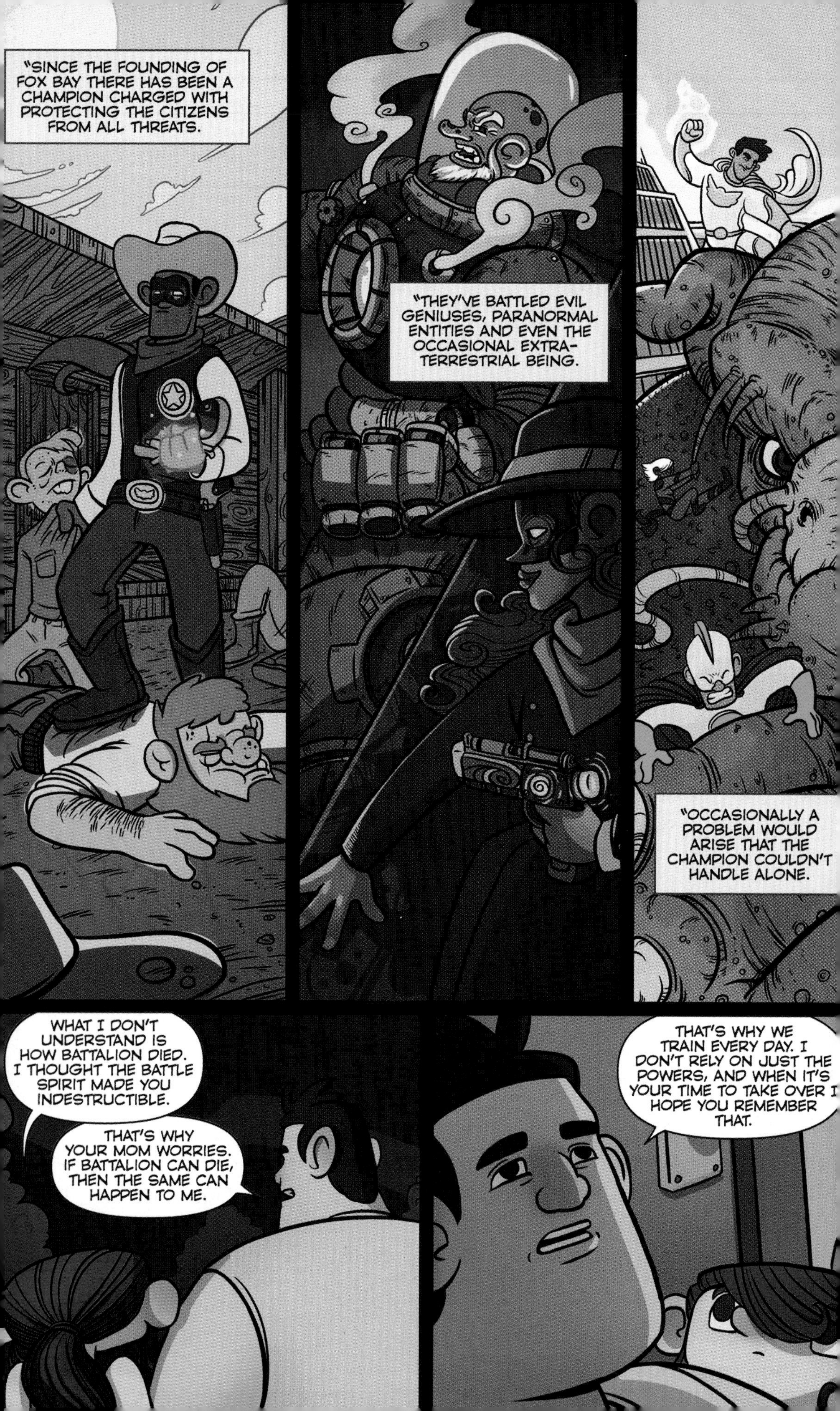
"SINCE THE FOUNDING OF FOX BAY THERE HAS BEEN A CHAMPION CHARGED WITH PROTECTING THE CITIZENS FROM ALL THREATS.
"THEY'VE BATTLED EVIL GENIUSES, PARANORMAL ENTITIES AND EVEN THE OCCASIONAL EXTRA-TERRESTRIAL BEING.
"OCCASIONALLY A PROBLEM WOULD ARISE THAT THE CHAMPION COULDN'T HANDLE ALONE.
WHAT I DON'T UNDERSTAND IS HOW BATTALION DIED. I THOUGHT THE BATTLE SPIRIT MADE YOU INDESTRUCTIBLE.
THAT'S WHY YOUR MOM WORRIES. IF BATTALION CAN DIE, THEN THE SAME CAN HAPPEN TO ME.
THAT'S WHY WE TRAIN EVERY DAY. I DON'T RELY ON JUST THE POWERS, AND WHEN IT'S YOUR TIME TO TAKE OVER I HOPE YOU REMEMBER THAT.

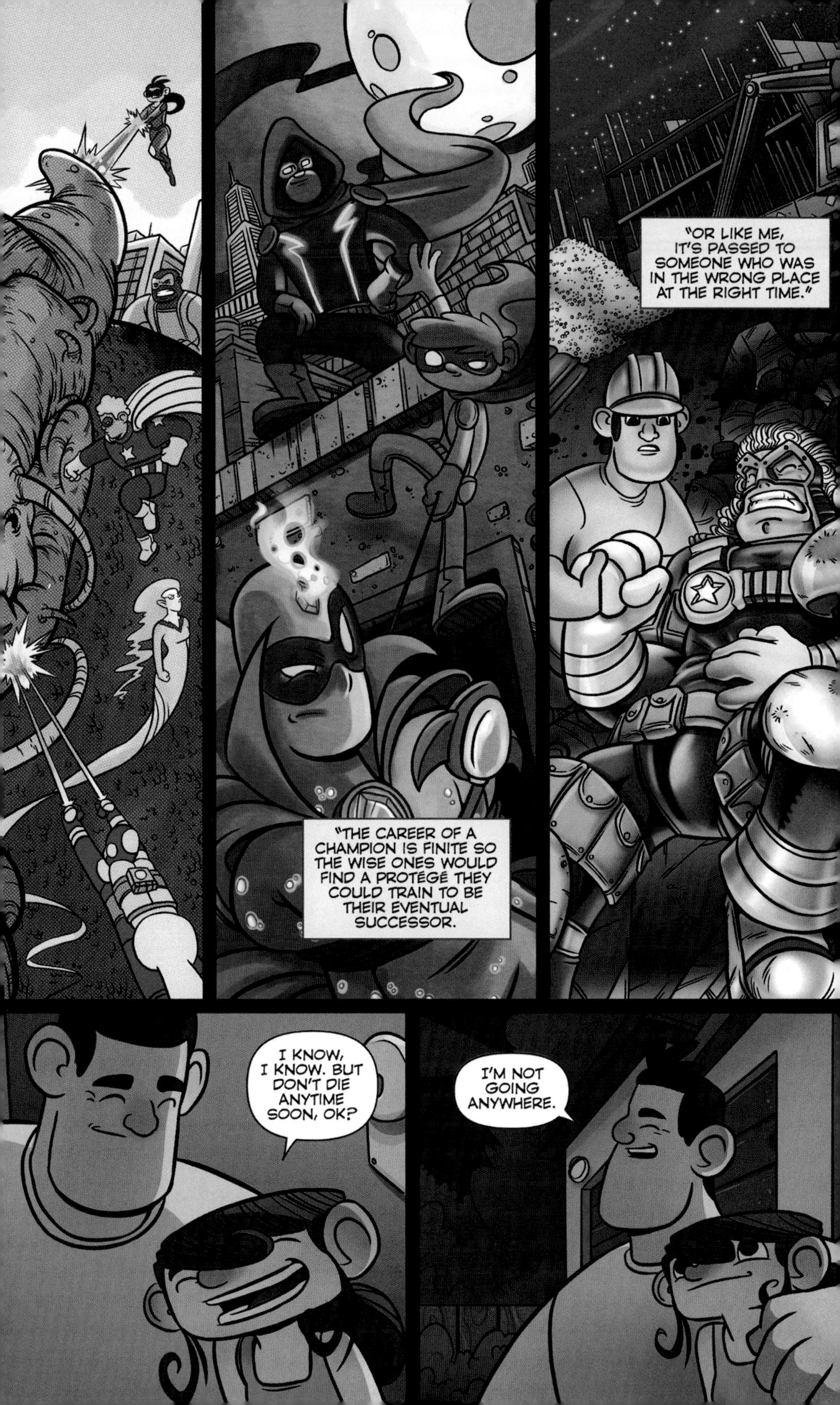
"THE CAREER OF A CHAMPION IS FINITE SO THE WISE ONES WOULD FIND A PROTÉGÉ THEY COULD TRAIN TO BE THEIR EVENTUAL SUCCESSOR.
"OR LIKE ME, IT'S PASSED TO SOMEONE WHO WAS IN THE WRONG PLACE AT THE RIGHT TIME."
I KNOW, I KNOW. BUT DON'T DIE ANYTIME SOON, OK?
I'M NOT GOING ANYWHERE.

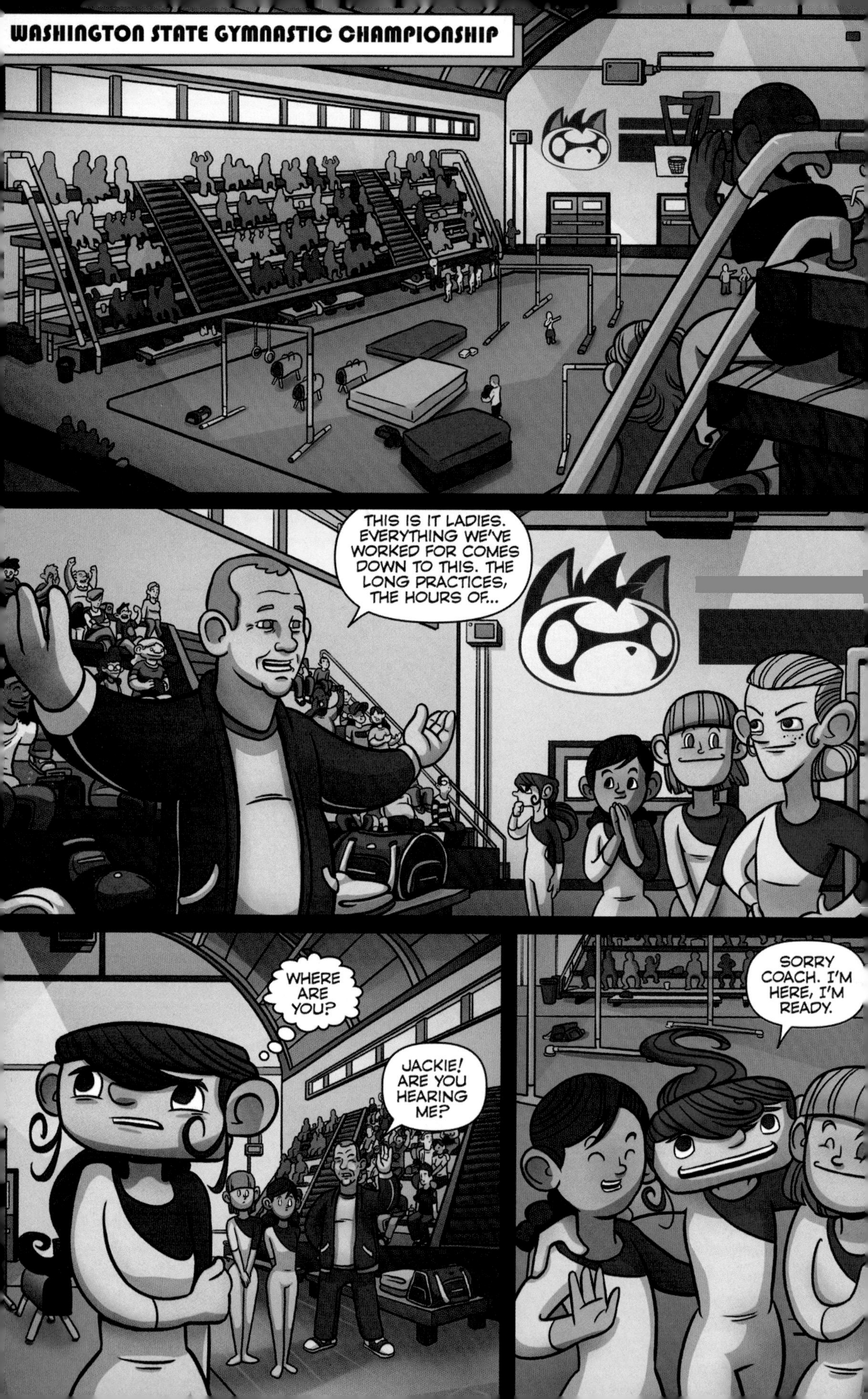
WASHINGTON STATE GYMNASTIC CHAMPIONSHIP
THIS IS IT LADIES. EVERYTHING WE'VE WORKED FOR COMES DOWN TO THIS. THE LONG PRACTICES, THE HOURS OF...
WHERE ARE YOU?
JACKIE! ARE YOU HEARING ME?
SORRY COACH. I'M HERE, I'M READY.

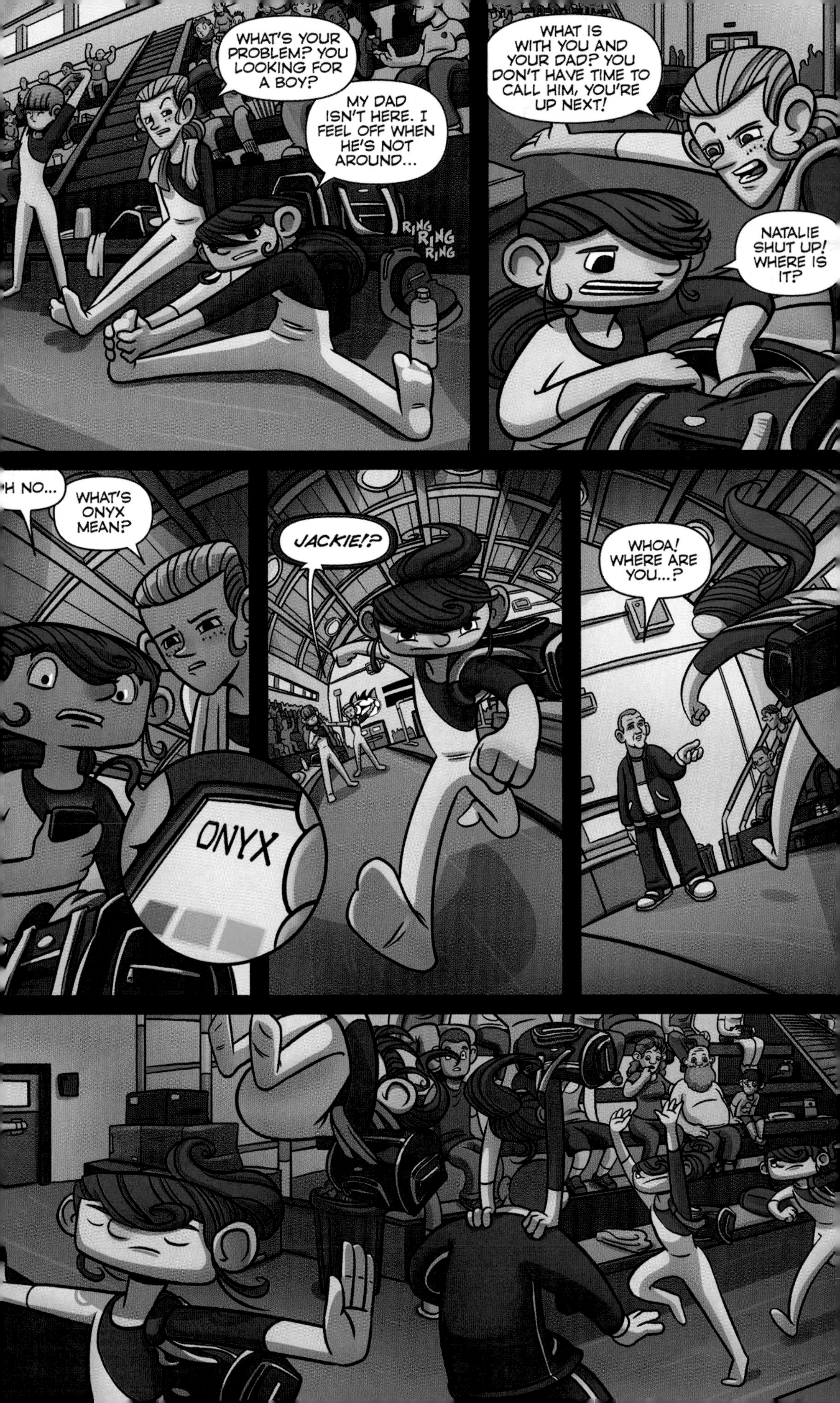

WHAT'S YOUR PROBLEM? YOU LOOKING FOR A BOY?
MY DAD ISN'T HERE. I FEEL OFF WHEN HE'S NOT AROUND...
RING RING RING
WHAT IS WITH YOU AND YOUR DAD? YOU DON'T HAVE TIME TO CALL HIM, YOU'RE UP NEXT!
NATALIE SHUT UP! WHERE IS IT?
H NO...
WHAT'S ONYX MEAN?
ONYX
JACKIE!?
WHOA! WHERE ARE YOU...?

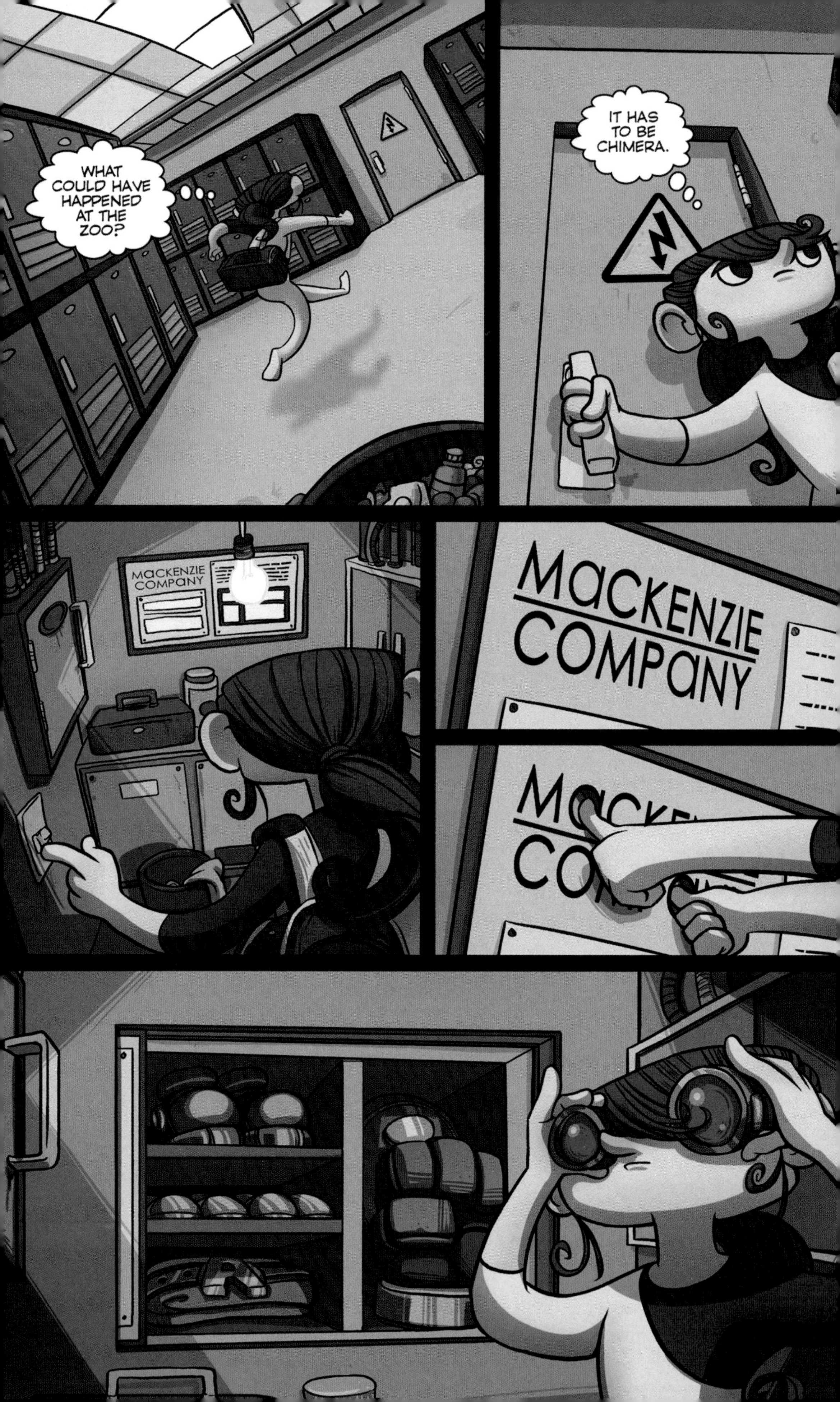
WHAT COULD HAVE HAPPENED AT THE ZOO?
IT HAS TO BE CHIMERA.
MACKENZIE COMPANY
MacKENZIE COMPany

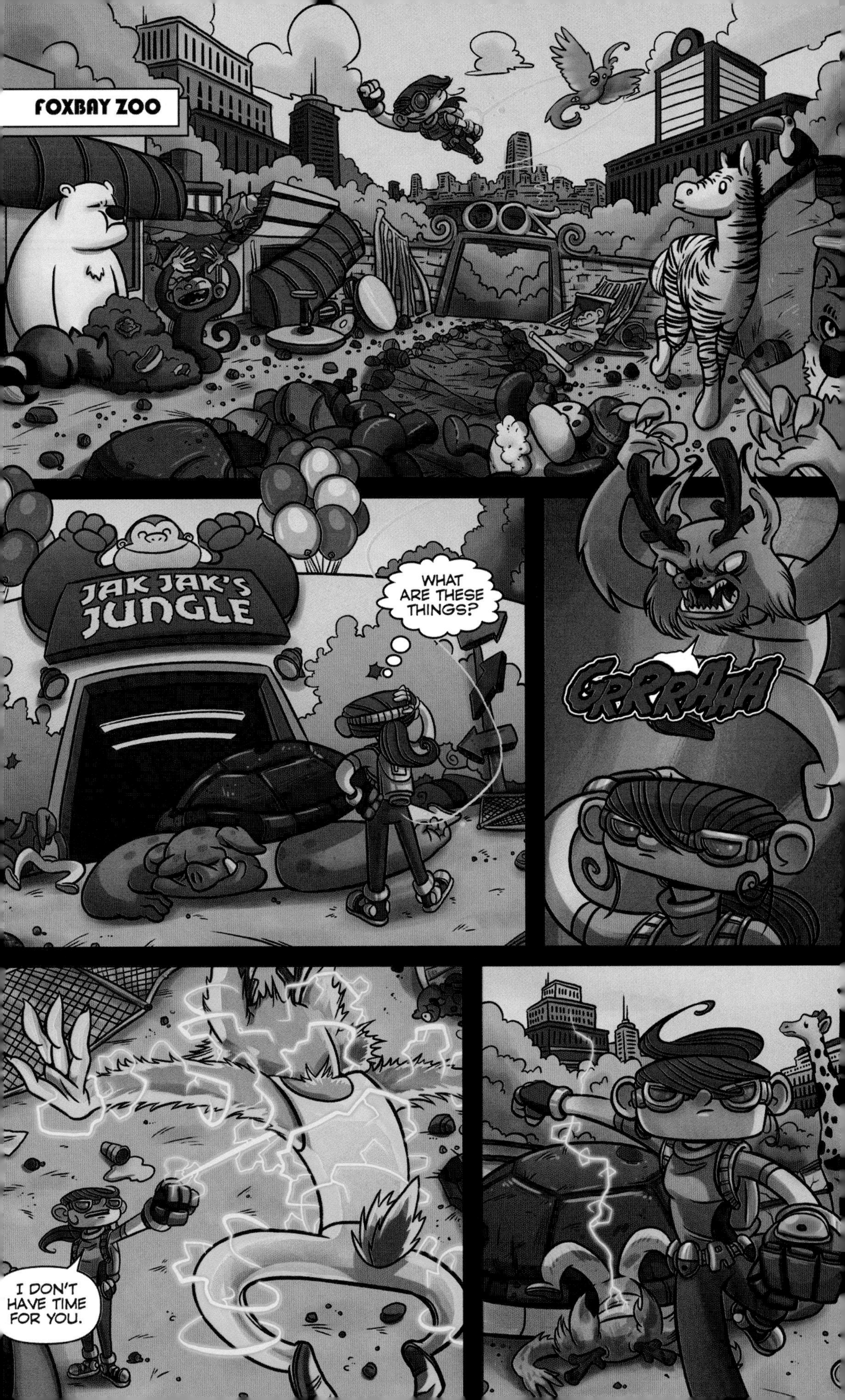
FOXBAY ZOO
JAK JAK'S JUNGLE
WHAT ARE THESE THINGS?
GRRRAAA
I DON'T HAVE TIME FOR YOU.

DAD!

DAD? AND YOU CALL ME IRRESPONSIBLE.

THIS WAS DESIGNED TO STRIP BATTLE JACK OF THE BATTLE SPIRIT, BUT I WONDER WHAT IT WOULD DO TO YOU?

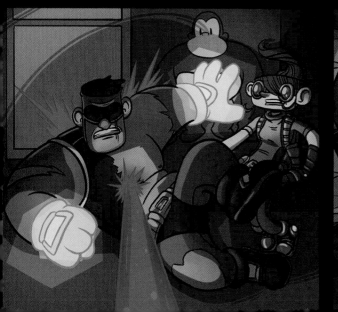

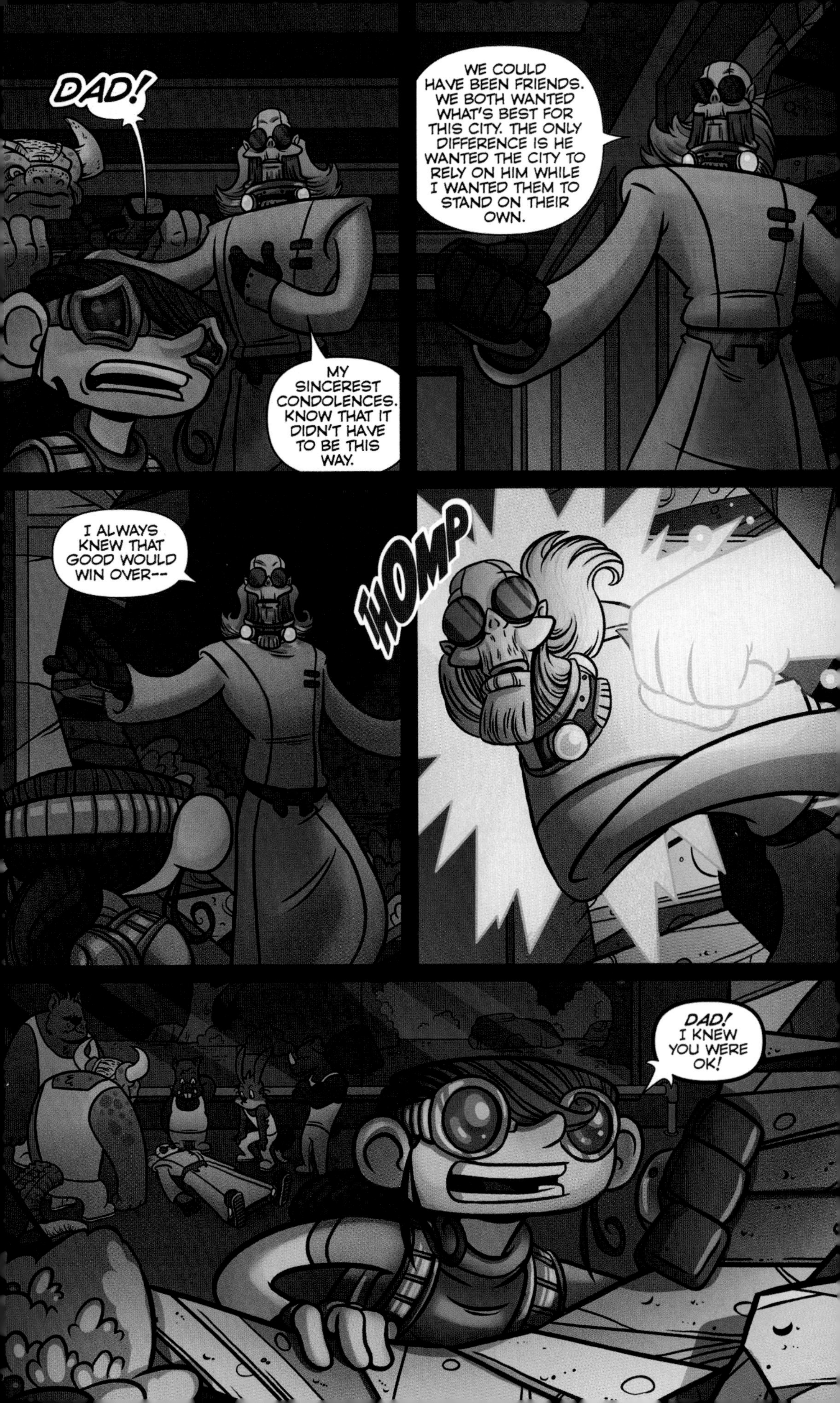
DAD!
MY SINCEREST CONDOLENCES. KNOW THAT IT DIDN'T HAVE TO BE THIS WAY.
WE COULD HAVE BEEN FRIENDS. WE BOTH WANTED WHAT'S BEST FOR THIS CITY. THE ONLY DIFFERENCE IS HE WANTED THE CITY TO RELY ON HIM WHILE I WANTED THEM TO STAND ON THEIR OWN.
I ALWAYS KNEW THAT GOOD WOULD WIN OVER--
THOMP
DAD! I KNEW YOU WERE OK!

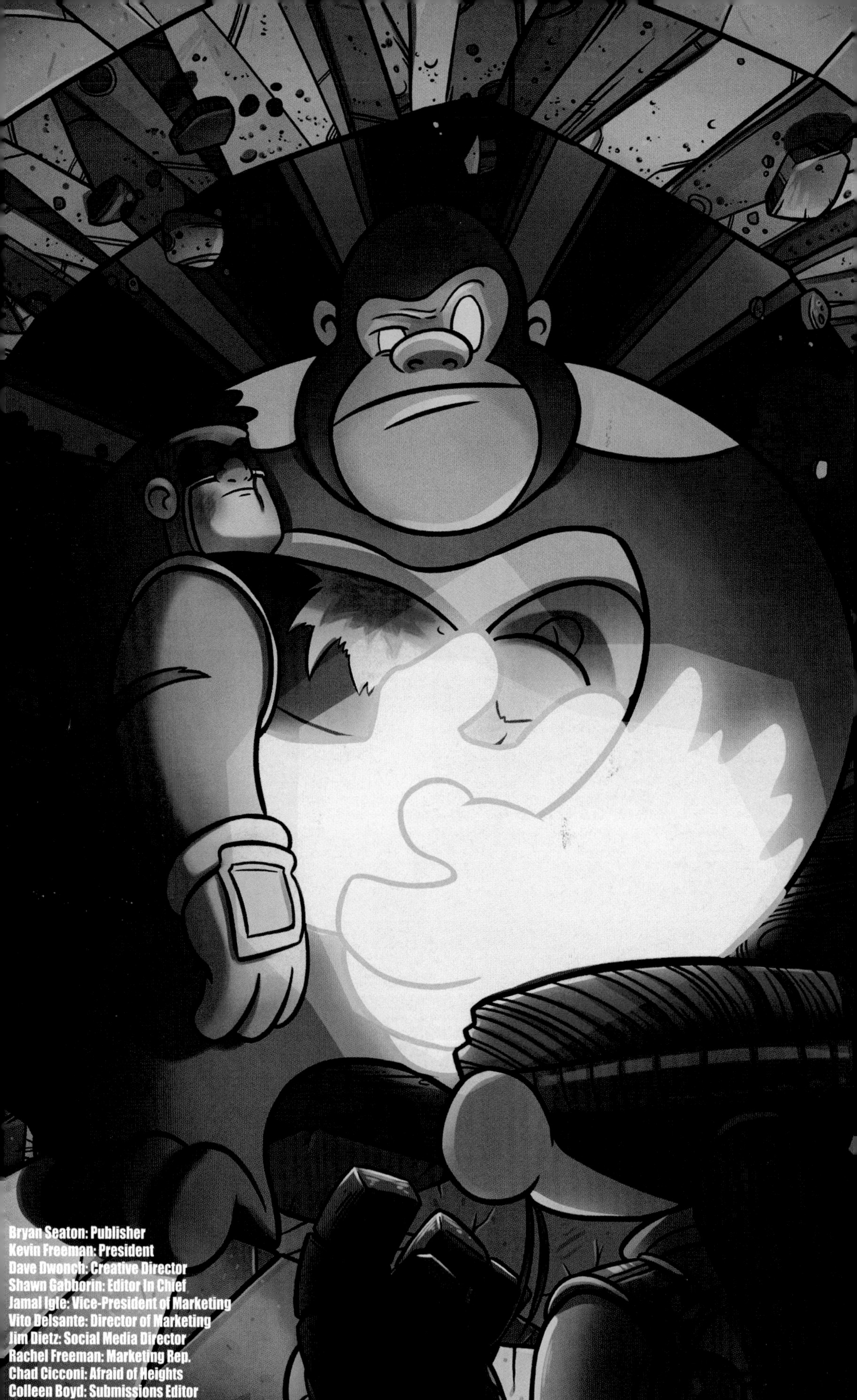

Bryan Seaton: Publisher
Kevin Freeman: President
Dave Dwonch: Creative Director
Shawn Gabborin: Editor In Chief
Jamal Igle: Vice-President of Marketing
Vito Delsante: Director of Marketing
Jim Dietz: Social Media Director
Rachel Freeman: Marketing Rep.
Chad Cicconi: Afraid of Heights
Colleen Boyd: Submissions Editor

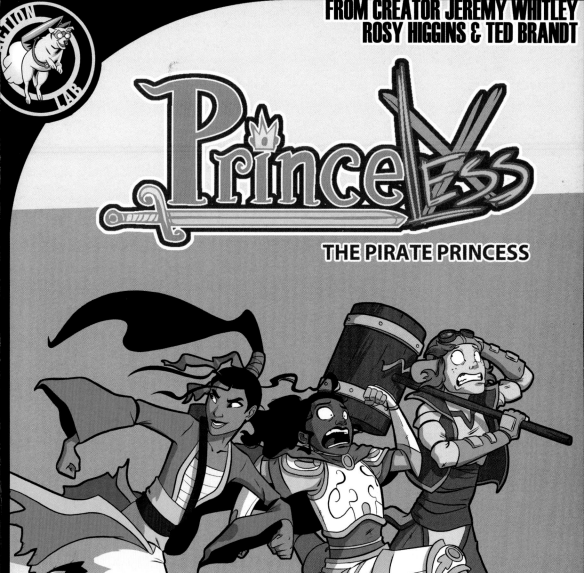

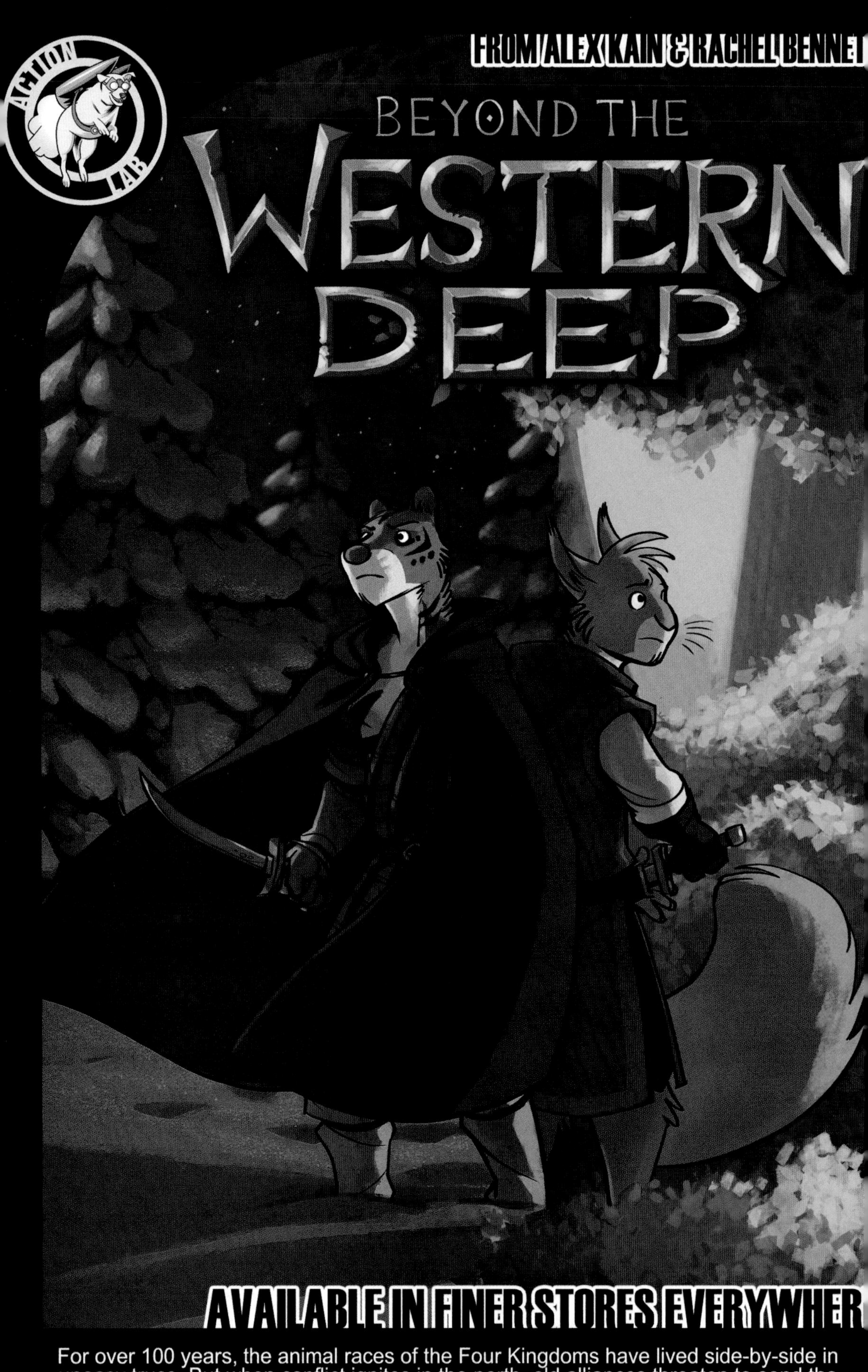
ACTION LAB
FROM ALEX KAIN & RACHEL BENNET
BEYOND THE
WESTERN
DEEP
AVAILABLE IN FINER STORES EVERYWHER

For over 100 years, the animal races of the Four Kingdoms have lived side-by-side in uneasy truce. But when conflict ignites in the north, old alliances threaten to send the world into chaos. Experience the beginnings of an epic all-ages fantasy in this first collected volume!

AVAILABLE IN FINER STORES EVERYWHERE

The shocking conclusion to the Nightmare Nursery saga! Destiny Harper is in deep trouble, and she will need the help of Rasket, Lycinda and the Vamplets themselves to thwart the plans of the evil Vammette. Will Destiny Harper get back home, or will she be trapped on the nightmare world of Gloomvania forever?

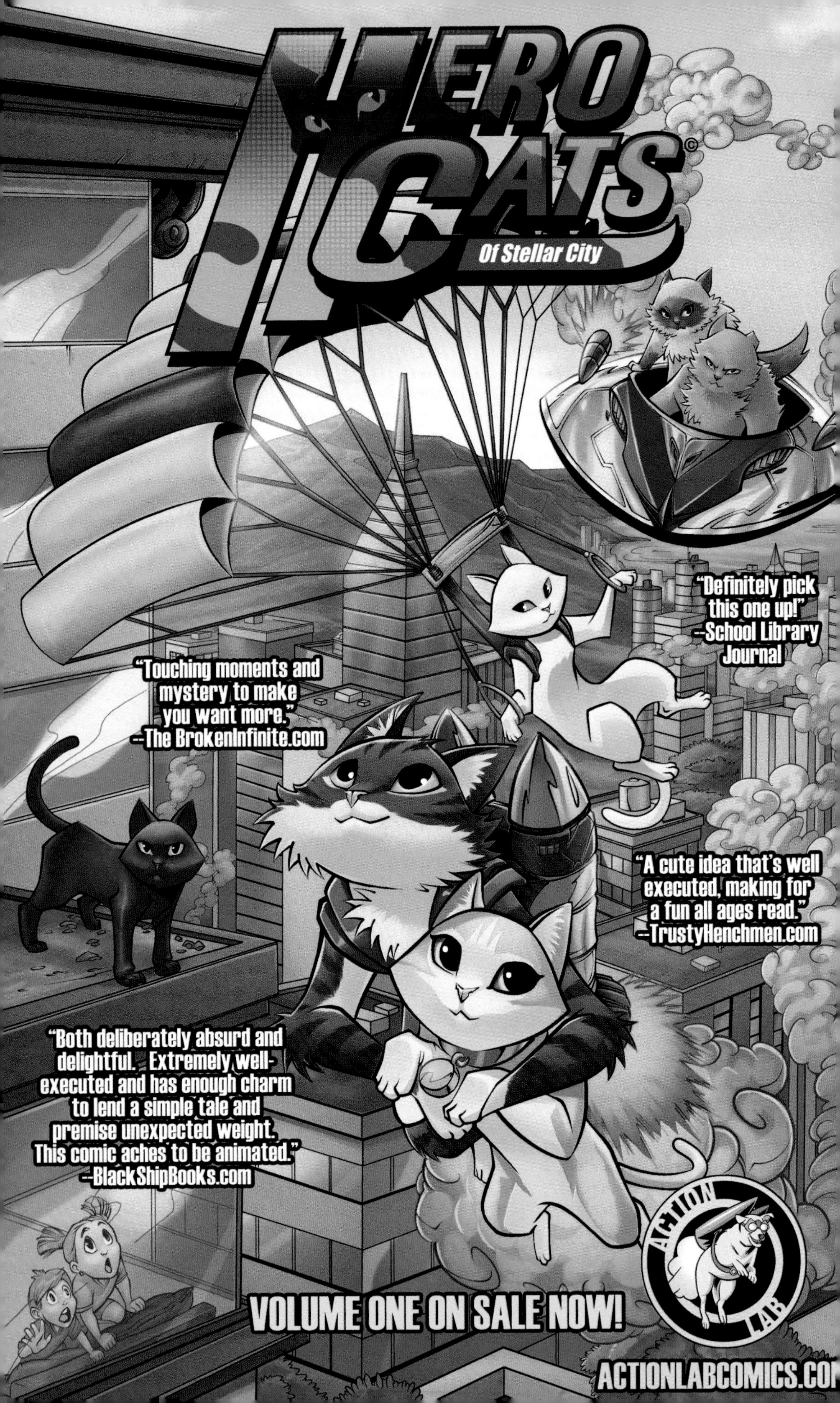

HERO CATS
Of Stellar City
"Definitely pick this one up!" --School Library Journal
"Touching moments and mystery to make you want more." --The BrokenInfinite.com
"A cute idea that's well executed, making for a fun all ages read." --TrustyHenchmen.com
"Both deliberately absurd and delightful. Extremely well-executed and has enough charm to lend a simple tale and premise unexpected weight. This comic aches to be animated." --BlackShipBooks.com
ACTION LAB
VOLUME ONE ON SALE NOW!
ACTIONLABCOMICS.COM

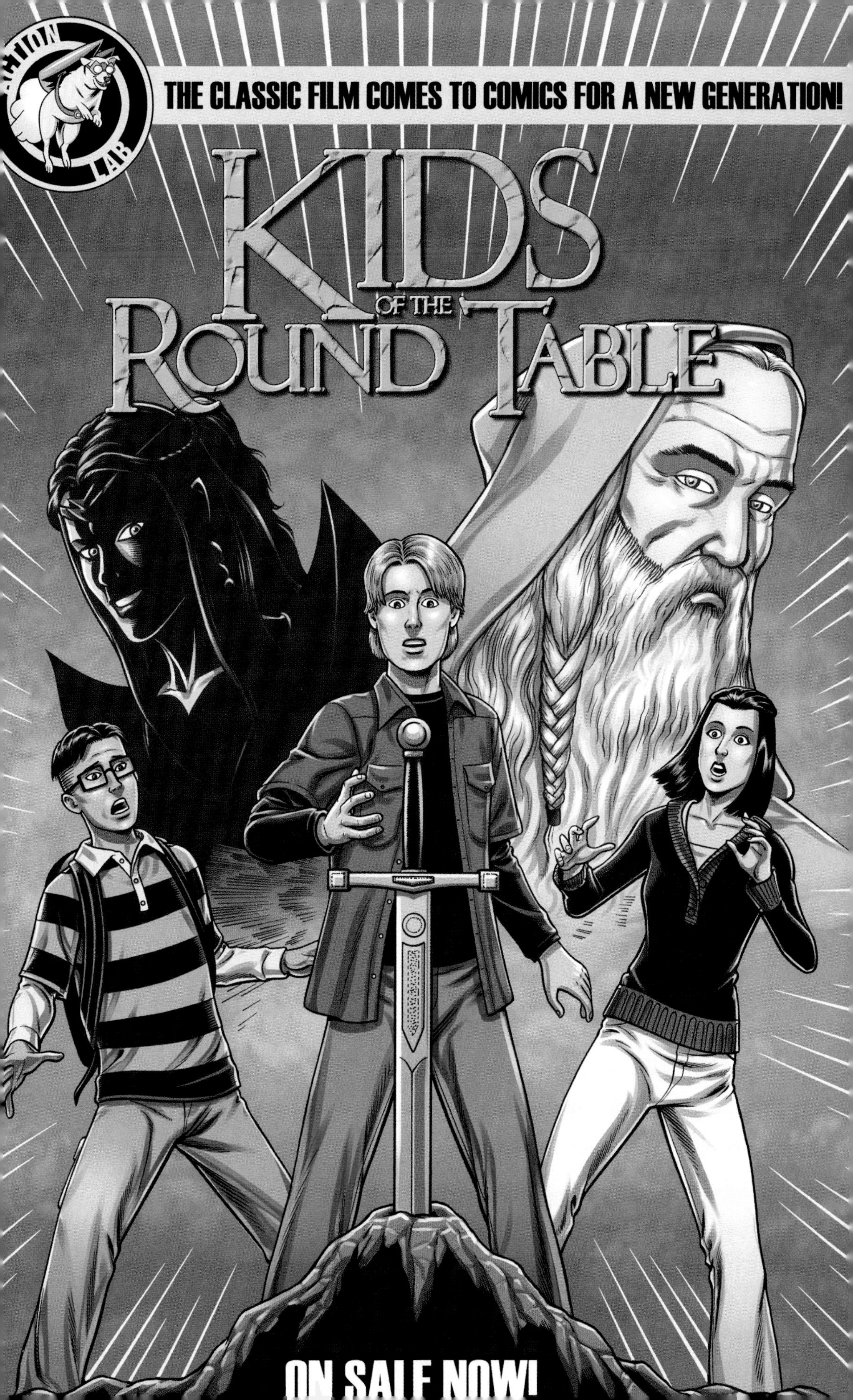
ACTION LAB
THE CLASSIC FILM COMES TO COMICS FOR A NEW GENERATION!
KIDS OF THE ROUND TABLE
ON SALE NOW!

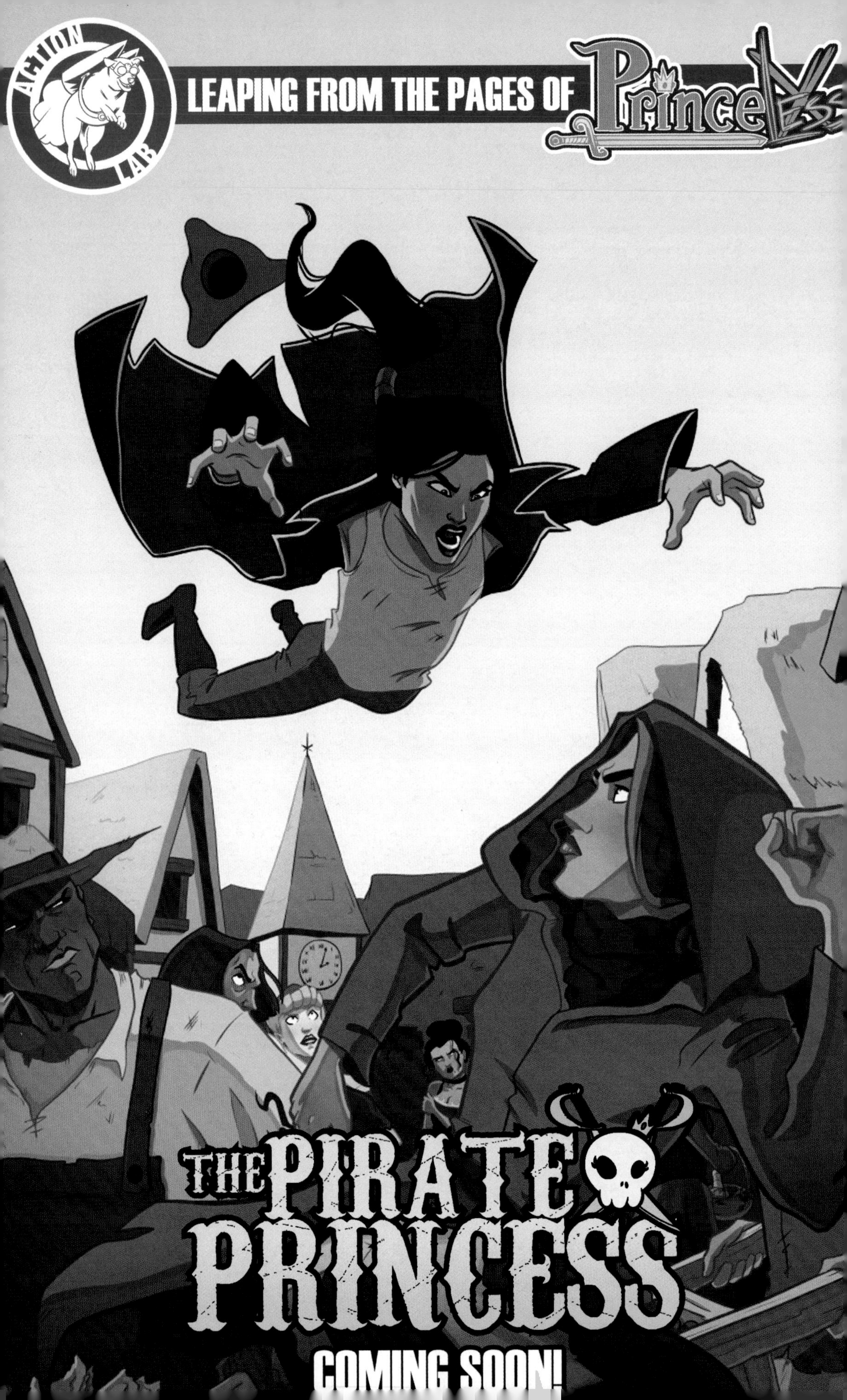
ACTION LAB
LEAPING FROM THE PAGES OF
Princeless
THE PIRATE PRINCESS
COMING SOON!

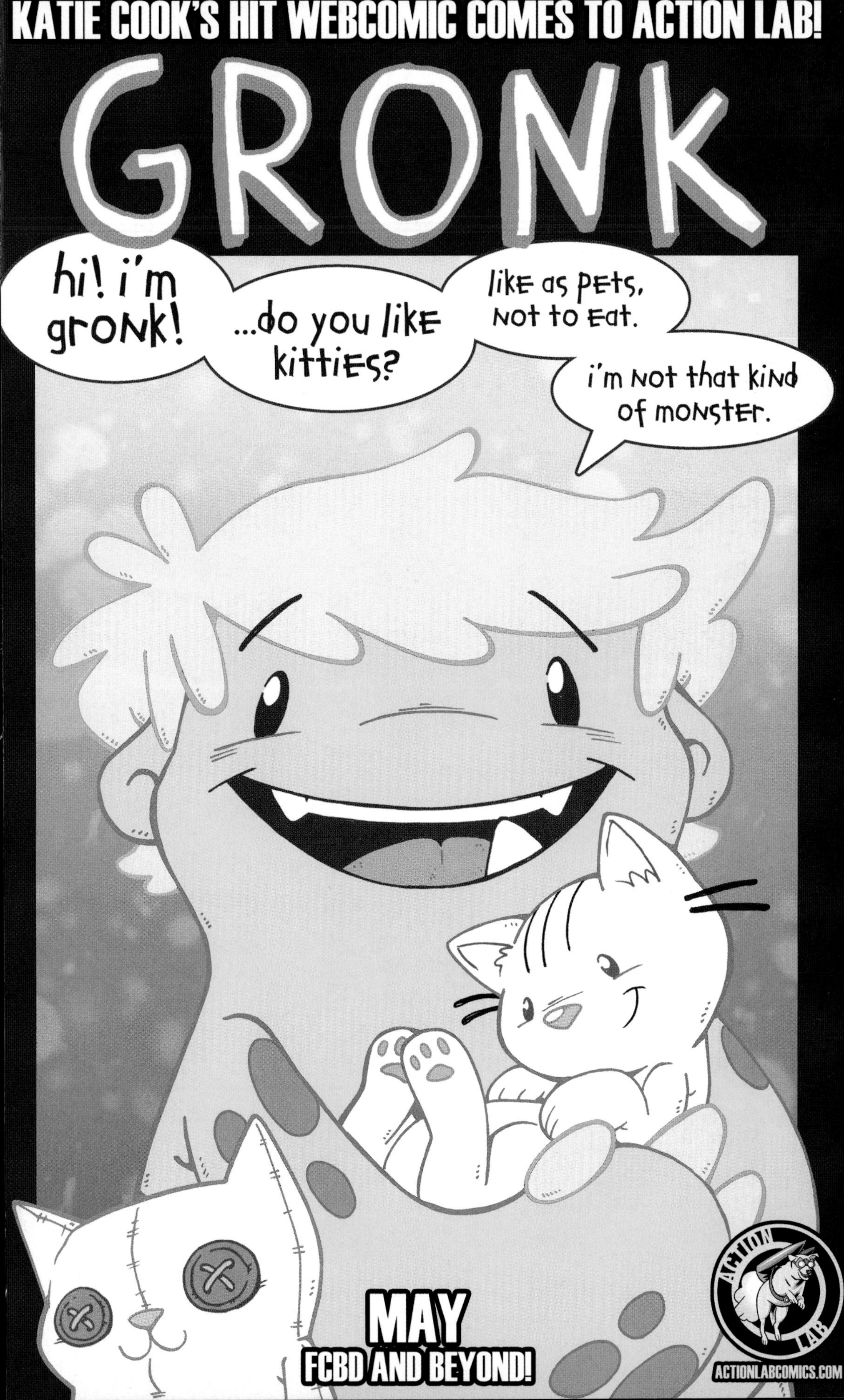
KATIE COOK'S HIT WEBCOMIC COMES TO ACTION LAB!
GRONK
hi! i'm gronk!
...do you like kitties?
like as pets, not to eat.
i'm not that kind of monster.
MAY
FCBD AND BEYOND!
ACTION LAB
ACTIONLABCOMICS.COM

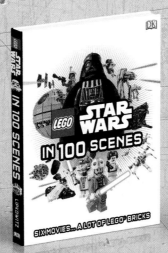
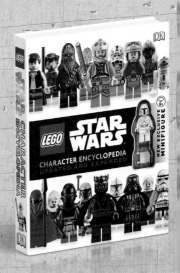
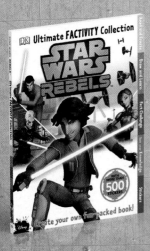

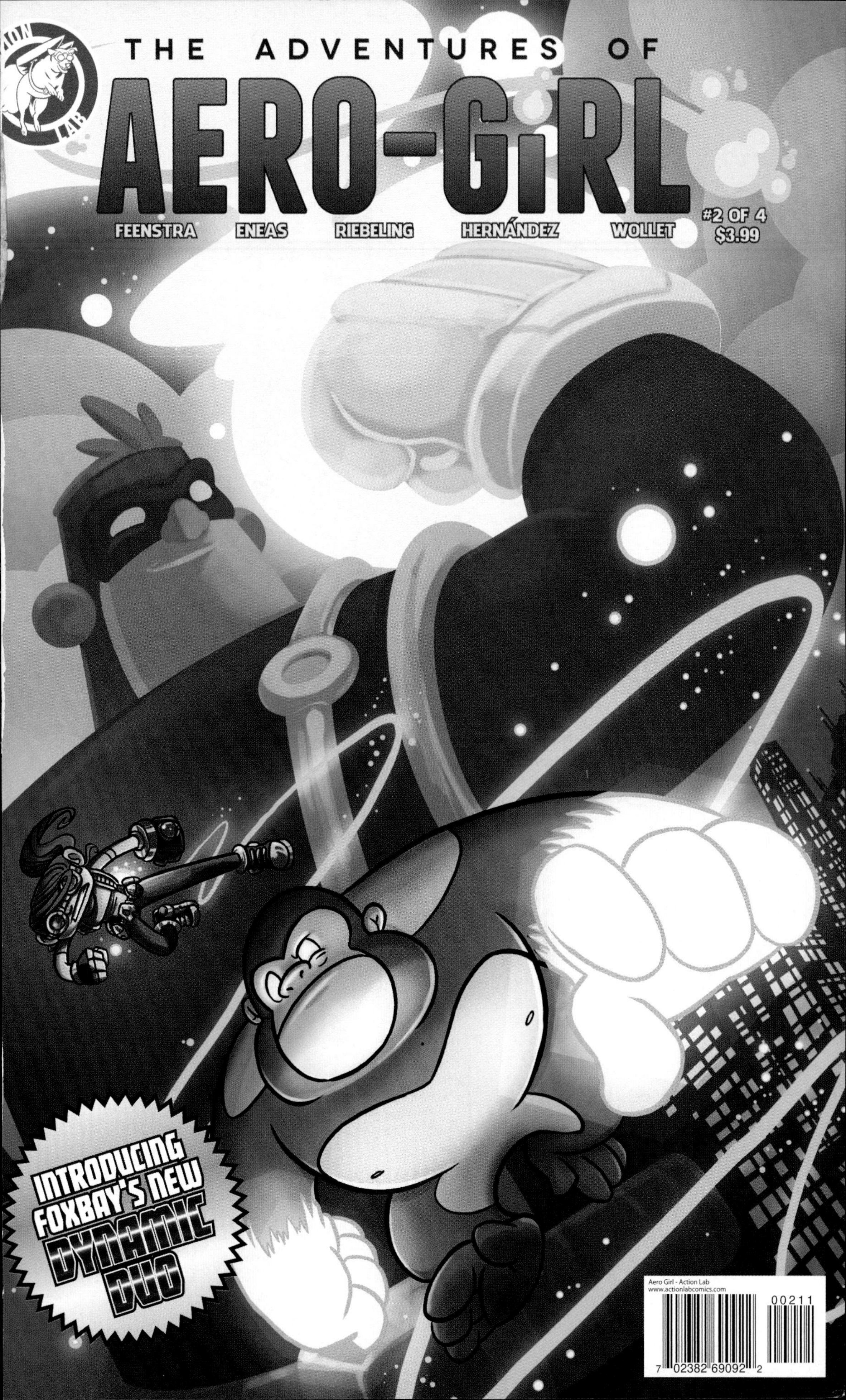

THE ADVENTURES OF
AERO-GIRL
FEENSTRA
ENEAS
RIEBELING
HERNÁNDEZ
WOLLET
#2 OF 4
$3.99
INTRODUCING FOXBAY'S NEW DYNAMIC DUO
Aero Girl - Action Lab
www.actionlabcomics.com
00211
7 02382 69092 2

FROM JAMES WRIGHT & JACKIE CROFT

NUTMEG

AVAILABLE IN FINER STORES EVERYWHER

Vol. 1 "Early Fall: Taste Buddies" collects issues 1-3 of Nutmeg, following 8th-grader Pop
Pepper's partnership with new girl Cassia Caraway and their plan to sabotage rich girl riv
Saffron Longfellow's brownie fundraiser, taking their first steps toward a life of crime.

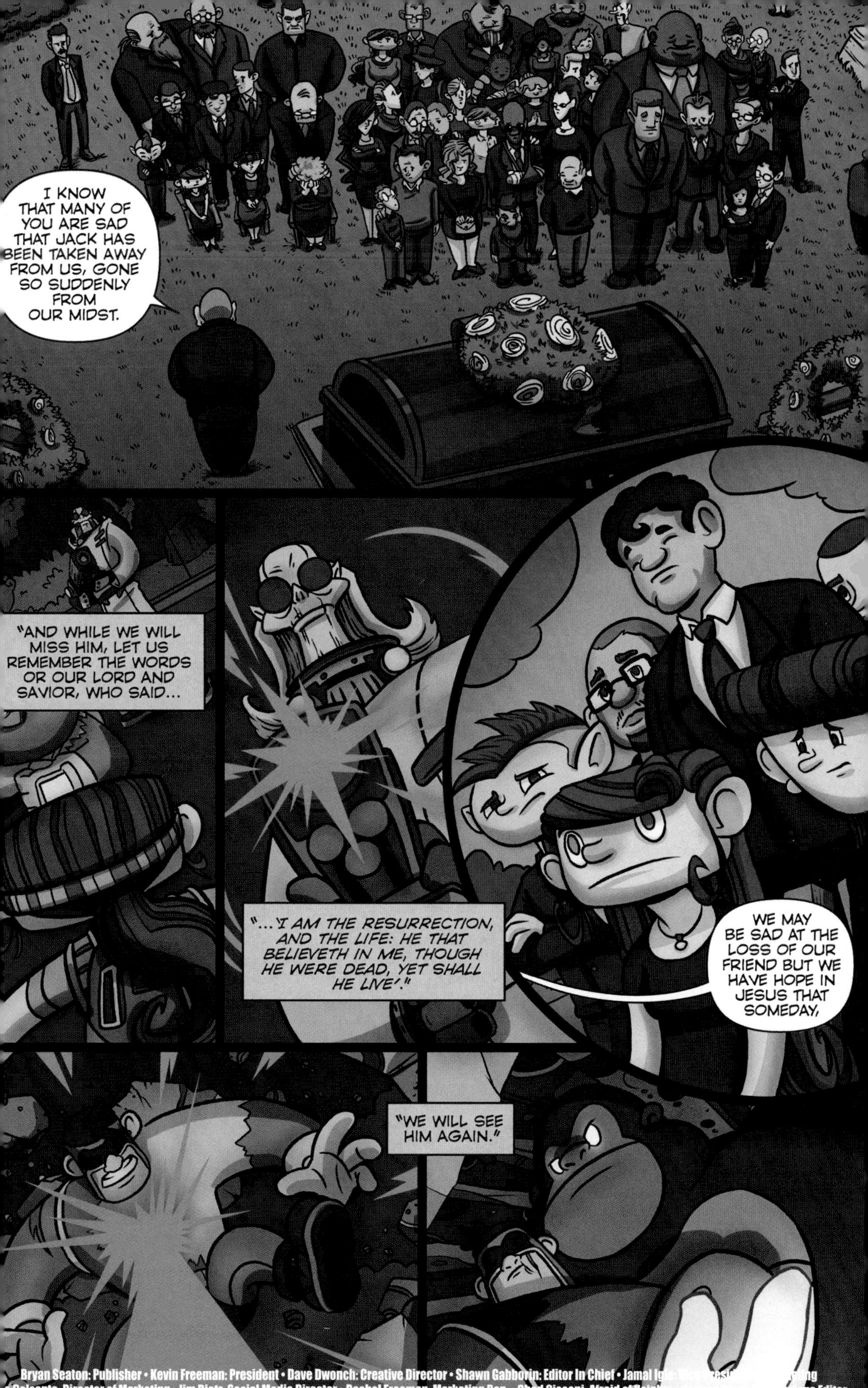

I KNOW THAT MANY OF YOU ARE SAD THAT JACK HAS BEEN TAKEN AWAY FROM US, GONE SO SUDDENLY FROM OUR MIDST.
"AND WHILE WE WILL MISS HIM, LET US REMEMBER THE WORDS OR OUR LORD AND SAVIOR, WHO SAID...
"...'I AM THE RESURRECTION, AND THE LIFE: HE THAT BELIEVETH IN ME, THOUGH HE WERE DEAD, YET SHALL HE LIVE'."
WE MAY BE SAD AT THE LOSS OF OUR FRIEND BUT WE HAVE HOPE IN JESUS THAT SOMEDAY,
"WE WILL SEE HIM AGAIN."

Bryan Seaton: Publisher • Kevin Freeman: President • Dave Dwonch: Creative Director • Shawn Gabborin: Editor In Chief • Jamal Igle: ...ing
o Delsante: Director of Marketing • Jim Dietz: Social Media Director • Rachel Freeman: Marketing Rep. • Chad Cicconi: Afraid of Heights • ...ions Editor

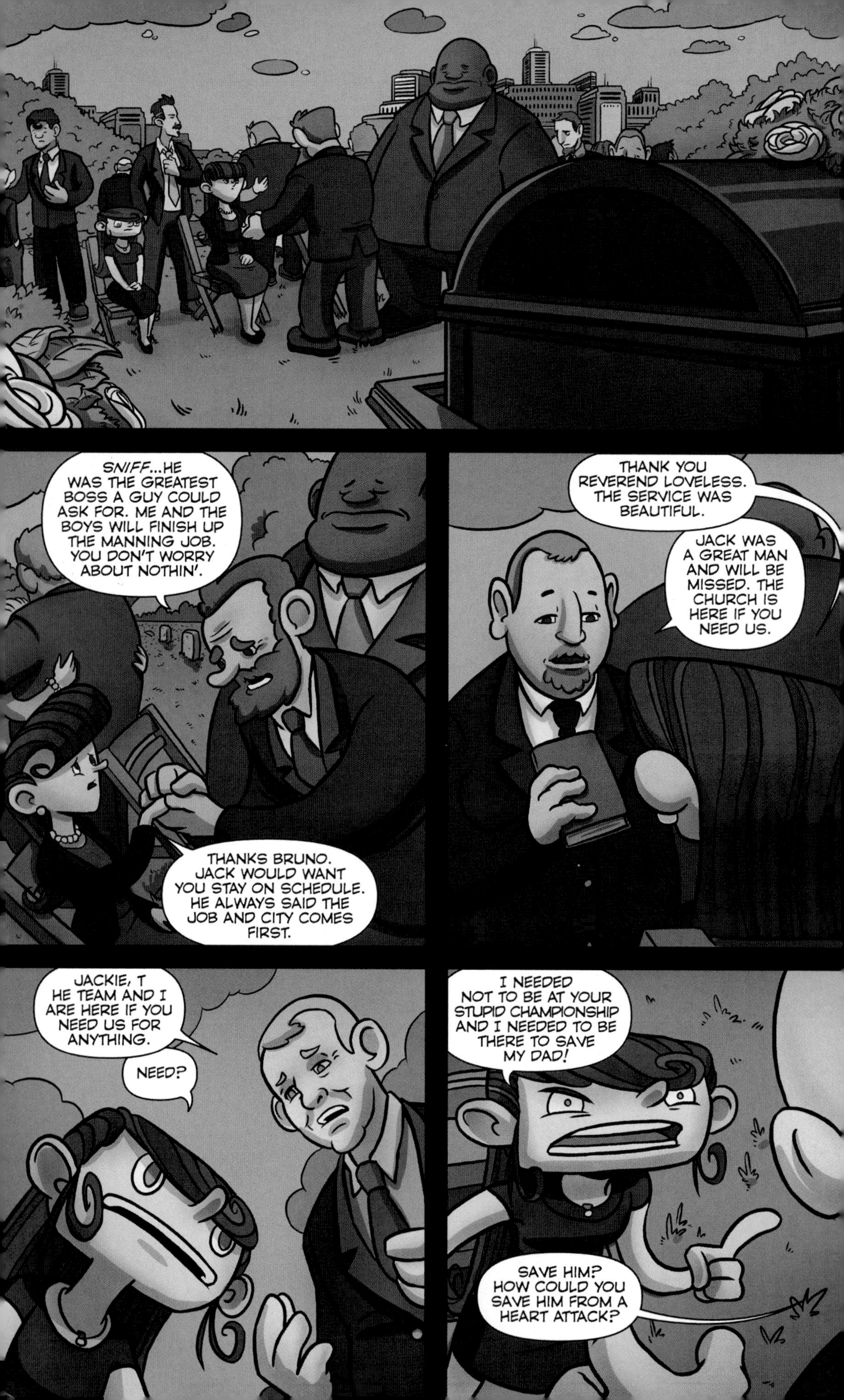
SNIFF...HE WAS THE GREATEST BOSS A GUY COULD ASK FOR. ME AND THE BOYS WILL FINISH UP THE MANNING JOB. YOU DON'T WORRY ABOUT NOTHIN'.
THANKS BRUNO. JACK WOULD WANT YOU STAY ON SCHEDULE. HE ALWAYS SAID THE JOB AND CITY COMES FIRST.
THANK YOU REVEREND LOVELESS. THE SERVICE WAS BEAUTIFUL.
JACK WAS A GREAT MAN AND WILL BE MISSED. THE CHURCH IS HERE IF YOU NEED US.
JACKIE, T HE TEAM AND I ARE HERE IF YOU NEED US FOR ANYTHING.
NEED?
I NEEDED NOT TO BE AT YOUR STUPID CHAMPIONSHIP AND I NEEDED TO BE THERE TO SAVE MY DAD!
SAVE HIM? HOW COULD YOU SAVE HIM FROM A HEART ATTACK?

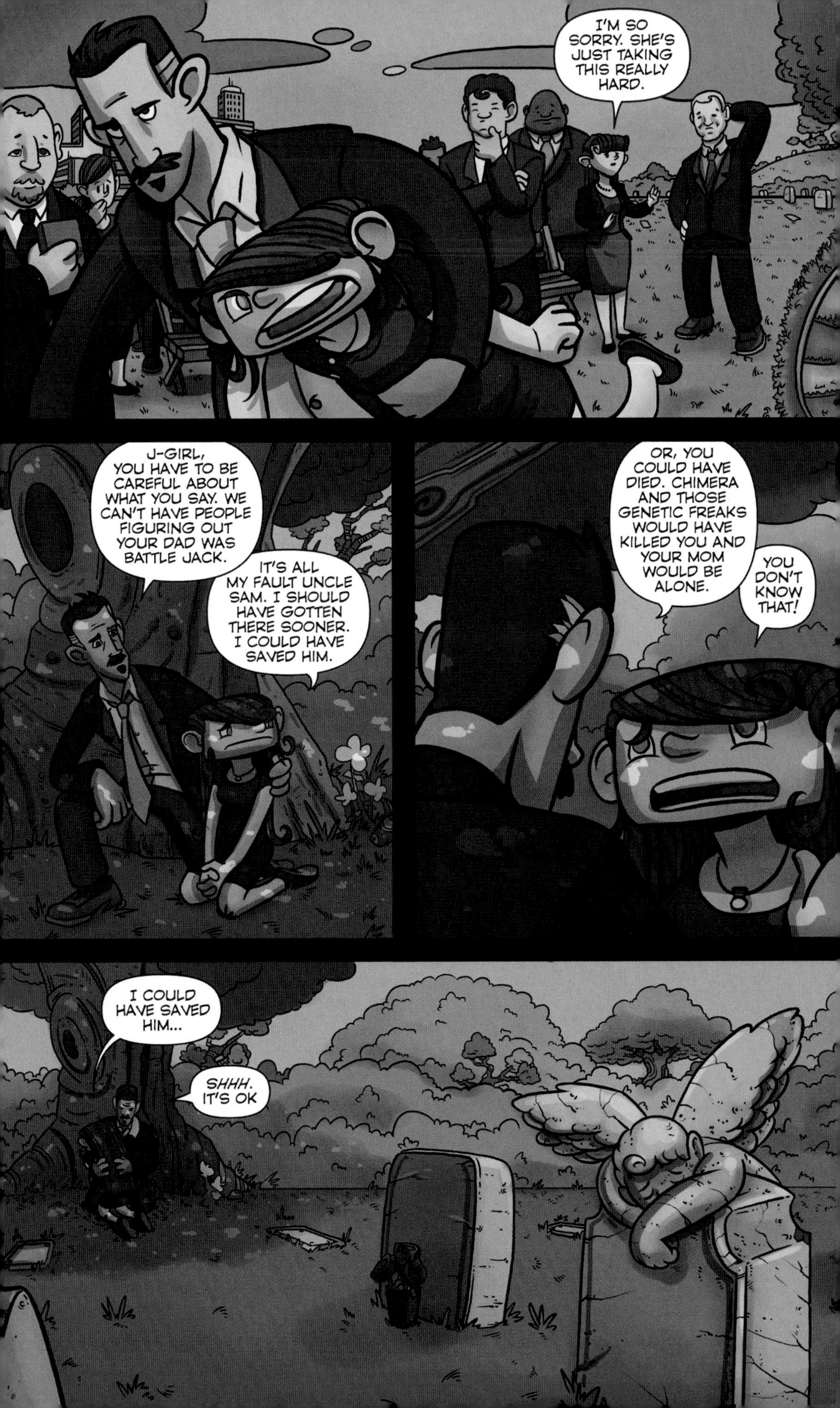

I'M SO SORRY. SHE'S JUST TAKING THIS REALLY HARD.
J-GIRL, YOU HAVE TO BE CAREFUL ABOUT WHAT YOU SAY. WE CAN'T HAVE PEOPLE FIGURING OUT YOUR DAD WAS BATTLE JACK.
IT'S ALL MY FAULT UNCLE SAM. I SHOULD HAVE GOTTEN THERE SOONER. I COULD HAVE SAVED HIM.
OR, YOU COULD HAVE DIED. CHIMERA AND THOSE GENETIC FREAKS WOULD HAVE KILLED YOU AND YOUR MOM WOULD BE ALONE.
YOU DON'T KNOW THAT!
I COULD HAVE SAVED HIM...
SHHH. IT'S OK

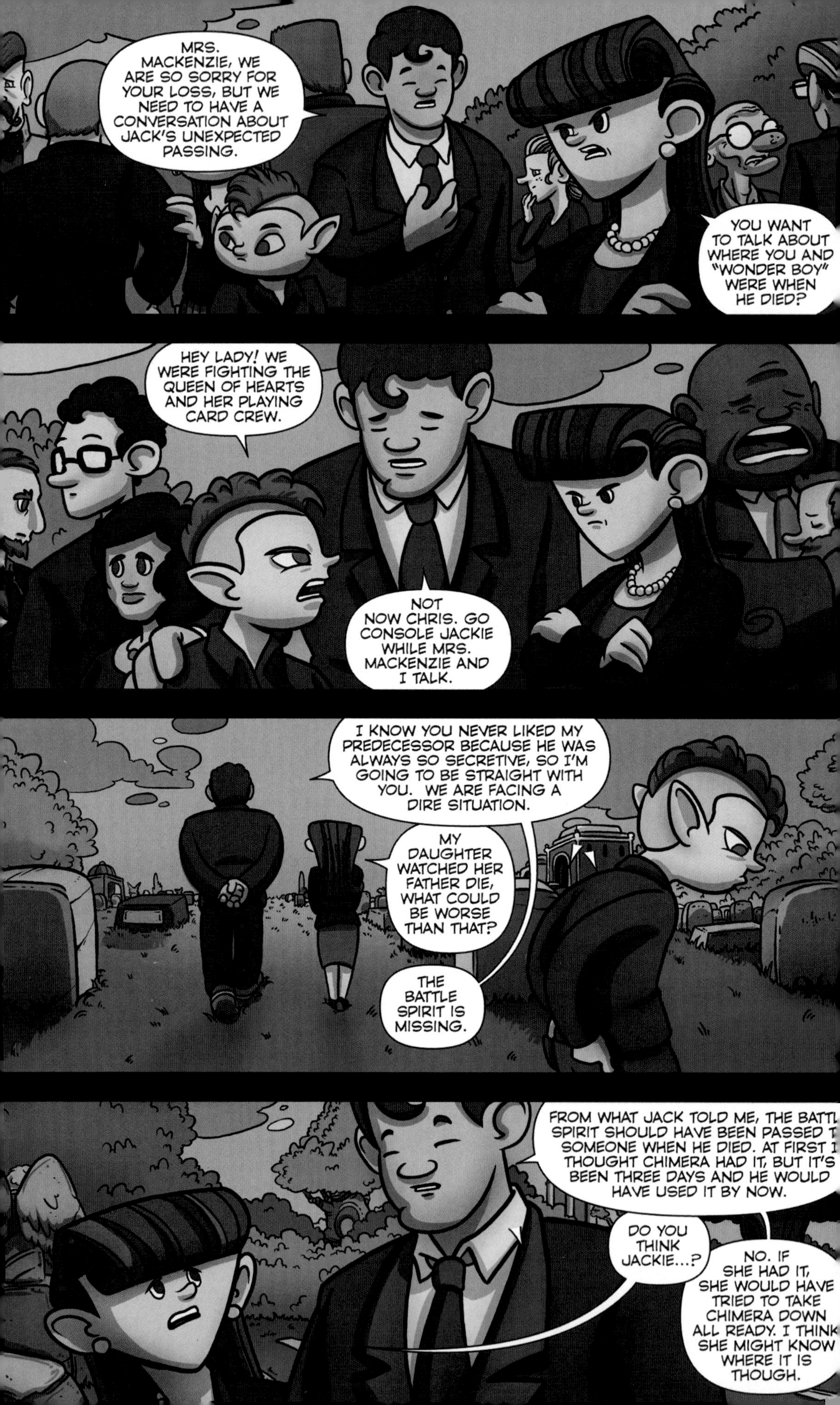
MRS. MACKENZIE, WE ARE SO SORRY FOR YOUR LOSS, BUT WE NEED TO HAVE A CONVERSATION ABOUT JACK'S UNEXPECTED PASSING.
YOU WANT TO TALK ABOUT WHERE YOU AND "WONDER BOY" WERE WHEN HE DIED?
HEY LADY! WE WERE FIGHTING THE QUEEN OF HEARTS AND HER PLAYING CARD CREW.
NOT NOW CHRIS. GO CONSOLE JACKIE WHILE MRS. MACKENZIE AND I TALK.
I KNOW YOU NEVER LIKED MY PREDECESSOR BECAUSE HE WAS ALWAYS SO SECRETIVE, SO I'M GOING TO BE STRAIGHT WITH YOU. WE ARE FACING A DIRE SITUATION.
MY DAUGHTER WATCHED HER FATHER DIE, WHAT COULD BE WORSE THAN THAT?
THE BATTLE SPIRIT IS MISSING.
FROM WHAT JACK TOLD ME, THE BATTL SPIRIT SHOULD HAVE BEEN PASSED T SOMEONE WHEN HE DIED. AT FIRST I THOUGHT CHIMERA HAD IT, BUT IT'S BEEN THREE DAYS AND HE WOULD HAVE USED IT BY NOW.
DO YOU THINK JACKIE...?
NO. IF SHE HAD IT, SHE WOULD HAVE TRIED TO TAKE CHIMERA DOWN ALL READY. I THINK SHE MIGHT KNOW WHERE IT IS THOUGH.

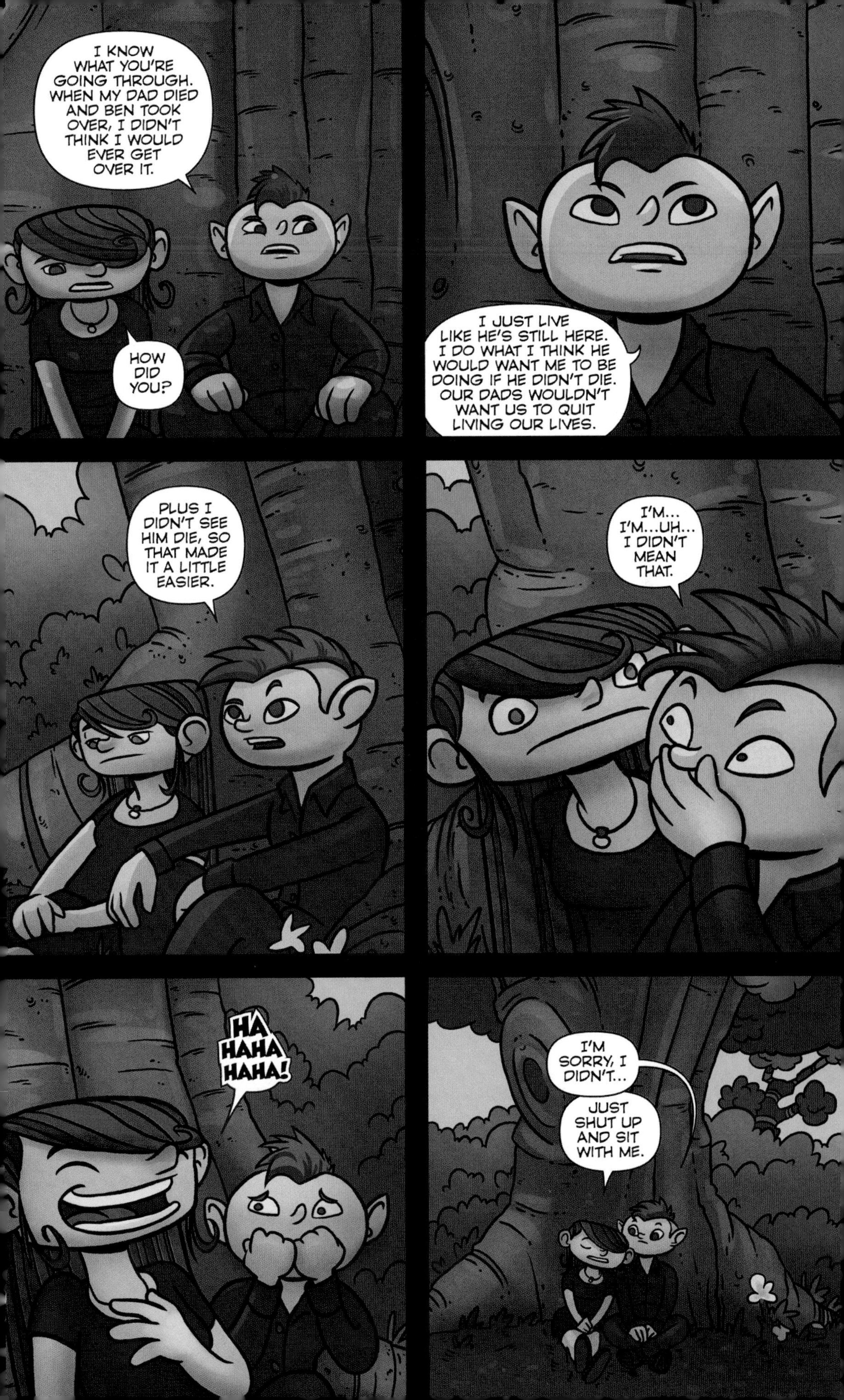
I KNOW WHAT YOU'RE GOING THROUGH. WHEN MY DAD DIED AND BEN TOOK OVER, I DIDN'T THINK I WOULD EVER GET OVER IT.
HOW DID YOU?
I JUST LIVE LIKE HE'S STILL HERE. I DO WHAT I THINK HE WOULD WANT ME TO BE DOING IF HE DIDN'T DIE. OUR DADS WOULDN'T WANT US TO QUIT LIVING OUR LIVES.
PLUS I DIDN'T SEE HIM DIE, SO THAT MADE IT A LITTLE EASIER.
I'M... I'M...UH... I DIDN'T MEAN THAT.
HA HAHA HAHA!
I'M SORRY, I DIDN'T...
JUST SHUT UP AND SIT WITH ME.

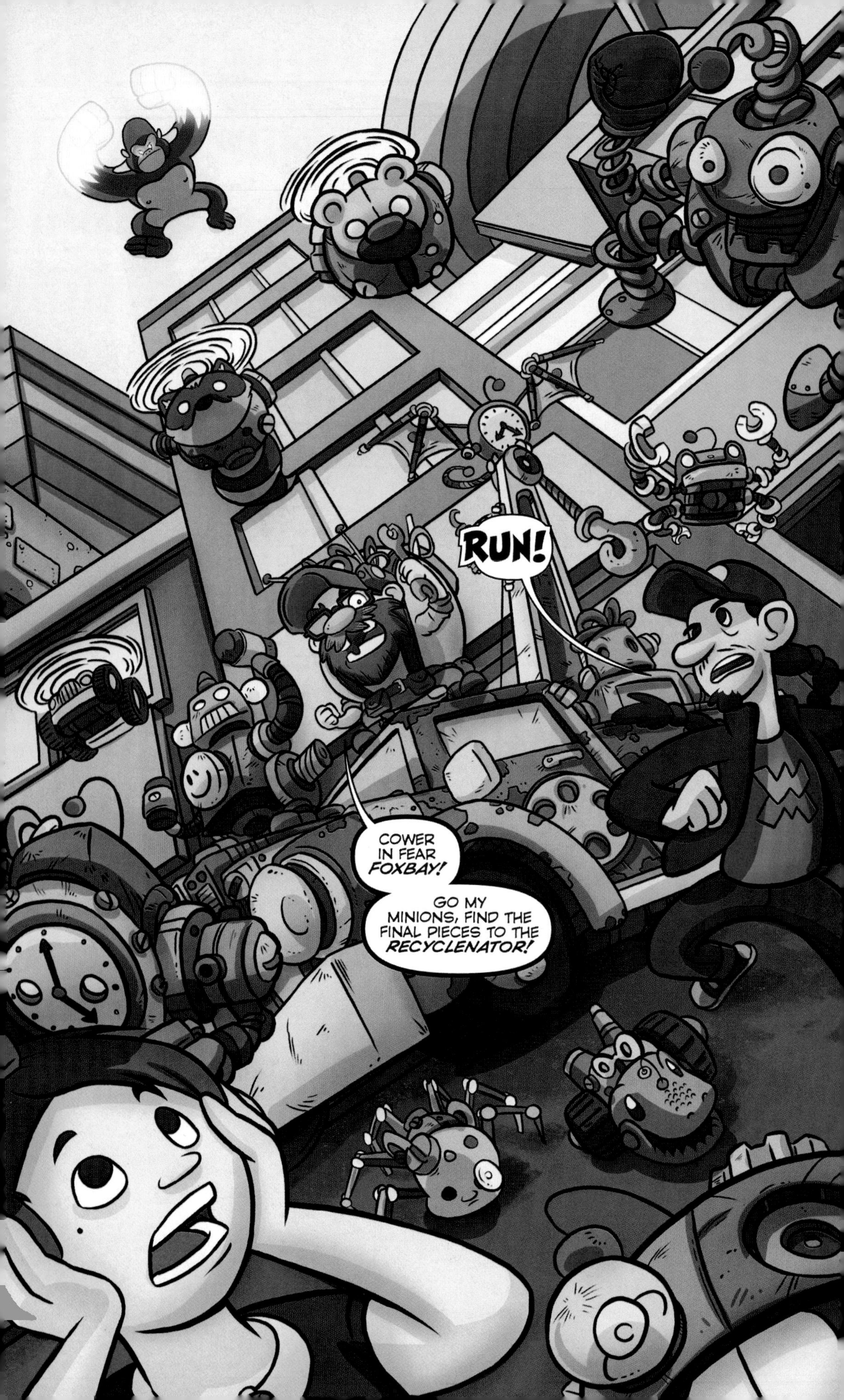
RUN!
COWER IN FEAR FOXBAY!
GO MY MINIONS, FIND THE FINAL PIECES TO THE RECYCLENATOR!

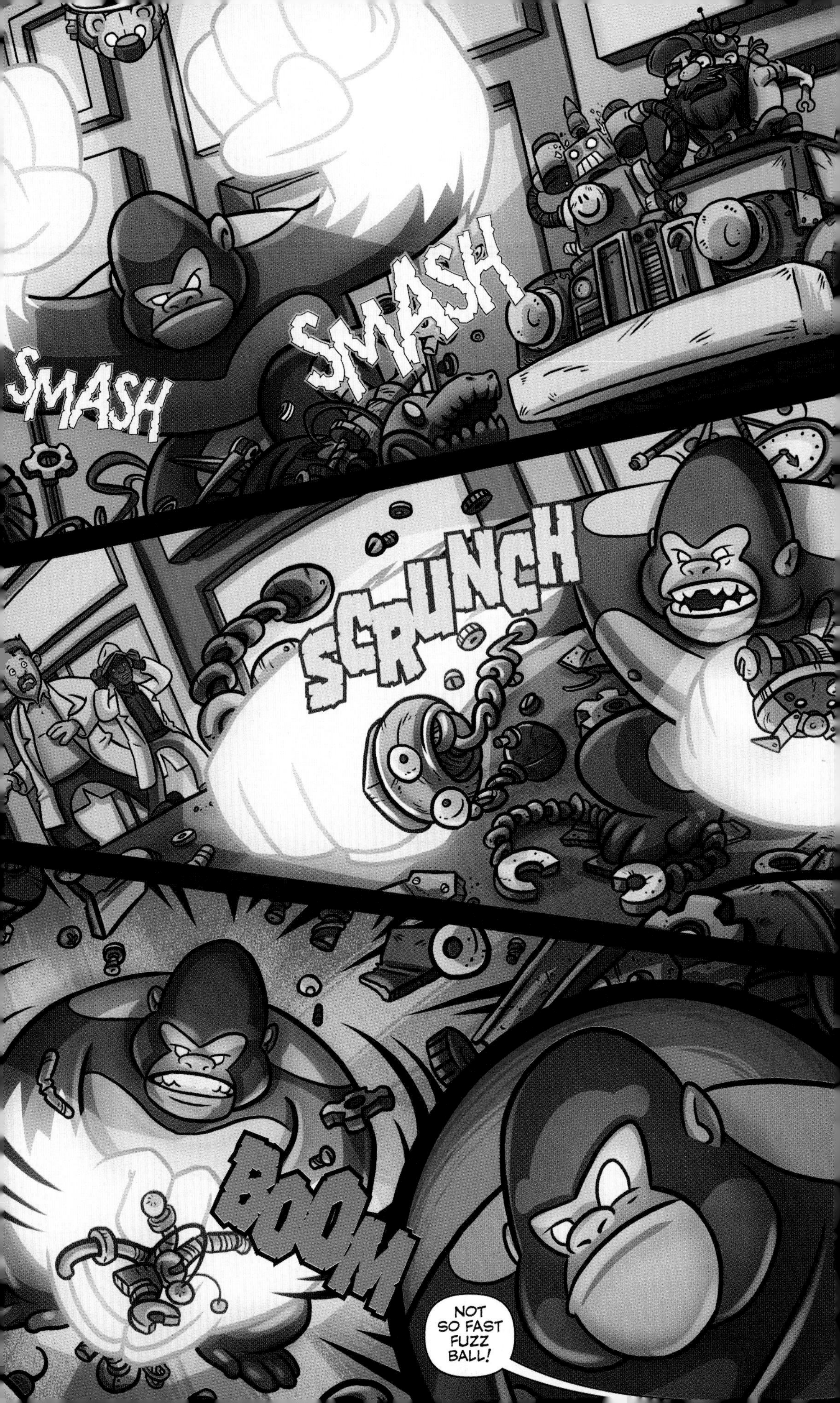
SMASH
SMASH
SCRUNCH
BOOM
NOT SO FAST FUZZ BALL!

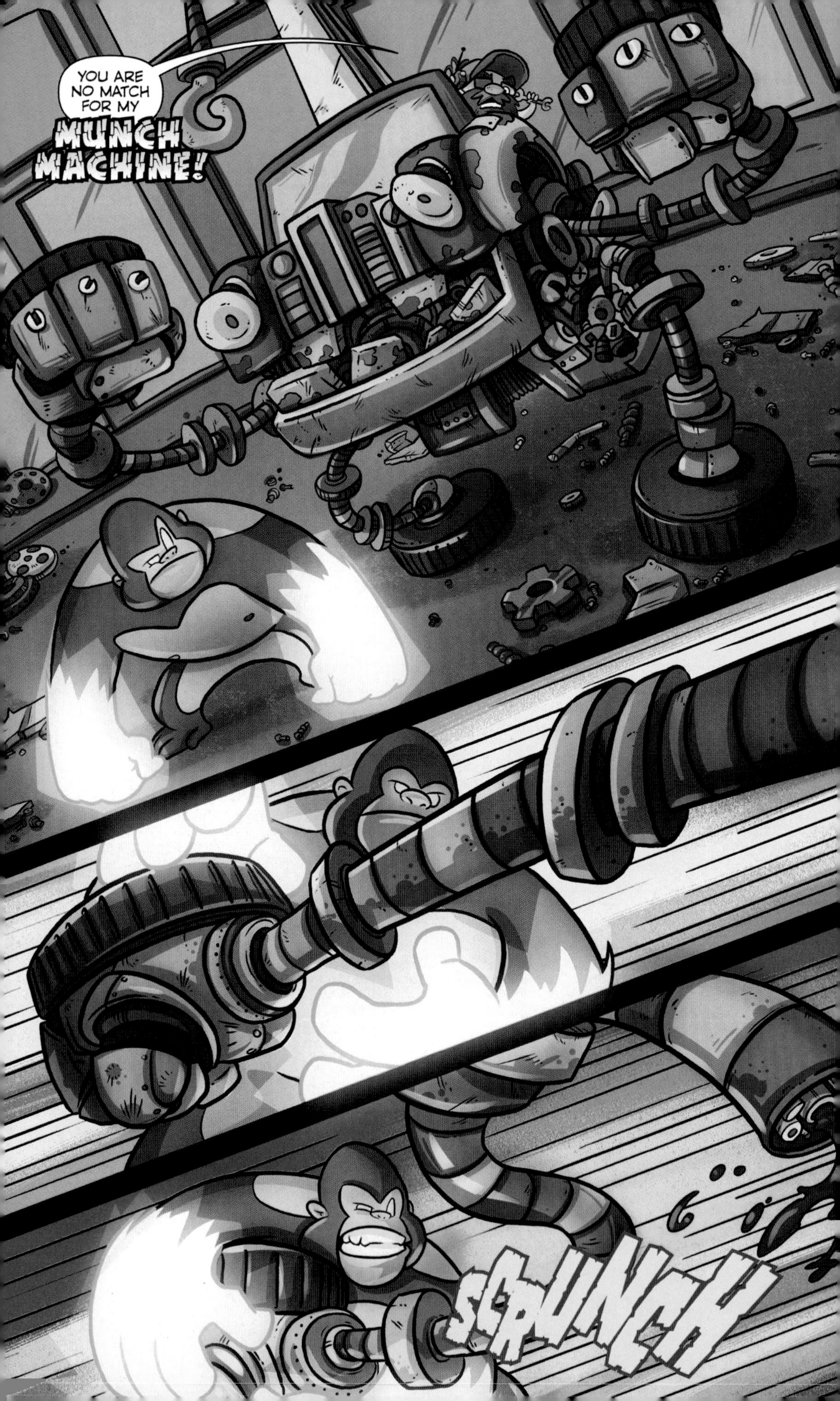
YOU ARE NO MATCH FOR MY
MUNCH MACHINE!
SCRUNCH

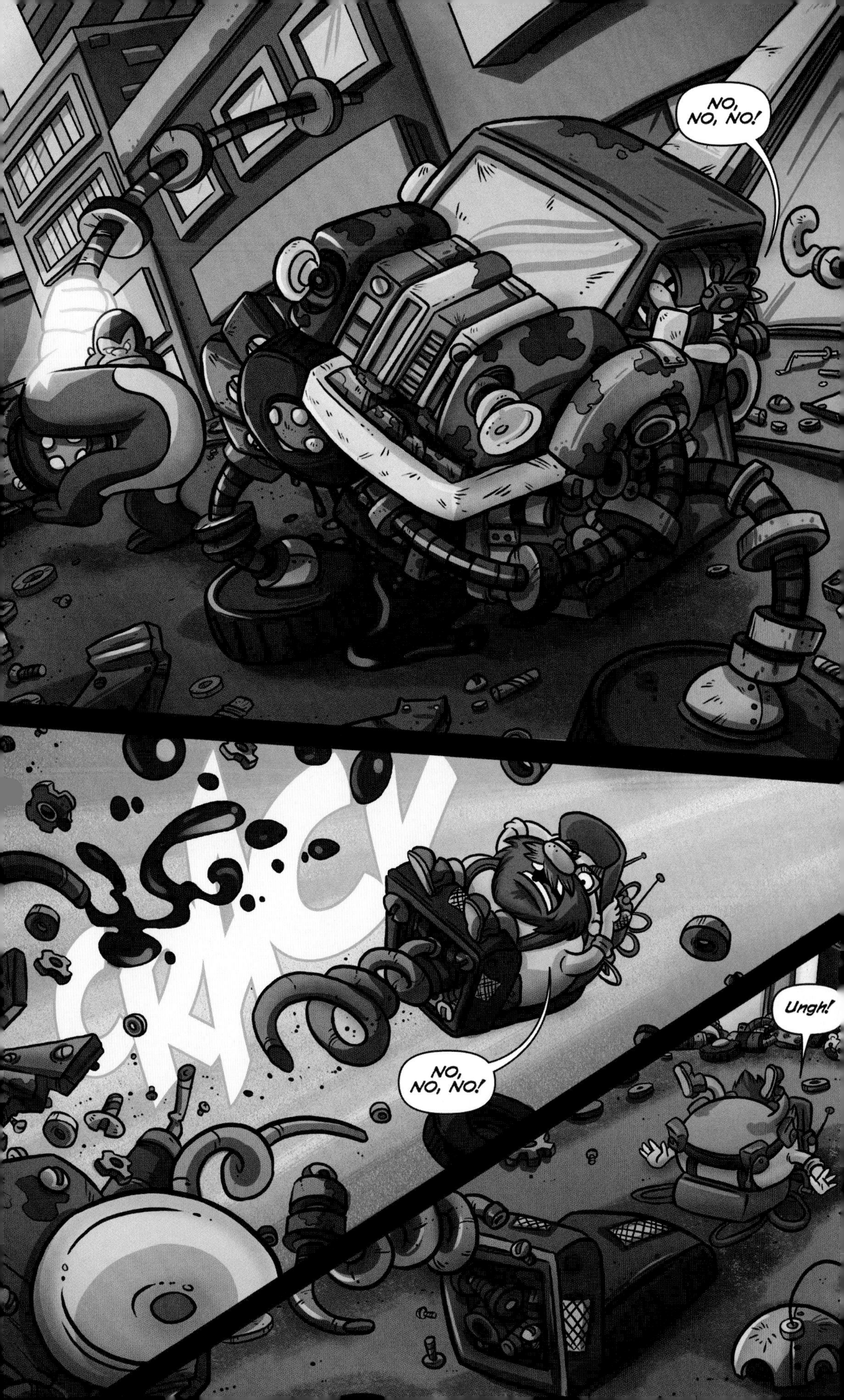
NO, NO, NO!
NO, NO, NO!
Ungh!

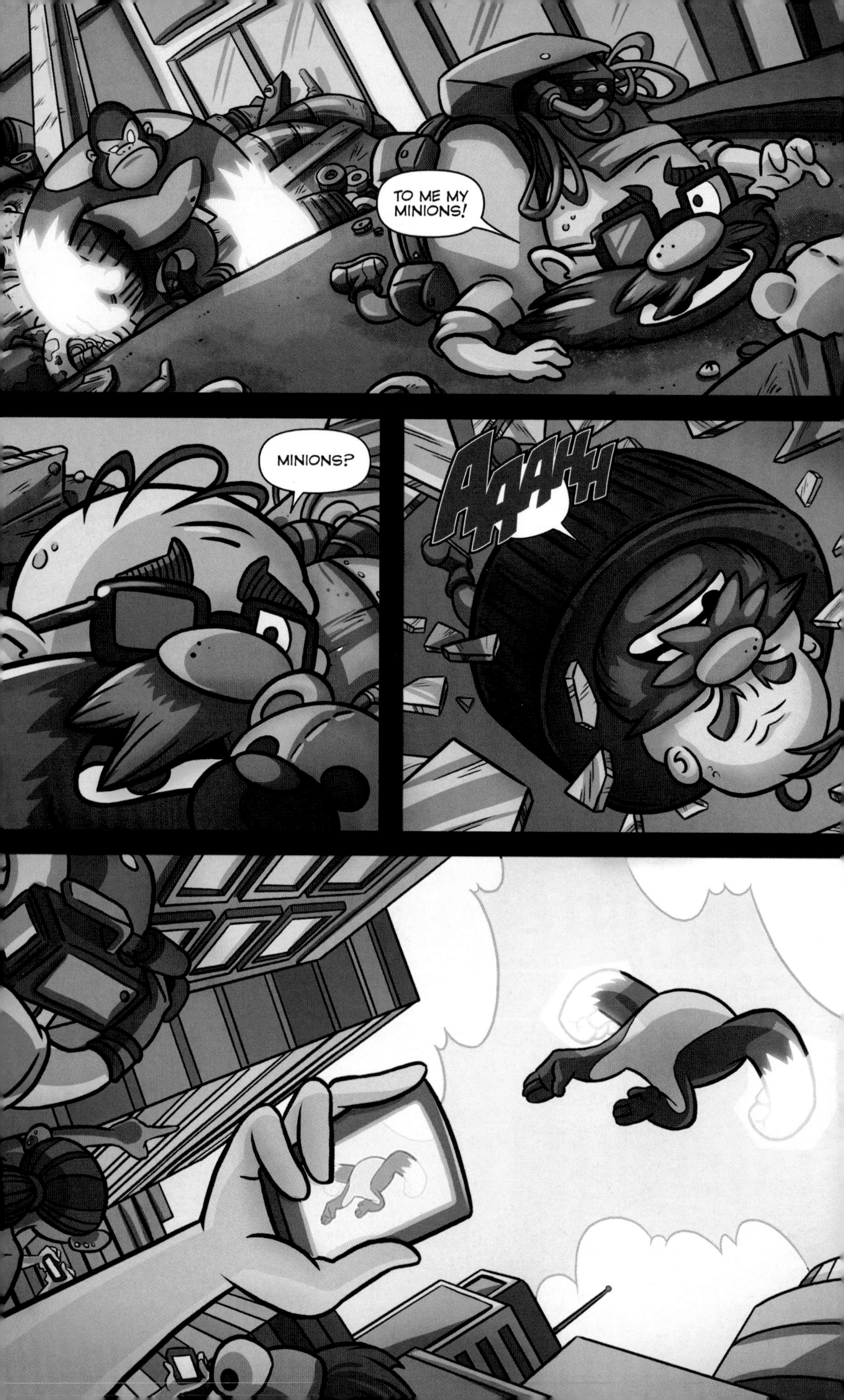
TO ME MY MINIONS!
MINIONS?
AAAHHH

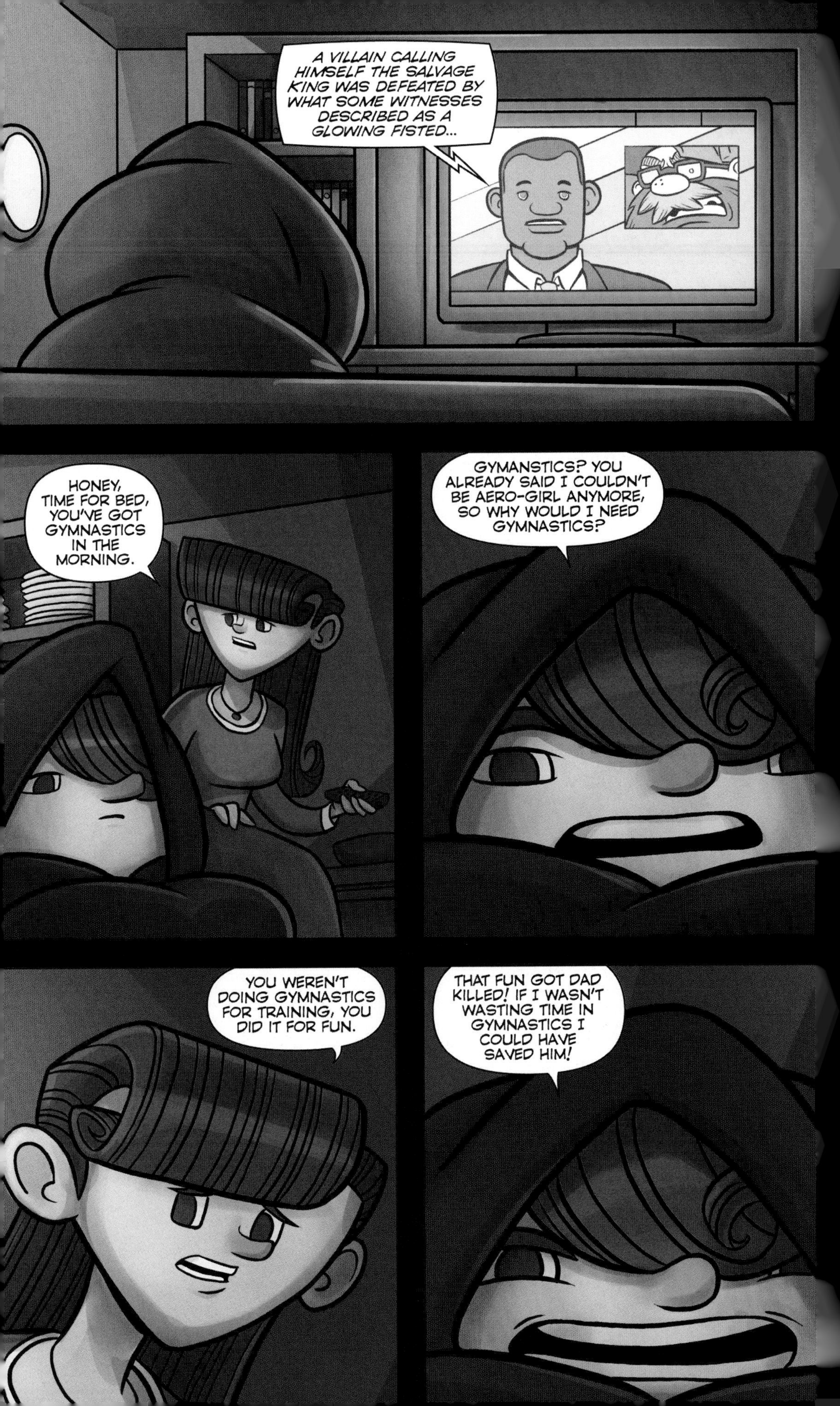
A VILLAIN CALLING HIMSELF THE SALVAGE KING WAS DEFEATED BY WHAT SOME WITNESSES DESCRIBED AS A GLOWING FISTED...
HONEY, TIME FOR BED, YOU'VE GOT GYMNASTICS IN THE MORNING.
GYMANSTICS? YOU ALREADY SAID I COULDN'T BE AERO-GIRL ANYMORE, SO WHY WOULD I NEED GYMNASTICS?
YOU WEREN'T DOING GYMNASTICS FOR TRAINING, YOU DID IT FOR FUN.
THAT FUN GOT DAD KILLED! IF I WASN'T WASTING TIME IN GYMNASTICS I COULD HAVE SAVED HIM!

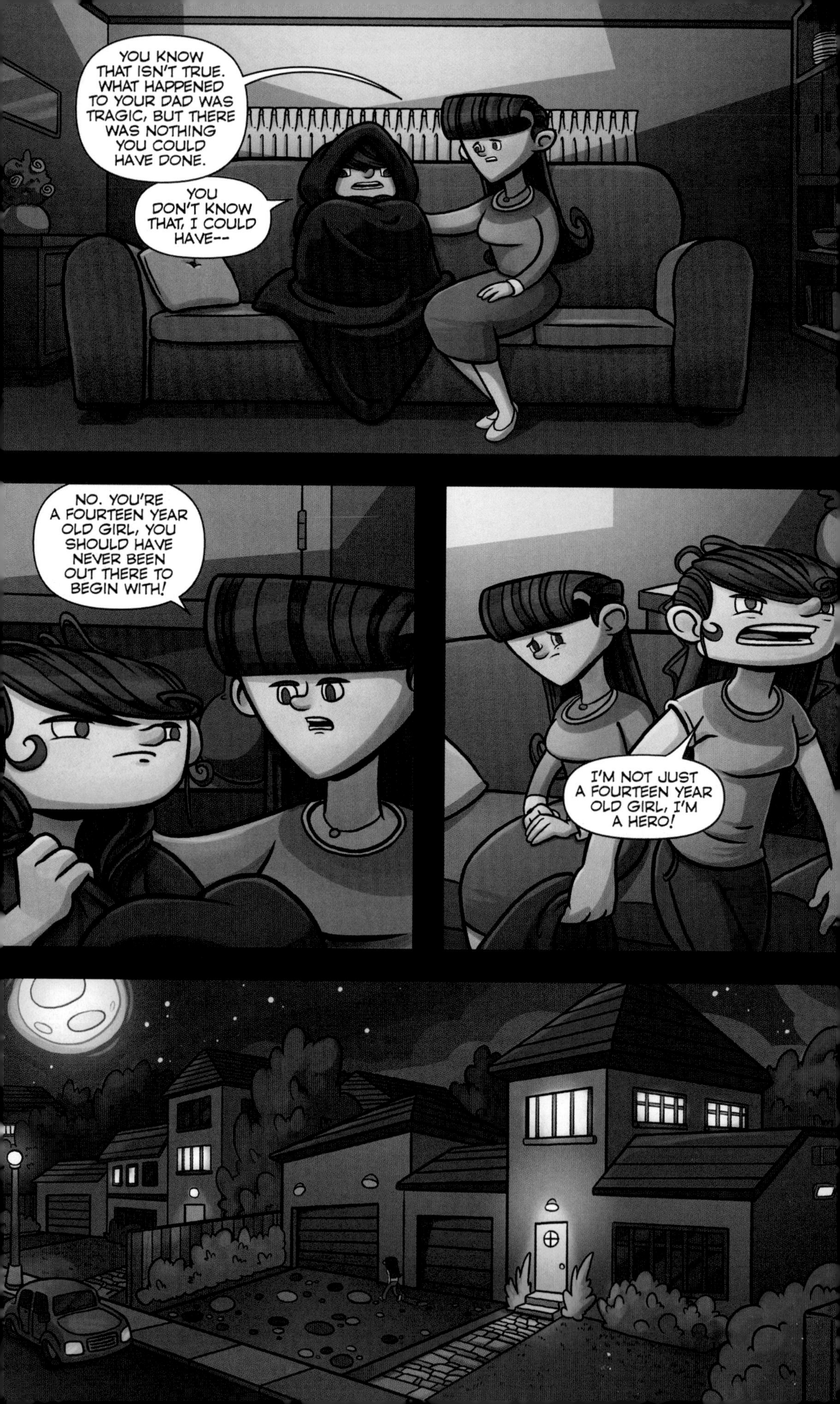
YOU KNOW THAT ISN'T TRUE. WHAT HAPPENED TO YOUR DAD WAS TRAGIC, BUT THERE WAS NOTHING YOU COULD HAVE DONE.
YOU DON'T KNOW THAT, I COULD HAVE--
NO. YOU'RE A FOURTEEN YEAR OLD GIRL, YOU SHOULD HAVE NEVER BEEN OUT THERE TO BEGIN WITH!
I'M NOT JUST A FOURTEEN YEAR OLD GIRL, I'M A HERO!

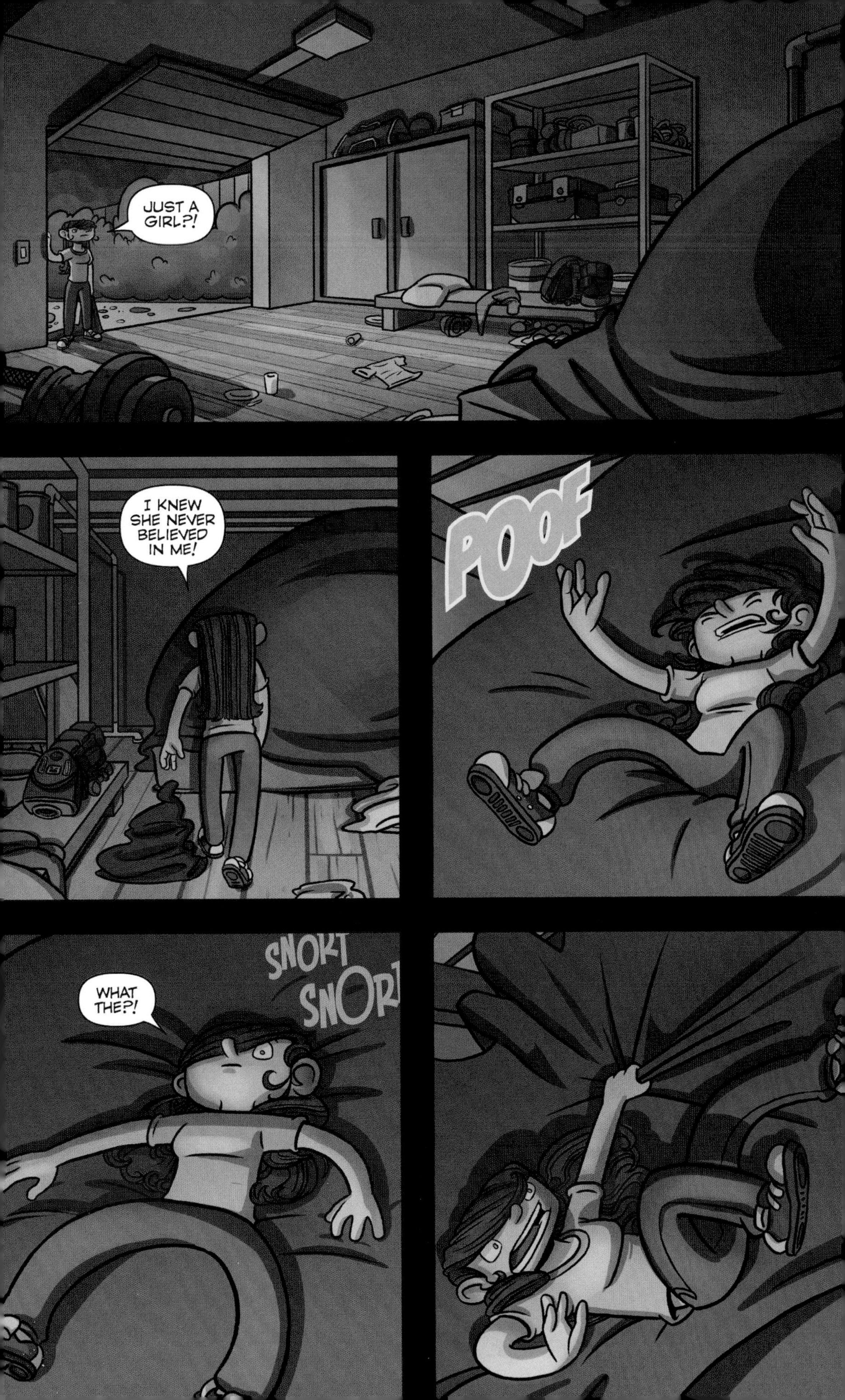
JUST A GIRL?!
I KNEW SHE NEVER BELIEVED IN ME!
POOF
WHAT THE?!
SNORT
SNORT

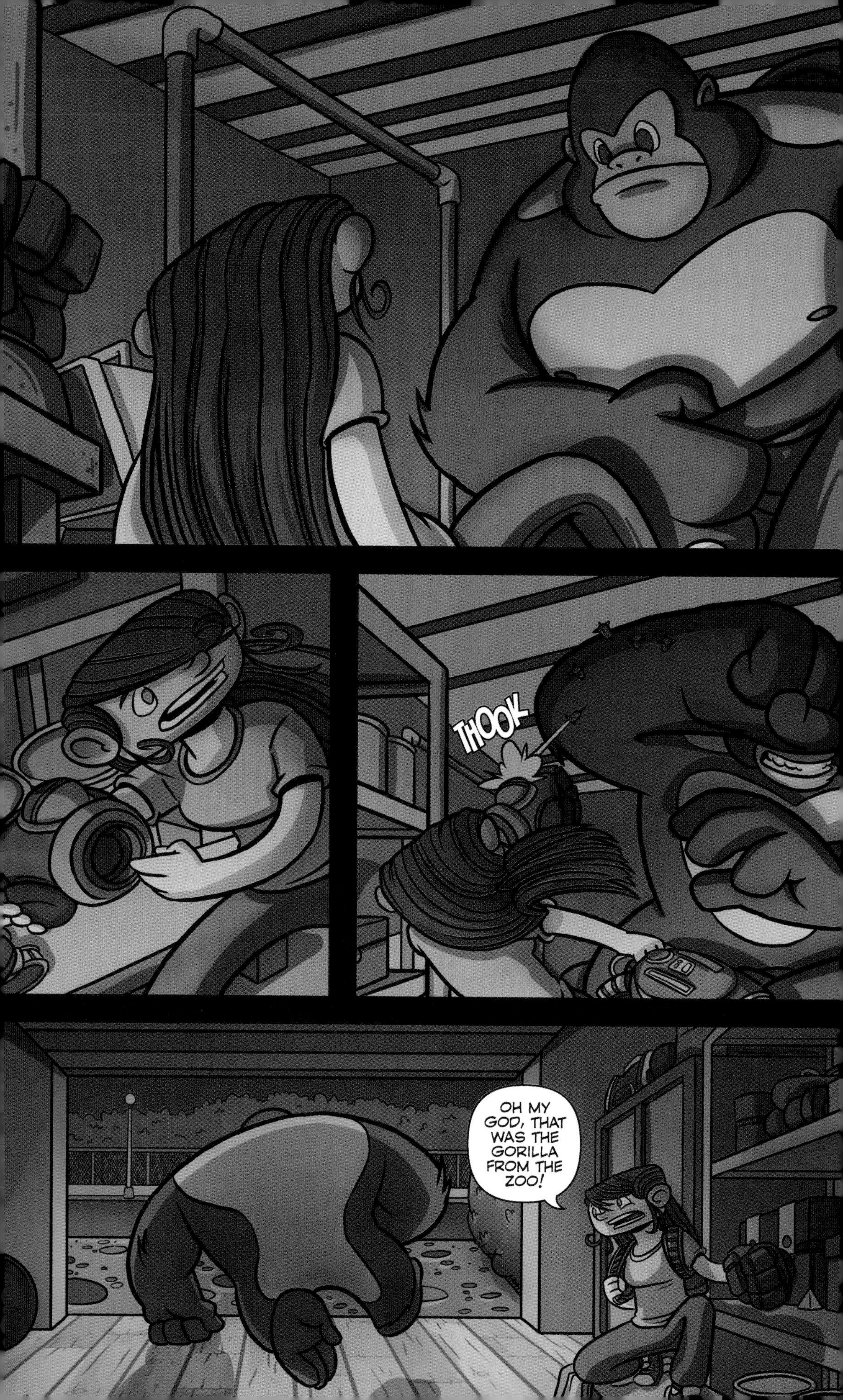
THOOK
OH MY GOD, THAT WAS THE GORILLA FROM THE ZOO!

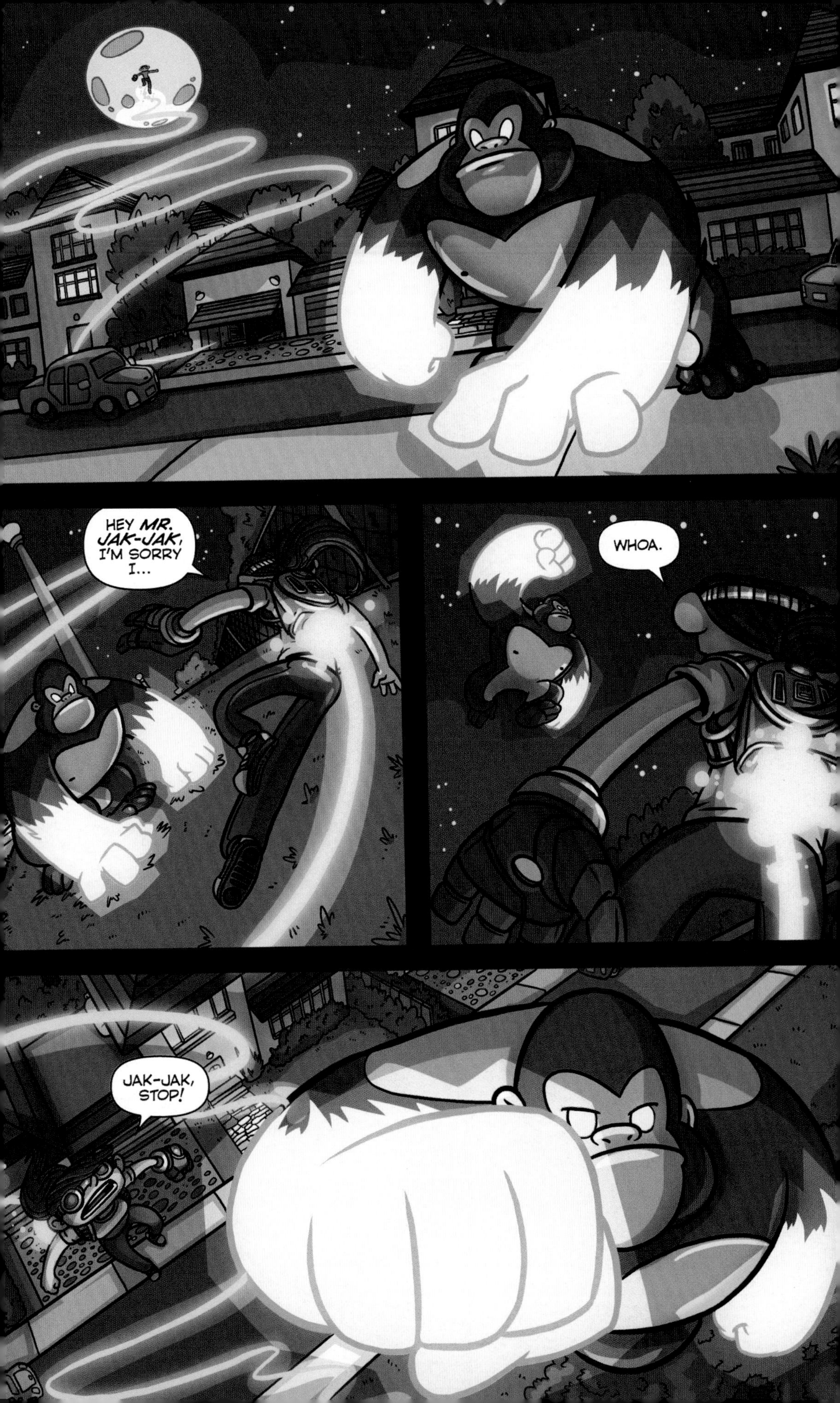
HEY *MR. JAK-JAK*, I'M SORRY I...
WHOA.
JAK-JAK, STOP!

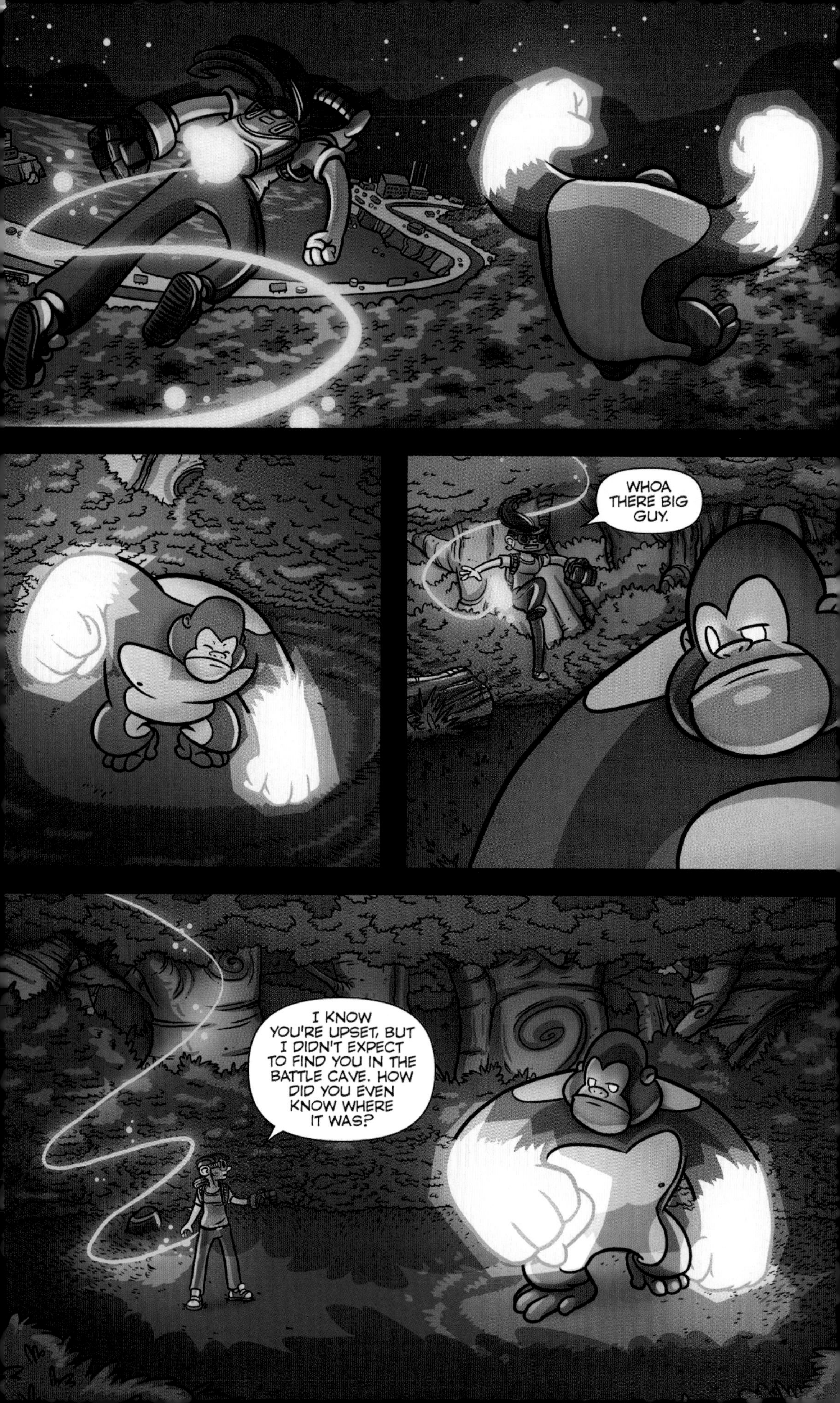
WHOA THERE BIG GUY.
I KNOW YOU'RE UPSET, BUT I DIDN'T EXPECT TO FIND YOU IN THE BATTLE CAVE. HOW DID YOU EVEN KNOW WHERE IT WAS?

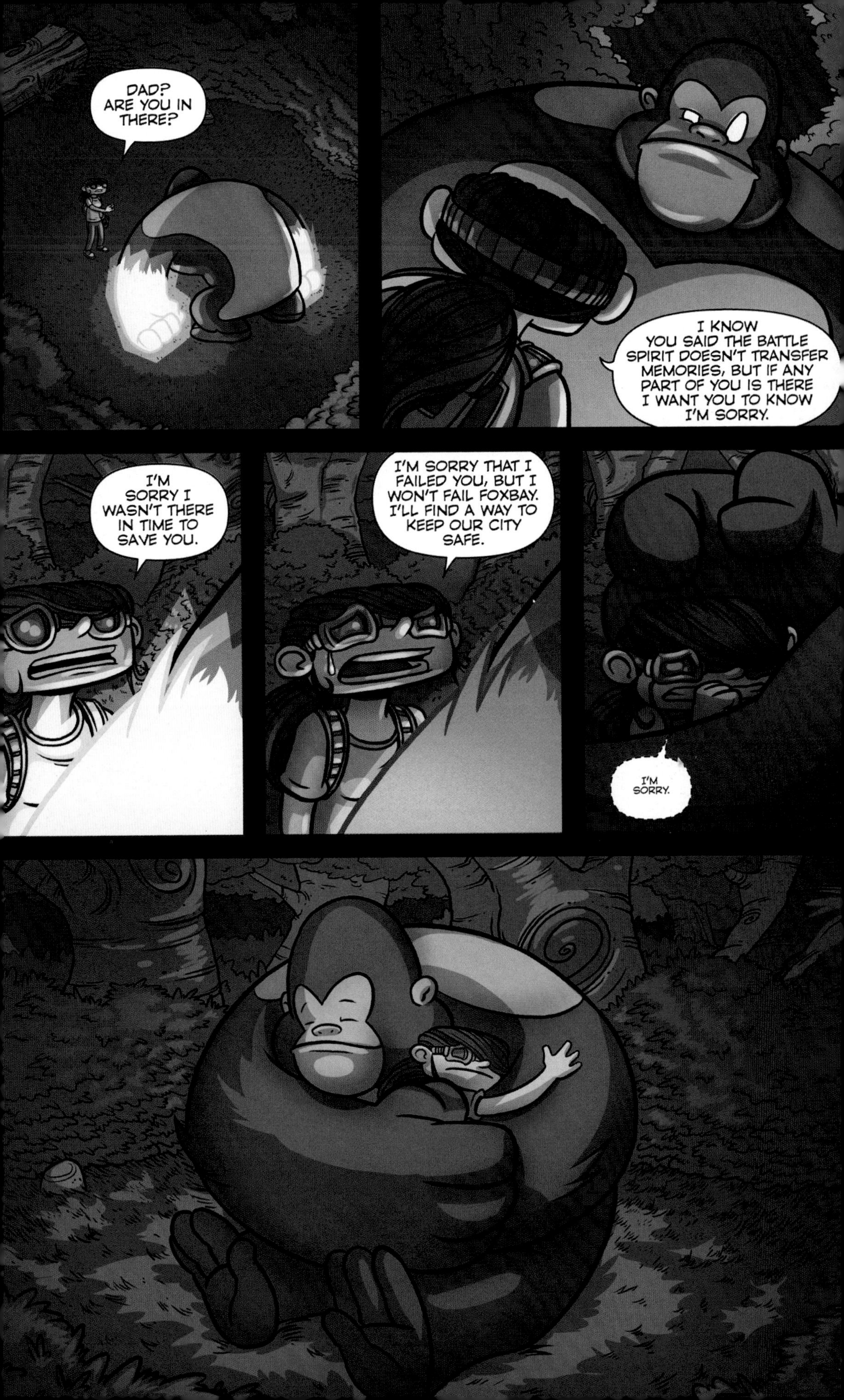
DAD? ARE YOU IN THERE?
I KNOW YOU SAID THE BATTLE SPIRIT DOESN'T TRANSFER MEMORIES, BUT IF ANY PART OF YOU IS THERE I WANT YOU TO KNOW I'M SORRY.
I'M SORRY I WASN'T THERE IN TIME TO SAVE YOU.
I'M SORRY THAT I FAILED YOU, BUT I WON'T FAIL FOXBAY. I'LL FIND A WAY TO KEEP OUR CITY SAFE.
I'M SORRY.

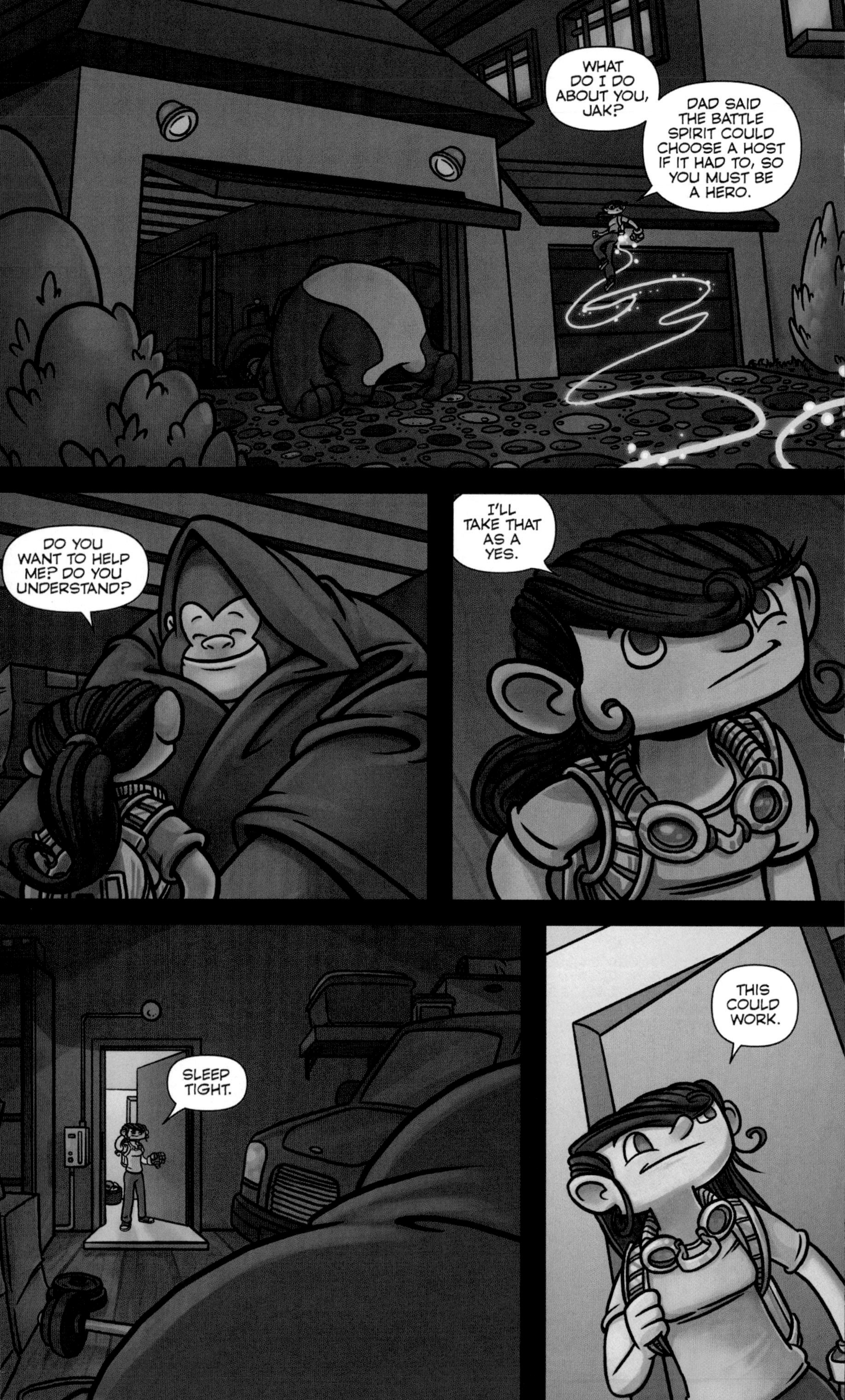
WHAT DO I DO ABOUT YOU, JAK?
DAD SAID THE BATTLE SPIRIT COULD CHOOSE A HOST IF IT HAD TO, SO YOU MUST BE A HERO.
DO YOU WANT TO HELP ME? DO YOU UNDERSTAND?
I'LL TAKE THAT AS A YES.
SLEEP TIGHT.
THIS COULD WORK.

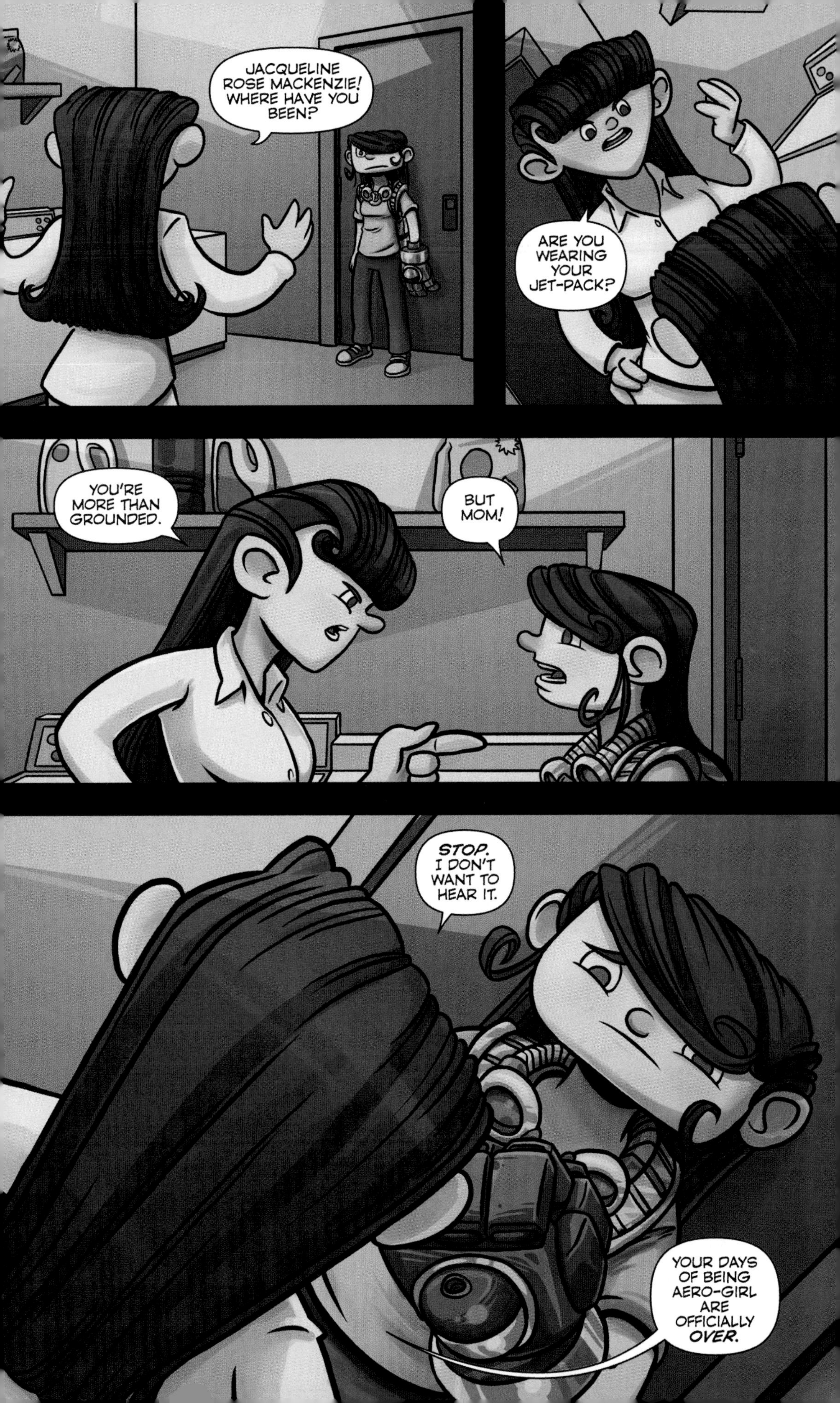
JACQUELINE ROSE MACKENZIE! WHERE HAVE YOU BEEN?
ARE YOU WEARING YOUR JET-PACK?
YOU'RE MORE THAN GROUNDED.
BUT MOM!
STOP. I DON'T WANT TO HEAR IT.
YOUR DAYS OF BEING AERO-GIRL ARE OFFICIALLY OVER.

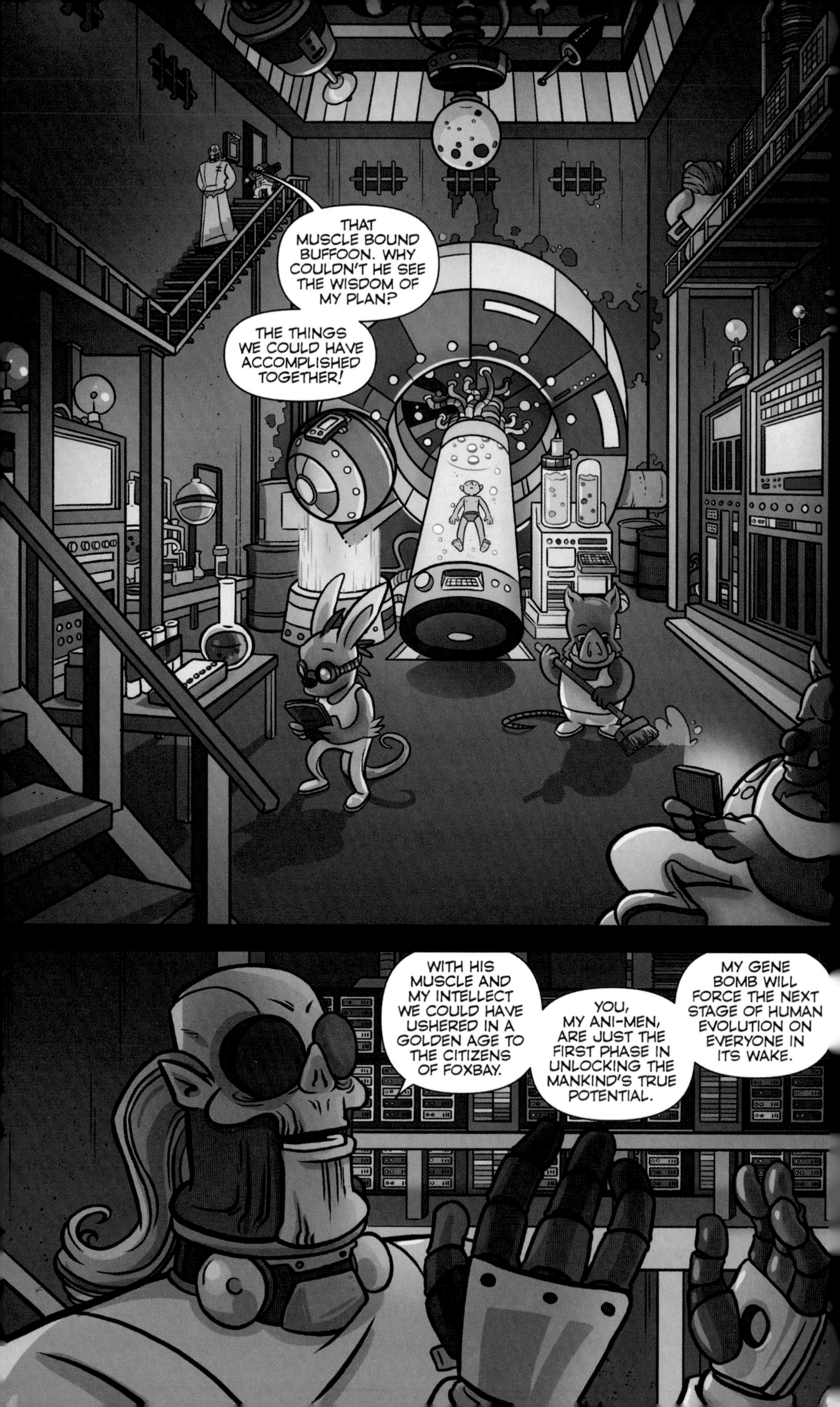
THAT MUSCLE BOUND BUFFOON. WHY COULDN'T HE SEE THE WISDOM OF MY PLAN?
THE THINGS WE COULD HAVE ACCOMPLISHED TOGETHER!
WITH HIS MUSCLE AND MY INTELLECT WE COULD HAVE USHERED IN A GOLDEN AGE TO THE CITIZENS OF FOXBAY.
YOU, MY ANI-MEN, ARE JUST THE FIRST PHASE IN UNLOCKING THE MANKIND'S TRUE POTENTIAL.
MY GENE BOMB WILL FORCE THE NEXT STAGE OF HUMAN EVOLUTION ON EVERYONE IN ITS WAKE.

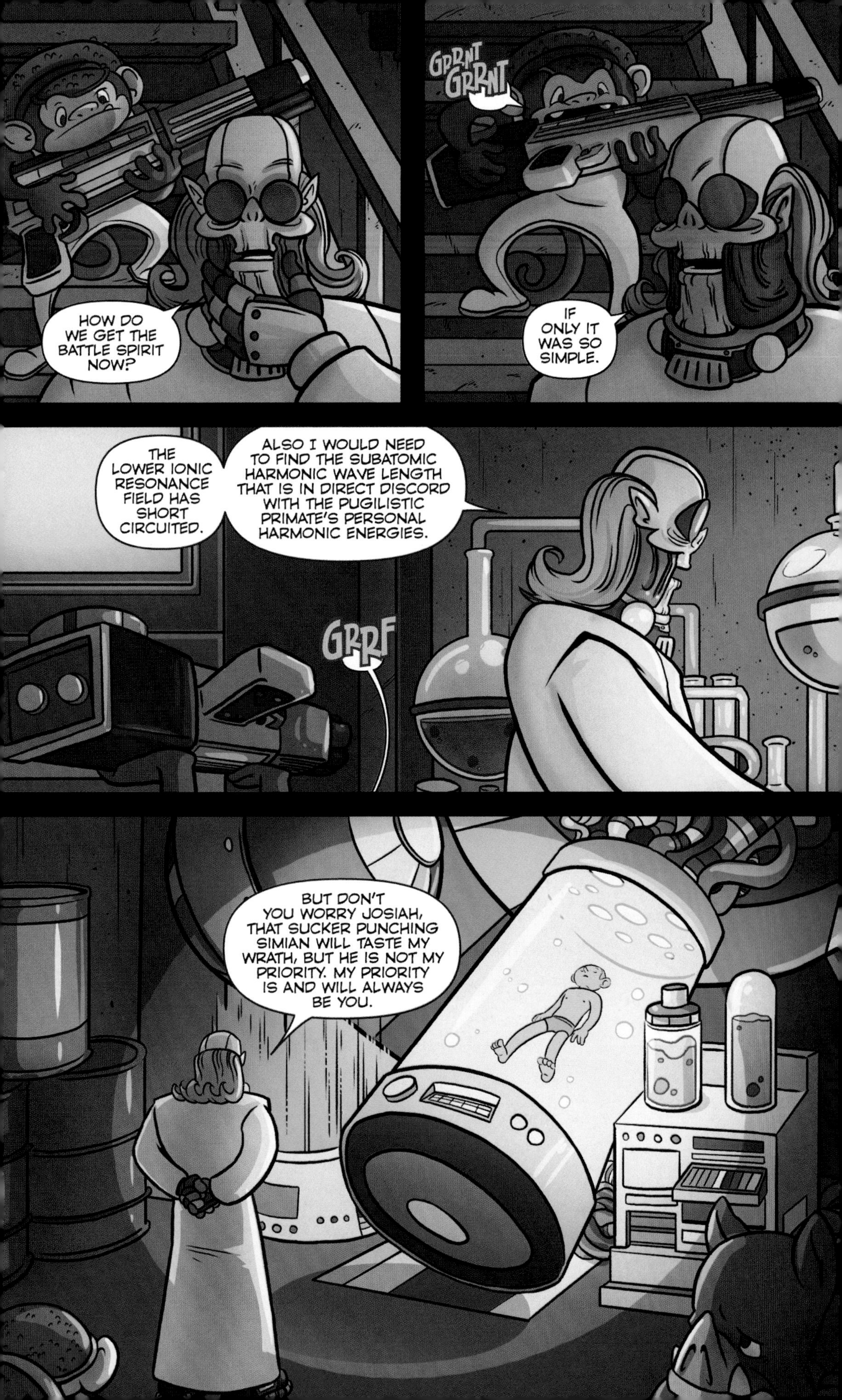
HOW DO WE GET THE BATTLE SPIRIT NOW?
GRRNT GRRNT
IF ONLY IT WAS SO SIMPLE.
THE LOWER IONIC RESONANCE FIELD HAS SHORT CIRCUITED.
ALSO I WOULD NEED TO FIND THE SUBATOMIC HARMONIC WAVE LENGTH THAT IS IN DIRECT DISCORD WITH THE PUGILISTIC PRIMATE'S PERSONAL HARMONIC ENERGIES.
GRRF
BUT DON'T YOU WORRY JOSIAH, THAT SUCKER PUNCHING SIMIAN WILL TASTE MY WRATH, BUT HE IS NOT MY PRIORITY. MY PRIORITY IS AND WILL ALWAYS BE YOU.

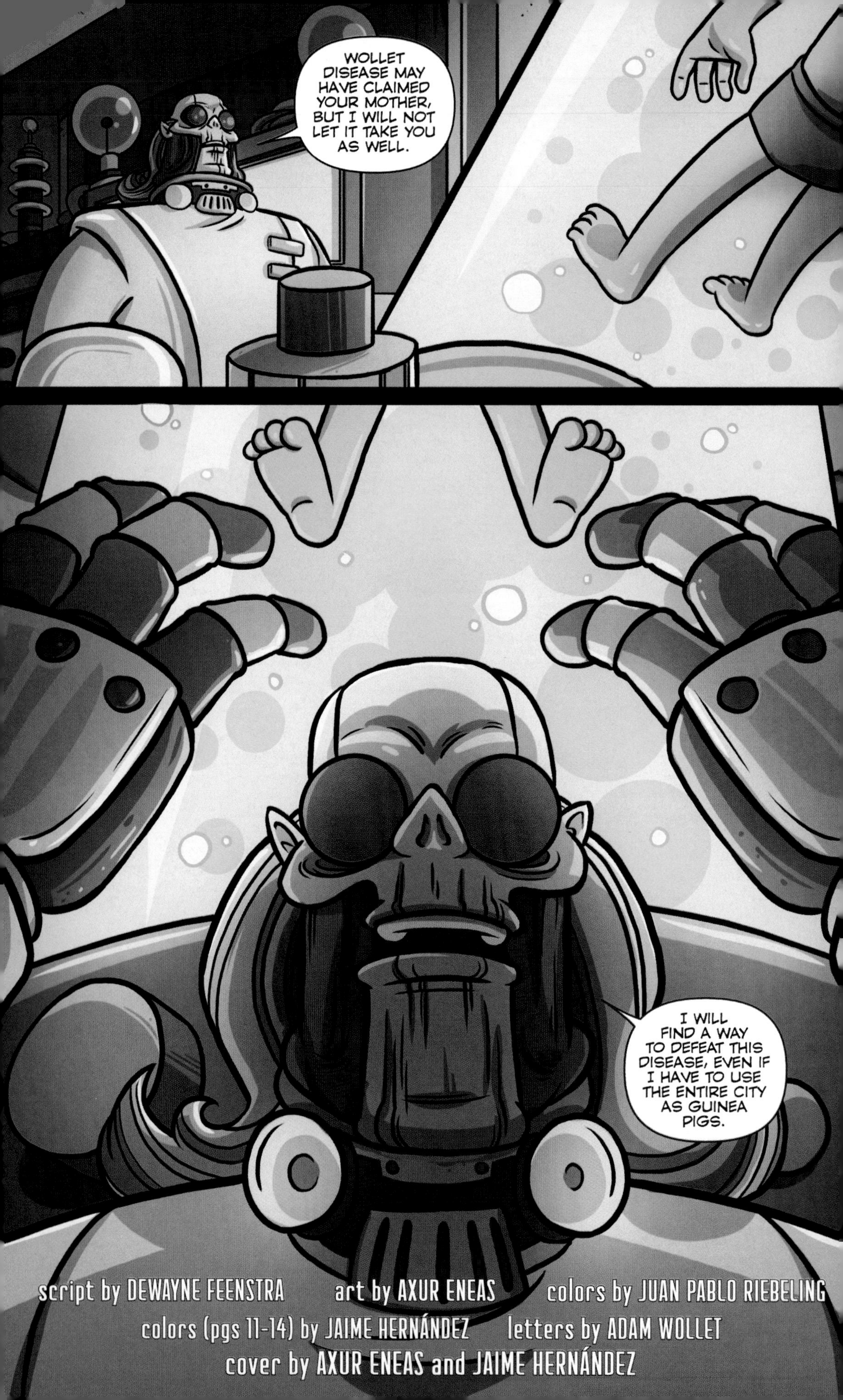
WOLLET DISEASE MAY HAVE CLAIMED YOUR MOTHER, BUT I WILL NOT LET IT TAKE YOU AS WELL.
I WILL FIND A WAY TO DEFEAT THIS DISEASE, EVEN IF I HAVE TO USE THE ENTIRE CITY AS GUINEA PIGS.

script by DEWAYNE FEENSTRA art by AXUR ENEAS colors by JUAN PABLO RIEBELING
colors (pgs 11-14) by JAIME HERNÁNDEZ letters by ADAM WOLLET
cover by AXUR ENEAS and JAIME HERNÁNDEZ

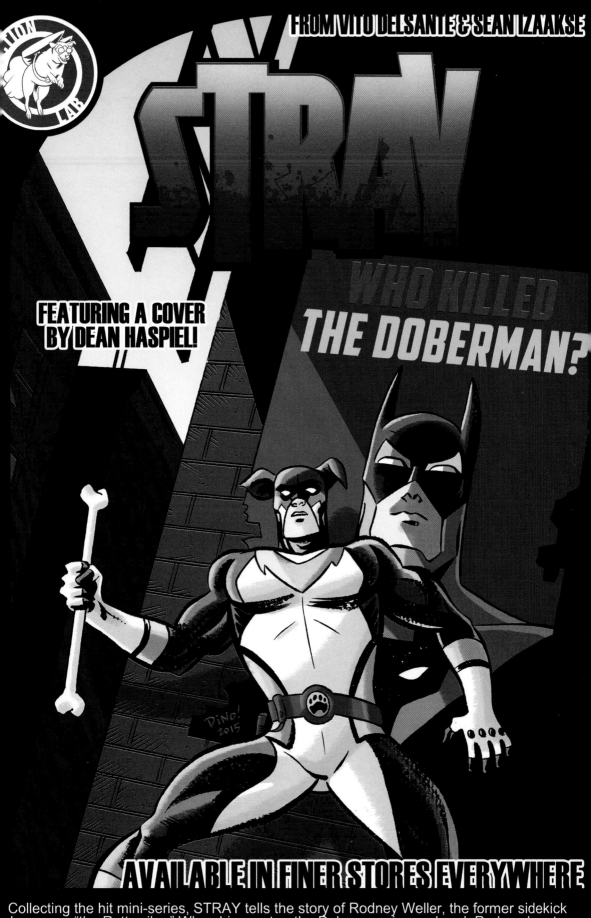

Collecting the hit mini-series, STRAY tells the story of Rodney Weller, the former sidekick known as "the Rottweiler." When his mentor, the Doberman, is murdered, Rodney has to decide if he wants to come back to the world of capes and masks and, if he does, who he wants to be. Cover by Emmy Award winner, Dean Haspiel (The Fox)! Collects Stray #1-4.

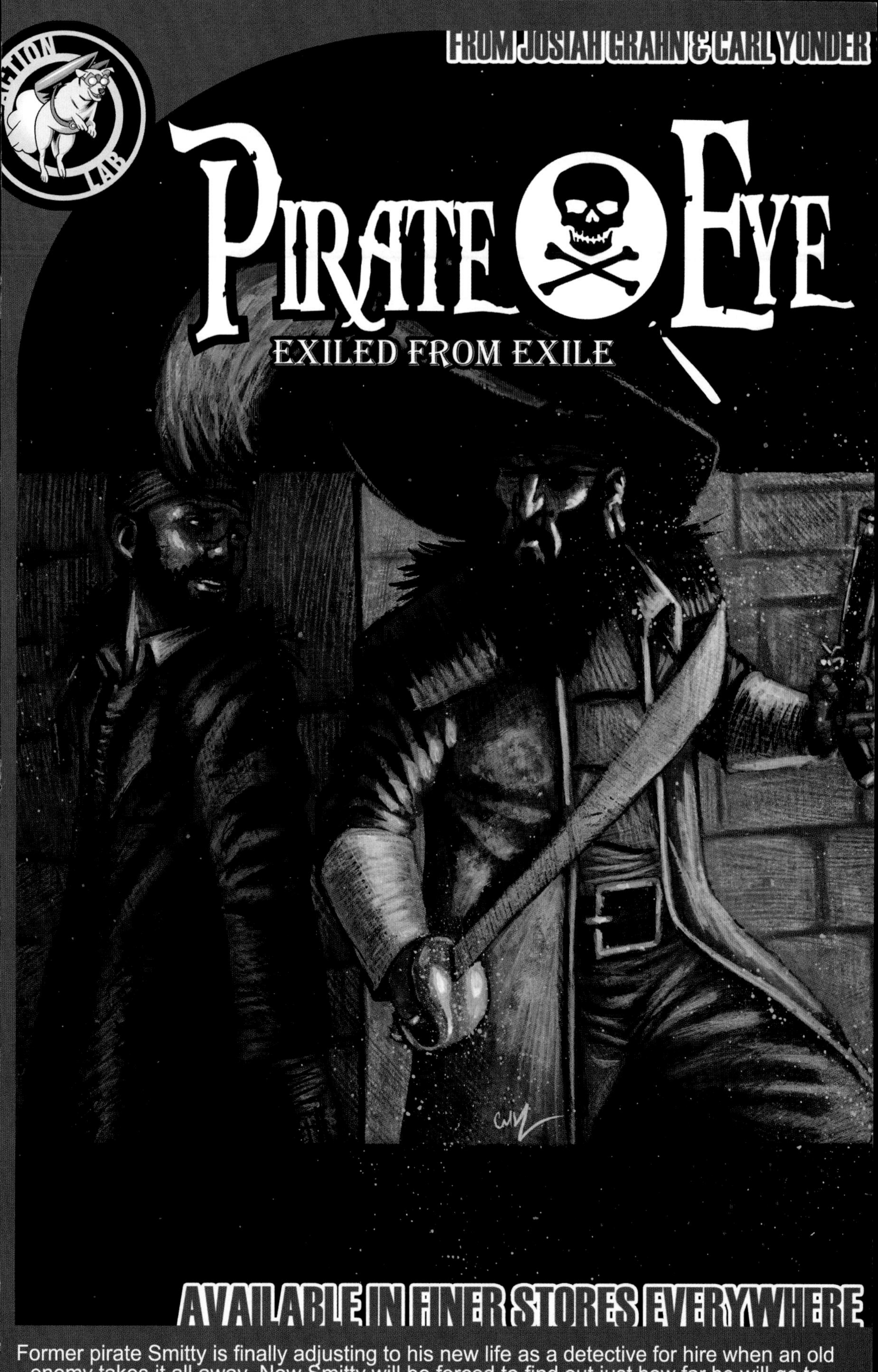
FROM JOSIAH GRAHN & CARL YONDER
PIRATE EYE
EXILED FROM EXILE
AVAILABLE IN FINER STORES EVERYWHERE

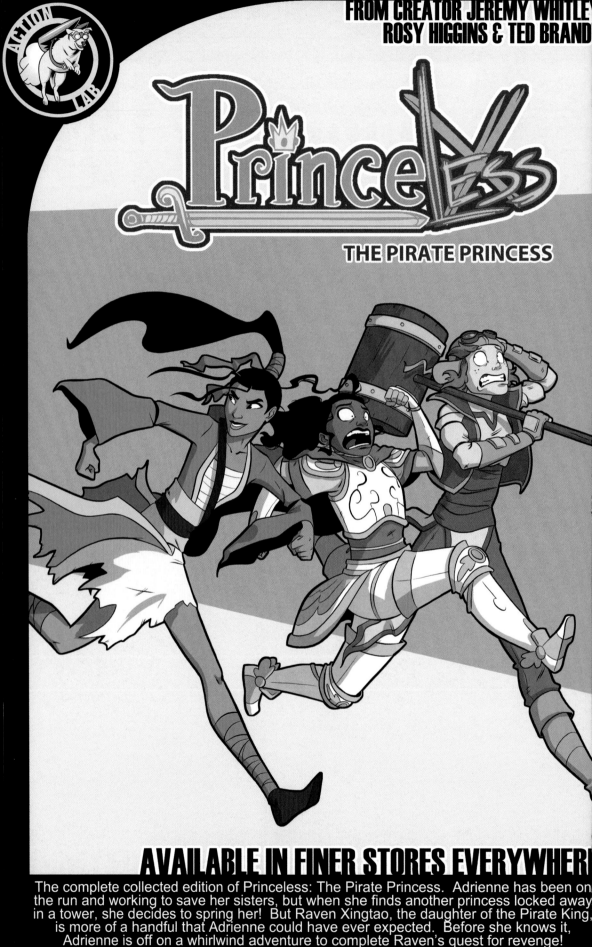

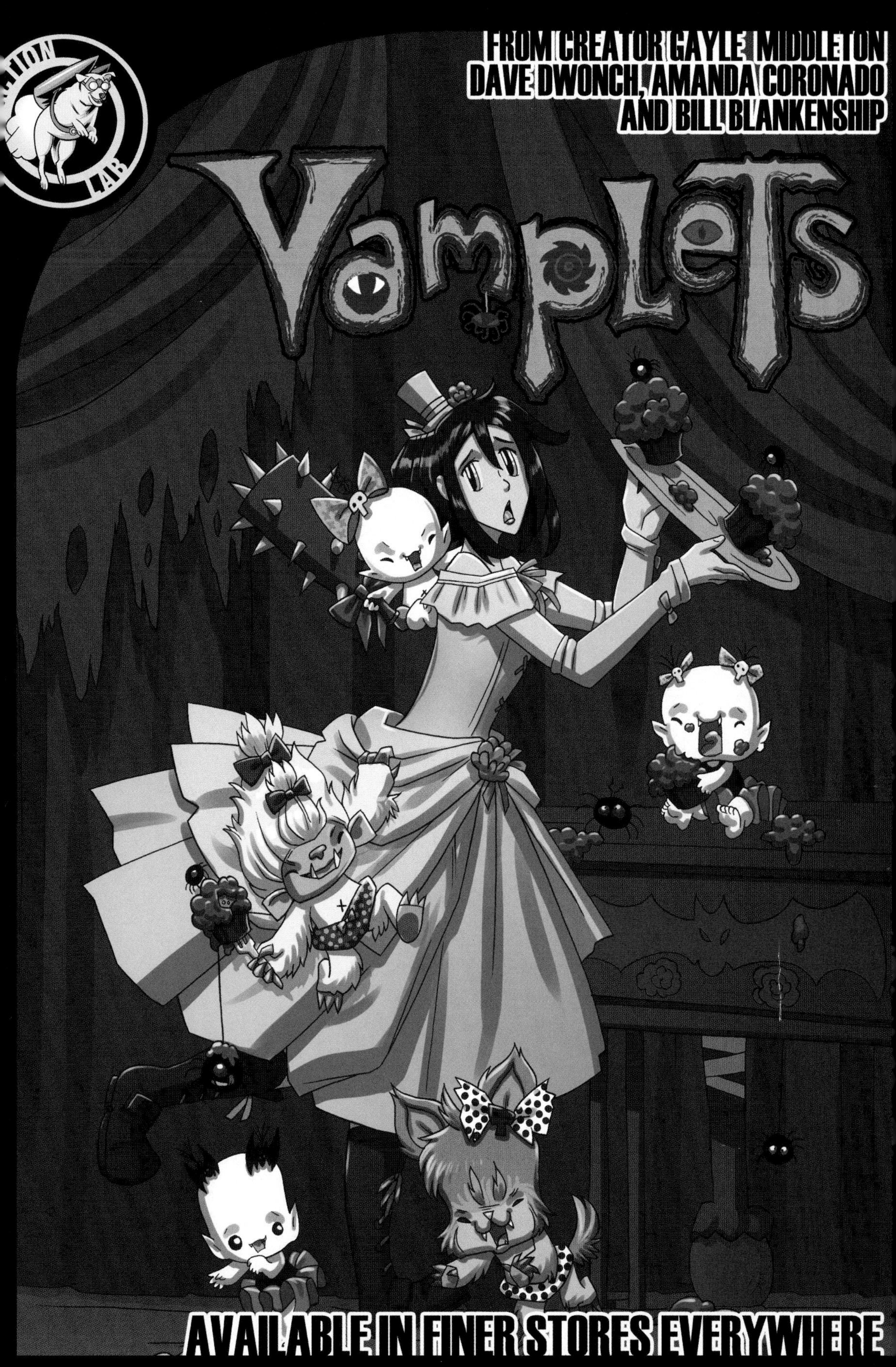
FROM CREATOR GAYLE MIDDLETON
DAVE DWONCH, AMANDA CORONADO
AND BILL BLANKENSHIP
VAMPLETS
AVAILABLE IN FINER STORES EVERYWHERE

The shocking conclusion to the Nightmare Nursery saga! Destiny Harper is in deep trouble, and she will need the help of Rasket, Lycinda and the Vamplets themselves to thwart the plans of the evil Vammette. Will Destiny Harper get back home, or will she be trapped on the nightmare world of Gloomvania forever?

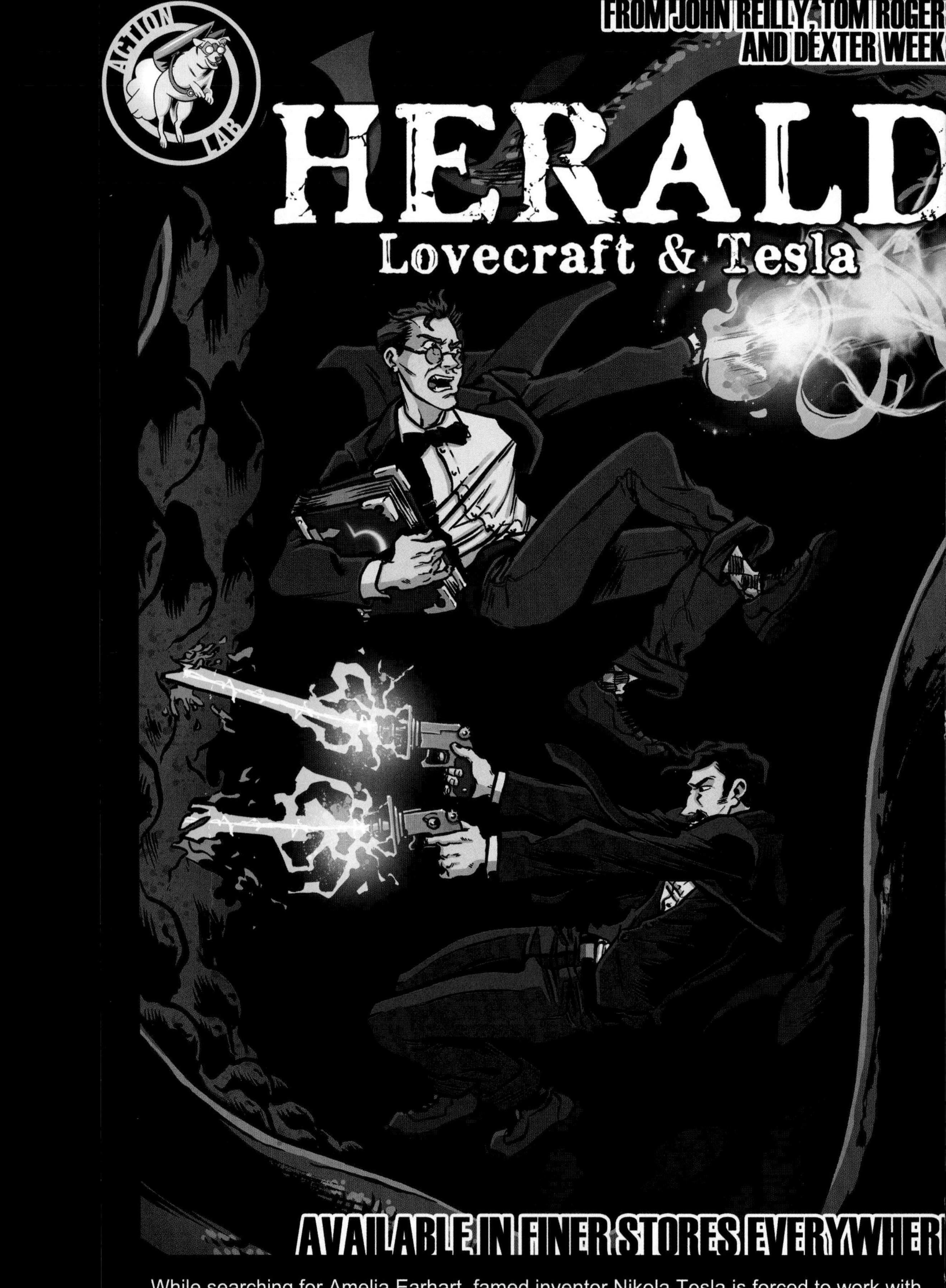
ACTION LAB
FROM JOHN REILLY, TOM ROGER
AND DEXTER WEEK
HERALD
Lovecraft & Tesla
AVAILABLE IN FINER STORES EVERYWHER

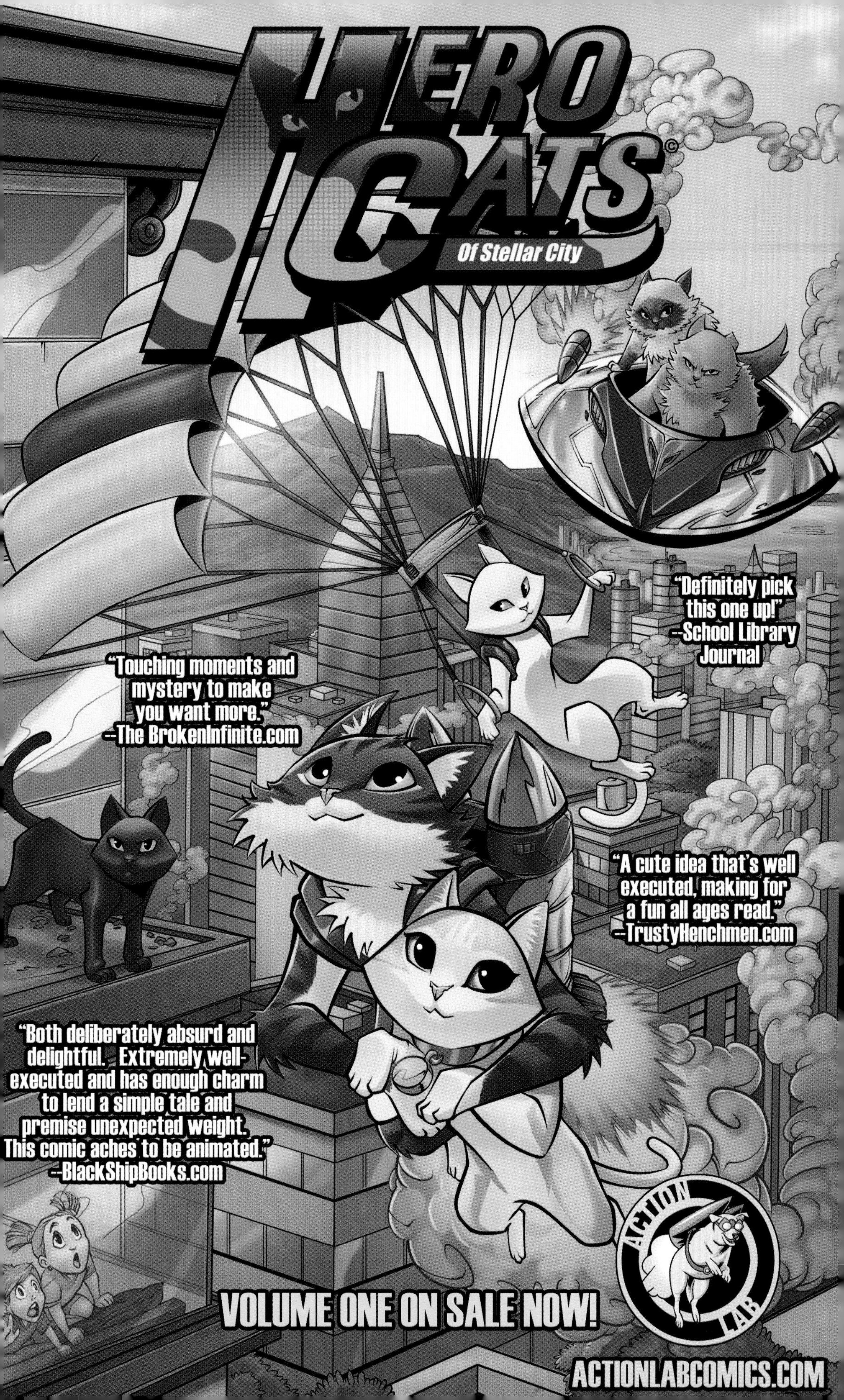

HERO CATS
Of Stellar City
"Definitely pick this one up!" --School Library Journal
"Touching moments and mystery to make you want more." --The BrokenInfinite.com
"A cute idea that's well executed, making for a fun all ages read." --TrustyHenchmen.com
"Both deliberately absurd and delightful. Extremely well-executed and has enough charm to lend a simple tale and premise unexpected weight. This comic aches to be animated." --BlackShipBooks.com
ACTION LAB
VOLUME ONE ON SALE NOW!
ACTIONLABCOMICS.COM

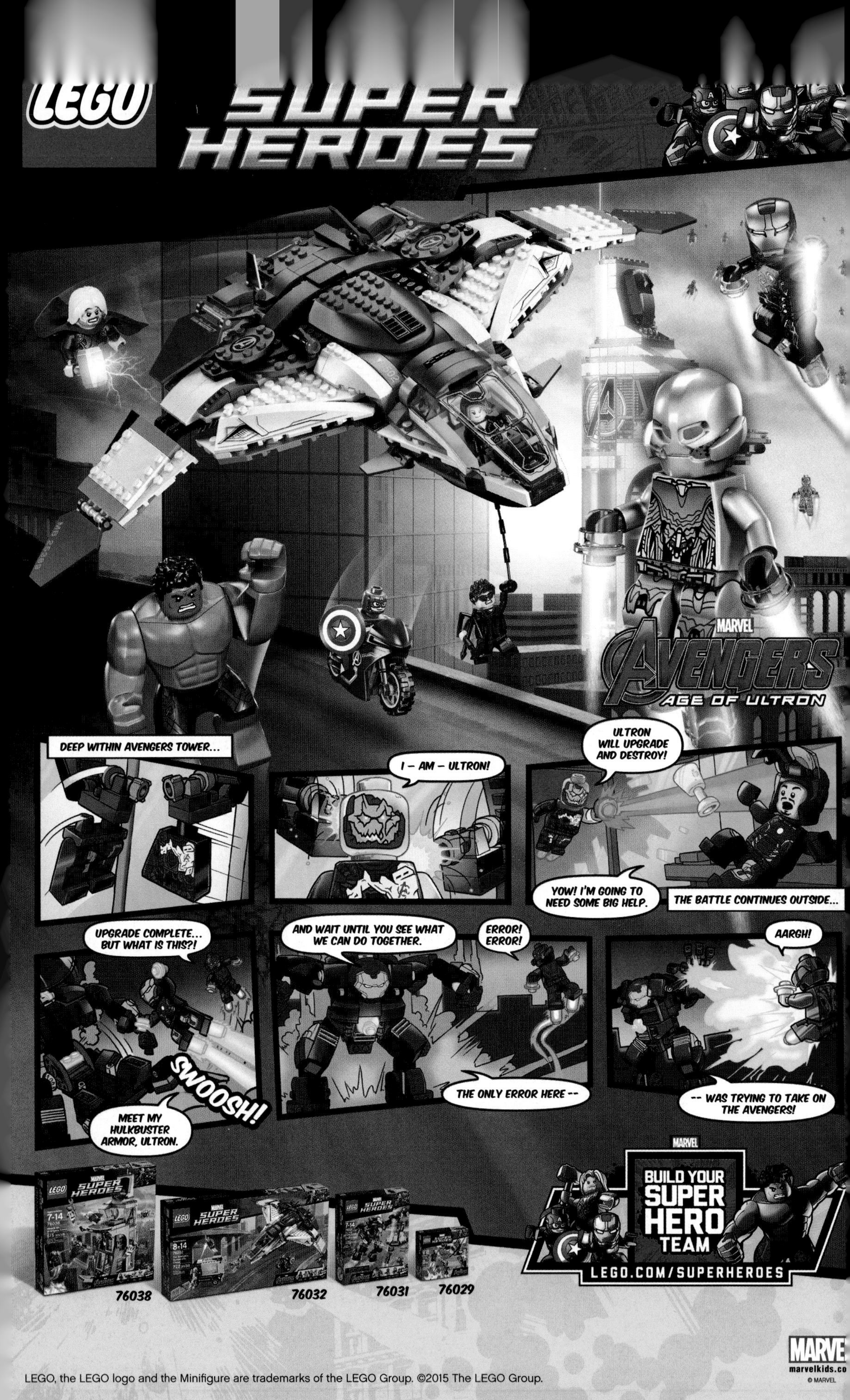

LEGO
SUPER HEROES
MARVEL
AVENGERS
AGE OF ULTRON
DEEP WITHIN AVENGERS TOWER...
I – AM – ULTRON!
ULTRON WILL UPGRADE AND DESTROY!
YOW! I'M GOING TO NEED SOME BIG HELP.
THE BATTLE CONTINUES OUTSIDE...
UPGRADE COMPLETE... BUT WHAT IS THIS?!
SWOOSH!
MEET MY HULKBUSTER ARMOR, ULTRON.
AND WAIT UNTIL YOU SEE WHAT WE CAN DO TOGETHER.
ERROR! ERROR!
THE ONLY ERROR HERE --
AARGH!
-- WAS TRYING TO TAKE ON THE AVENGERS!
76038
76032
76031
76029
MARVEL
BUILD YOUR SUPER HERO TEAM
LEGO.COM/SUPERHEROES
MARVEL
marvelkids.co
© MARVEL

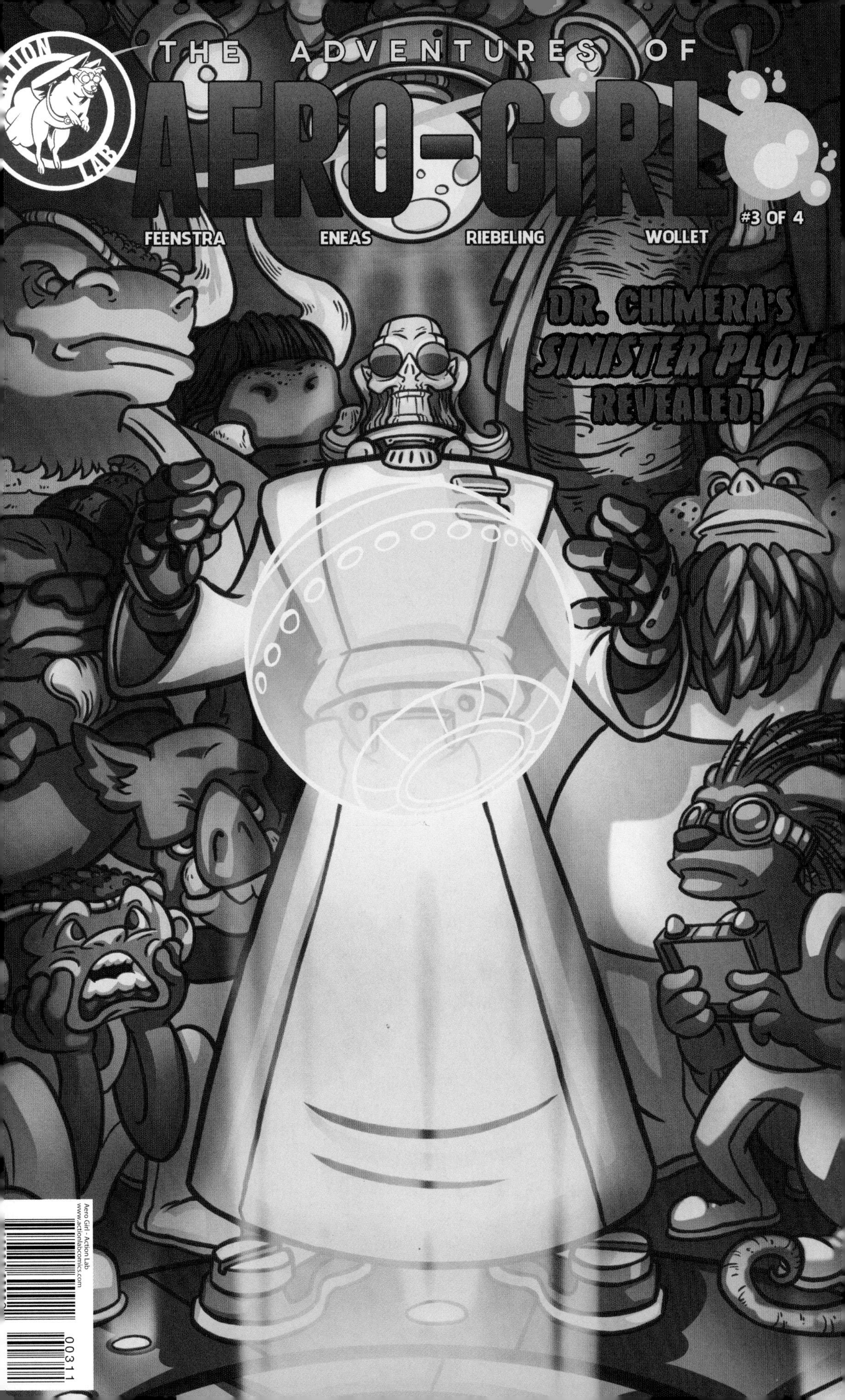
ACTION LAB
THE ADVENTURES OF
AERO-GIRL
#3 OF 4
FEENSTRA
ENEAS
RIEBELING
WOLLET
DR. CHIMERA'S SINISTER PLOT REVEALED!
Aero Girl - Action Lab
www.actionlabcomics.com
00311

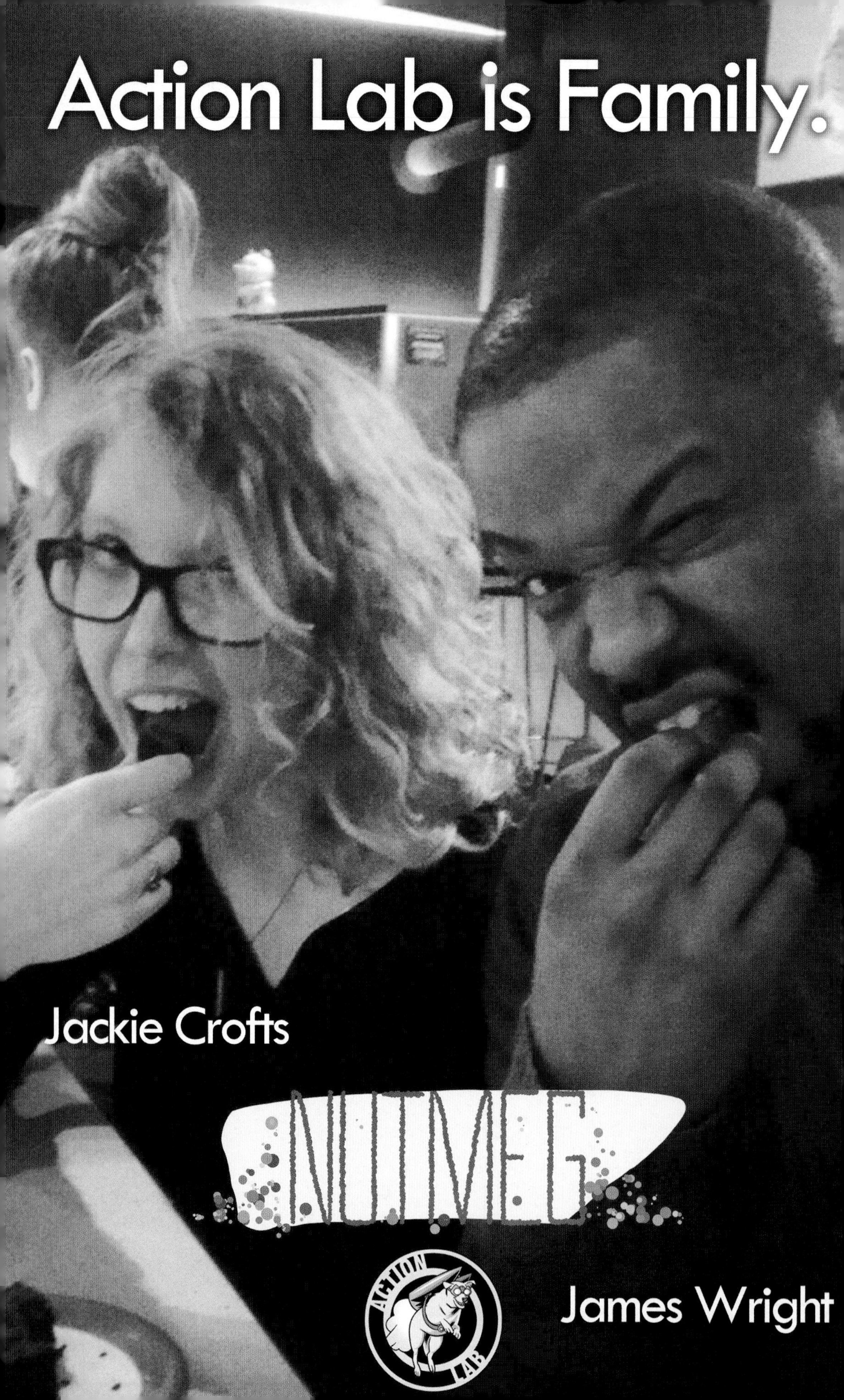
Action Lab is Family.
Jackie Crofts
NUTMEG
ACTION LAB
James Wright

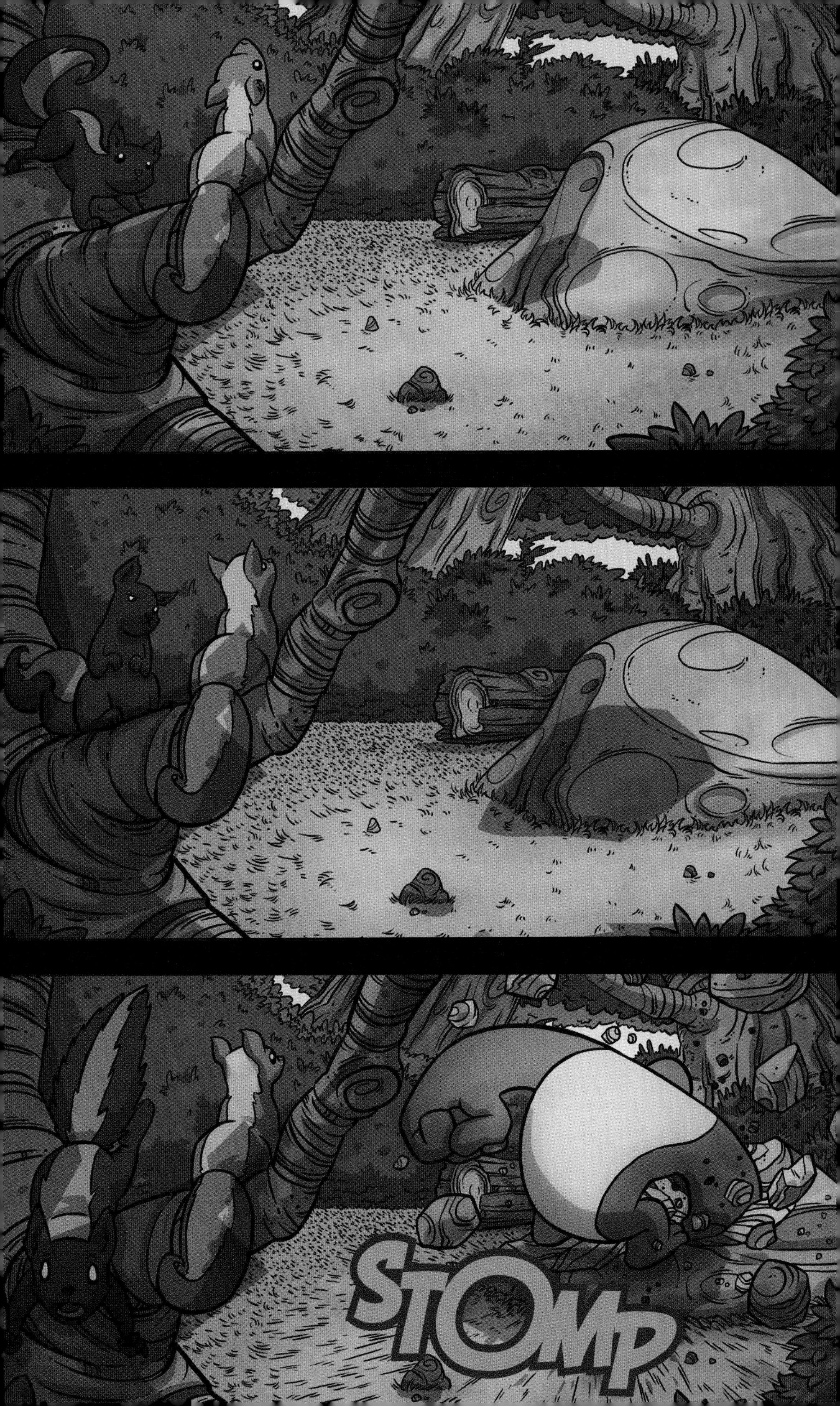
STOMP

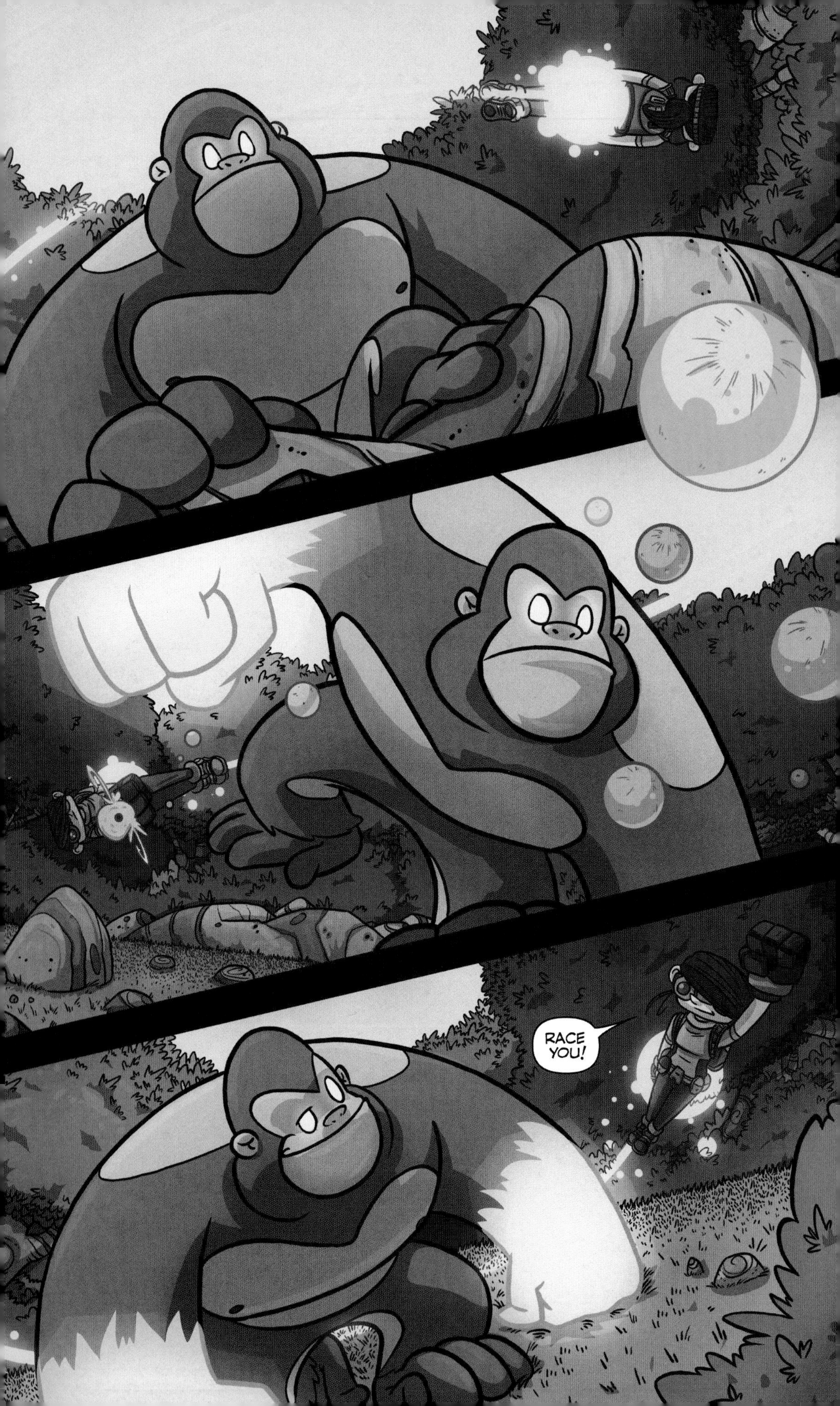
RACE YOU!

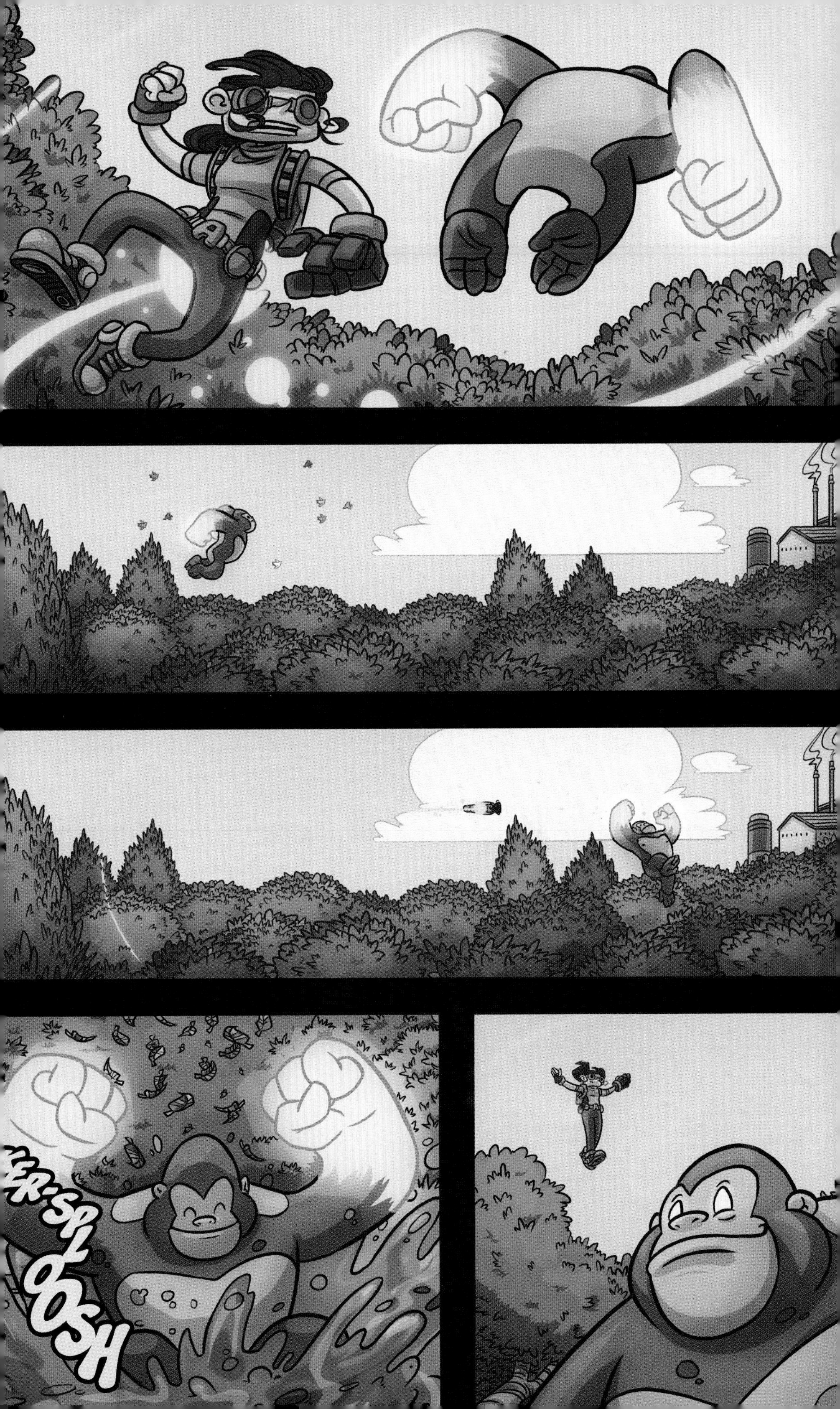
ER-SPLOOSH

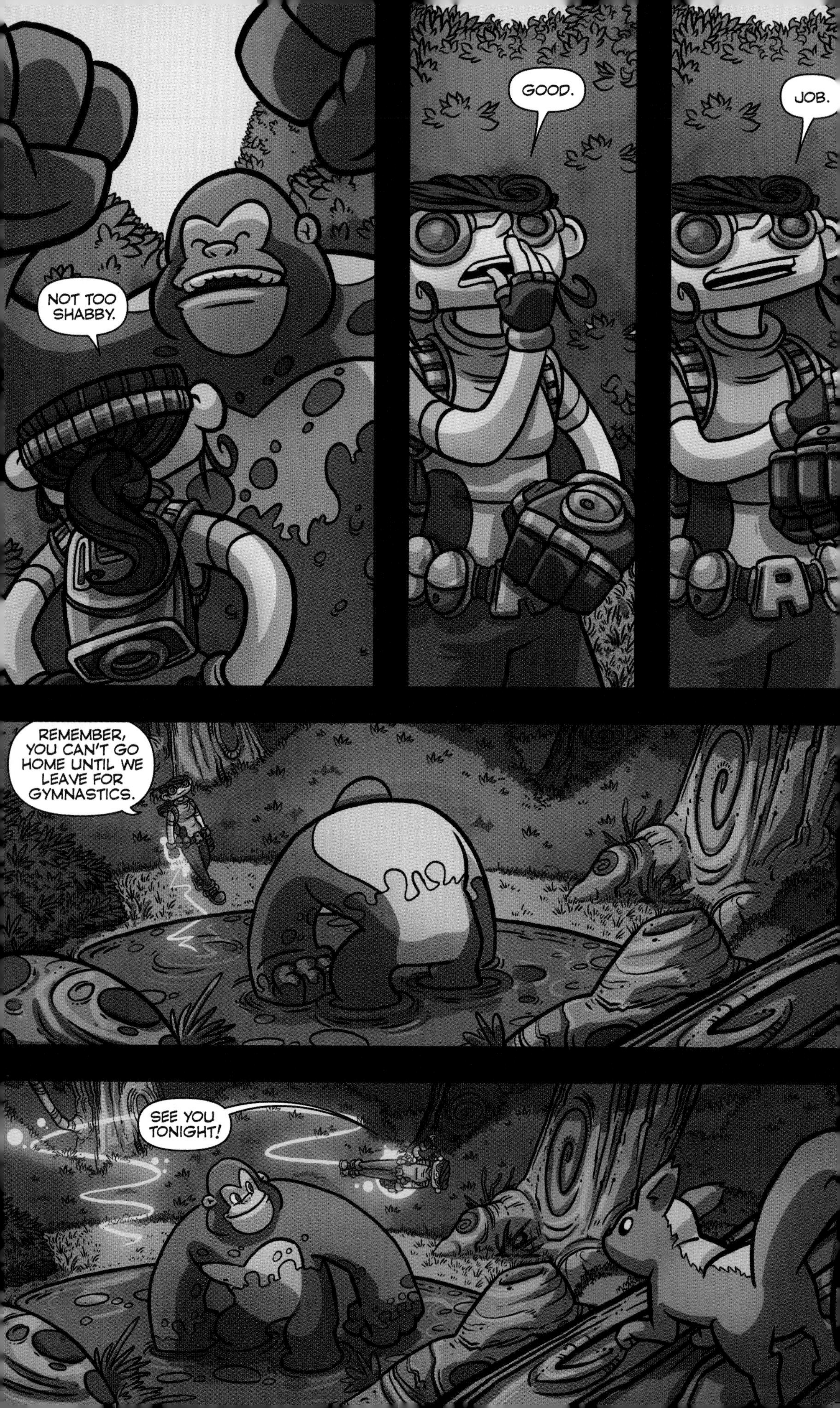
NOT TOO SHABBY.
GOOD.
JOB.
REMEMBER, YOU CAN'T GO HOME UNTIL WE LEAVE FOR GYMNASTICS.
SEE YOU TONIGHT!

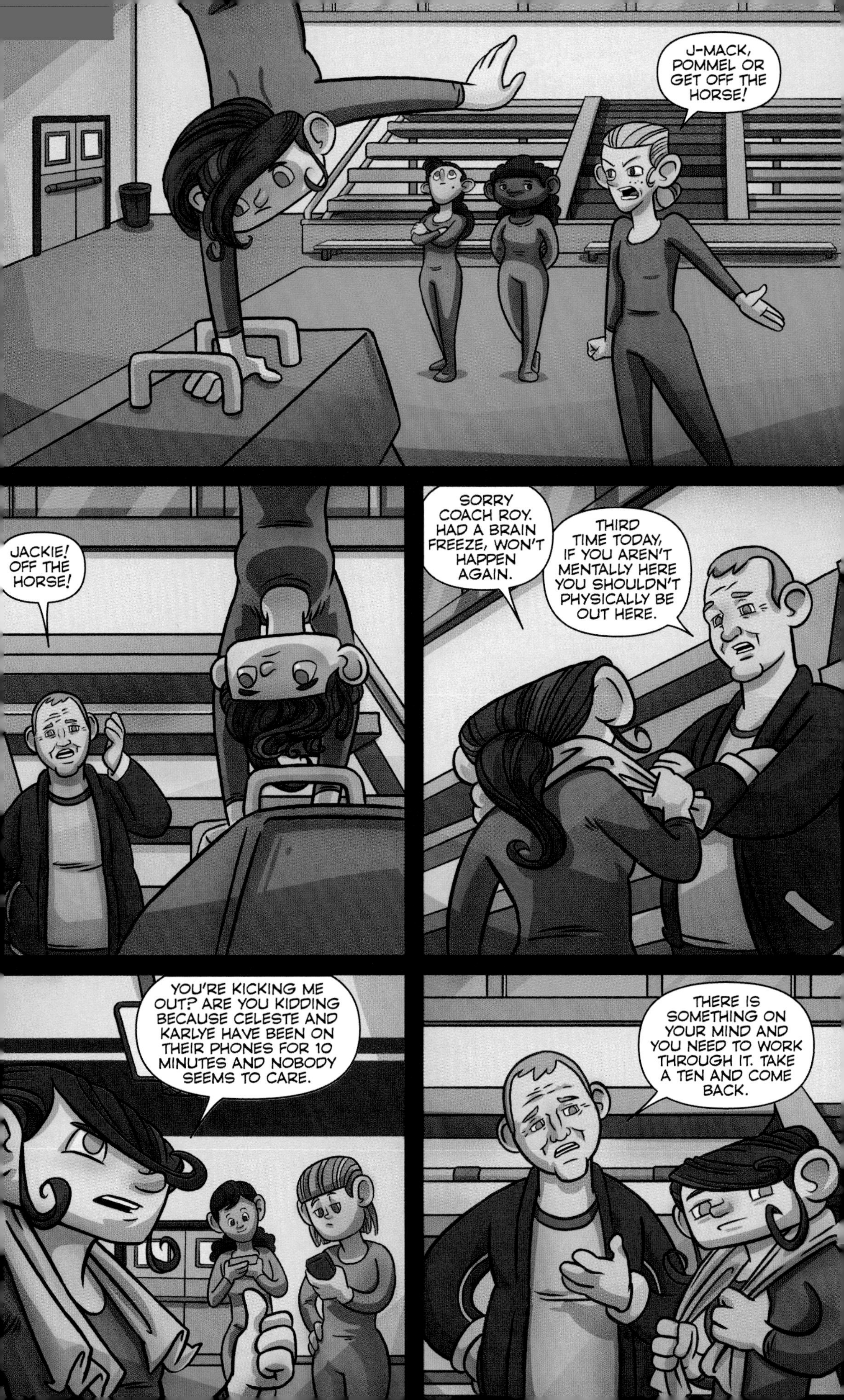
J-MACK, POMMEL OR GET OFF THE HORSE!
JACKIE! OFF THE HORSE!
SORRY COACH ROY. HAD A BRAIN FREEZE, WON'T HAPPEN AGAIN.
THIRD TIME TODAY, IF YOU AREN'T MENTALLY HERE YOU SHOULDN'T PHYSICALLY BE OUT HERE.
YOU'RE KICKING ME OUT? ARE YOU KIDDING BECAUSE CELESTE AND KARLYE HAVE BEEN ON THEIR PHONES FOR 10 MINUTES AND NOBODY SEEMS TO CARE.
THERE IS SOMETHING ON YOUR MIND AND YOU NEED TO WORK THROUGH IT. TAKE A TEN AND COME BACK.

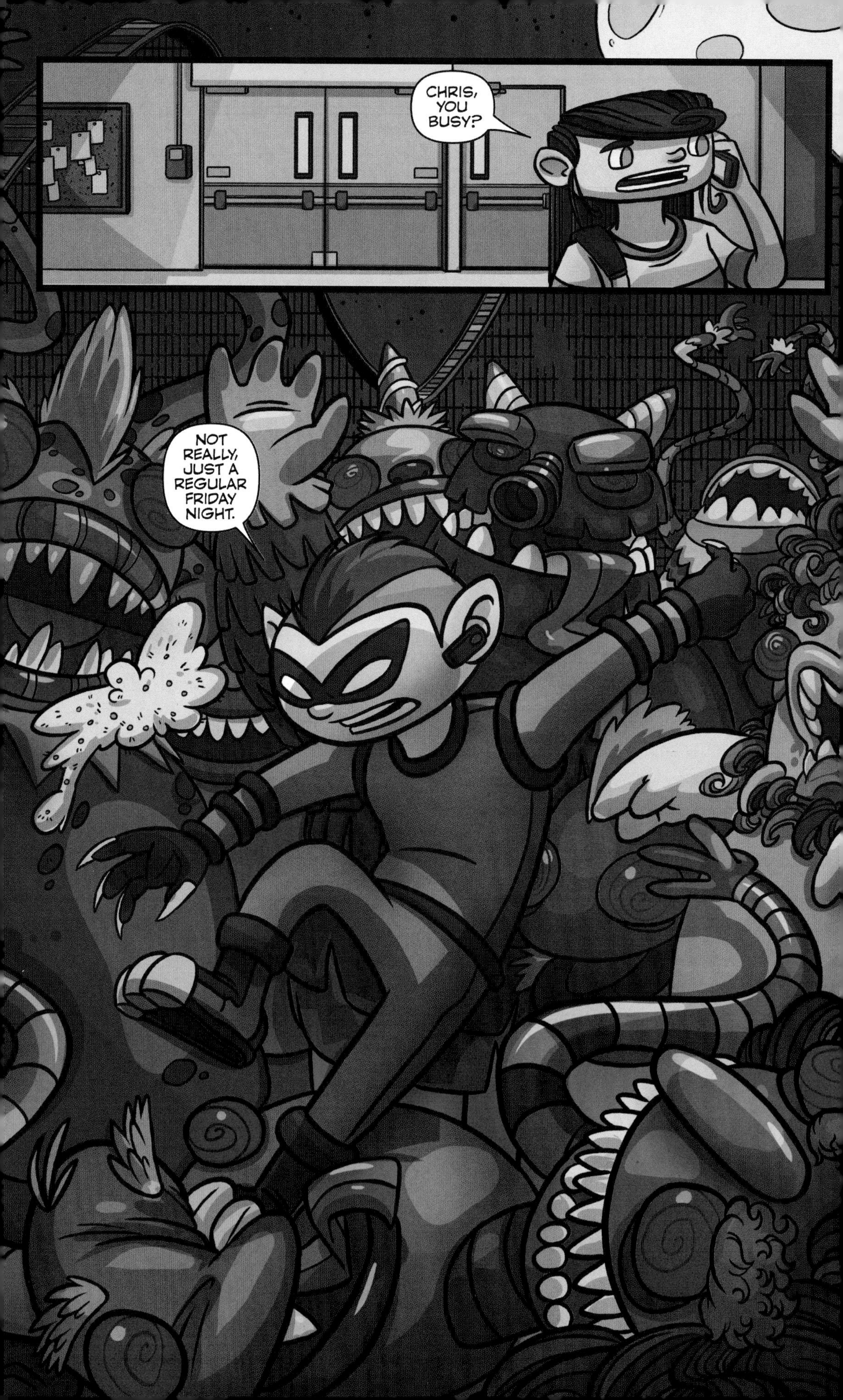
CHRIS, YOU BUSY?
NOT REALLY, JUST A REGULAR FRIDAY NIGHT.

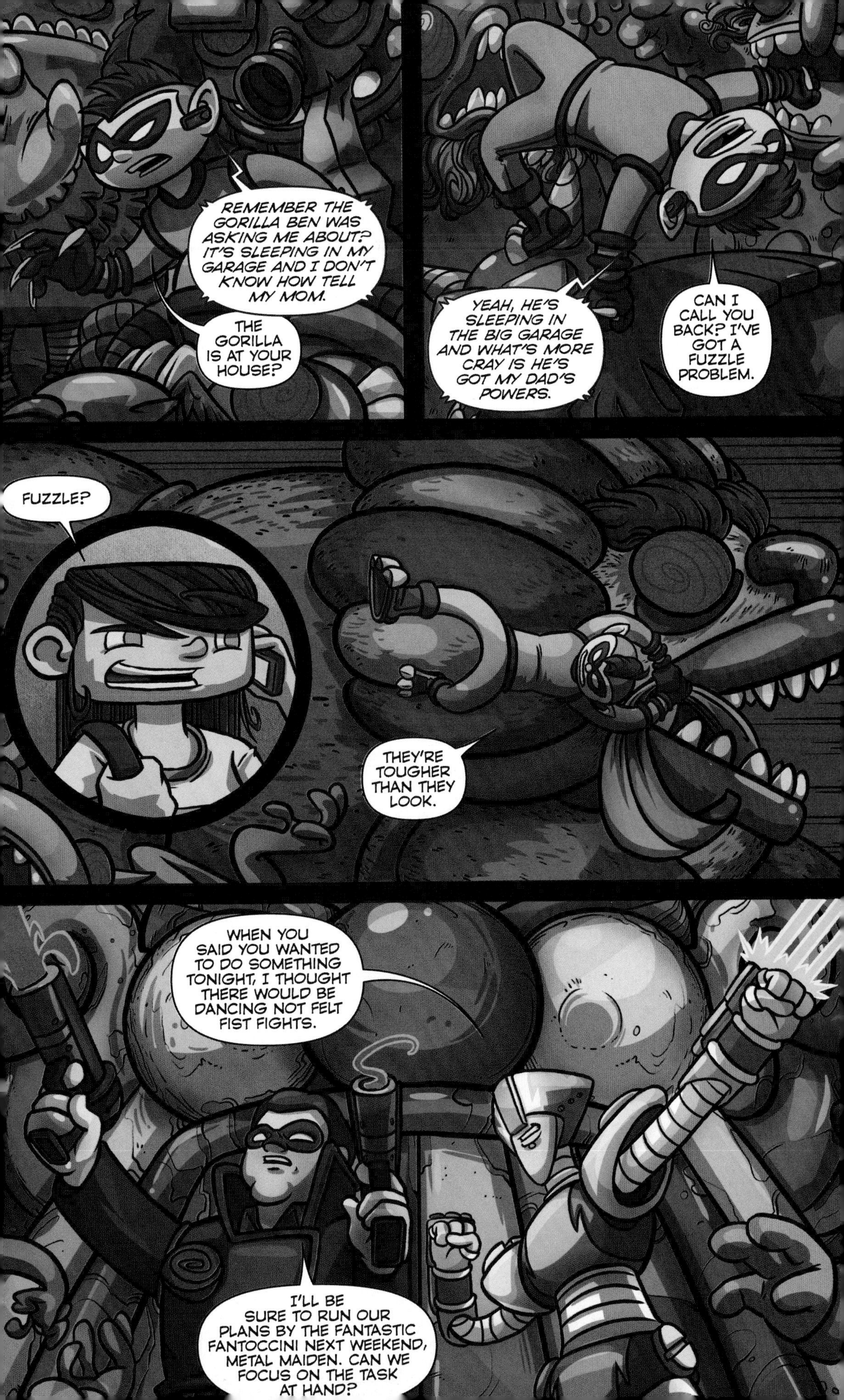
REMEMBER THE GORILLA BEN WAS ASKING ME ABOUT? IT'S SLEEPING IN MY GARAGE AND I DON'T KNOW HOW TELL MY MOM.
THE GORILLA IS AT YOUR HOUSE?
YEAH, HE'S SLEEPING IN THE BIG GARAGE AND WHAT'S MORE CRAY IS HE'S GOT MY DAD'S POWERS.
CAN I CALL YOU BACK? I'VE GOT A FUZZLE PROBLEM.
FUZZLE?
THEY'RE TOUGHER THAN THEY LOOK.
WHEN YOU SAID YOU WANTED TO DO SOMETHING TONIGHT, I THOUGHT THERE WOULD BE DANCING NOT FELT FIST FIGHTS.
I'LL BE SURE TO RUN OUR PLANS BY THE FANTASTIC FANTOCCINI NEXT WEEKEND, METAL MAIDEN. CAN WE FOCUS ON THE TASK AT HAND?

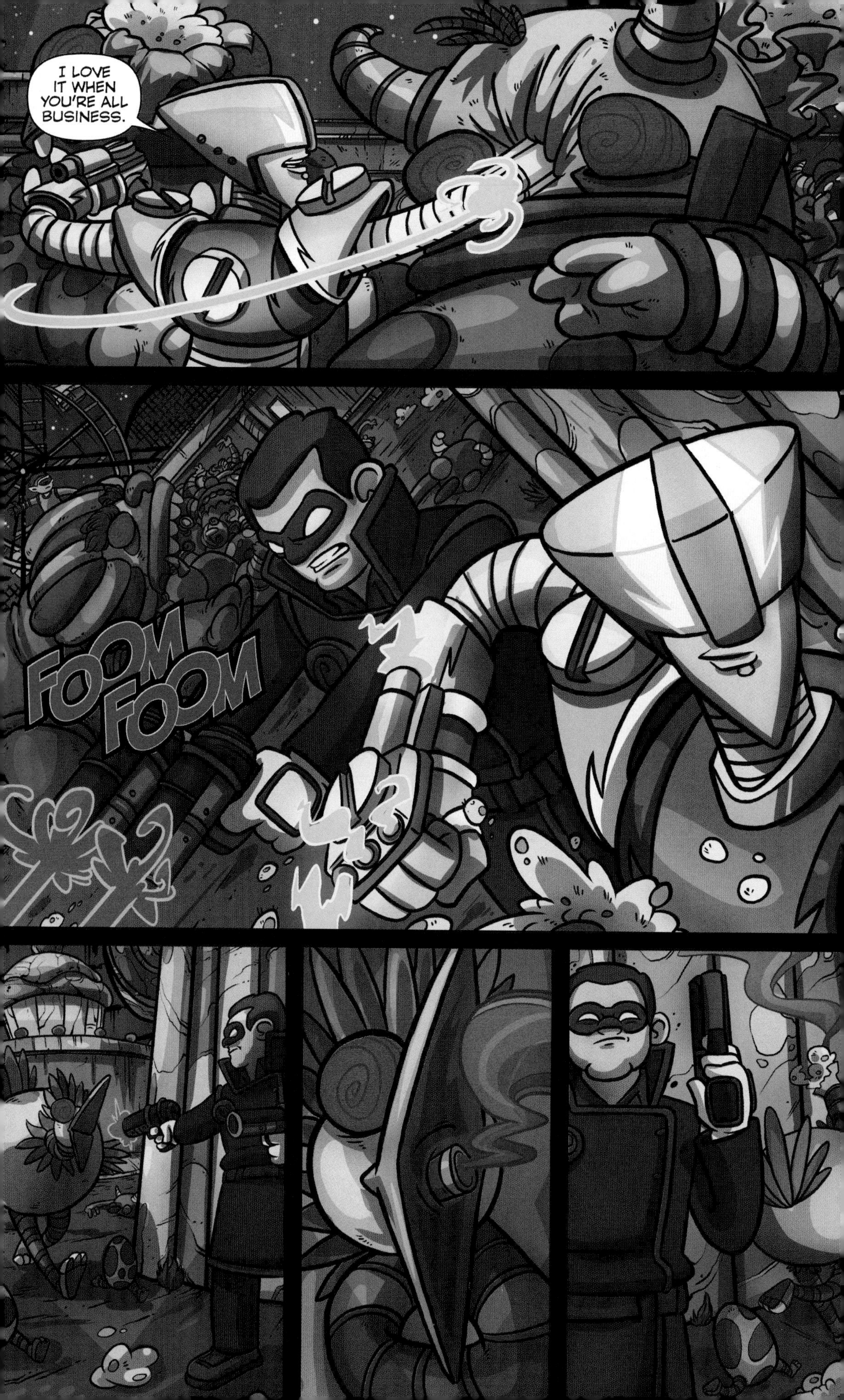
I LOVE IT WHEN YOU'RE ALL BUSINESS.
FOOM FOOM

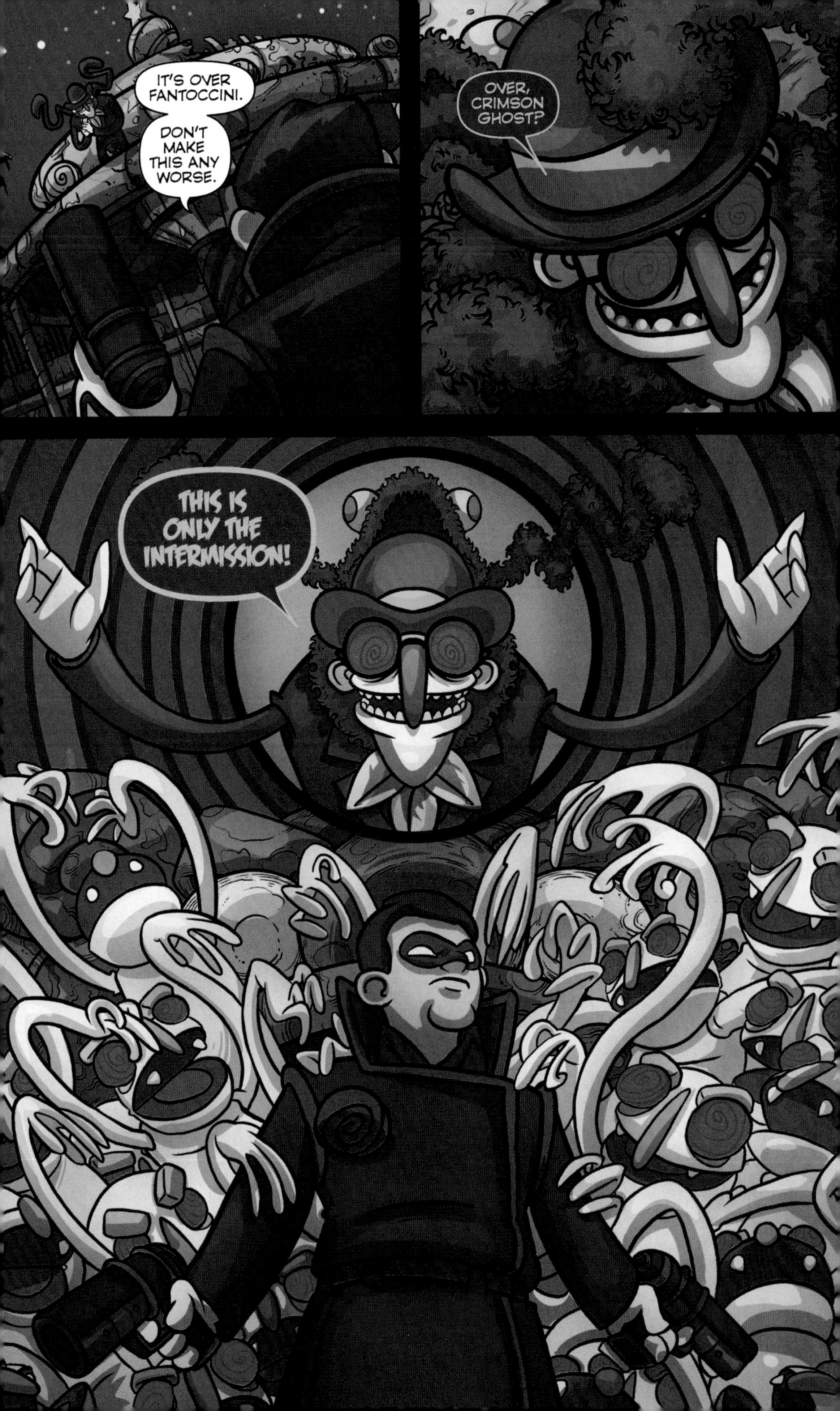

IT'S OVER FANTOCCINI.
DON'T MAKE THIS ANY WORSE.
OVER, CRIMSON GHOST?
THIS IS ONLY THE INTERMISSION!

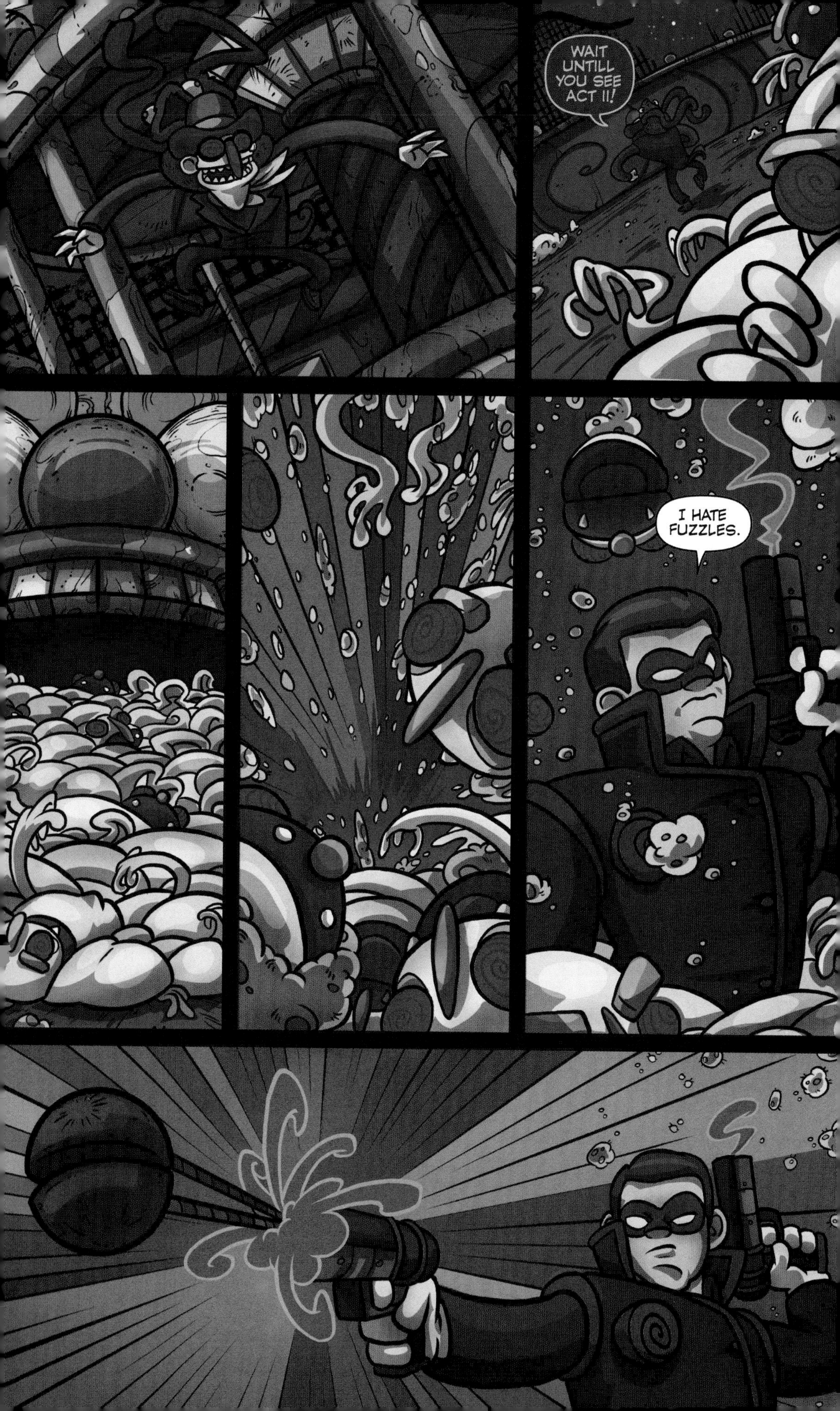
WAIT UNTILL YOU SEE ACT II!
I HATE FUZZLES.

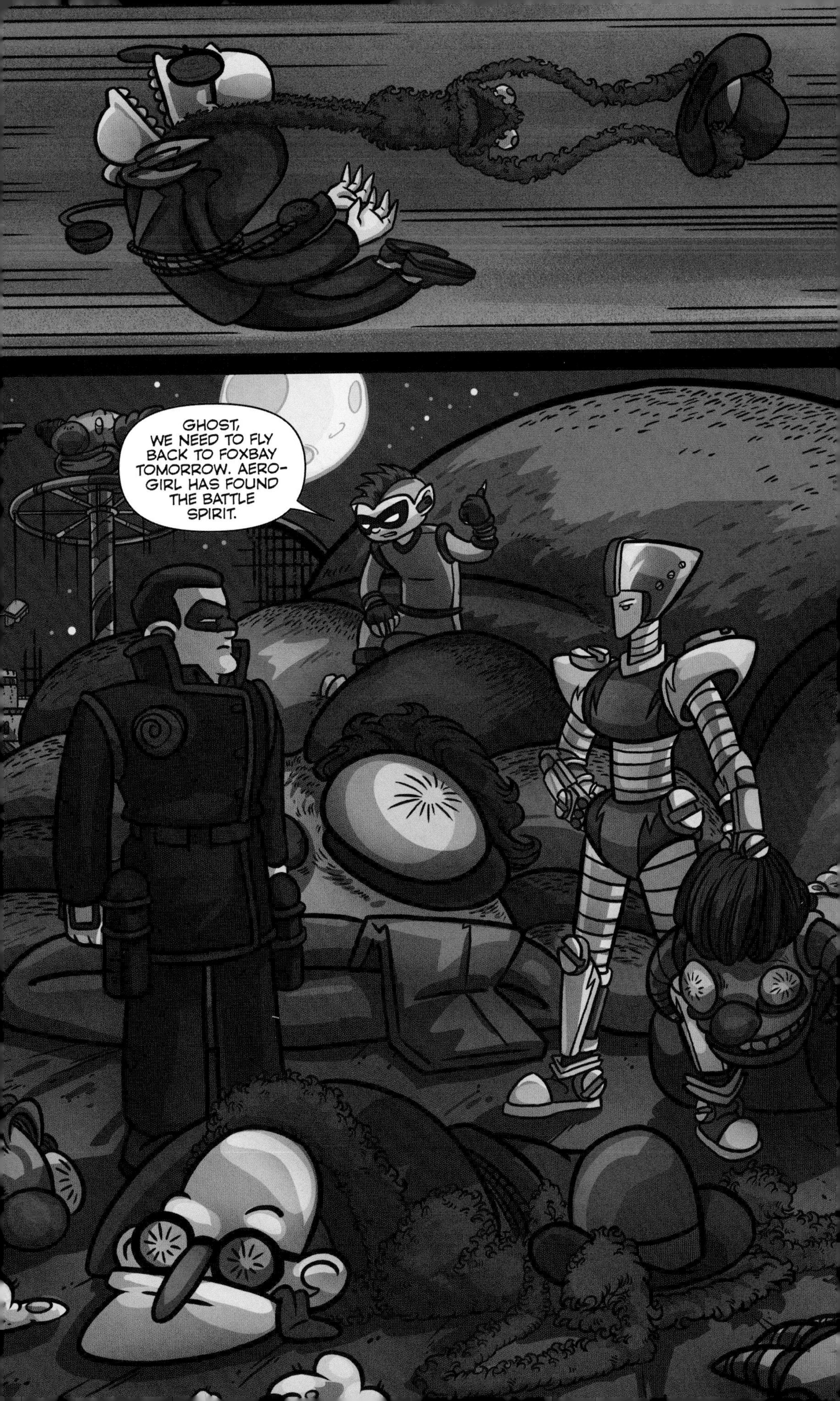
GHOST, WE NEED TO FLY BACK TO FOXBAY TOMORROW. AERO-GIRL HAS FOUND THE BATTLE SPIRIT.

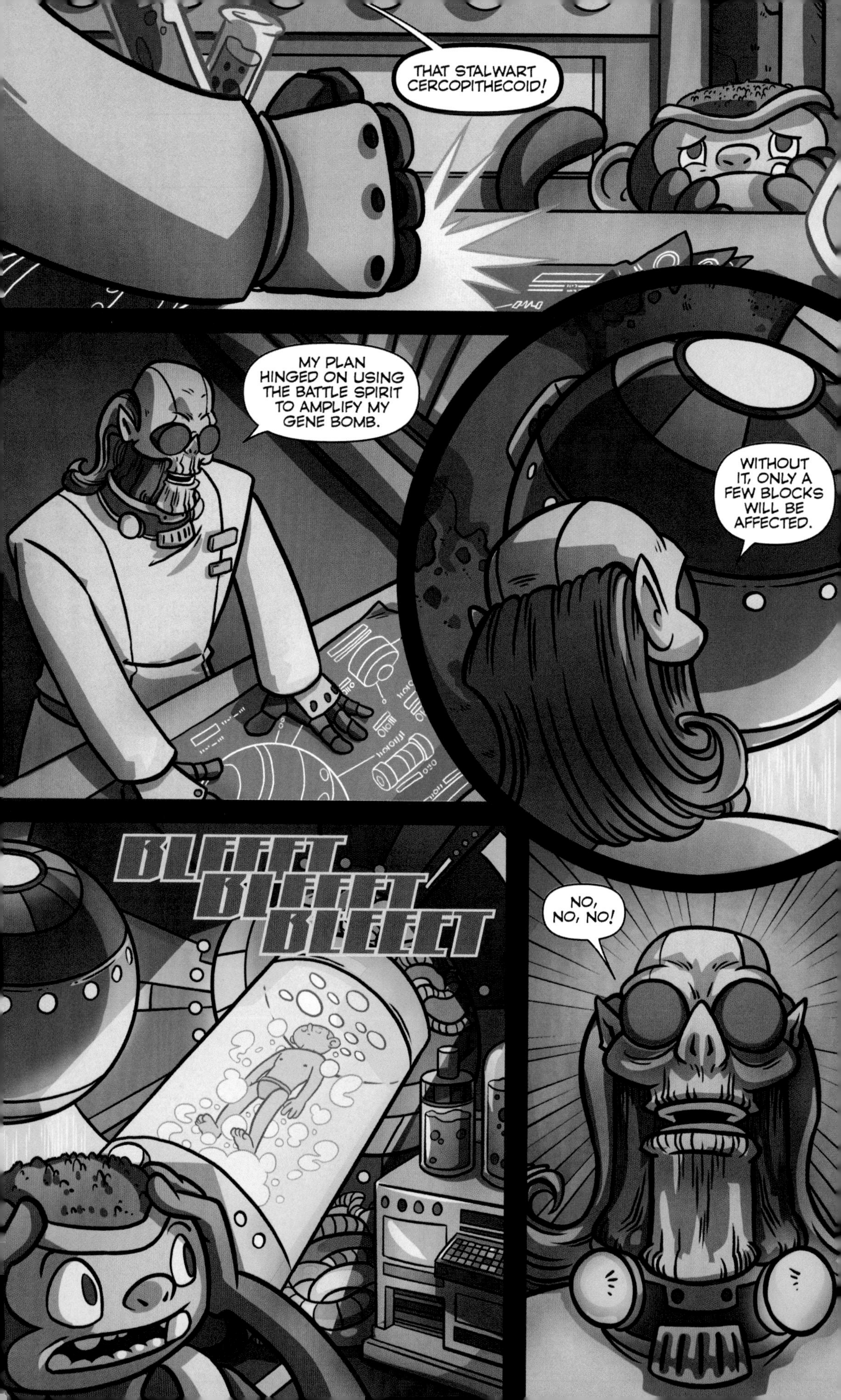
THAT STALWART CERCOPITHECOID!
MY PLAN HINGED ON USING THE BATTLE SPIRIT TO AMPLIFY MY GENE BOMB.
WITHOUT IT, ONLY A FEW BLOCKS WILL BE AFFECTED.
BLEEET
BLEEET
BLEEET
NO, NO, NO!

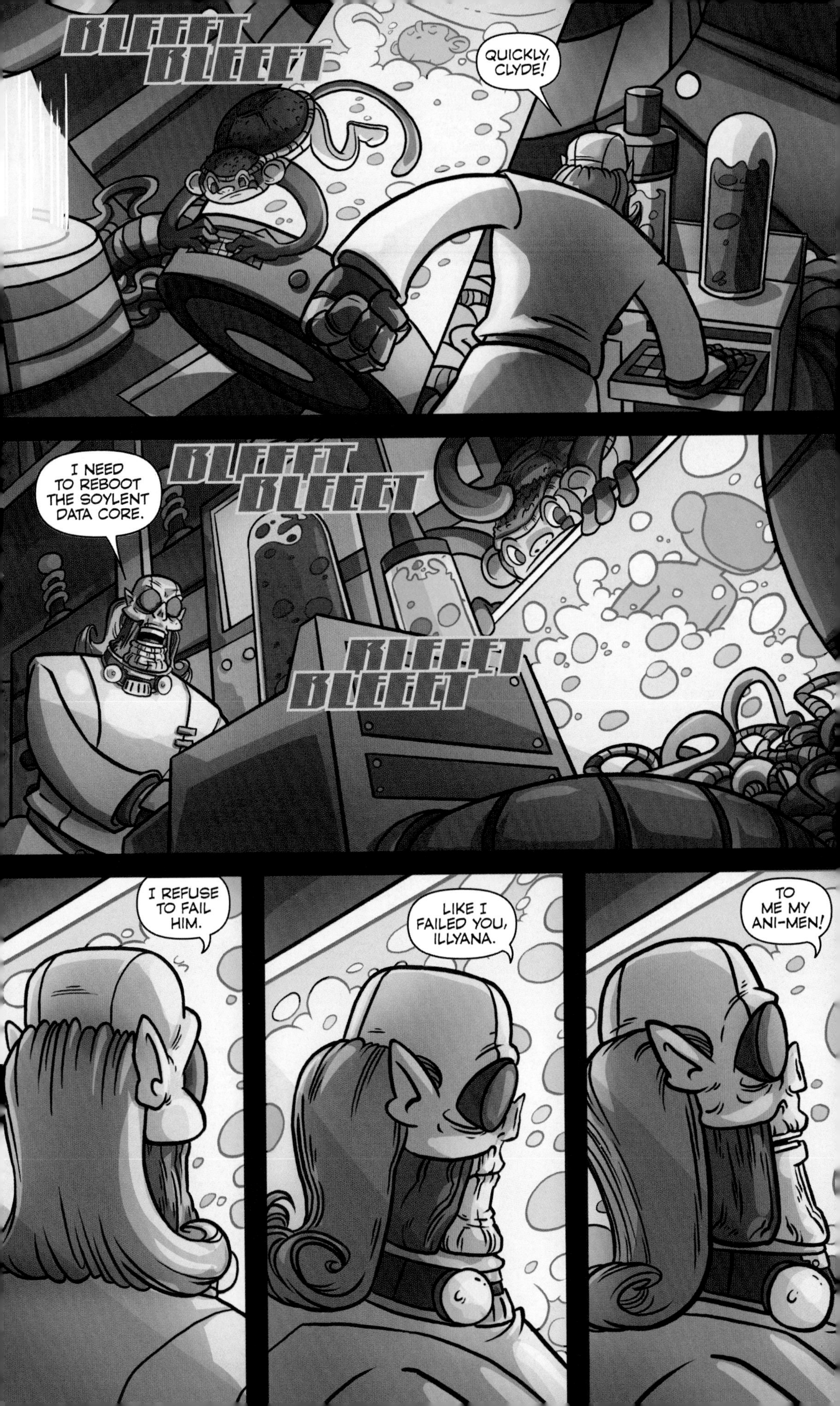
BLEEET BLEEET
QUICKLY, CLYDE!
I NEED TO REBOOT THE SOYLENT DATA CORE.
BLEEET BLEEET
BLEEET BLEEET
I REFUSE TO FAIL HIM.
LIKE I FAILED YOU, ILLYANA.
TO ME MY ANI-MEN!

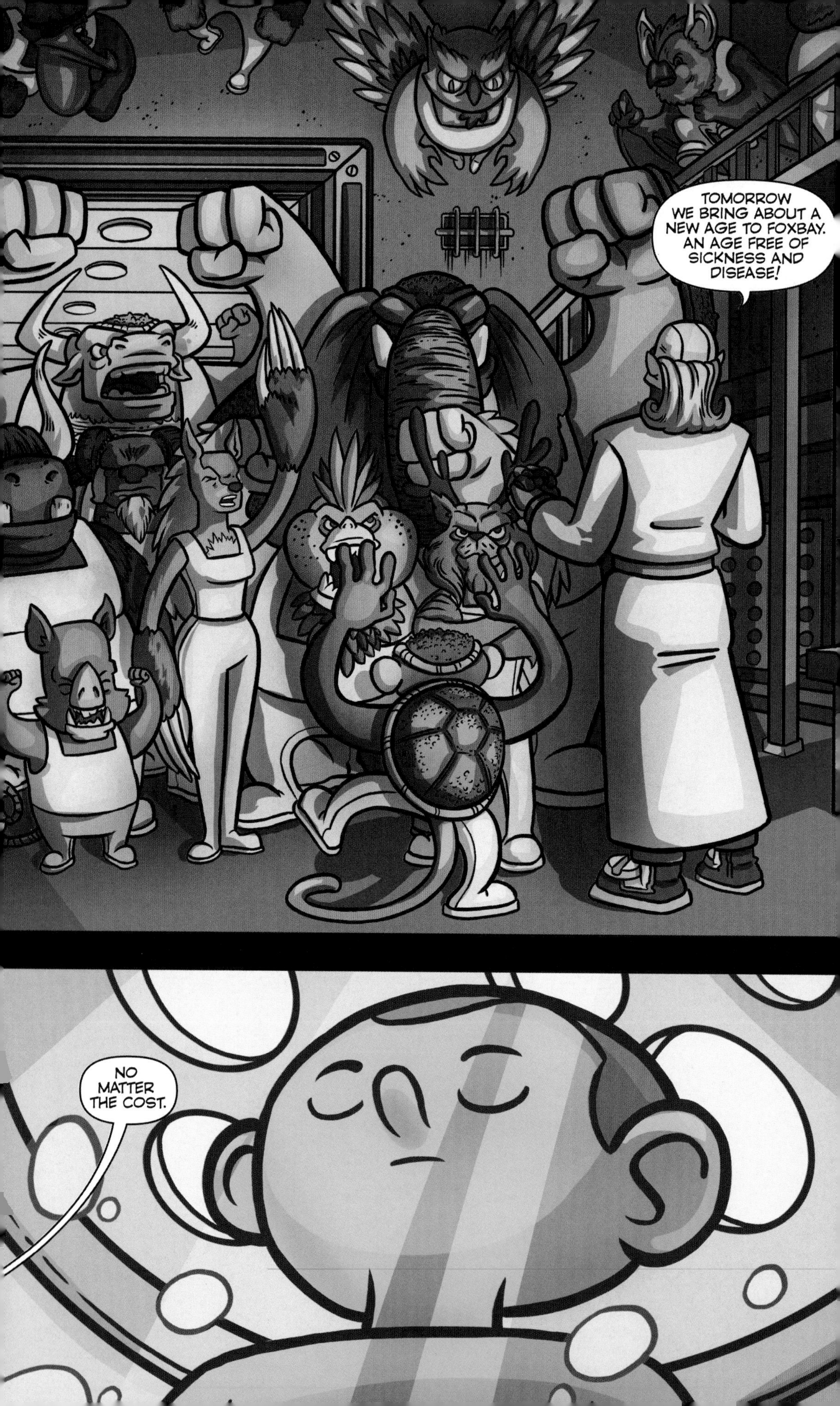
TOMORROW WE BRING ABOUT A NEW AGE TO FOXBAY. AN AGE FREE OF SICKNESS AND DISEASE!
NO MATTER THE COST.

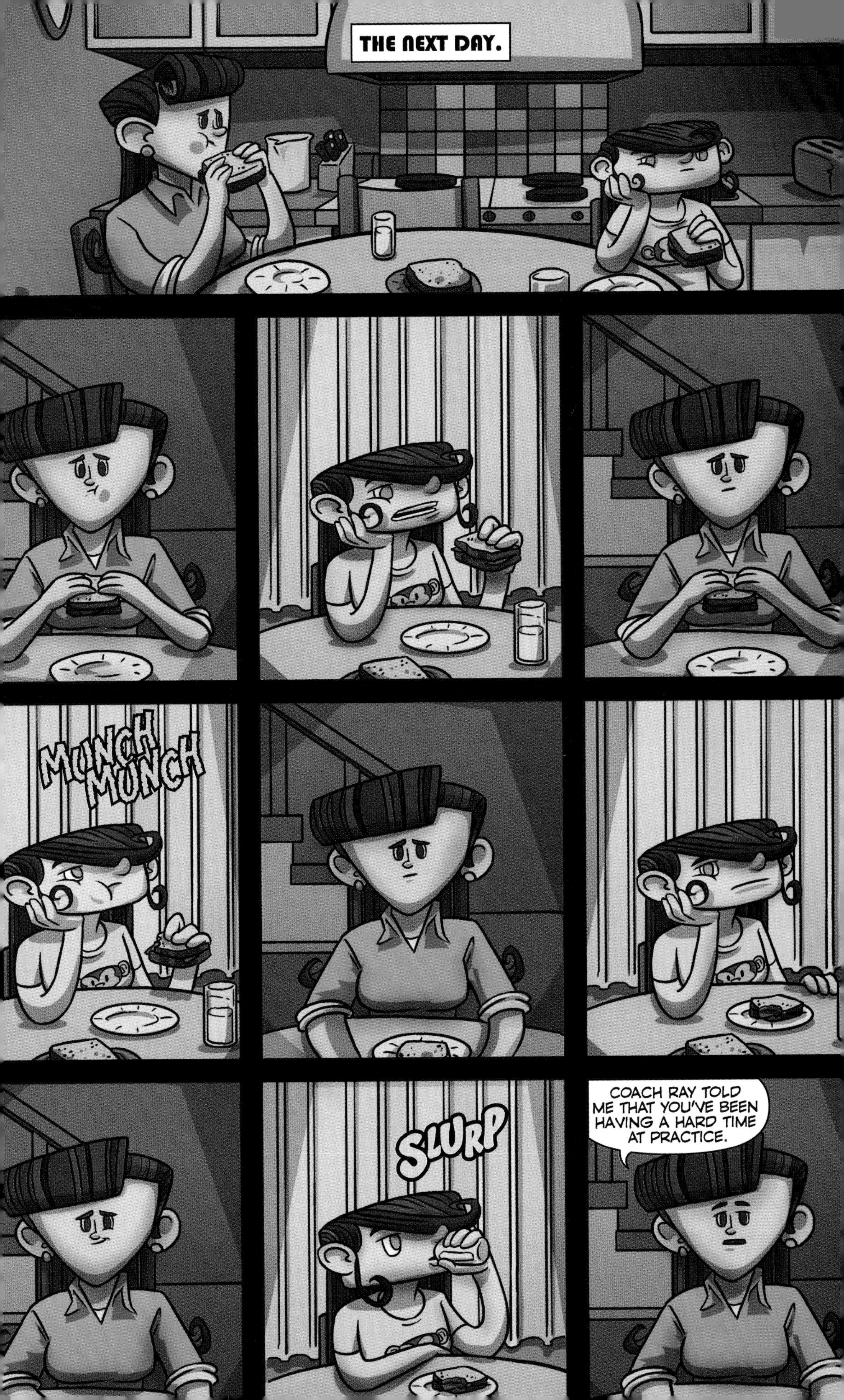
THE NEXT DAY.
MUNCH MUNCH
SLURP
COACH RAY TOLD ME THAT YOU'VE BEEN HAVING A HARD TIME AT PRACTICE.

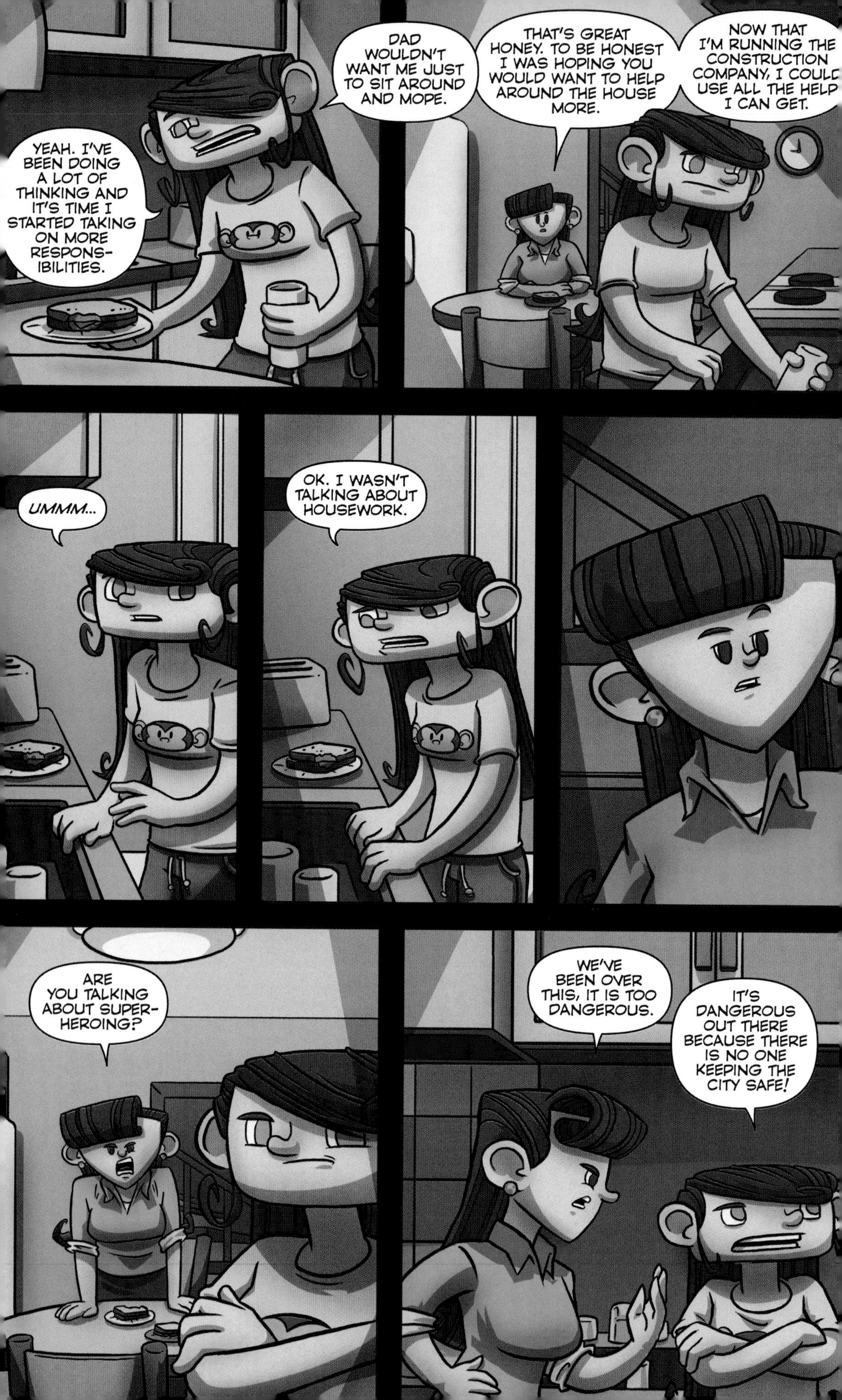
YEAH. I'VE BEEN DOING A LOT OF THINKING AND IT'S TIME I STARTED TAKING ON MORE RESPONS-IBILITIES.
DAD WOULDN'T WANT ME JUST TO SIT AROUND AND MOPE.
THAT'S GREAT HONEY. TO BE HONEST I WAS HOPING YOU WOULD WANT TO HELP AROUND THE HOUSE MORE.
NOW THAT I'M RUNNING THE CONSTRUCTION COMPANY, I COULD USE ALL THE HELP I CAN GET.
UMMM...
OK. I WASN'T TALKING ABOUT HOUSEWORK.
ARE YOU TALKING ABOUT SUPER-HEROING?
WE'VE BEEN OVER THIS, IT IS TOO DANGEROUS.
IT'S DANGEROUS OUT THERE BECAUSE THERE IS NO ONE KEEPING THE CITY SAFE!

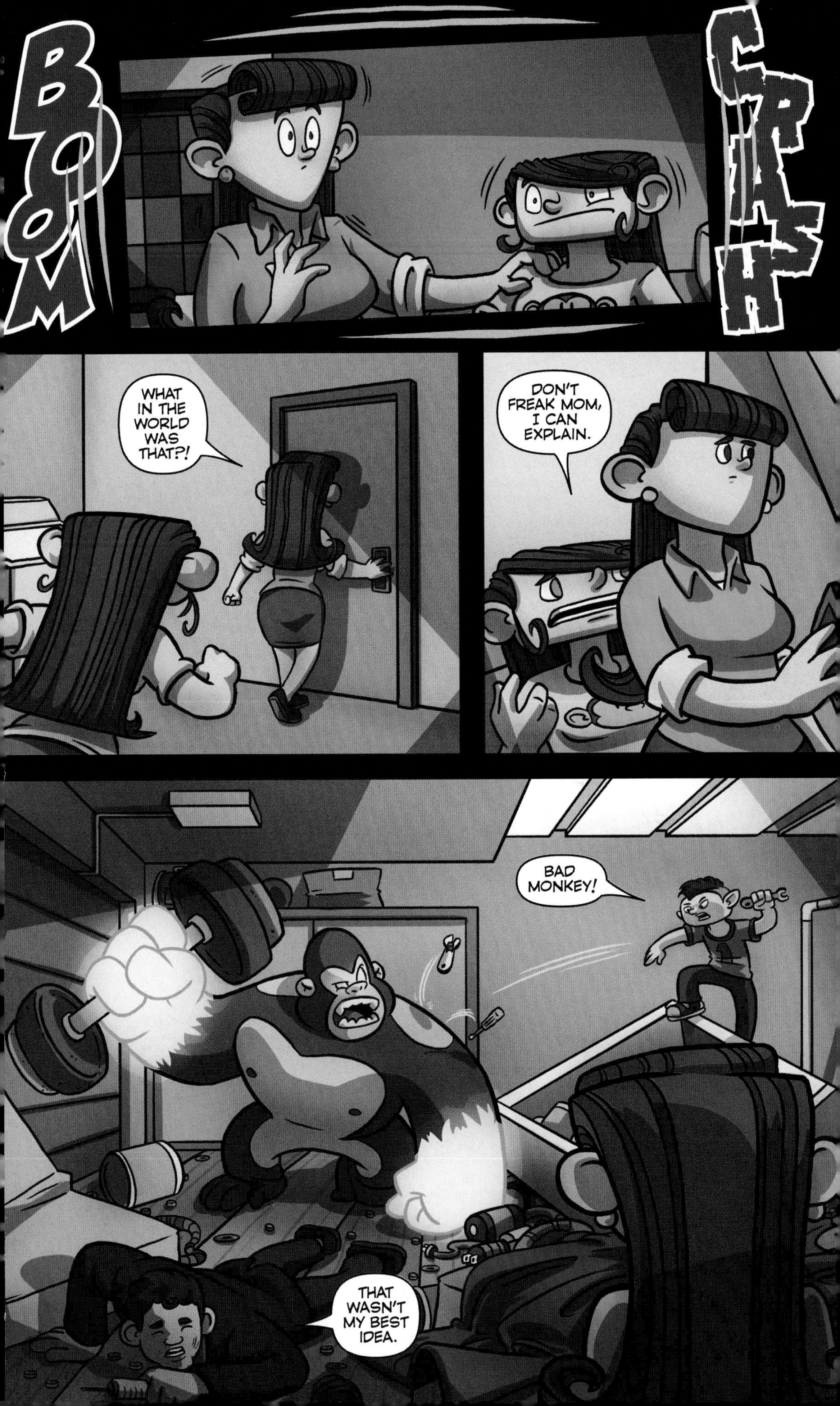
BOOM
CRASH
WHAT IN THE WORLD WAS THAT?!
DON'T FREAK MOM, I CAN EXPLAIN.
BAD MONKEY!
THAT WASN'T MY BEST IDEA.

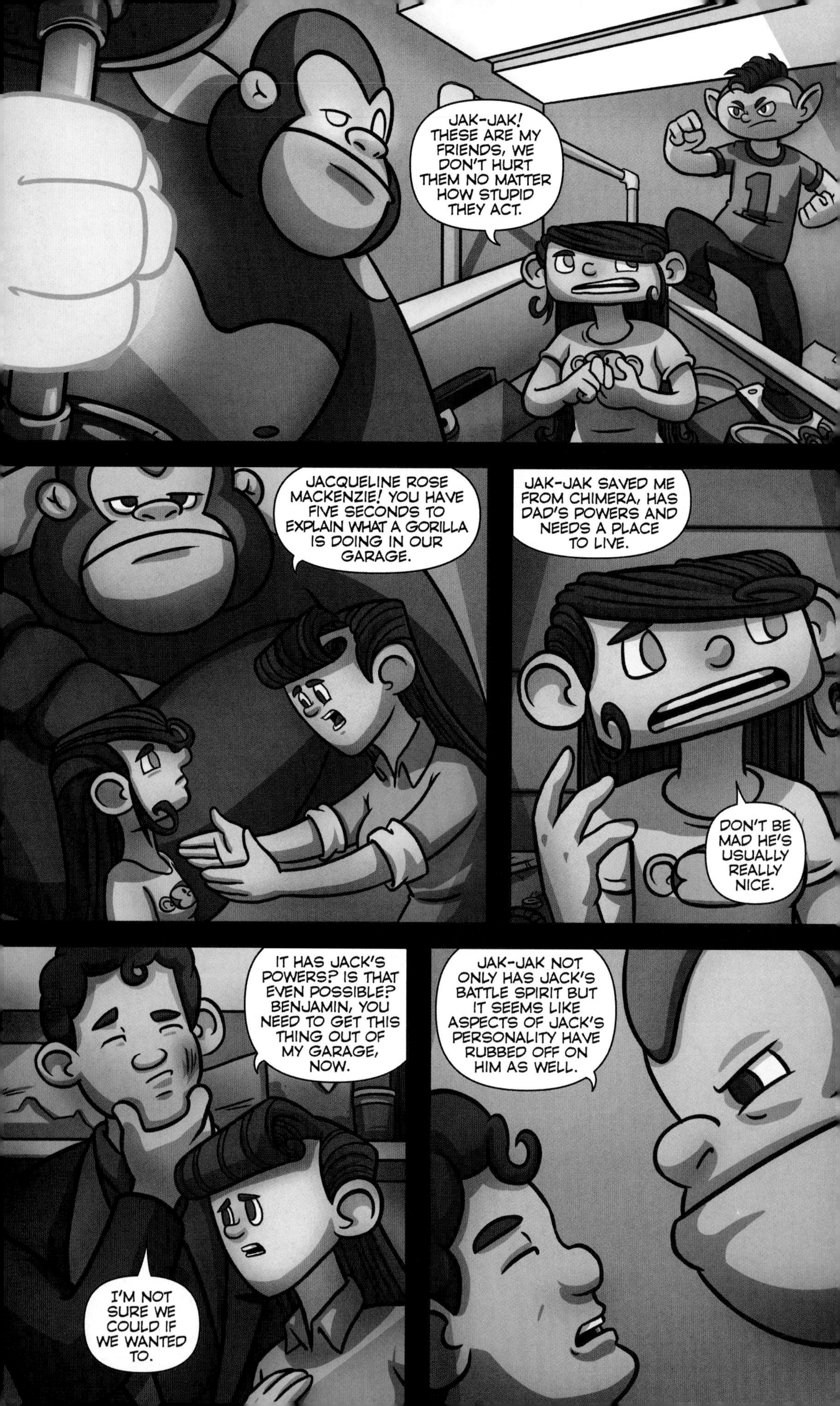
JAK-JAK! THESE ARE MY FRIENDS, WE DON'T HURT THEM NO MATTER HOW STUPID THEY ACT.
JACQUELINE ROSE MACKENZIE! YOU HAVE FIVE SECONDS TO EXPLAIN WHAT A GORILLA IS DOING IN OUR GARAGE.
JAK-JAK SAVED ME FROM CHIMERA, HAS DAD'S POWERS AND NEEDS A PLACE TO LIVE.
DON'T BE MAD HE'S USUALLY REALLY NICE.
IT HAS JACK'S POWERS? IS THAT EVEN POSSIBLE? BENJAMIN, YOU NEED TO GET THIS THING OUT OF MY GARAGE, NOW.
I'M NOT SURE WE COULD IF WE WANTED TO.
JAK-JAK NOT ONLY HAS JACK'S BATTLE SPIRIT BUT IT SEEMS LIKE ASPECTS OF JACK'S PERSONALITY HAVE RUBBED OFF ON HIM AS WELL.

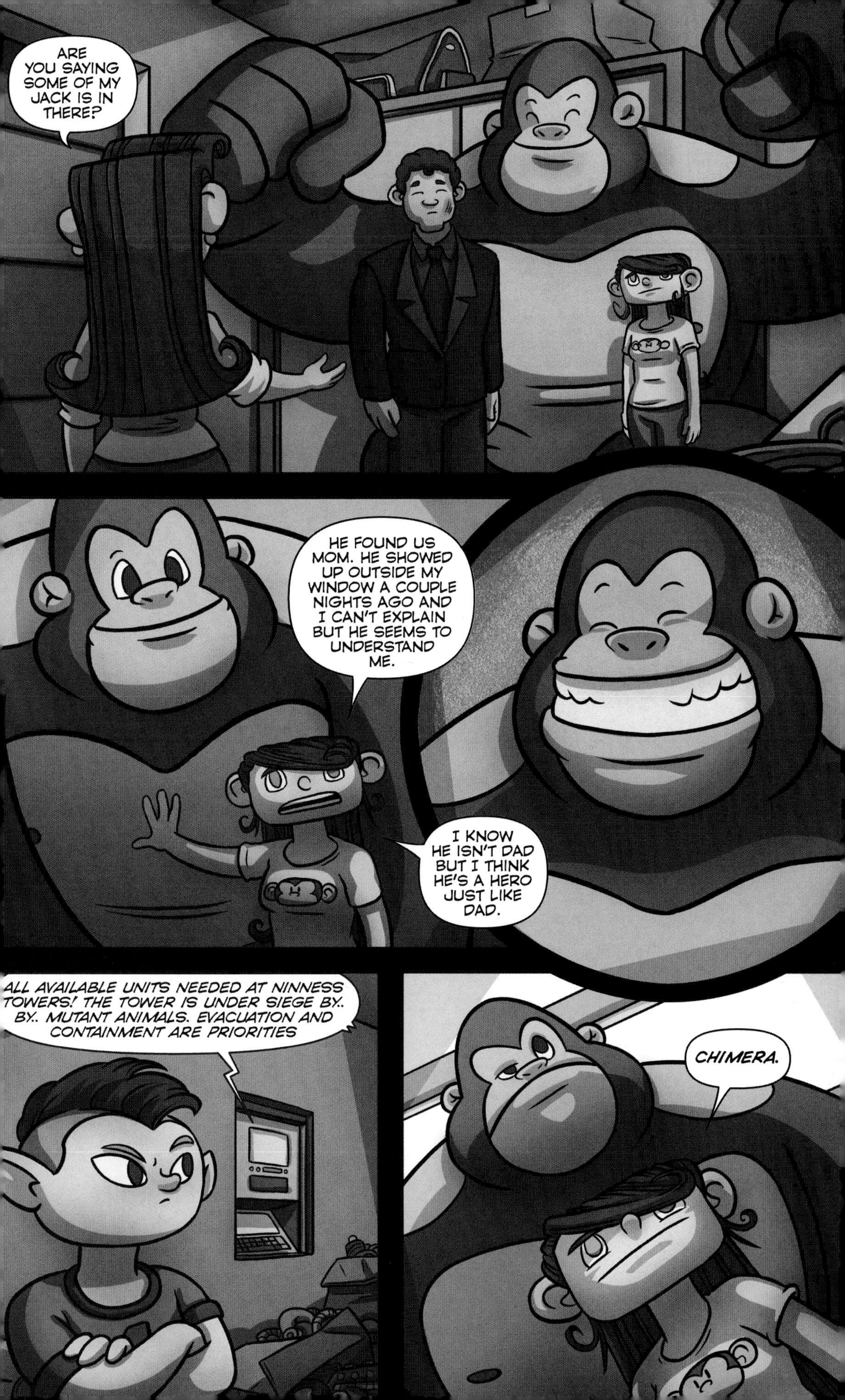
ARE YOU SAYING SOME OF MY JACK IS IN THERE?
HE FOUND US MOM. HE SHOWED UP OUTSIDE MY WINDOW A COUPLE NIGHTS AGO AND I CAN'T EXPLAIN BUT HE SEEMS TO UNDERSTAND ME.
I KNOW HE ISN'T DAD BUT I THINK HE'S A HERO JUST LIKE DAD.
ALL AVAILABLE UNITS NEEDED AT NINNESS TOWERS! THE TOWER IS UNDER SIEGE BY.. BY.. MUTANT ANIMALS. EVACUATION AND CONTAINMENT ARE PRIORITIES
CHIMERA.

WE HAVE TO STOP HIM. YOU GUYS HAVE COSTUMES ON YOU?

MEET YOU THERE.

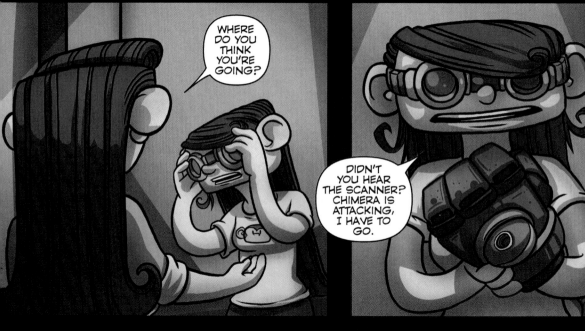

WHERE DO YOU THINK YOU'RE GOING?

DIDN'T YOU HEAR THE SCANNER? CHIMERA IS ATTACKING, I HAVE TO GO.

I'VE TOLD YOU, THAT PART OF YOUR LIFE IS OVER.

BEN AND CHRIS ARE ON THEIR WAY...

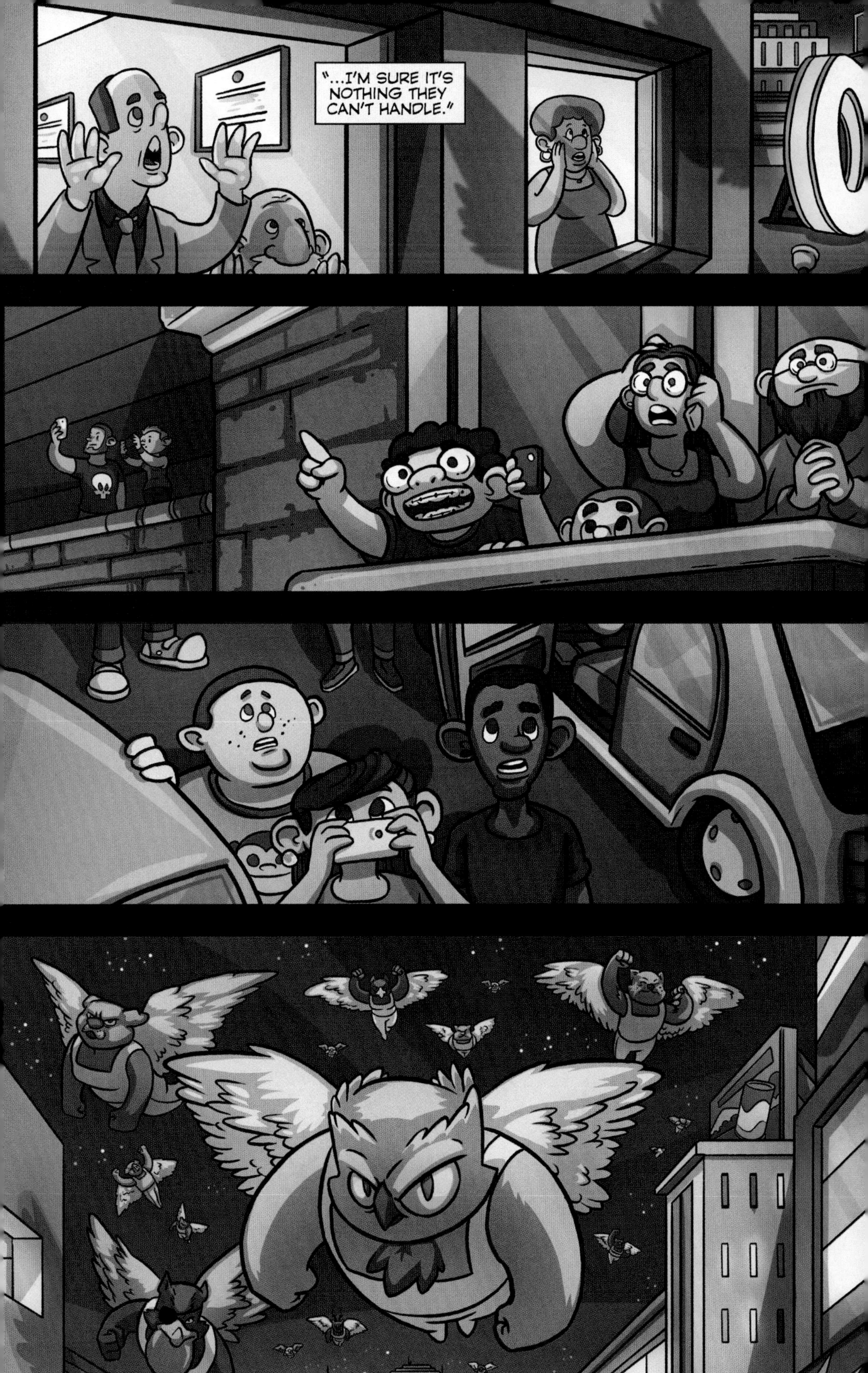
"...I'M SURE IT'S NOTHING THEY CAN'T HANDLE."

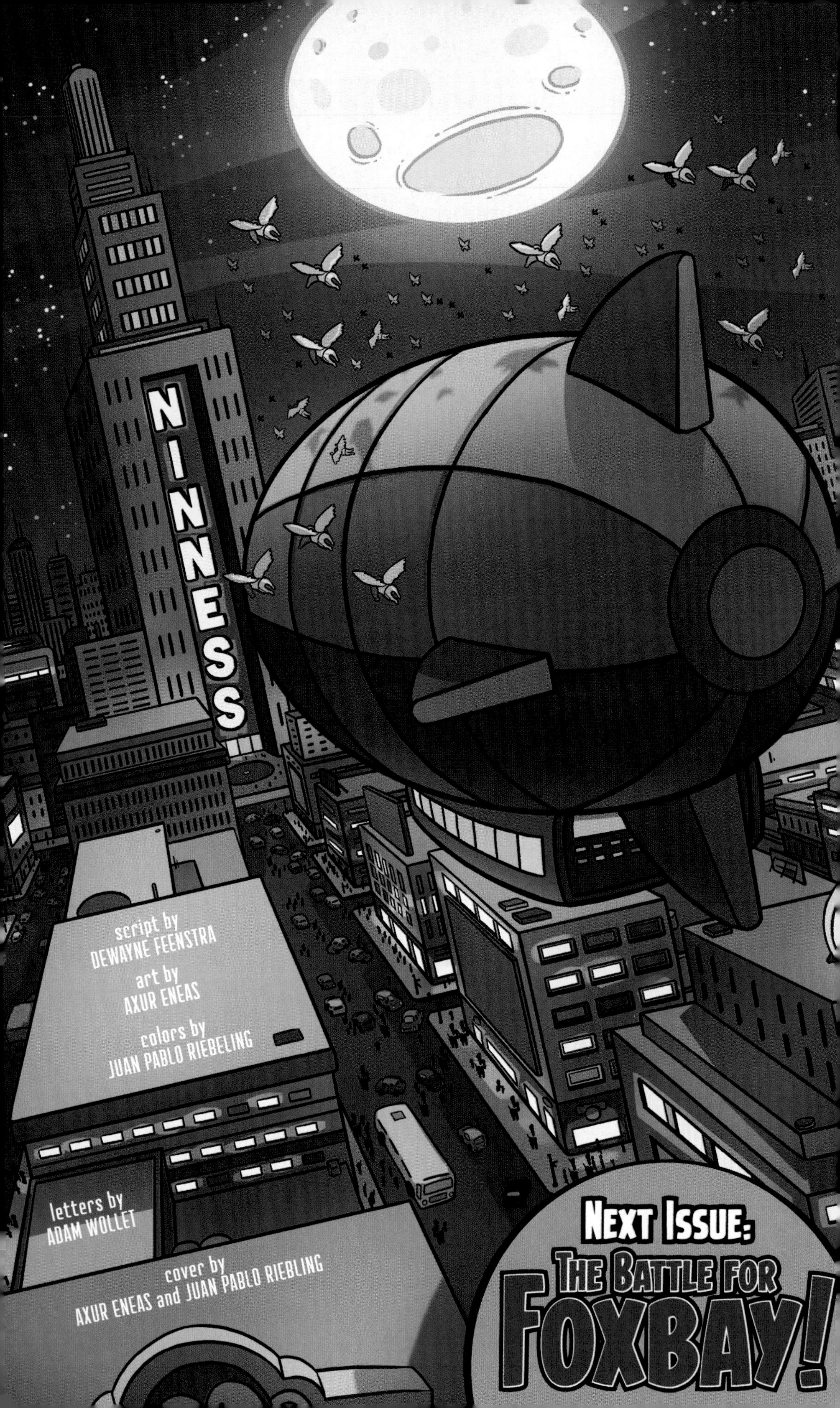
NINNESS
script by
DEWAYNE FEENSTRA
art by
AXUR ENEAS
colors by
JUAN PABLO RIEBELING
letters by
ADAM WOLLET
cover by
AXUR ENEAS and JUAN PABLO RIEBLING
NEXT ISSUE:
THE BATTLE FOR
FOXBAY!

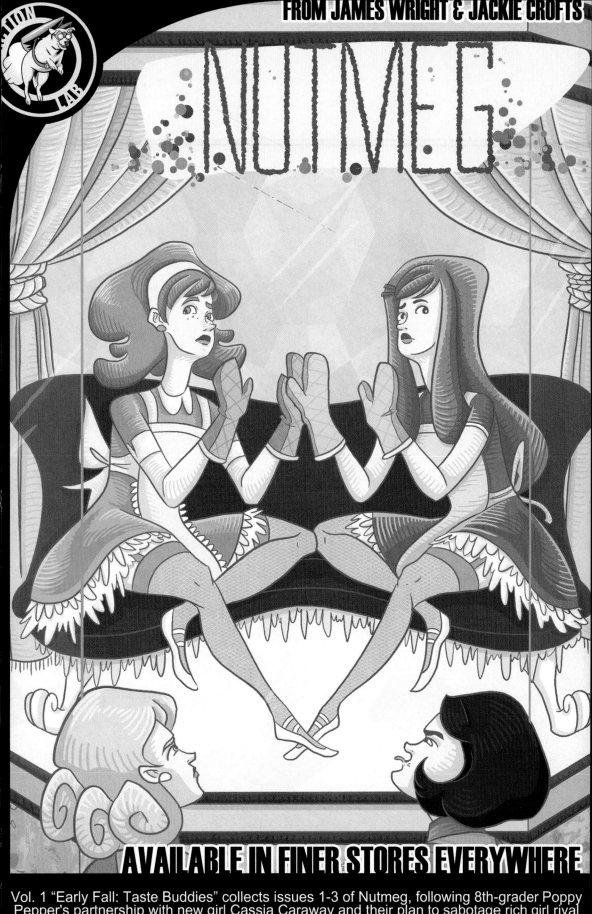

FROM JAMES WRIGHT & JACKIE CROFTS

N.U.T.M.E.G

AVAILABLE IN FINER STORES EVERYWHERE

Vol. 1 "Early Fall: Taste Buddies" collects issues 1-3 of Nutmeg, following 8th-grader Poppy Pepper's partnership with new girl Cassia Caraway and their plan to sabotage rich girl rival Saffron Longfellow's brownie fundraiser, taking their first steps toward a life of crime.

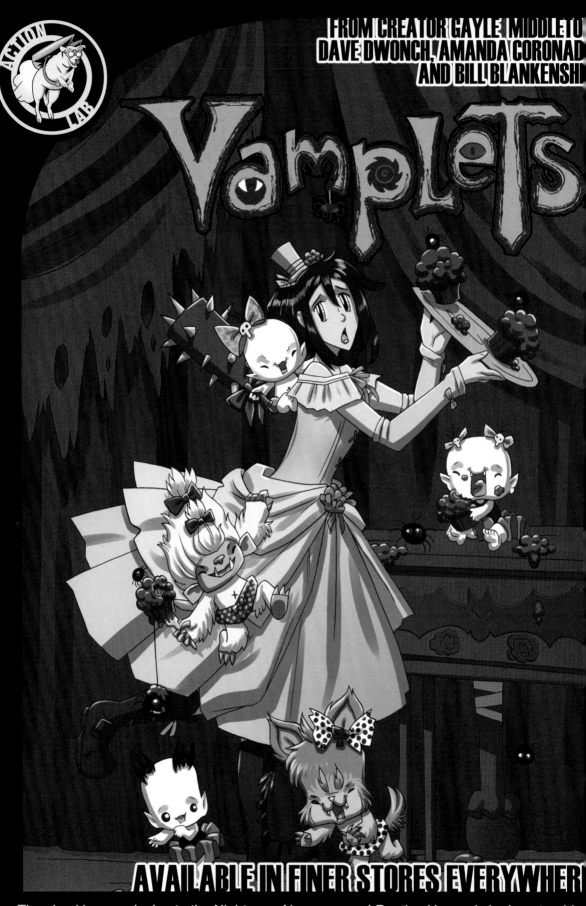

The shocking conclusion to the Nightmare Nursery saga! Destiny Harper is in deep trouble and she will need the help of Rasket, Lycinda and the Vamplets themselves to thwart the plans of the evil Vammette. Will Destiny Harper get back home, or will she be trapped on th nightmare world of Gloomvania forever?

Collecting the hit mini-series, STRAY tells the story of Rodney Weller, the former sidekick known as "the Rottweiler." When his mentor, the Doberman, is murdered, Rodney has to decide if he wants to come back to the world of capes and masks and, if he does, who he

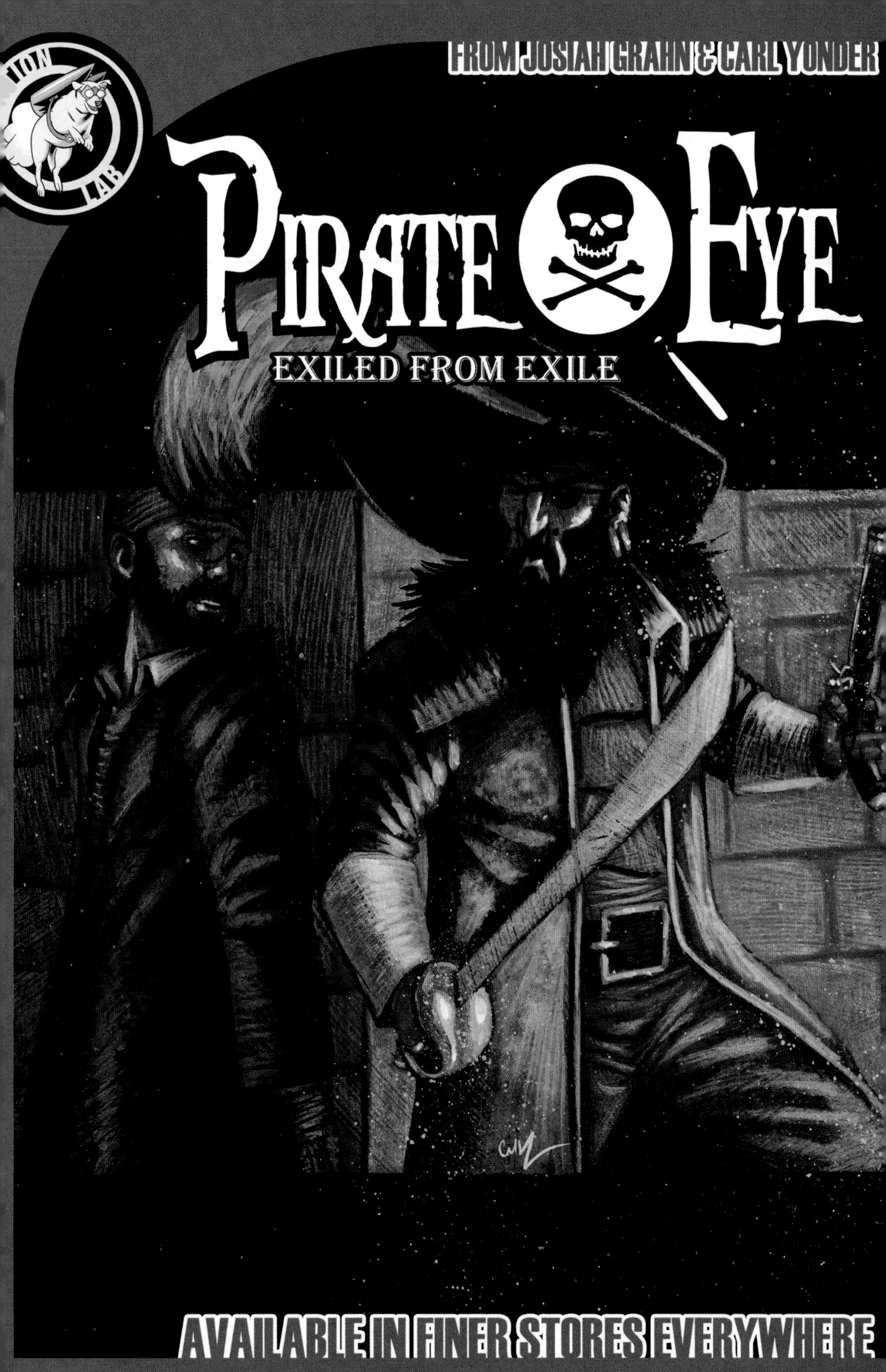

FROM JOSIAH GRAHN & CARL YONDER

PIRATE EYE

EXILED FROM EXILE

AVAILABLE IN FINER STORES EVERYWHERE

Former pirate Smitty is finally adjusting to his new life as a detective for hire when an old enemy takes it all away. Now Smitty will be forced to find out just how far he will go to stay alive, to retrieve what he's lost and to take revenge. Collects the critically-acclaimed Pirate Eye: Exiled from Exile #1-4.

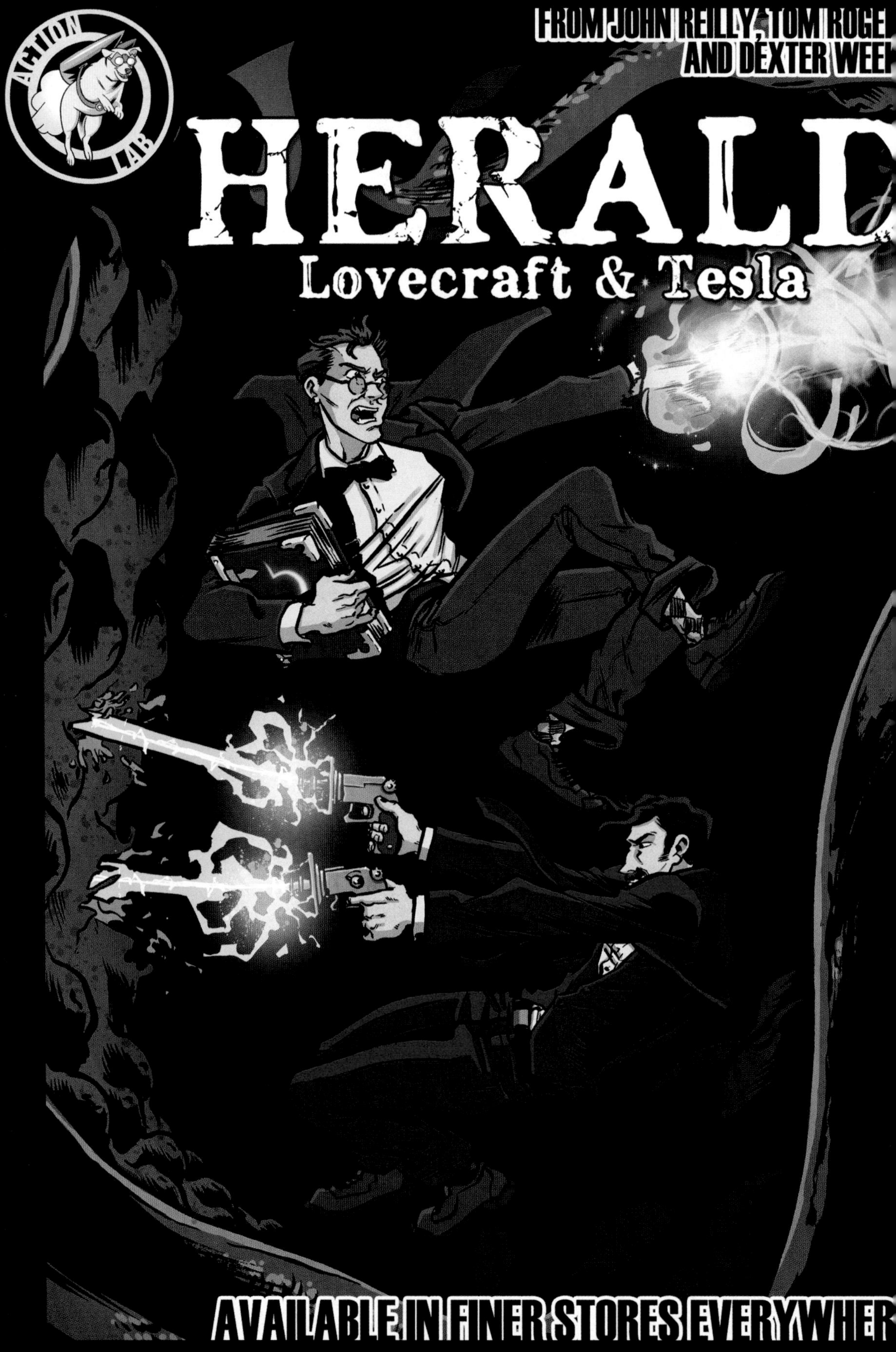
ACTION LAB
FROM JOHN REILLY, TOM ROGE
AND DEXTER WEE
HERALD
Lovecraft & Tesla
AVAILABLE IN FINER STORES EVERYWHER

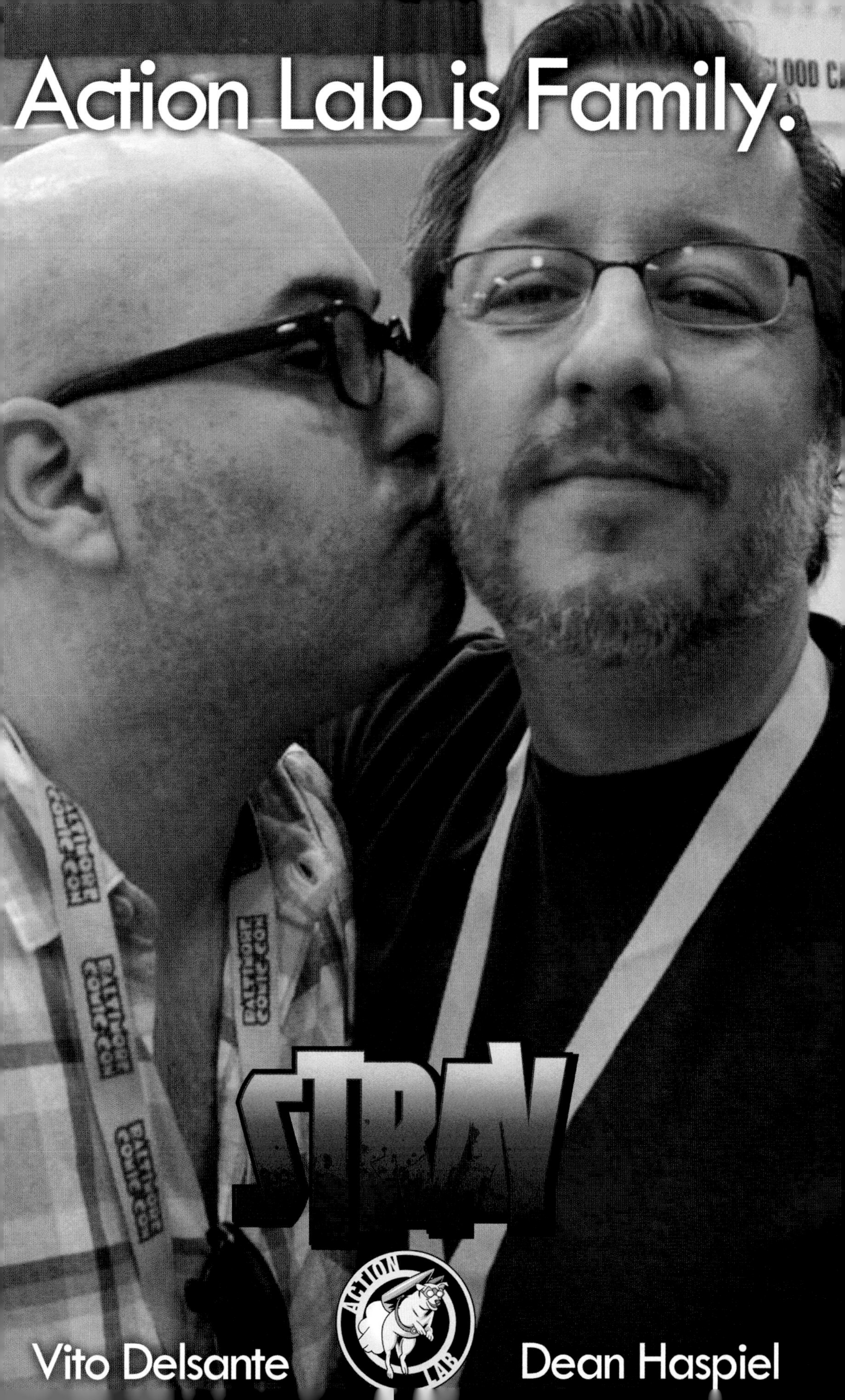

Action Lab is Family.
BALTIMORE COMIC-CON
STRAY
ACTION LAB
Vito Delsante
Dean Haspiel

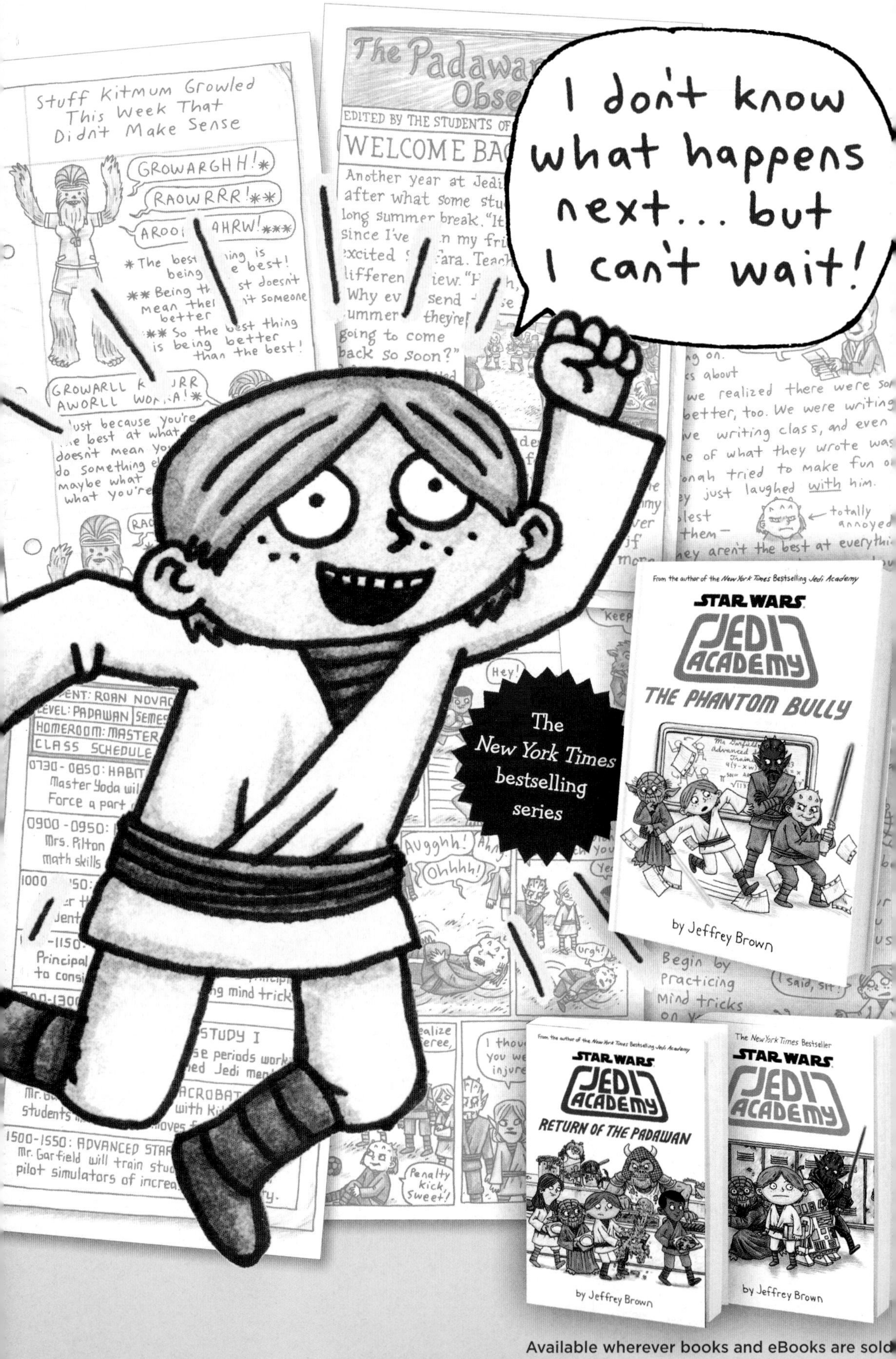

I don't know what happens next... but I can't wait!
The New York Times bestselling series
From the author of the New York Times Bestselling Jedi Academy
STAR WARS
JEDI ACADEMY
THE PHANTOM BULLY
by Jeffrey Brown
From the author of the New York Times Bestselling Jedi Academy
STAR WARS
JEDI ACADEMY
RETURN OF THE PADAWAN
by Jeffrey Brown
The New York Times Bestseller
STAR WARS
JEDI ACADEMY
by Jeffrey Brown

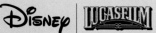

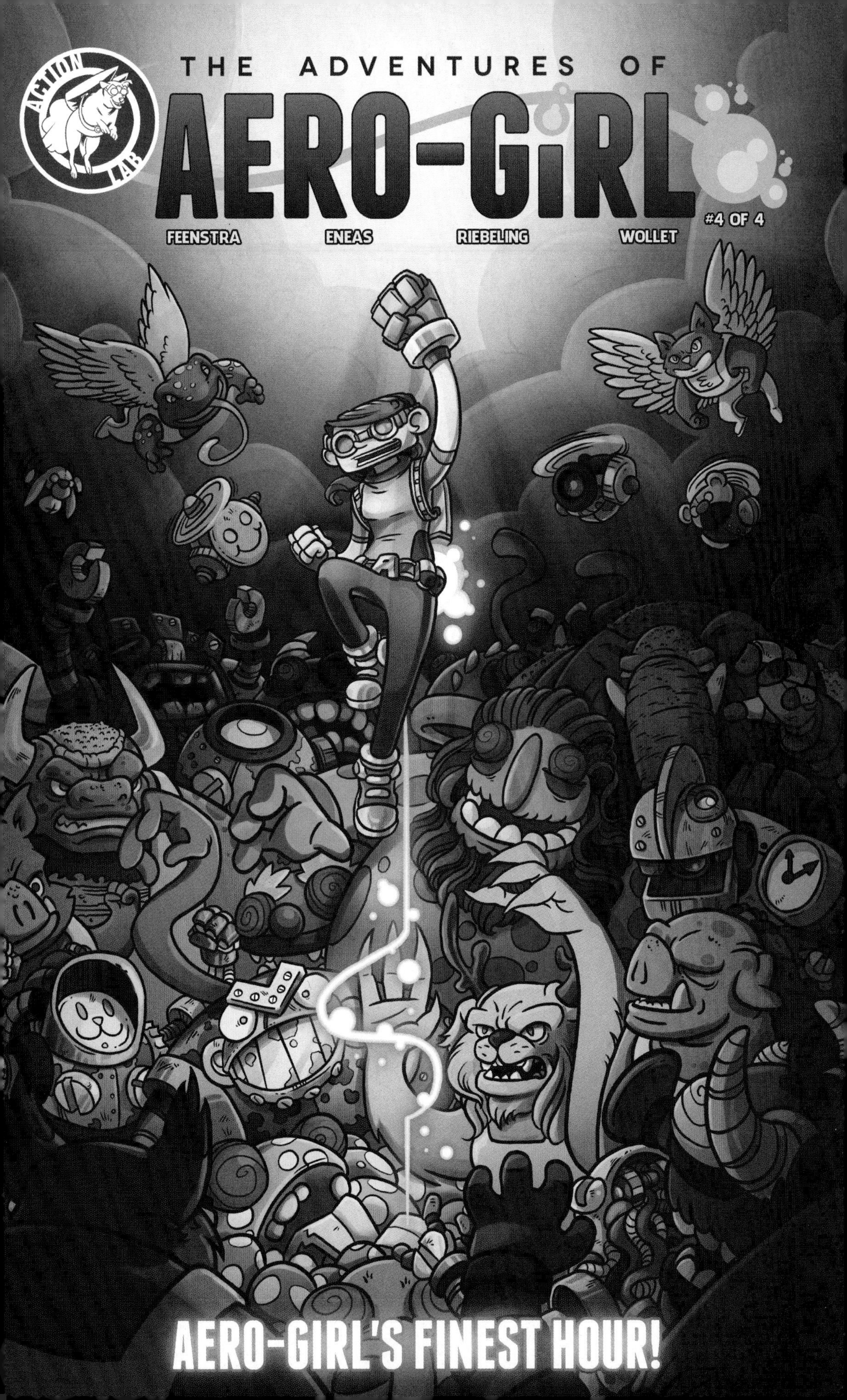
ACTION LAB
THE ADVENTURES OF
AERO-GiRL
#4 OF 4
FEENSTRA
ENEAS
RIEBELING
WOLLET
AERO-GIRL'S FINEST HOUR!

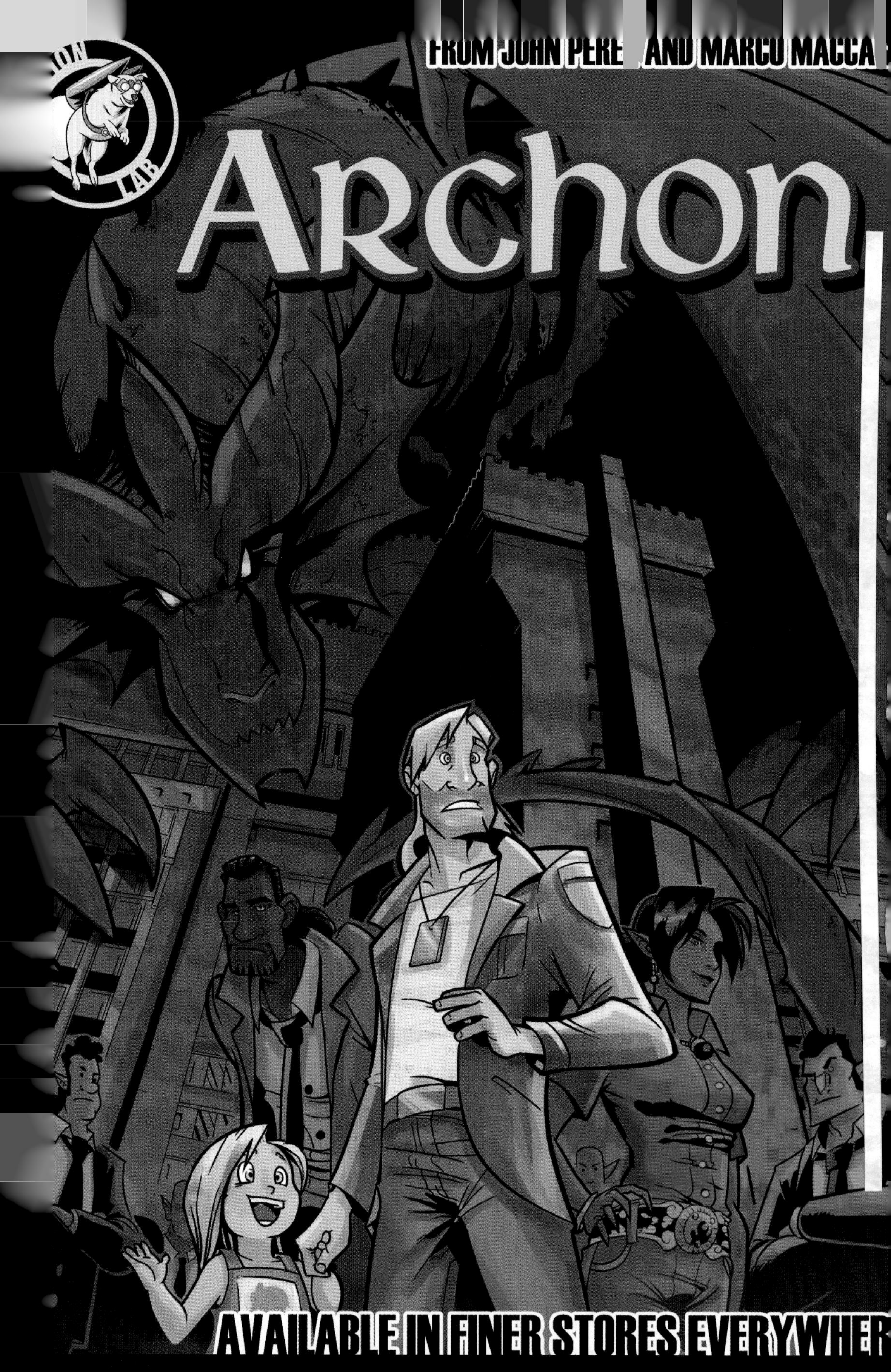
FROM JOHN PERE AND MARCO MACCA
Archon
AVAILABLE IN FINER STORES EVERYWHER

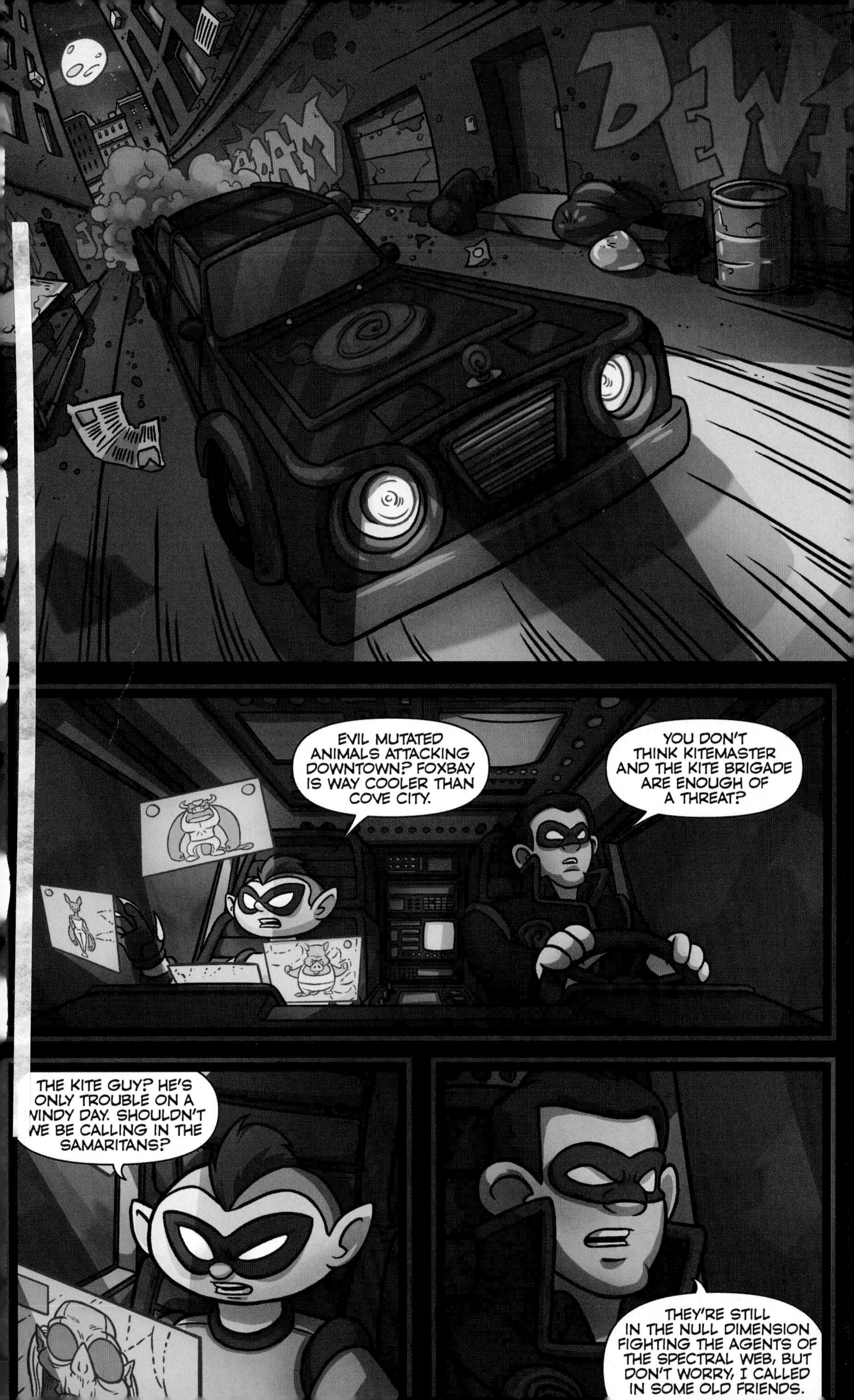
EVIL MUTATED ANIMALS ATTACKING DOWNTOWN? FOXBAY IS WAY COOLER THAN COVE CITY.
YOU DON'T THINK KITEMASTER AND THE KITE BRIGADE ARE ENOUGH OF A THREAT?
THE KITE GUY? HE'S ONLY TROUBLE ON A WINDY DAY. SHOULDN'T WE BE CALLING IN THE SAMARITANS?
THEY'RE STILL IN THE NULL DIMENSION FIGHTING THE AGENTS OF THE SPECTRAL WEB, BUT DON'T WORRY, I CALLED IN SOME OLD FRIENDS.

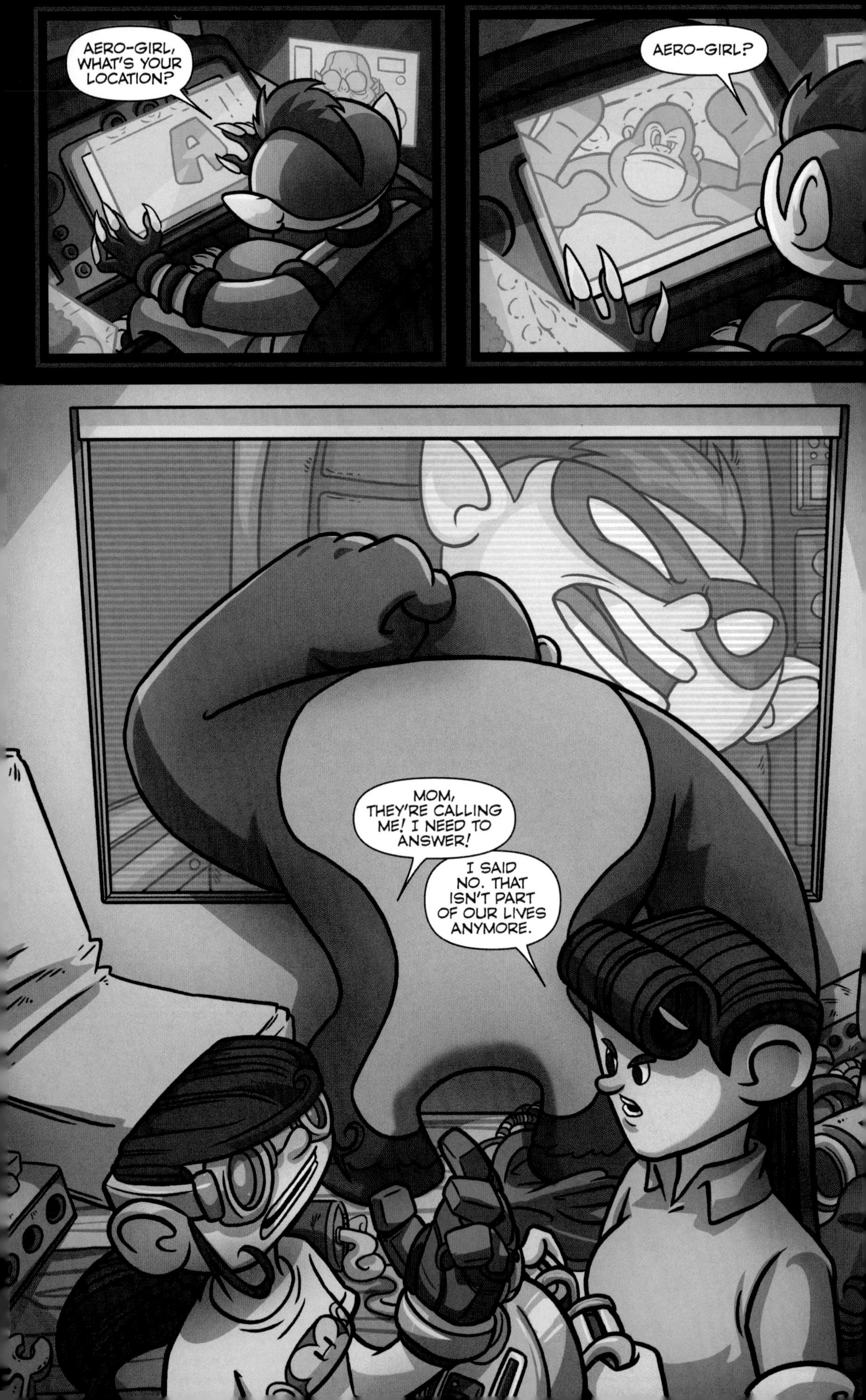
AERO-GIRL, WHAT'S YOUR LOCATION?
AERO-GIRL?
MOM, THEY'RE CALLING ME! I NEED TO ANSWER!
I SAID NO. THAT ISN'T PART OF OUR LIVES ANYMORE.

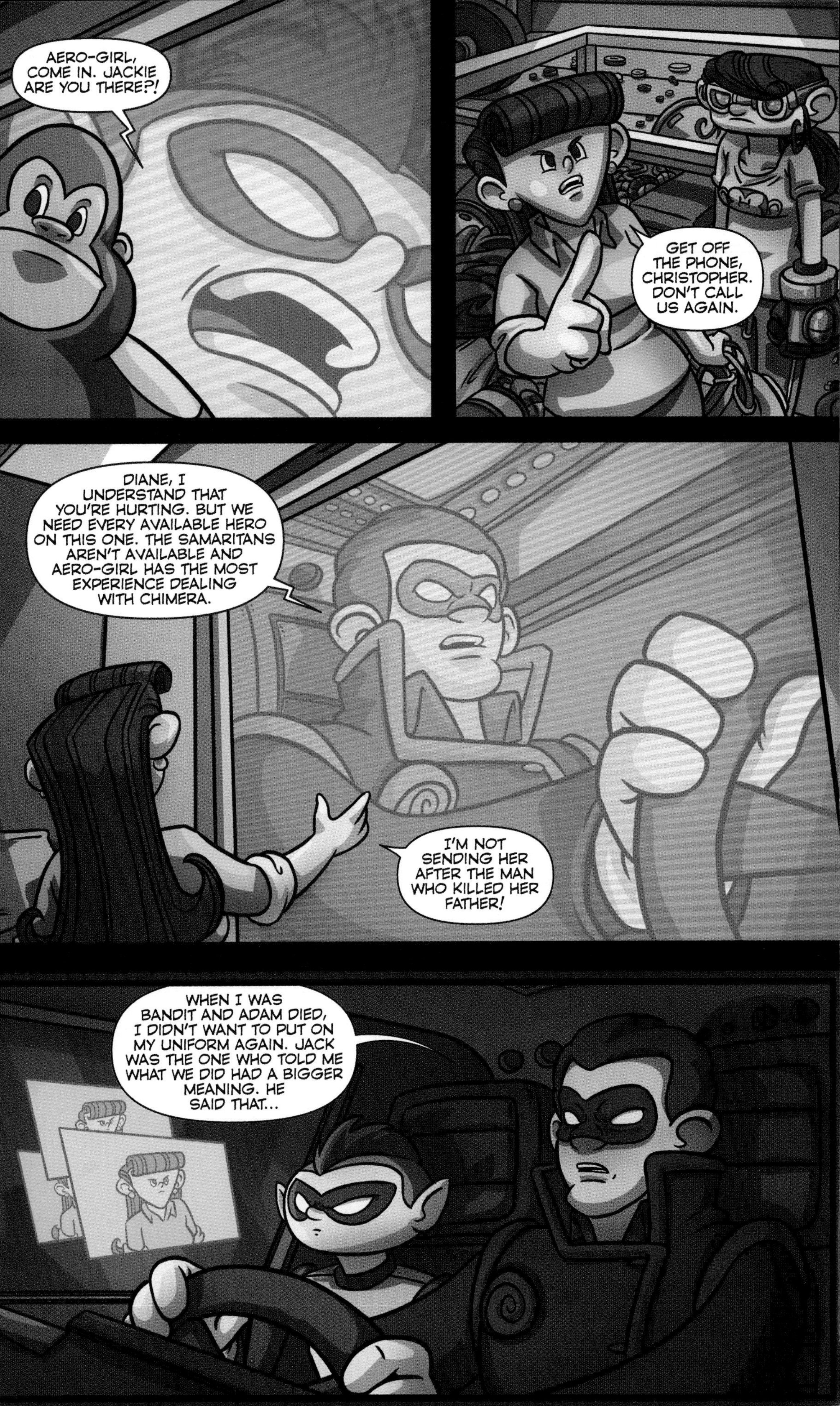

AERO-GIRL, COME IN. JACKIE ARE YOU THERE?!
GET OFF THE PHONE, CHRISTOPHER. DON'T CALL US AGAIN.
DIANE, I UNDERSTAND THAT YOU'RE HURTING. BUT WE NEED EVERY AVAILABLE HERO ON THIS ONE. THE SAMARITANS AREN'T AVAILABLE AND AERO-GIRL HAS THE MOST EXPERIENCE DEALING WITH CHIMERA.
I'M NOT SENDING HER AFTER THE MAN WHO KILLED HER FATHER!
WHEN I WAS BANDIT AND ADAM DIED, I DIDN'T WANT TO PUT ON MY UNIFORM AGAIN. JACK WAS THE ONE WHO TOLD ME WHAT WE DID HAD A BIGGER MEANING. HE SAID THAT...

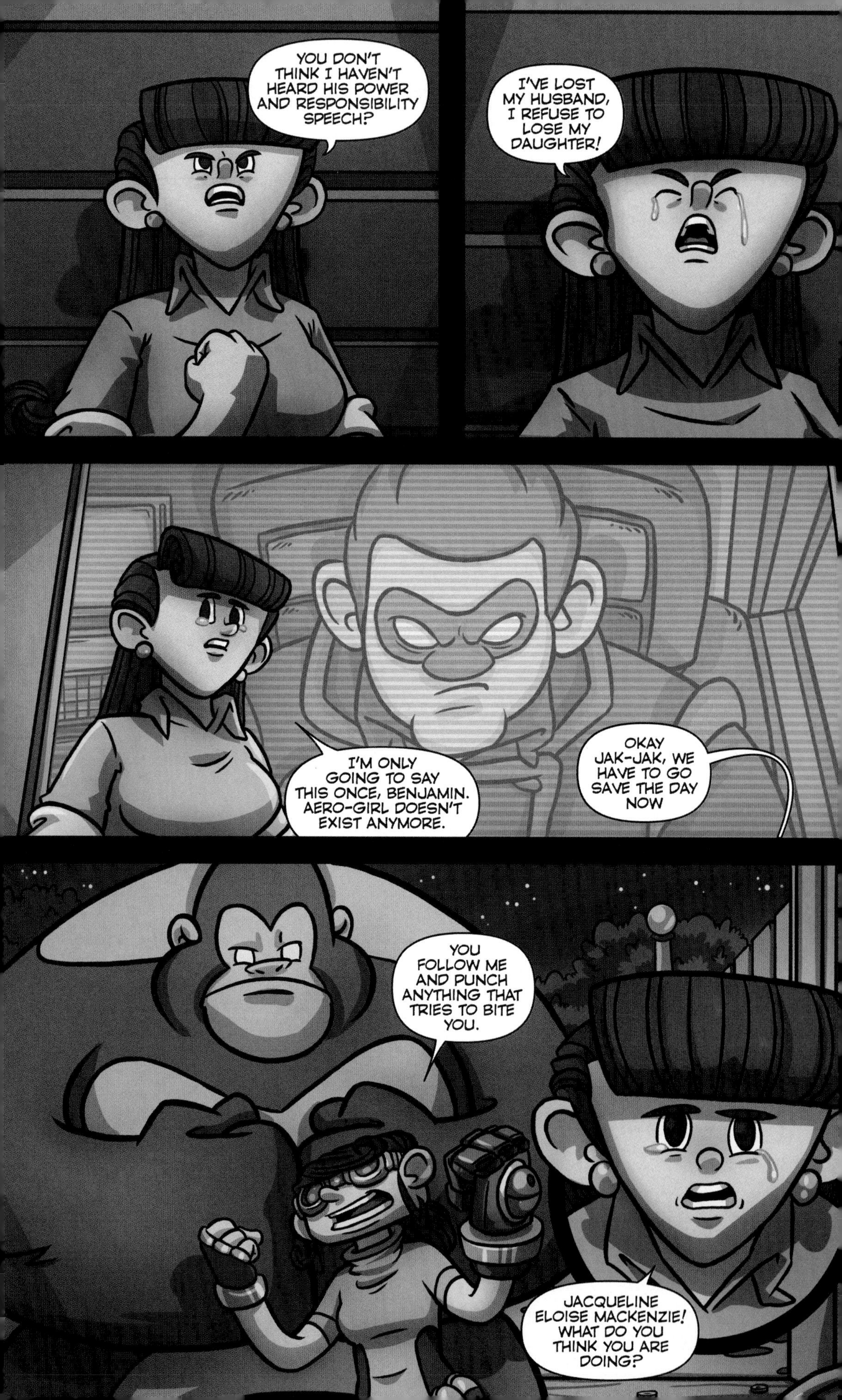
YOU DON'T THINK I HAVEN'T HEARD HIS POWER AND RESPONSIBILITY SPEECH?
I'VE LOST MY HUSBAND, I REFUSE TO LOSE MY DAUGHTER!
I'M ONLY GOING TO SAY THIS ONCE, BENJAMIN. AERO-GIRL DOESN'T EXIST ANYMORE.
OKAY JAK-JAK, WE HAVE TO GO SAVE THE DAY NOW
YOU FOLLOW ME AND PUNCH ANYTHING THAT TRIES TO BITE YOU.
JACQUELINE ELOISE MACKENZIE! WHAT DO YOU THINK YOU ARE DOING?

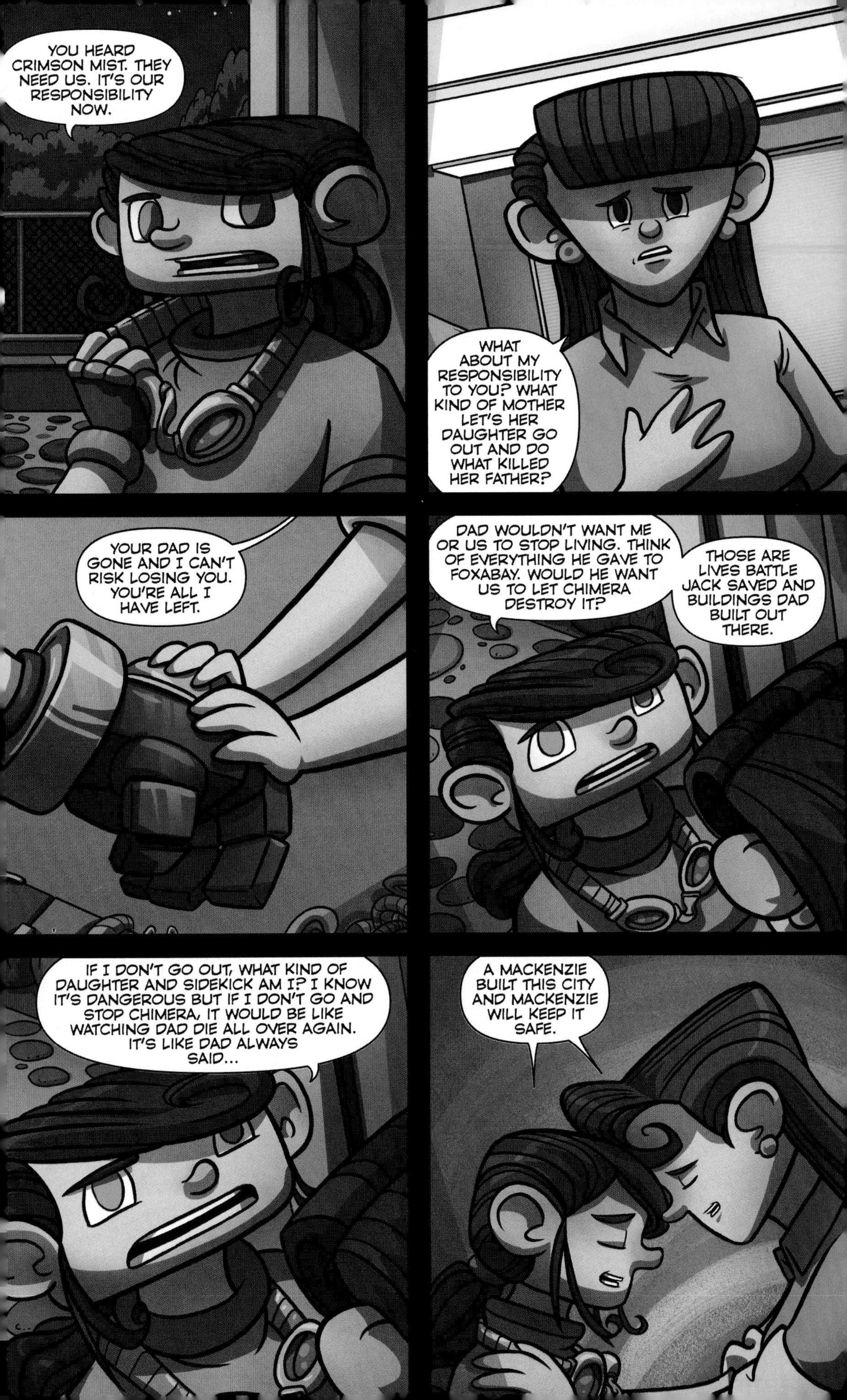
YOU HEARD CRIMSON MIST. THEY NEED US. IT'S OUR RESPONSIBILITY NOW.
WHAT ABOUT MY RESPONSIBILITY TO YOU? WHAT KIND OF MOTHER LET'S HER DAUGHTER GO OUT AND DO WHAT KILLED HER FATHER?
YOUR DAD IS GONE AND I CAN'T RISK LOSING YOU. YOU'RE ALL I HAVE LEFT.
DAD WOULDN'T WANT ME OR US TO STOP LIVING. THINK OF EVERYTHING HE GAVE TO FOXABAY. WOULD HE WANT US TO LET CHIMERA DESTROY IT?
THOSE ARE LIVES BATTLE JACK SAVED AND BUILDINGS DAD BUILT OUT THERE.
IF I DON'T GO OUT, WHAT KIND OF DAUGHTER AND SIDEKICK AM I? I KNOW IT'S DANGEROUS BUT IF I DON'T GO AND STOP CHIMERA, IT WOULD BE LIKE WATCHING DAD DIE ALL OVER AGAIN. IT'S LIKE DAD ALWAYS SAID...
A MACKENZIE BUILT THIS CITY AND MACKENZIE WILL KEEP IT SAFE.

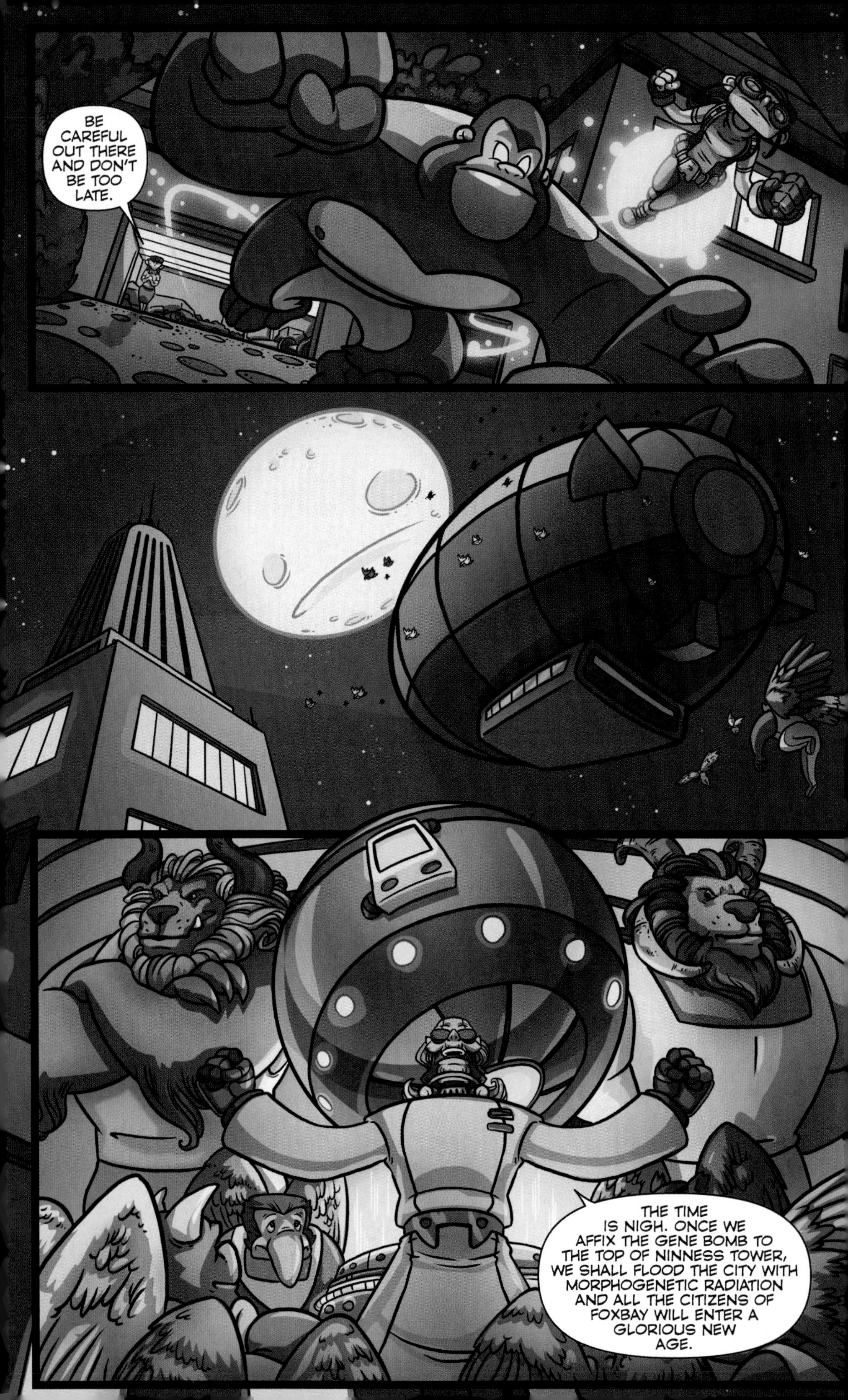
BE CAREFUL OUT THERE AND DON'T BE TOO LATE.
THE TIME IS NIGH. ONCE WE AFFIX THE GENE BOMB TO THE TOP OF NINNESS TOWER, WE SHALL FLOOD THE CITY WITH MORPHOGENETIC RADIATION AND ALL THE CITIZENS OF FOXBAY WILL ENTER A GLORIOUS NEW AGE.

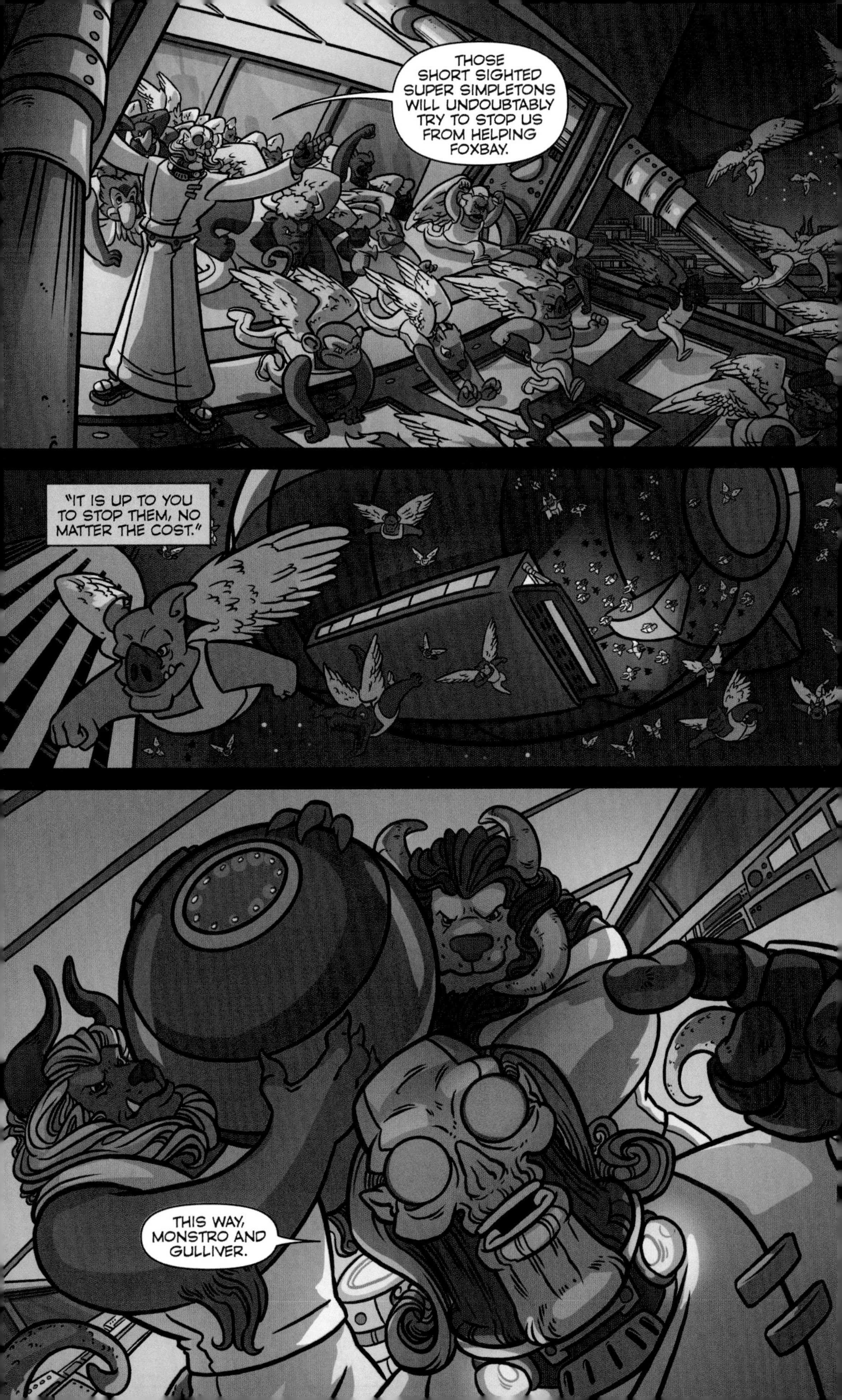
THOSE SHORT SIGHTED SUPER SIMPLETONS WILL UNDOUBTABLY TRY TO STOP US FROM HELPING FOXBAY.
"IT IS UP TO YOU TO STOP THEM, NO MATTER THE COST."
THIS WAY, MONSTRO AND GULLIVER.

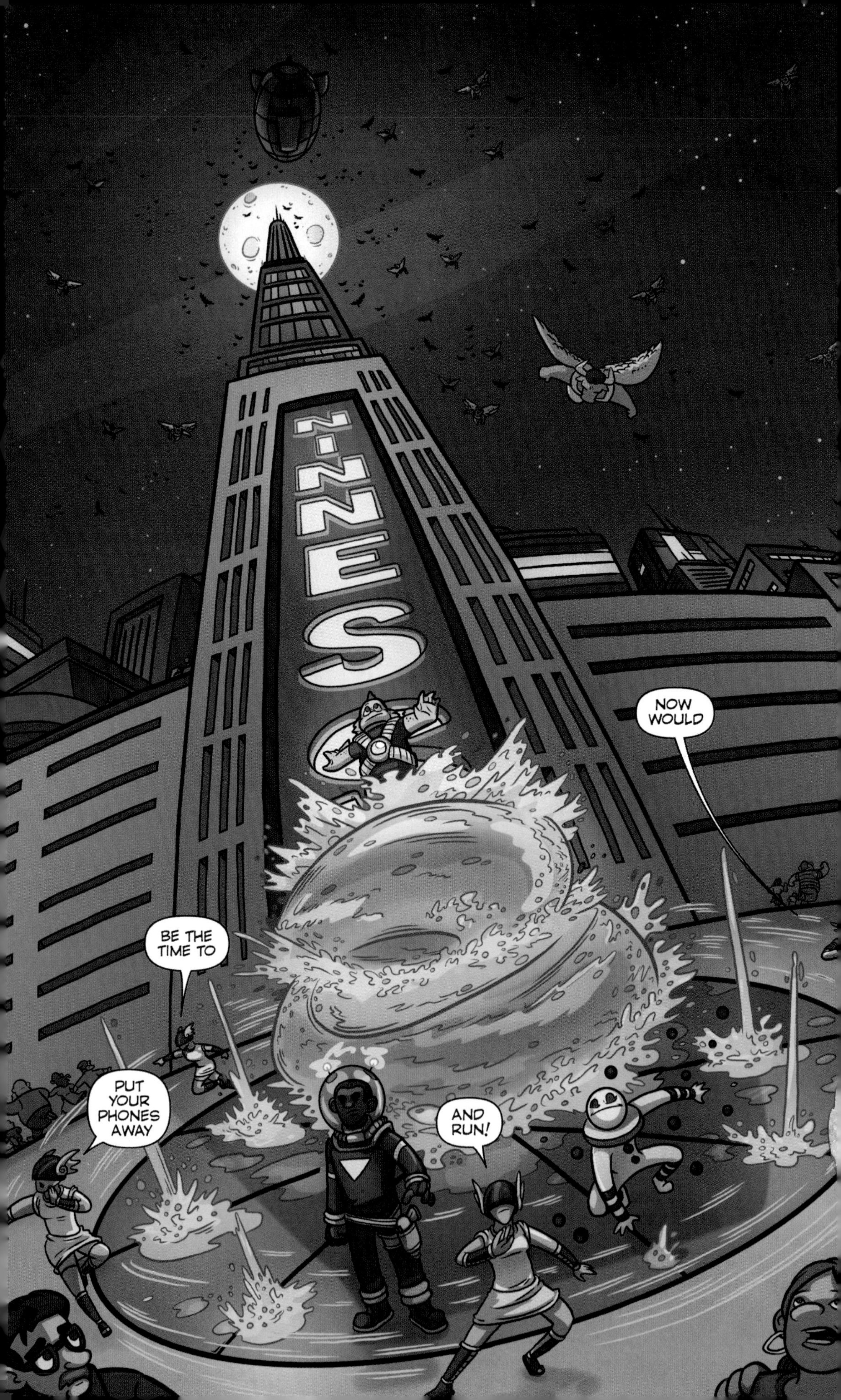
NINNES
NOW WOULD
BE THE TIME TO
PUT YOUR PHONES AWAY
AND RUN!

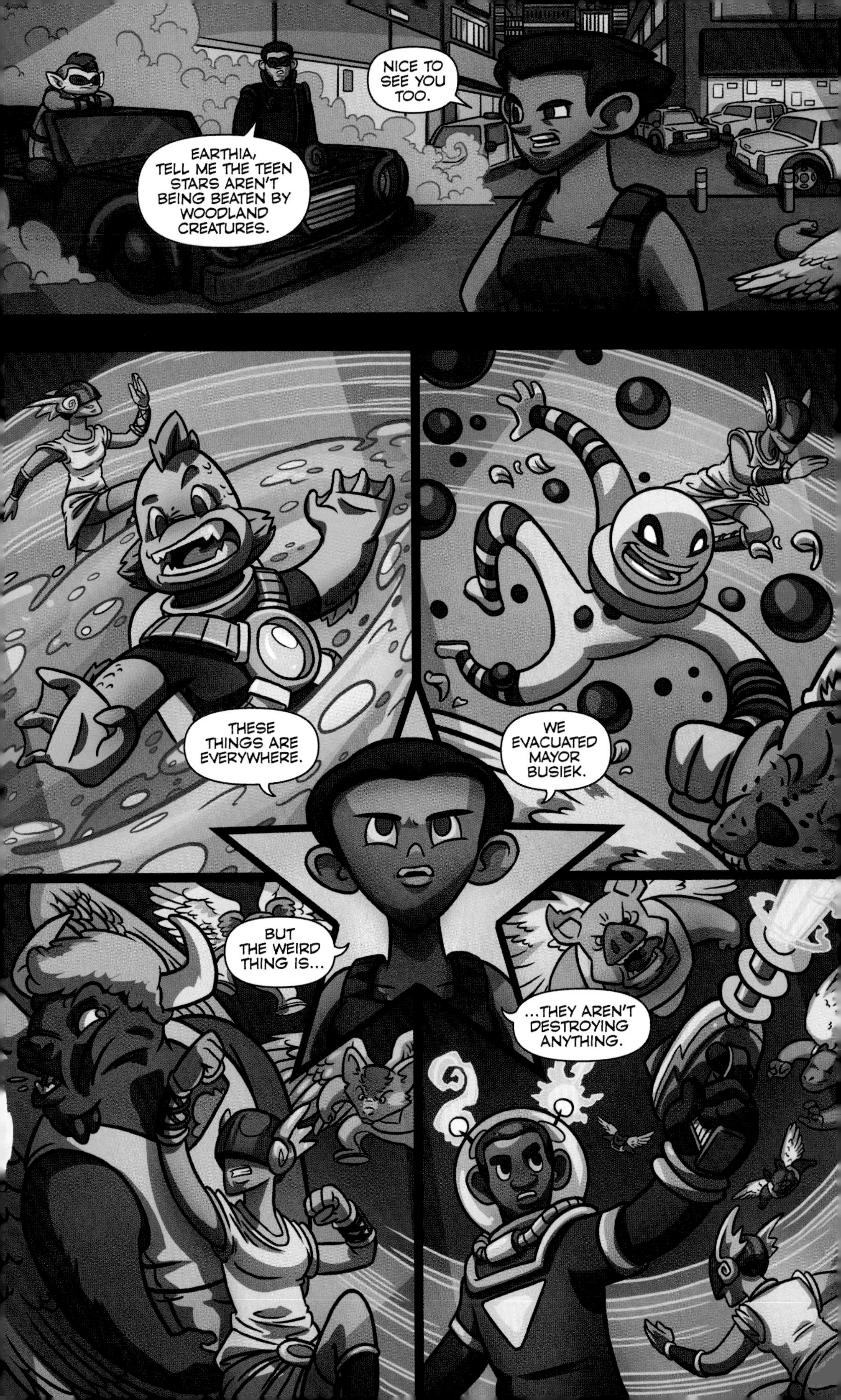
NICE TO SEE YOU TOO.
EARTHIA, TELL ME THE TEEN STARS AREN'T BEING BEATEN BY WOODLAND CREATURES.
THESE THINGS ARE EVERYWHERE.
WE EVACUATED MAYOR BUSIEK.
BUT THE WEIRD THING IS...
...THEY AREN'T DESTROYING ANYTHING.

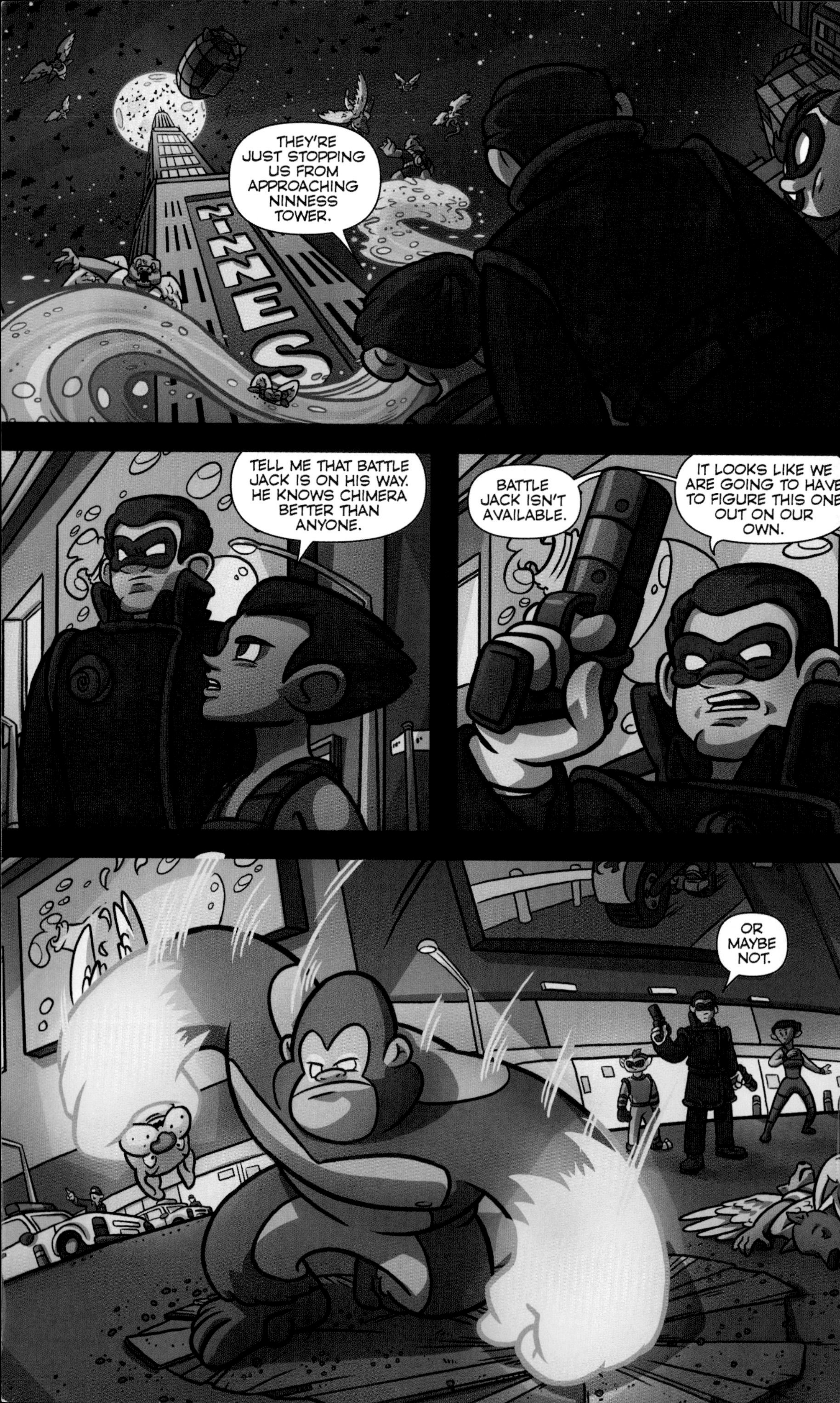
THEY'RE JUST STOPPING US FROM APPROACHING NINNESS TOWER.
NINNES
TELL ME THAT BATTLE JACK IS ON HIS WAY. HE KNOWS CHIMERA BETTER THAN ANYONE.
BATTLE JACK ISN'T AVAILABLE.
IT LOOKS LIKE WE ARE GOING TO HAVE TO FIGURE THIS ONE OUT ON OUR OWN.
OR MAYBE NOT.

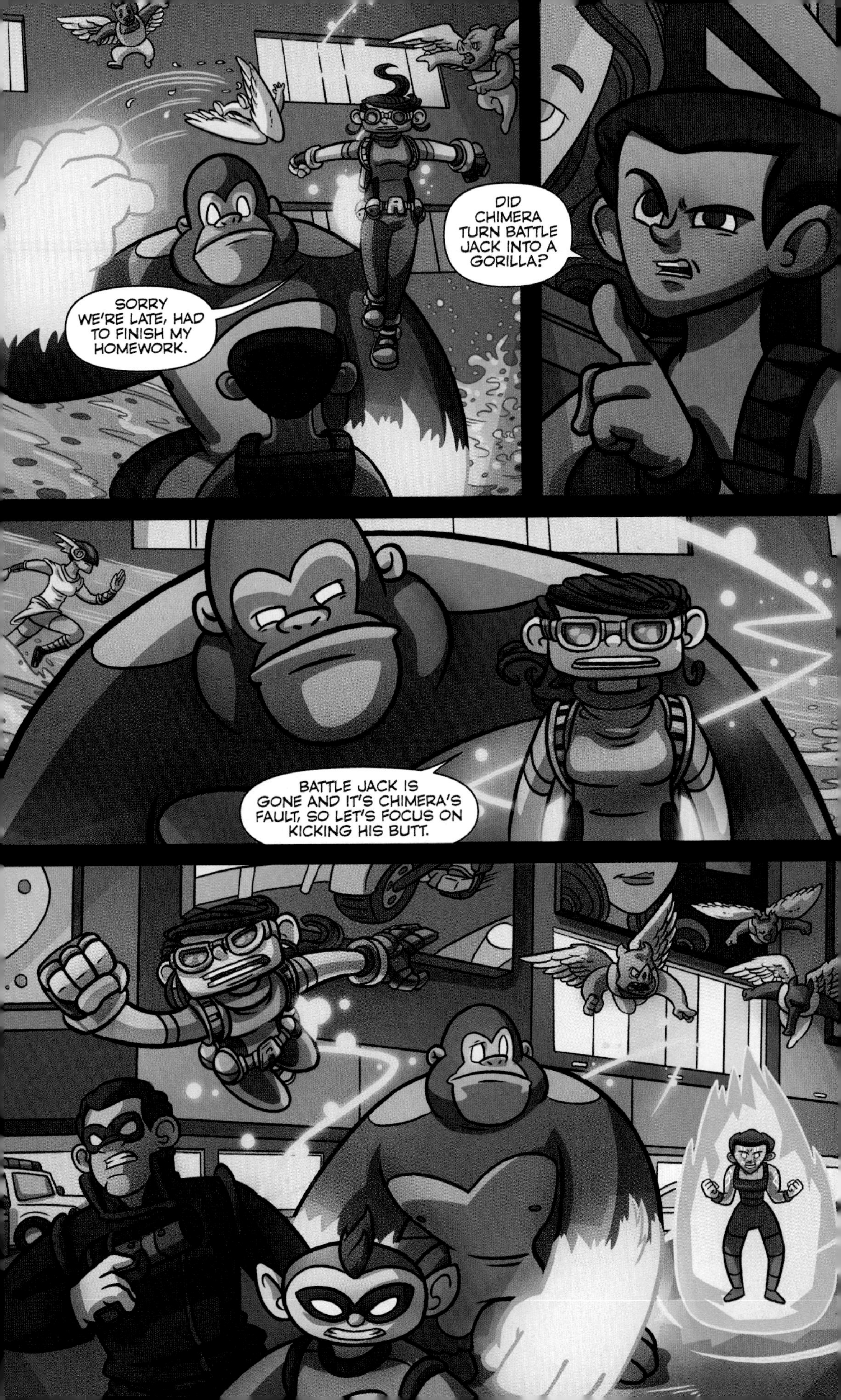
DID CHIMERA TURN BATTLE JACK INTO A GORILLA?
SORRY WE'RE LATE, HAD TO FINISH MY HOMEWORK.
BATTLE JACK IS GONE AND IT'S CHIMERA'S FAULT, SO LET'S FOCUS ON KICKING HIS BUTT.

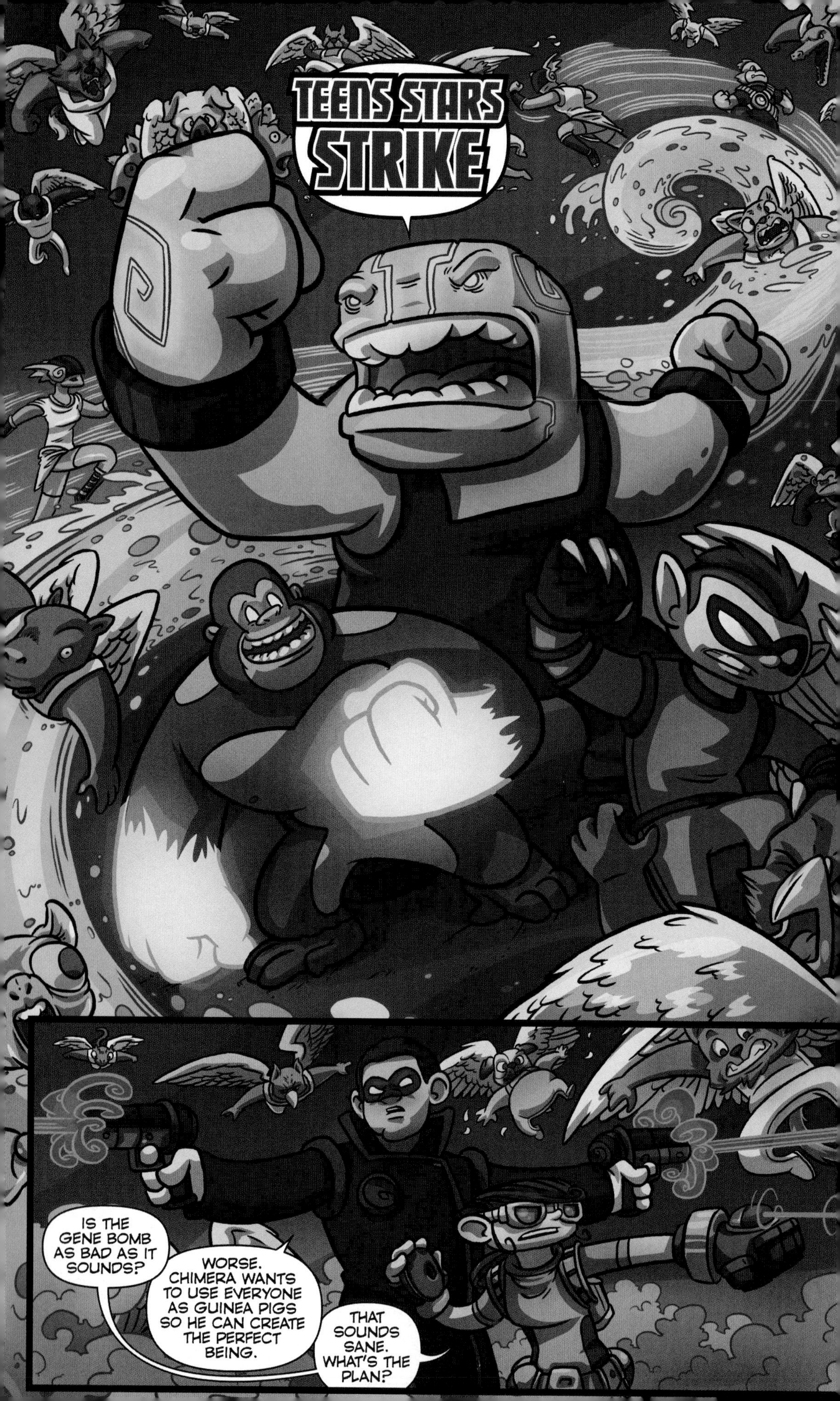
TEENS STARS STRIKE
IS THE GENE BOMB AS BAD AS IT SOUNDS?
WORSE. CHIMERA WANTS TO USE EVERYONE AS GUINEA PIGS SO HE CAN CREATE THE PERFECT BEING.
THAT SOUNDS SANE. WHAT'S THE PLAN?

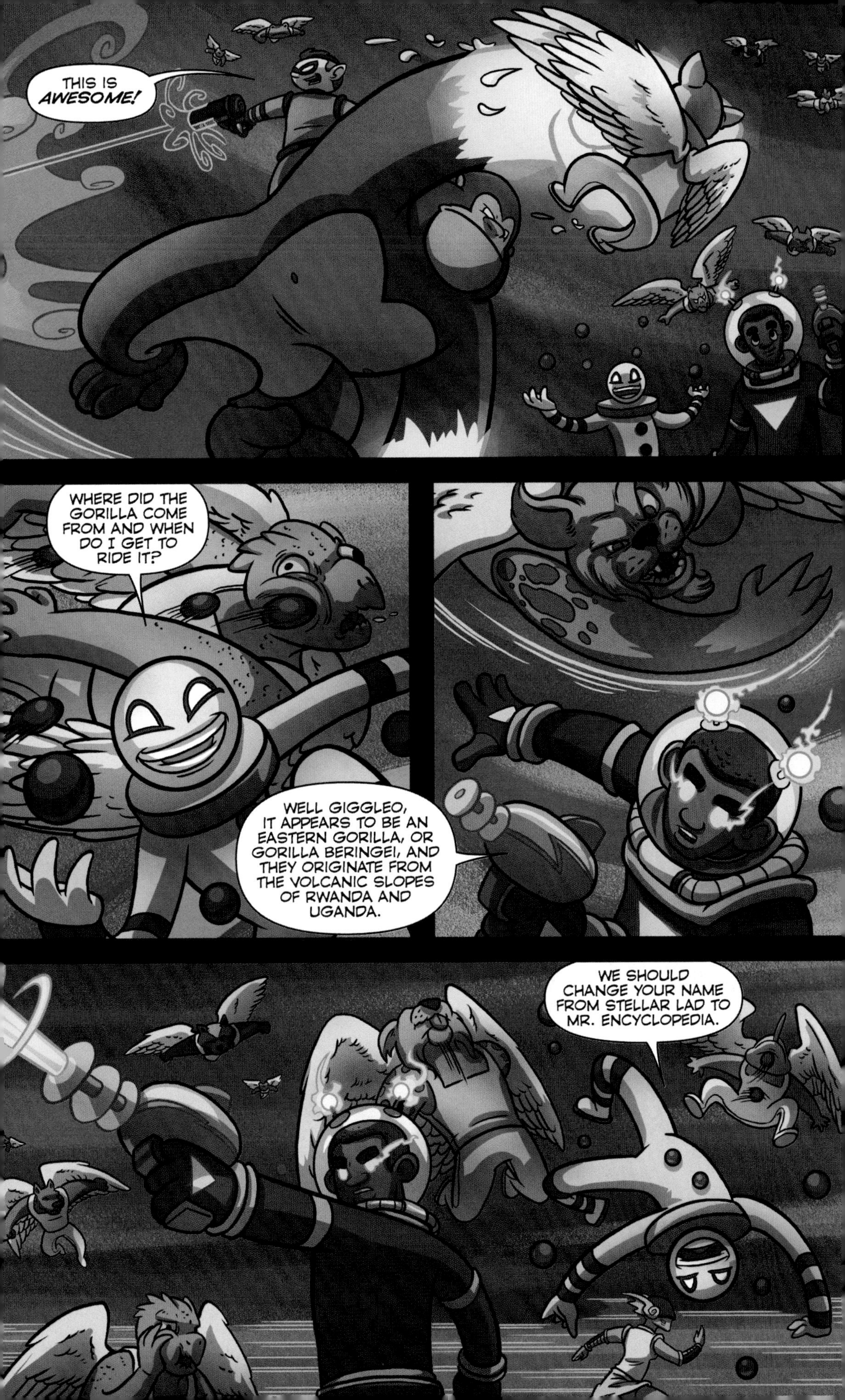
THIS IS AWESOME!
WHERE DID THE GORILLA COME FROM AND WHEN DO I GET TO RIDE IT?
WELL GIGGLEO, IT APPEARS TO BE AN EASTERN GORILLA, OR GORILLA BERINGEI, AND THEY ORIGINATE FROM THE VOLCANIC SLOPES OF RWANDA AND UGANDA.
WE SHOULD CHANGE YOUR NAME FROM STELLAR LAD TO MR. ENCYCLOPEDIA.

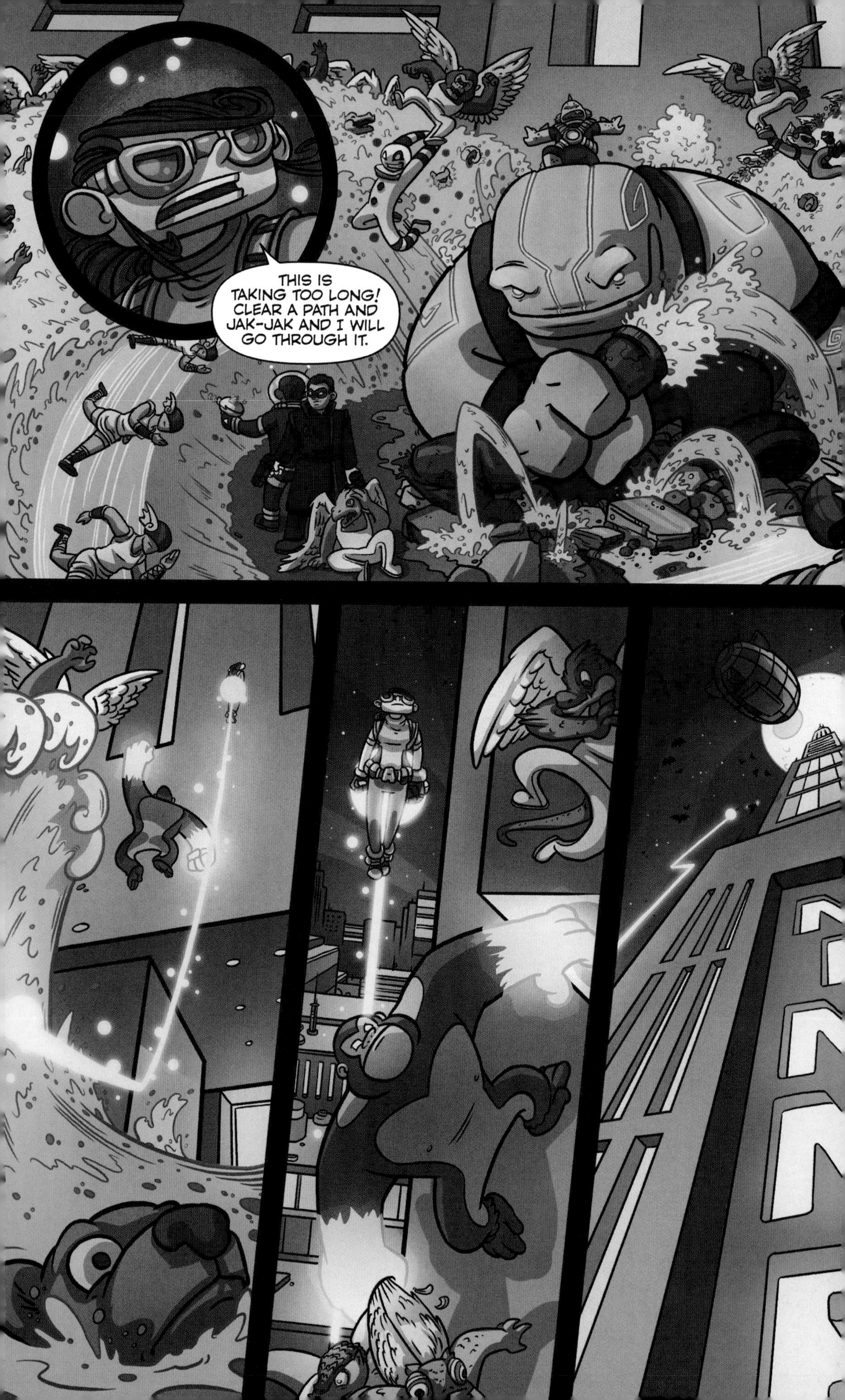
THIS IS TAKING TOO LONG! CLEAR A PATH AND JAK-JAK AND I WILL GO THROUGH IT.

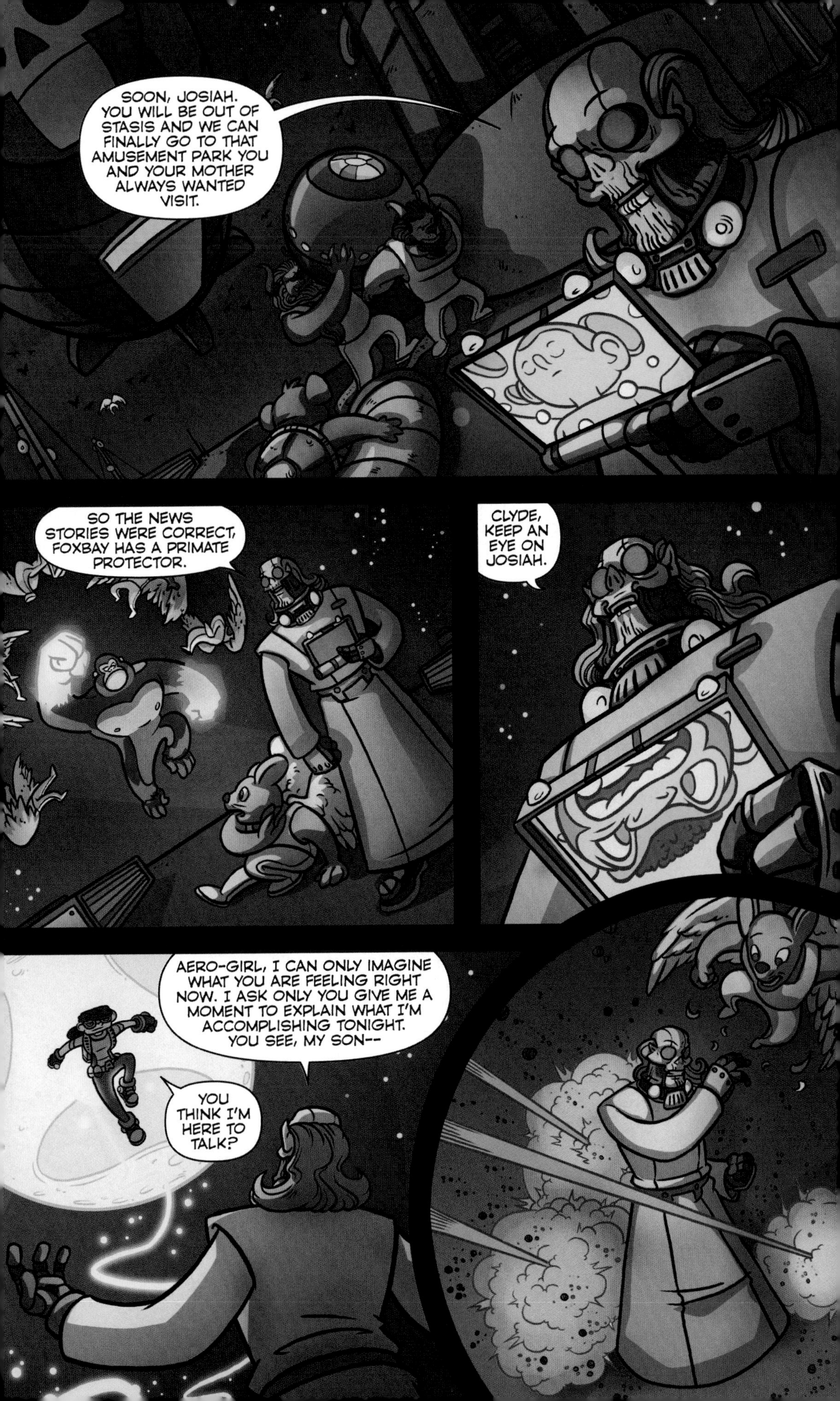
SOON, JOSIAH. YOU WILL BE OUT OF STASIS AND WE CAN FINALLY GO TO THAT AMUSEMENT PARK YOU AND YOUR MOTHER ALWAYS WANTED VISIT.
SO THE NEWS STORIES WERE CORRECT, FOXBAY HAS A PRIMATE PROTECTOR.
CLYDE, KEEP AN EYE ON JOSIAH.
AERO-GIRL, I CAN ONLY IMAGINE WHAT YOU ARE FEELING RIGHT NOW. I ASK ONLY YOU GIVE ME A MOMENT TO EXPLAIN WHAT I'M ACCOMPLISHING TONIGHT. YOU SEE, MY SON--
YOU THINK I'M HERE TO TALK?

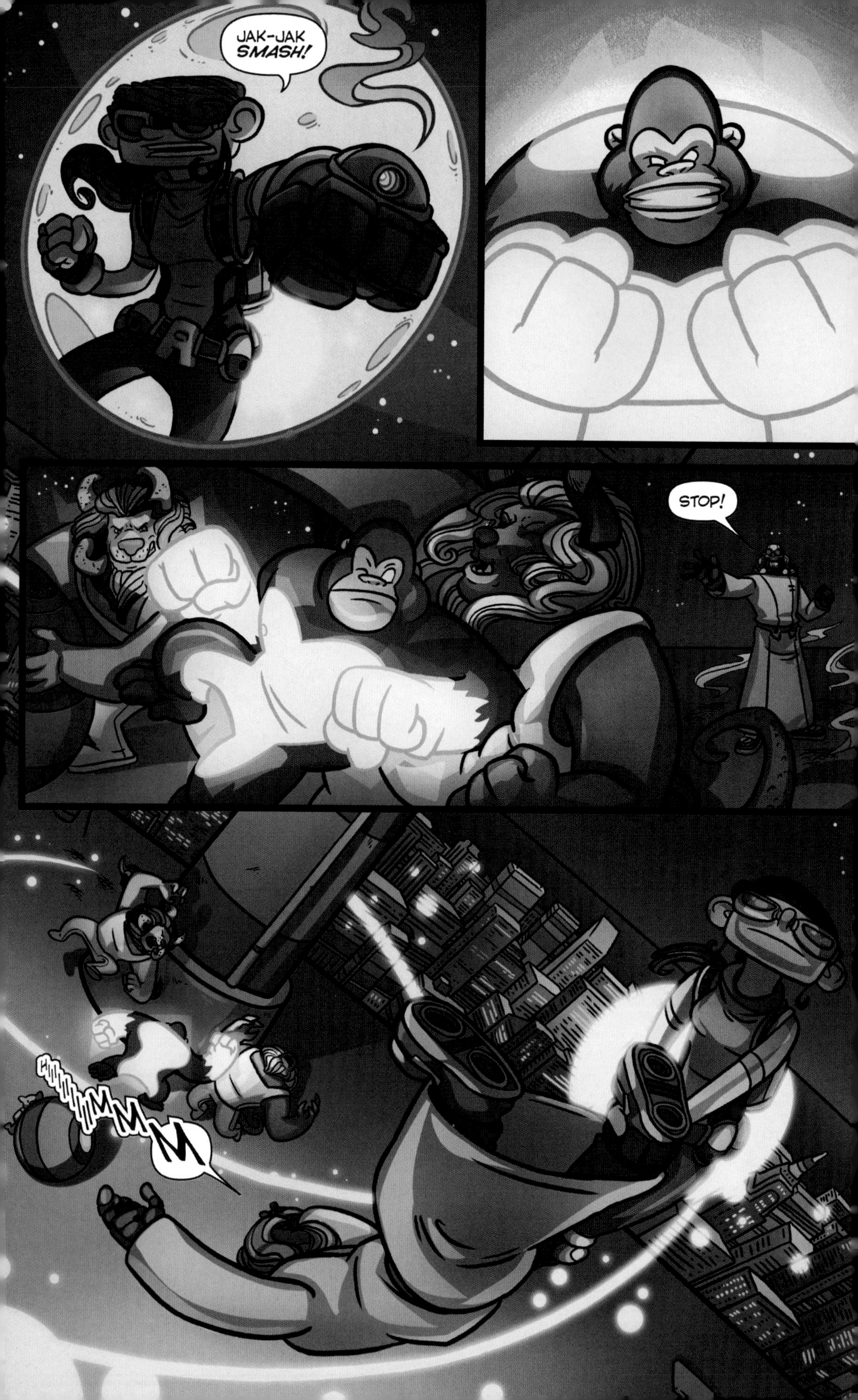
JAK-JAK SMASH!
STOP!
MMMM

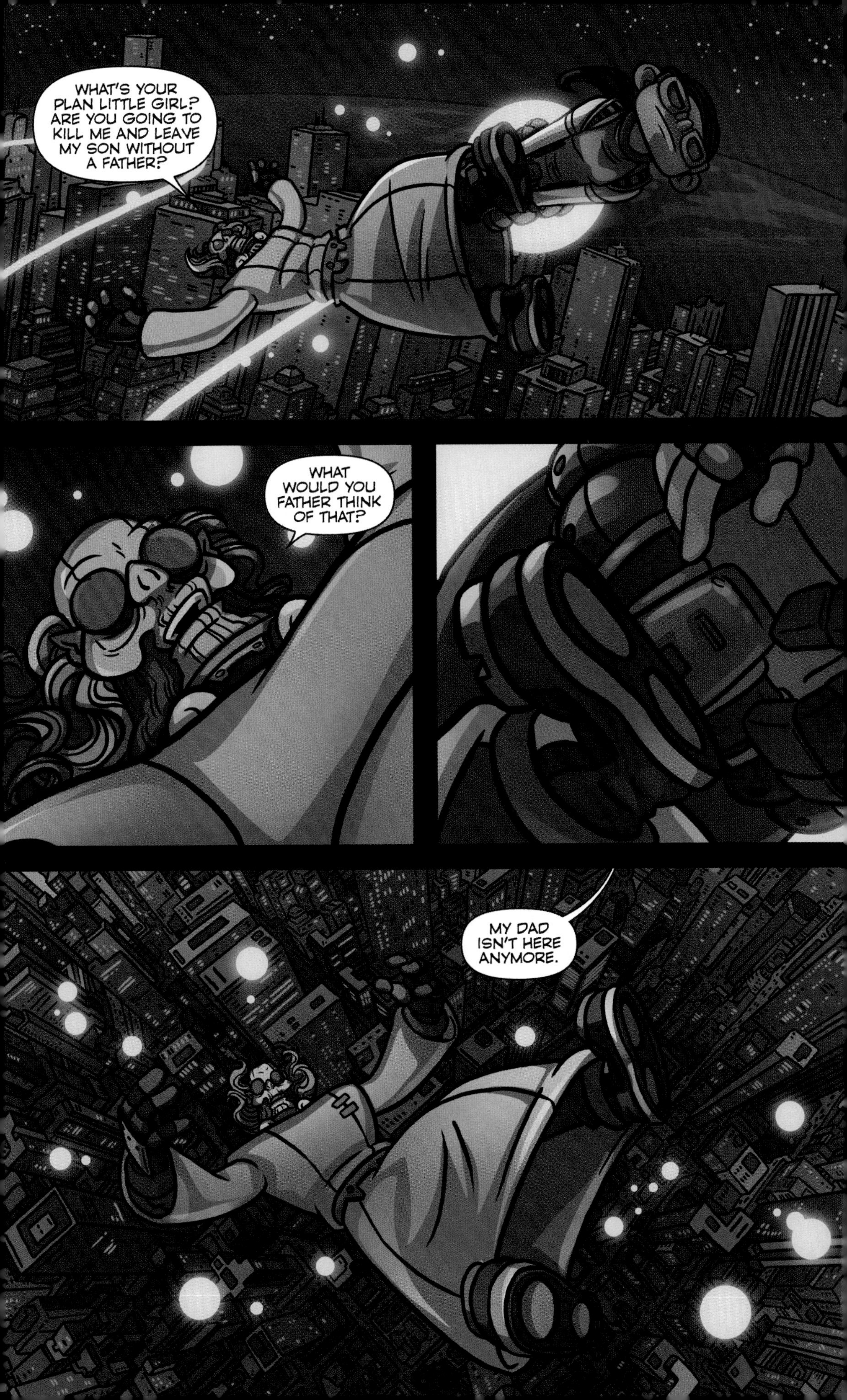
WHAT'S YOUR PLAN LITTLE GIRL? ARE YOU GOING TO KILL ME AND LEAVE MY SON WITHOUT A FATHER?
WHAT WOULD YOU FATHER THINK OF THAT?
MY DAD ISN'T HERE ANYMORE.

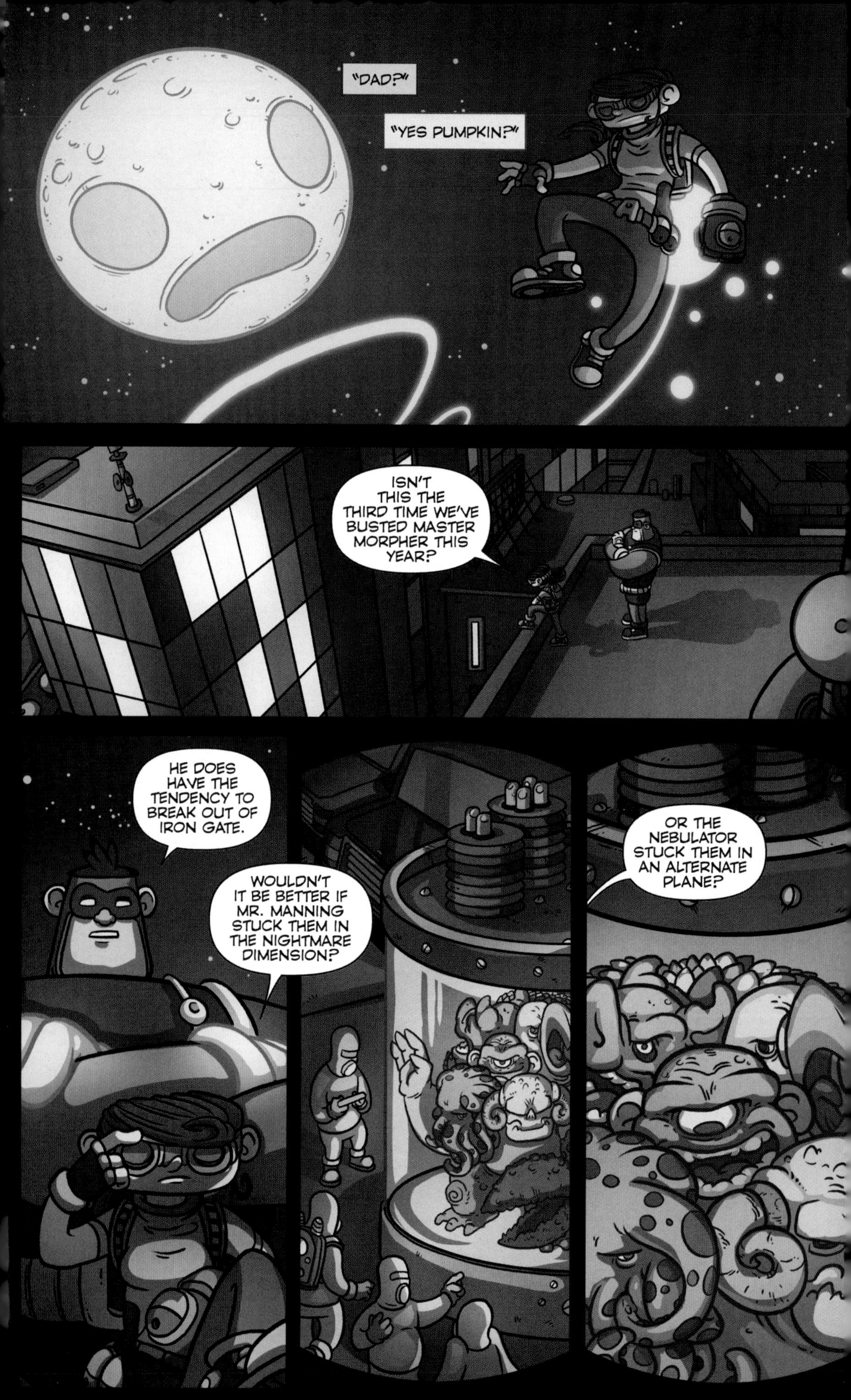
"DAD?"
"YES PUMPKIN?"
ISN'T THIS THE THIRD TIME WE'VE BUSTED MASTER MORPHER THIS YEAR?
HE DOES HAVE THE TENDENCY TO BREAK OUT OF IRON GATE.
WOULDN'T IT BE BETTER IF MR. MANNING STUCK THEM IN THE NIGHTMARE DIMENSION?
OR THE NEBULATOR STUCK THEM IN AN ALTERNATE PLANE?

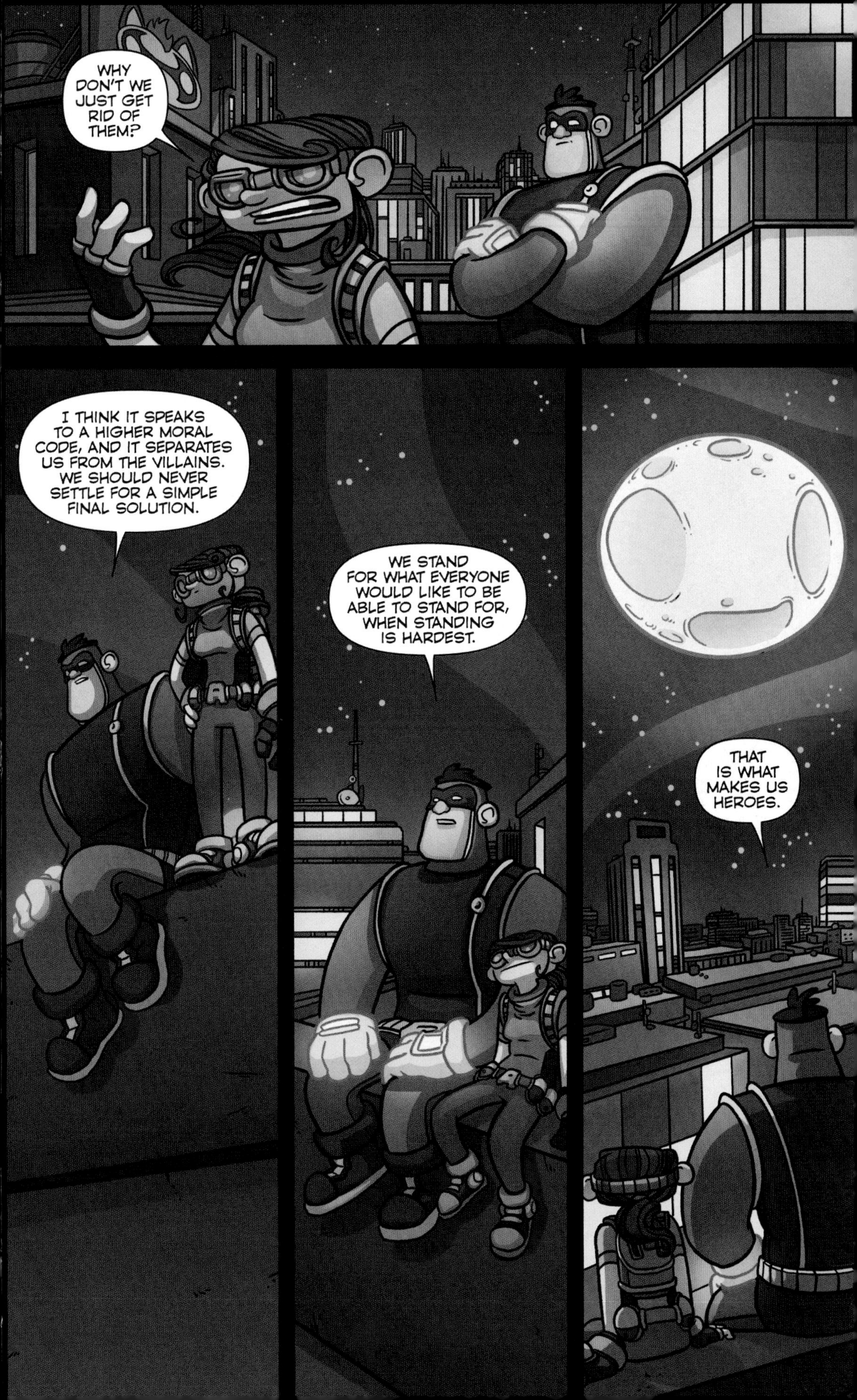
WHY DON'T WE JUST GET RID OF THEM?
I THINK IT SPEAKS TO A HIGHER MORAL CODE, AND IT SEPARATES US FROM THE VILLAINS. WE SHOULD NEVER SETTLE FOR A SIMPLE FINAL SOLUTION.
WE STAND FOR WHAT EVERYONE WOULD LIKE TO BE ABLE TO STAND FOR, WHEN STANDING IS HARDEST.
THAT IS WHAT MAKES US HEROES.

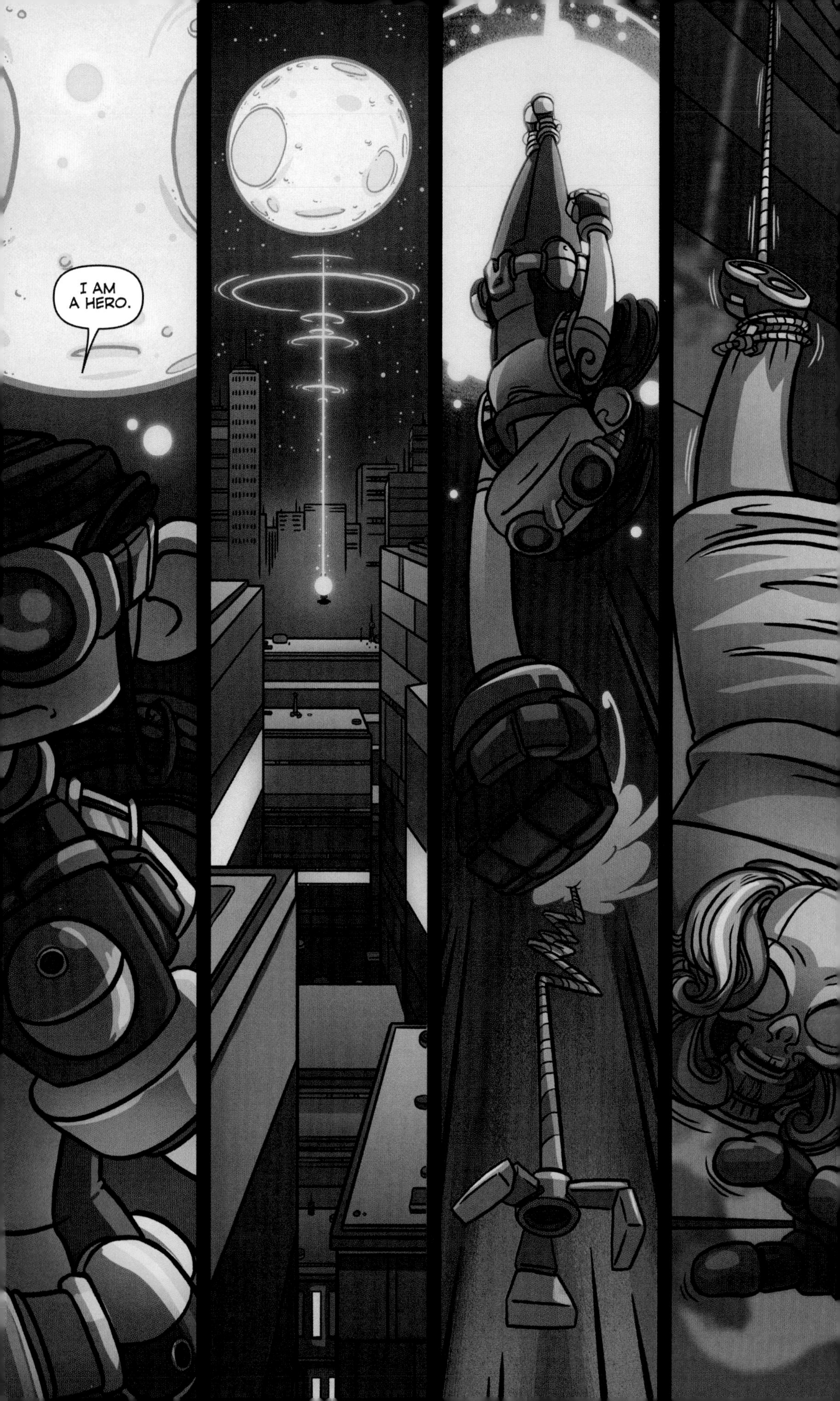
I AM A HERO.

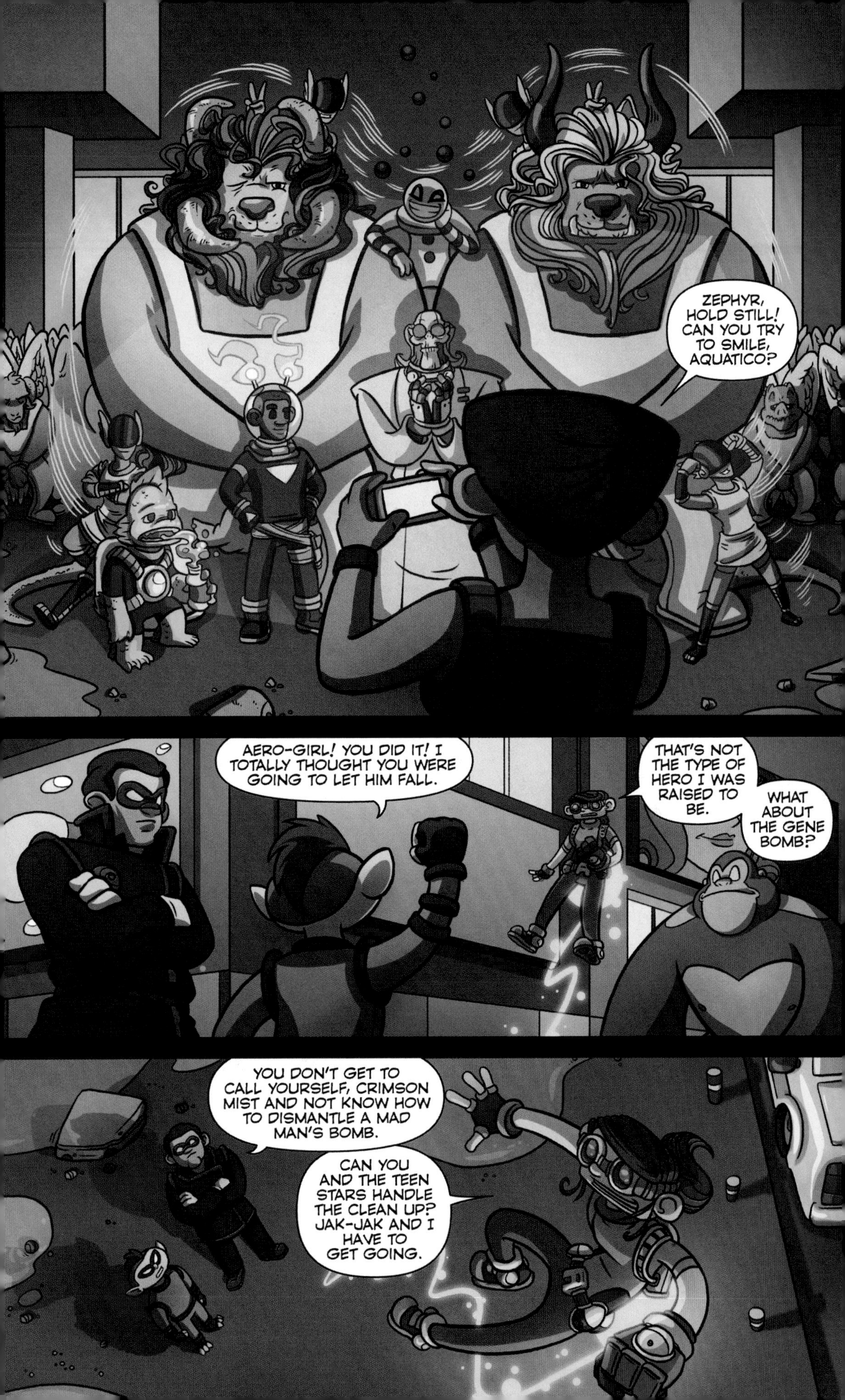
ZEPHYR, HOLD STILL! CAN YOU TRY TO SMILE, AQUATICO?
AERO-GIRL! YOU DID IT! I TOTALLY THOUGHT YOU WERE GOING TO LET HIM FALL.
THAT'S NOT THE TYPE OF HERO I WAS RAISED TO BE.
WHAT ABOUT THE GENE BOMB?
YOU DON'T GET TO CALL YOURSELF, CRIMSON MIST AND NOT KNOW HOW TO DISMANTLE A MAD MAN'S BOMB.
CAN YOU AND THE TEEN STARS HANDLE THE CLEAN UP? JAK-JAK AND I HAVE TO GET GOING.

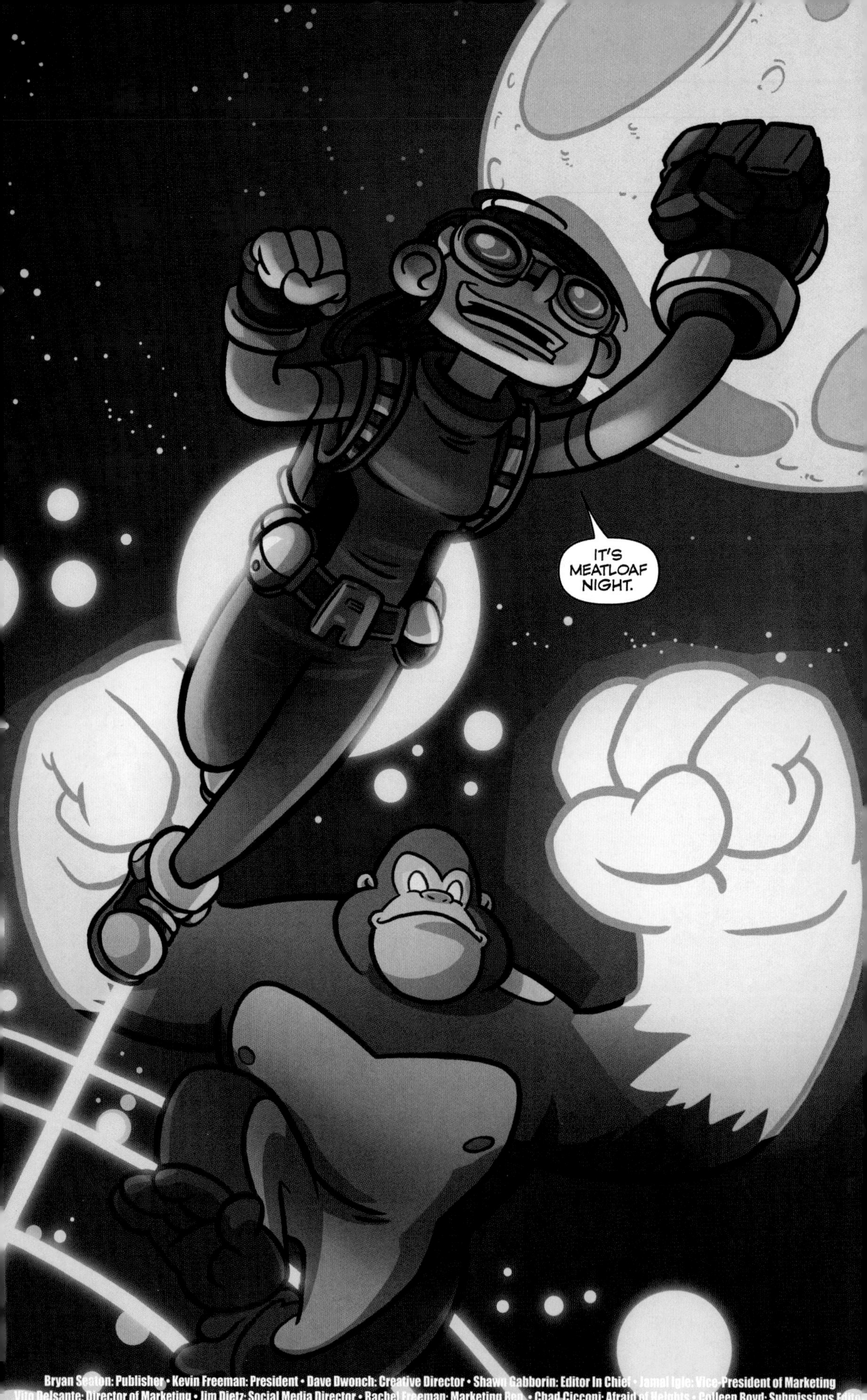
IT'S MEATLOAF NIGHT.

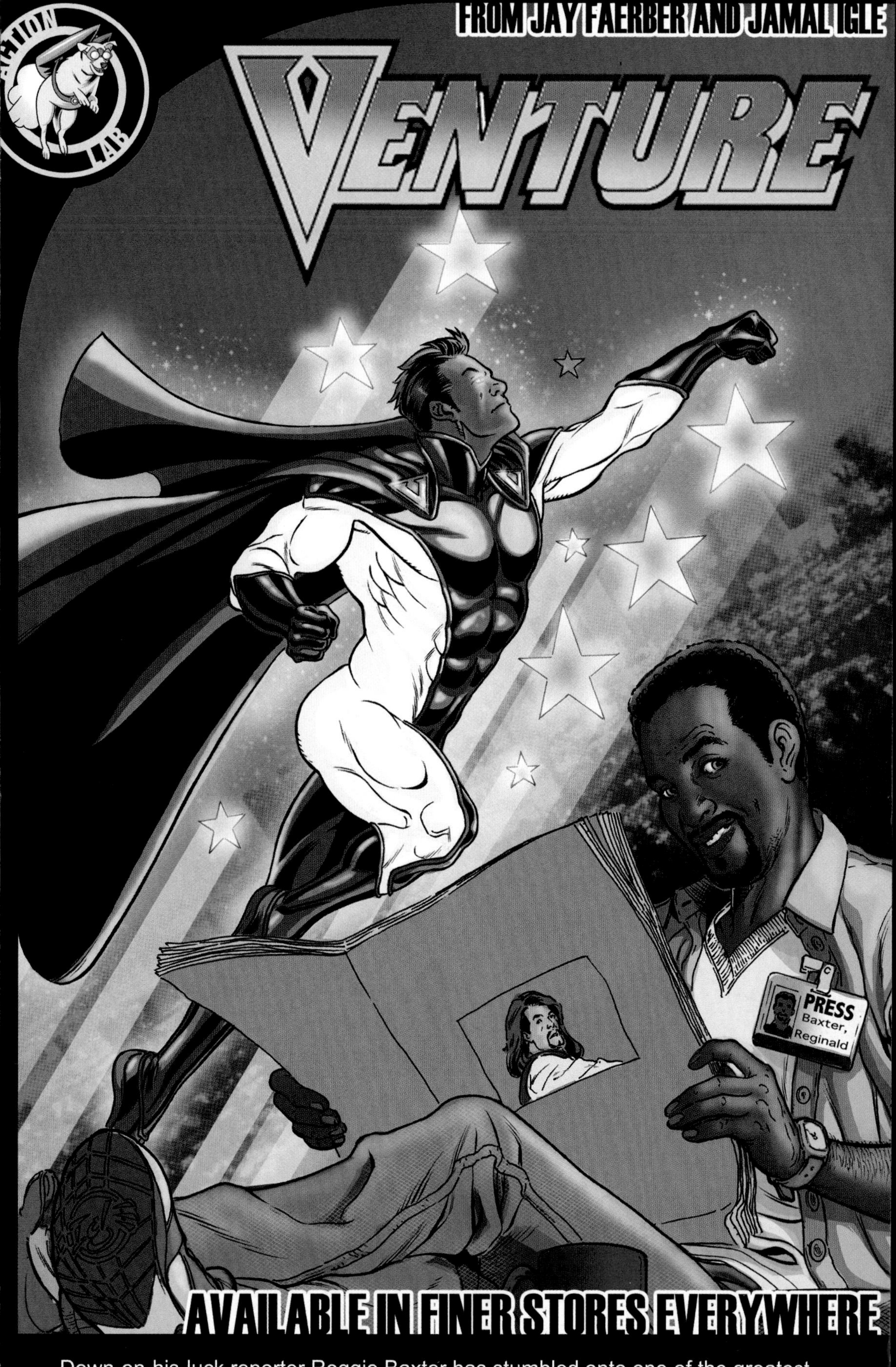
FROM JAY FAERBER AND JAMAL IGLE
ACTION LAB
VENTURE
PRESS
Baxter, Reginald
AVAILABLE IN FINER STORES EVERYWHERE

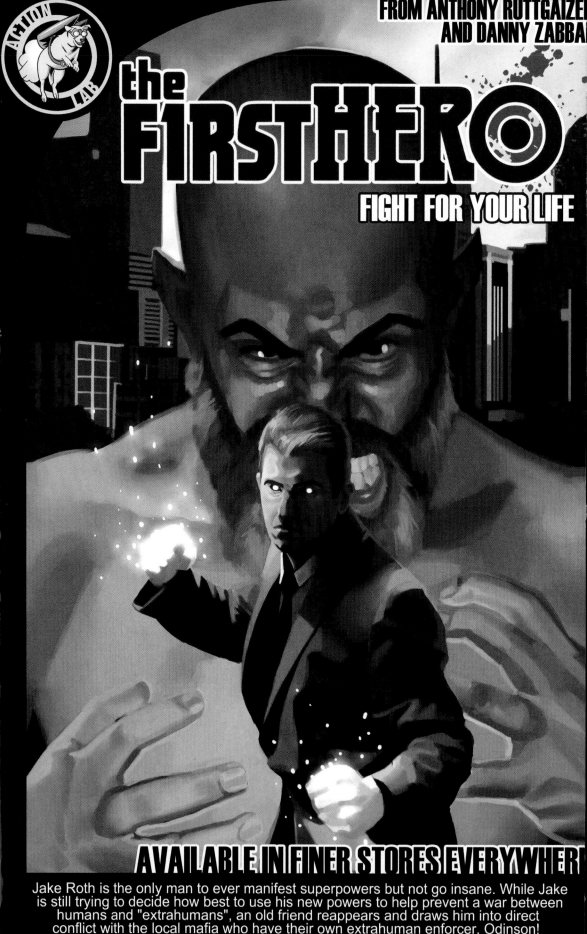

FROM ANTHONY RUTTGAIZER
AND DANNY ZABBAL

the **FIRSTHERO**

FIGHT FOR YOUR LIFE

ACTION LAB

AVAILABLE IN FINER STORES EVERYWHERE!

Jake Roth is the only man to ever manifest superpowers but not go insane. While Jake
is still trying to decide how best to use his new powers to help prevent a war between
humans and "extrahumans", an old friend reappears and draws him into direct
conflict with the local mafia who have their own extrahuman enforcer, Odinson!

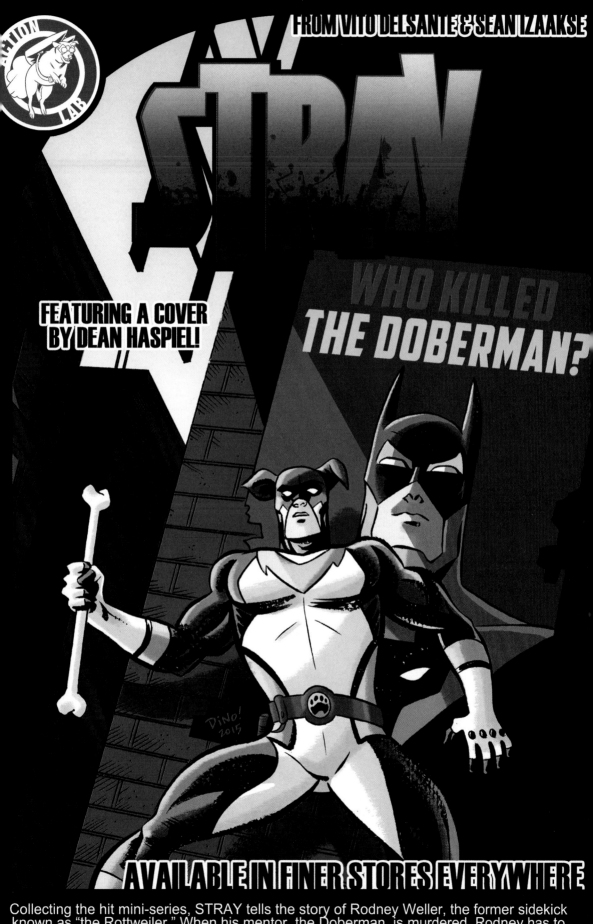

FROM VITO DELSANTE & SEAN IZAAKSE

STRAY

FEATURING A COVER BY DEAN HASPIEL!

WHO KILLED THE DOBERMAN?

DiNo! 2015

AVAILABLE IN FINER STORES EVERYWHERE

Collecting the hit mini-series, STRAY tells the story of Rodney Weller, the former sidekick known as "the Rottweiler." When his mentor, the Doberman, is murdered, Rodney has to decide if he wants to come back to the world of capes and masks and, if he does, who he wants to be. Cover by Emmy Award winner, Dean Haspiel (The Fox)! Collects Stray #1-4.

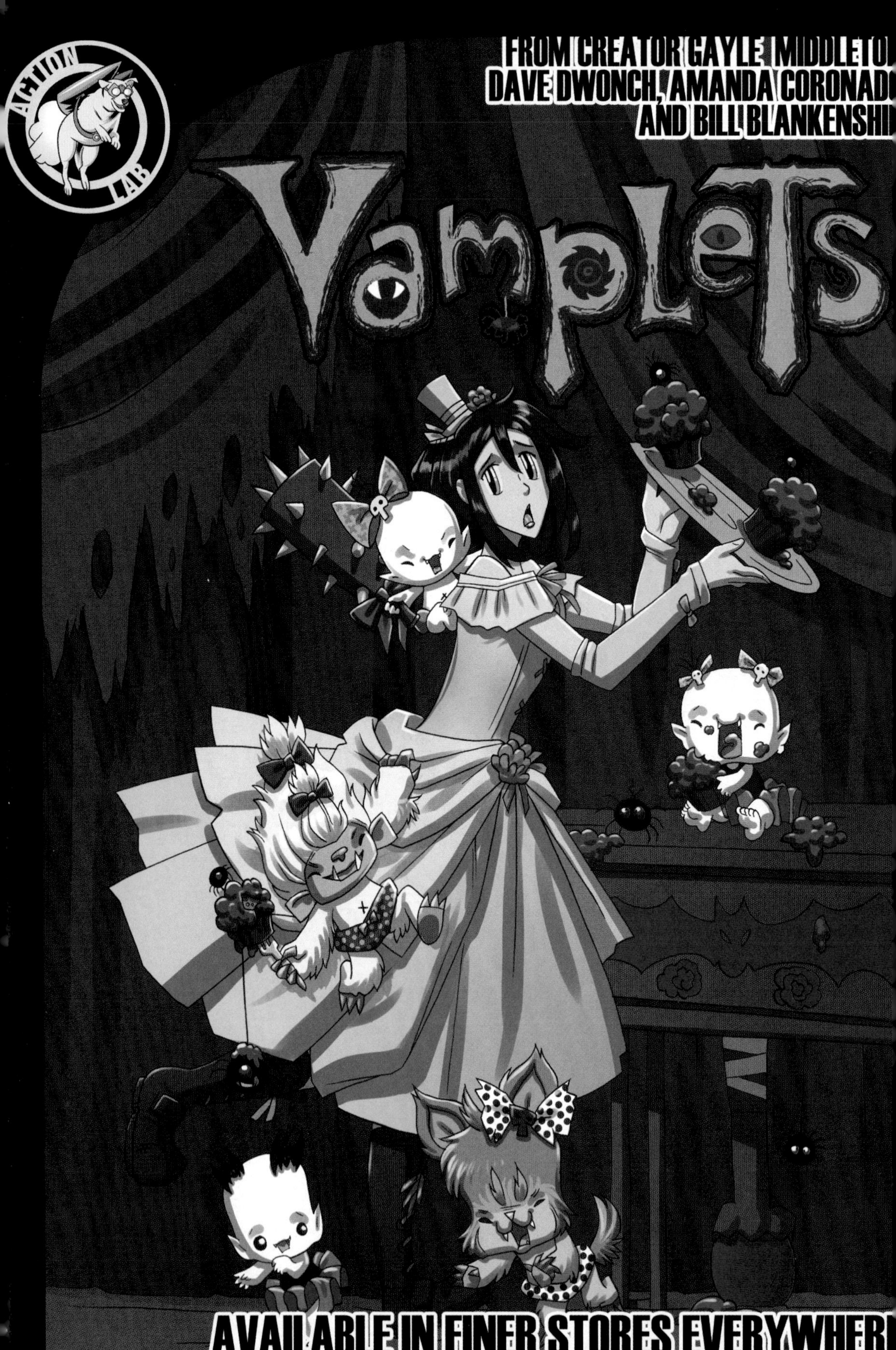
ACTION LAB
FROM CREATOR GAYLE MIDDLETO-
DAVE DWONCH, AMANDA CORONAD-
AND BILL BLANKENSHI-
VAMPLETS
AVAILABLE IN FINER STORES EVERYWHER-

The shocking conclusion to the Nightmare Nursery saga! Destiny Harper is in deep trouble, and she will need the help of Rasket, Lycinda and the Vamplets themselves to thwart the plans of the evil Vammette. Will Destiny Harper get back home, or will she be trapped on the nightmare world of Gloomvania forever?

READ MORE NOW

Aero Girl - Action Lab
www.actionlabcomics.com
00411
7 02382 69092 2

ACTIONLABCOMICS.COM